A

ge

A Deadly Exchange

Sheryl Jane Stafford

Writer's Showcase
San Jose New York Lincoln Shanghai

A Deadly Exchange

Writer's Showcase
an imprint of iUniverse.com, Inc.

For information address:
iUniverse.com, Inc.
5220 S 16th, Ste. 200
Lincoln, NE 68512
www.iuniverse.com

ISBN: 0-595-15677-0

Printed in the United States of America

This book is dedicated to my mother, Jane McWilliams Coleman, the most loving and compassionate woman I have ever known.

Contents

PROLOGUE

Morgan Cay, Bahamas

Special Agent William Driggers crashed through the underbrush leaving broken limbs and pitted earth in his wake. Pursued by drug runners, he pounded over stony loam beneath a canopy of Bahama pines. Twenty yards back, the hounds whined and strained at their leashes as they converged on his trail. The intensity of their baying rose and fell as they lost then rediscovered his scent.

Like a quarterback with the ball, Driggers snaked through the woods making tight S's around the trees. Inside his broad chest he felt the drumming of his heart as it labored to circulate his precious nine pints of blood. Like two failing pistons, his muscular arms pumped erratically; from his dry throat came a high-pitched wheeze.

The night gave him an edge. Darkness shrouded the forest of casuarina trees and enabled him to hide from the pack. The dogs, however, were nosing the dry underbrush and leading the hunters directly to him. He heard their footfalls and rapid-fire Spanish reverberating among the trees.

The airfield was a short distance away, about a half mile. A former marathon runner, Driggers knew he could cover that distance in four minutes. The terrain ahead was rough, pitted with broken limerock, but maybe, just maybe…

The splintering limbs and agitated dogs sounded close. When he paused for a moment to get his bearings, he glanced left to right, then behind him. He had no choice except to press on and hope that he would soon come to the winding road that would lead him to the airfield.

Stunted thatch palms and poisonwood hindered his passage as he stumbled to the edge of the forest and scanned the periphery for the road. It lay some hundred yards away. Without hesitating, he bolted toward it. Suddenly a bullet singed his left ear. *Close.* He hunkered down, tried to make himself a smaller target. Driggers heard his heart, a miniature percussion band, keeping time in his ears. His feet, like Mercury's at the beginning of the chase, felt like ballast. Only his adrenaline and determination to escape propelled him forward. Again there was a shot, off to his right this time.

No longer camouflaged by the timber, Driggers expected one of those small missiles to pierce his flesh. Ever since he had seen the movie, *Fantastic Voyage*, he had thought of his body in a larger, more detailed way. He imagined a hollow point striking him at an incredible rate of speed and knocking him to the ground like a wounded buffalo.

He wasn't afraid of pain, at least not at the moment. That would come later. What he feared most was that these hopped-up sociopaths would ultimately make him tell everything before they killed him. If he understood anything about them, it was that they were the most animated when they were systematically torturing someone to death. On several violent occasions Driggers had stood by while their interrogators expertly administered the punishment du jour. Electric shocks, dental drills, spiked chairs, all manner of weapons from the mundane to the exotic, were their instruments of persuasion. Operating undercover, he had been forced to watch silently with feigned indifference while some wretched soul pleaded to die.

Before him Driggers saw the soft blue runway lights paralleling the landing strip. He didn't hear the drone of a plane overhead, an unusual occurrence for the private airport that saw transports heavily laden with drugs coming and going twenty-four hours a day.

As his Nike tennis shoes crunched across the shell driveway that led to the terminal entrance, Driggers veered left and away from the traveled, more dangerous path. He was elated when he saw the silver birds standing on the tarmac and an unexpected jolt of energy lightened his step. The long runway and parking area appeared to be empty.

A green and white Bonanza airplane offered the nearest means of escape. Crouching, Driggers quickly removed the chocks from in front of the wheels. Without looking back, he opened the cockpit door, stepped on the wing and scrambled inside, locking the door behind him. The cabin smelled familiar, like old leather and stale tobacco.

Oh, no, there they are, the scouts.

Crossing the runway and loping toward the plane, the panting, lathery dogs were closing in on their quarry. Sensing that the climax of the chase was at hand, they nipped at each other's hindquarters as they jockeyed for position at the head of the pack. Obviously he was safe from the canines, but the two-legged beasts behind them posed a deadly threat.

When he couldn't stop his hands from shaking, he knotted them into fists and held them against his chest for a moment. Calmer now, he instinctively located the master switch, turned on the battery, cracked the throttle a quarter of an inch and hit the primer twice.

When he glanced up, he saw the men closing in like rabid jackals. Several of them charged up the runway excitedly waving their guns. A kid, maybe sixteen years old, arrived at the plane well ahead of the others. The boy's face contorted with rage. He shook his M16 at Driggers and ordered him in Spanish to give it up. Undaunted, Driggers extricated his Smith and Wesson .38 from his pants pocket and aimed it at him. When the young Columbian spotted the gun, he quickly ducked beneath the belly of the plane.

Driggers felt his blood pulsing through his veins, his lungs expanding and contracting, the music of his heart…playing. *God, I don't want to die.* His mind was unable to focus, but his fingers miraculously located the ignition key and turned it. The propeller fluttered once, twice, three times before catching. He gently advanced the throttle a hair.

From beneath the plane there were muffled shots, barely audible over the roar of the engine. Driggers felt the tires deflate and the plane settle like an enormous beast that had been brought to its knees. At that precise moment, he accepted that escape from this Bahama outback was no longer an option.

Recognizing that his capture was inevitable, his pursuers seemed less intent on killing. To return with him alive would bring high praise from Raoul, *el jefe.* As they surrounded the plane, their dark eyes were charged with excitement.

Driggers wanted to shoot at them through the window, go out in a blaze of glory, but he was afraid they might respond by simply wounding him and taking him prisoner. Once captured, he would be forced to endure a prolonged, agonizing death and in the end when he talked, and he would talk, he might reveal something that would jeopardize the lives of other DEA agents. That would never do.

Driggers had not planned to die like this. He was always realistic, of course, and had expected that his demise would be, at the very least, colorful. After all, he was the one who had chosen to embrace the underworld in order to expose it.

His right hand trembled as he raised the revolver and inserted the blue barrel in his mouth. His nostrils flared at the smell of Hoppe's No.9 gun solvent; his tongue recoiled from the bitter steel. He paused for a few seconds, allowed his thoughts to turn inward.

For a brief moment he thought about his father, alone and waiting to die in the Bayfront Nursing Home. *Sorry, Pop.* Driggers was glad that he had no one else. Otherwise, he thought, I could never have lived so recklessly.

He wondered whether his life would pass before his eyes but doubted there would be enough time. *Do it!* He leaned back against the seat, trembling. *No choice! Do it now!* He used his left hand to steady his right. *Do it!*

Someone cracked a window. Cool air flowed into the cabin. Voices. A hand reached for him. He fired.

What used to be Driggers slumped over the wheel, its startled eyes fixed on the blood-spattered controls.

CHAPTER ONE

Mission Harbor, Bahamas

Tyrone paced the dock, alternately glancing at the harbor master's office and his Timex wrist watch. Two p.m.. As usual, Z. was late.

Antsy, he sat down on a piling, tapped a Salem Light cigarette from its pack, lit it, and inhaled the cool mentholated smoke. From behind his sunglasses, he studied the long wooden dock and marine vessels that lined its flanks. Beneath him, the old timber gently swayed.

At twenty-three, Tyrone was an impressive black male, tall and muscular with unwavering dark eyes. He had inherited his mother's high cheekbones, his father's full lips.

After several quick puffs, he flicked the butt into the clear water and watched it drift beneath the dock. When he looked up, there was Z. shuffling toward him. Tyrone's mirrored glasses reflected a painfully thin, unwashed man of twenty-one who approached in his characteristic manner with his head cocked to the right and down. He wore a faded green tank top with the words "Born to Run" stamped across the front. Z.'s eyes, vacant and pale, focused on Tyrone's feet.

"Goddammit, Z, where have you been?"

"Hey, man, you know my old lady. When she's in the mood, I gotta be ready. I don't get that much."

Z. straightened up for a second and grinned.

"Are you talking about Laticia?"

"Yeah, Laticia."

"She's not your old lady, asshole. She runs with Danny and them. She's a damn whore, and an ugly one at that."

Z. glanced away, folded his arms across his chest.

"Laticia loves me."

"Whatever. Now pay attention, because I don't want to repeat myself. Tomorrow morning some heavy dude from Miami is gonna show up. He's gonna march his fat ass down to this dock and get on a sailboat that has coke fiberglassed in its locker. We, that's you and me, are supposed to stash the stuff and build a wall around it. Are you listening?"

Z. nodded.

"This has got to be done right. It's goddamn critical. You may not give a shit about your future, but I've got plans. And that doesn't include getting fucked up by…"

"You know what your problem is man?"

"Yeah, what?"

"You worry too much."

Tyrone looked down, inhaled, began again. "This job has got to be done right. Got that?"

"Yeah, man, I hear you."

"You'd better. Now show me which boat it is."

Tyrone trailed behind Z. as he ambled down the dock. He noticed that Z.'s cut-off jeans had a gaping hole in the rear seam.

Three charter boats, each thirty-two feet long, were tied up like ducklings alongside the wooden pier. Clones from the factory with white hulls, blue stripes, and plaid upholstery, there was no one characteristic that distinguished them. Because of generations of renters who had no pride of ownership, they even bore the same scuff marks, rips in their sail covers, and dents in their hulls. Either for convenience or more likely for lack of imagination, the charter service had chosen similar names. As they proceeded passed each boat, Z. read the three boat names aloud.

"*Amour. Amity. Amani.*"

He watched Z. scratch his dirty blond head and a feeling of apprehension washed over Tyrone. *Oh, Jesus.* Z. padded back and fourth beside the three boats, his rubber thongs flapping.

"Okay," Tyrone said after a few minutes, "which boat did Danny tell you to put the bags on?"

Z. plucked at the hem of his tank top and a flicker of panic crossed his eyes.

"Which boat," Z. said and licked his lips, "h-m-m."

Tyrone looked up at the sky and said through clenched teeth, "You mean to tell me you don't know which boat we're supposed to put the coke on? You mean to tell me, you dipshit, that you fuckin' don't remember?"

Z. flinched and withdrew from Tyrone's withering glare.

"Now listen, bro," Z. said as he raised the palms of his hands in front of him, "Don't piss your pants. I got it written down on a piece of paper."

"Okay, so let me see it," Tyrone said through a tight jaw.

While Z. groped inside his pockets, a knot of American tourists strolled by. A young blond woman balancing a fat-cheeked baby on her right hip looked at them curiously and continued up the dock. Z. withdrew a faded gasoline receipt with something scrawled across its face. Tyrone could see that the writing was smeared and blurry.

Sweat formed on Z.'s brow. He stared at the receipt, rubbed his nose, then wiped his hand on his pants.

"Now wait a minute. Wait a minute," Z. said. "I remember now. Oh, yeah, it was a name that I've never heard before, kind 'a foreign sounding. Danny and me talked about what a weird name it was. I asked him what it meant, but he didn't know."

"And?"

"He didn't know."

"No, shit for brains, which boat is it?"

"Uh, it's this one right here," he said and pointed.

Tyrone felt the earth move. For a moment, he glared at Z. and imagined how wonderful it would feel to strangle him. It would almost be worth it.

"Is Danny home?" Tyrone said.

"Beats me. Him and Jimbo were goin' to Miami today, but I don't know when."

Tyrone bit down on his lip, jingled the coins in his pocket.

"I'll be right back," he told Z. "You stay put. Don't move."

Z. nodded and extracted a joint from his shirt pocket. "Okay, bro," he called after Tyrone.

At the dingy phone booth outside the harbor master's office, Tyrone counted out some coins and deposited them into the pay phone. While rummaging in his pocket, he noticed the unmistakable smell of urine wafting from the littered floor, dried chewing gum on the ledge, and a crumpled pack of Marlboros at his feet. He tried not to touch anything. Removing a list of phone numbers from his wallet, he located Danny's new number and dialed. After several rings and no answer, he hung up the receiver, retrieved the coins from the return slot, and reinserted them. Again scanning his list, he selected another number and dialed. After three rings, Danny's girlfriend, Ariel, said a breathy hello.

"Ariel, this is Tyrone."

"Hey, baby, what's up?"

"Is Danny there?"

"No, sweetie, Mr. Bigshot left early this morning in the plane. Would he tell me where he's going? I don't think so. Asshole."

"Shit."

"Uh, you want me to give him a message when I see him?"

"When will he be back? Tonight?"

"Like I said, I don't know where he went or how long he'll be gone."

Tyrone exhaled into the receiver.

"Hey, boy, wanna come over later? I'll give you a dime."

A leer came to Tyrone's lips and he felt a warm tingling in his groin. He remembered Ariel the way he had last seen her at Danny's. Her firm, white buttocks were covered only by the thong strap that disappeared between their full cheeks and her breasts, like two overripe melons, strained to escape confinement from her skimpy bathing suit top.

"Well?" Ariel said.

Tyrone was tempted, but only mildly. Staying in one piece and getting along with Danny was a strong incentive to keep his distance. Danny was his ticket into the Cartel. He might even work his way up to lieutenant. Doing a few lines of coke with Ariel and sticking it inside that supple white body would be a real pleasure, but if Danny ever found out… Unconsciously, he shook his head.

"Can't tonight, babe," he said. "Not that I wouldn't like to, uh, spend some time with you. It's just that I have important business, and…"

"Just think about it. I'll be here until ten. Who knows, you might change your mind."

"Maybe. Tell Danny I'm looking for him. If you see him tonight, make sure he calls me at my place after midnight. It's important."

"Will do."

"Later."

He hung up the receiver and for a full minute continued to grasp it like a lifeline. When he returned to the dock, Tyrone found that Z. had removed the hatch boards from the sailboat, *Amani,* and was busy taking gear from the hanging wet locker.

"This goes here. This goes there." he was saying aloud to himself.

Tyrone squatted in the companionway and looked down at him.

"Okay, mother-fucker, pay attention. If you screw up this deal, it's both our asses. I don't give a shit if Danny is dating your cousin. We'll both be jacked up if we put the coke on the wrong boat."

"Look, man, I know it's this boat, I swear. Everything's cool. Why don't you help me get my tools from the car and we'll get started."

Tyrone closed his eyes and wished that fate had not teamed him with this idiot who could easily get them both into serious trouble. *How shitty. My first big chance to become a player and I end up with this moron.*

He climbed back onto the dock and waited for Z. to join him. When they returned with their tools, fiberglass, and plywood, they began to prepare the hanging wet locker for the cocaine. Using thin lumber, they cut several pieces that would form another wall inside the narrow closet. This wall would cover the plastic-wrapped packages of coke once they were stacked and in place. After a second trip to Z.'s car, they returned with a red Igloo ice chest containing the bagged cocaine.

The preceding Saturday when air travel to the Bahamas was heavy, the shipment had been flown to Mission Harbor from Columbia. Before its departure the coca leaves had been crushed in a press and transformed into cocaine sulfate or pasta. When hydrochloric acid was added, other chemicals were eliminated. The final product, cocaine hydrochloride, was then chopped into a fine white powder and packaged.

"Wouldn't you like to take one of these home?" Z. said as he waved a bag in the air.

"Don't say that. Shit, don't even think it. Just hand them to me, one at a time. All of them."

"Bummer," Z. said as he began passing the bags to Tyrone.

Tyrone ignored him while he stacked the packages one on top of the other, flat against the existing wall. Z. then handed him the strips of cut plywood which he positioned over the bags. Using half inch nails, Tyrone tapped the boards into place.

"Lookin' good, bro," Z. said.

On the boat's dinette table, Z. measured and cut the cloth that would be glassed to the plywood.

"Make sure it's even," Tyrone said. "This has gotta be neat."

"You act like I don't know nothin.'"

While Z. rechecked his measurements, Tyrone smeared caulk around the edges of the new wood.

"Cloth's ready," Z. said.

Tyrone fitted the fabric to the new wall and hammered it in place with short, thin tacks. He then opened a can of resin, added white pigment, and stirred.

"I got finishing resin," he told Z. over his shoulder, "so we'll be able to sand it in a few hours."

When the pigment and resin were mixed to his satisfaction, Tyrone followed with the catalyst and stirred again.

"We have to hurry," Tyrone said. "We only have about twenty minutes before this stuff gets hard."

Using a brush, Tyrone saturated the glass cloth with resin while Z. peered over his shoulder.

"Get back, asshole! You're crowdin' me!"

"Sorry, bro."

When the job was completed, the cabin reeked with the pungent odor of new fiberglass and Tyrone felt his sinus passages crackle.

"Let's get out 'a here for a while," Tyrone said. "We'll have to wait a few hours before we can paint."

Z. nodded and followed Tyrone up the companionway and out of the cabin.

Three hours later they returned to the boat with a pint of off-white paint and a bristle brush. Tyrone knelt down and patted the wall.

"Yep, it's ready," he said.

Using a Stanley Surform tool for finishing, Tyrone went over the rough spots in the glass, then followed with sandpaper.

"Go ahead and open the can," Tyrone said.

"Can I paint?" Z. said.

"Yeah, but stir it first."

While Z. dabbed at the new interior, Tyrone leaned back and smoked a cigarette.

Oh, Mama, this ought 'a put me in solid with Danny. It's only the beginning.

Night covered their part of the world like an inverted black bowl. Outside the boat, thatch palms rustled in the light breeze and the dock creaked.

Chapter Two

Bahama Bank

Ten knots of wind hit the mainsheet driving the thirty-two-foot sail-boat through the water. The sloop moved beneath mountainous clouds that had begun building early in the day.

Alexandra Spencer, thirty-five, reclined on the fore deck, basking in the remaining warmth of the sun as she studied the many shades of blue around her. She had never seen a place that was quite so breathtaking.

She sighed, stretched her long tan legs and considered whether or not she needed to slather on another handful of sunscreen. Her freckles were rapidly multiplying under the bright Bahama sun. She stifled a yawn with the back of her hand as she peered over the railing to view the water surging passed the bow. The sea below was so transparent that she could see purple fans and reddish-brown starfish flourishing on the Bahama Bank.

Although Alex was unaware of it, she would never be more beautiful. Her face was smooth and taut, her expression both wise and innocent. She looked at the world through soulful brown eyes, moved with a body that was both strong and lithe.

With each passing hour, Alex felt more assured that she and Matt had made the right decision to buy the *Amani*. There were sacrifices, of course, and they would not have been able to own such an expensive boat if they hadn't been willing to leave it in charter for seven years. When she first heard they could purchase a yacht with only a down payment, she was ecstatic. It had taken her a while to convince Matt, but eventually he came around. They put ten thousand dollars down on a Pearson 323 and then the Yacht Charter Service took over. The Service maintained and insured the boat while making payments to the manufacturer with proceeds from the boat's rental. They were always obligated, of course, to make the monthly payment if the boat sat idle, but in seven years there had only been a few. At last the boat belonged to them. Though worn from constant use, it could easily be made whole again with a little love and a lot of soap and water.

Yes, they had paid their dues. Now there was time, endless days and nights to swim, sail, walk deserted beaches, make love. There would be solitude, quiet dinners, no phones or alarm clocks, no dogs barking.

Alex heard Matt sharing a weather report on the VHF radio with the skipper of another boat. She admired his ability to navigate and digest weather information, to fine tune the sails like a sensitive lover. His oneness with the wind and water were a result of the training he received while in the Navy. He had sat at the controls of airplanes, primarily fighter jets, for twenty-five years, and after he retired, the most logical transition for him was to convert his skills from the air to the sea.

Alex lounged on the bow, seemingly content, thinking about how perfect everything was, but beneath the surface she was disturbed by a vague sense that danger lay ahead. But how could that be? Certainly this was an adventure but unlike Columbus or Ponce de Leon who faced unknown perils, they were equipped with up-to-date charts and modern navigational gear. Matt had pointed out that if they exercised good judgment, they had nothing to fear. Alex refused to let anything, especially her own unfounded premonitions, spoil this precious day.

She concentrated on Matt who always made her feel safe. After eight years of marriage, they had both begun to feel an inner peace that neither of them had known before. She admitted publicly, much to his amusement, that she hog-tied him and dragged him to the alter. He would have been satisfied to live with her informally and indefinitely. She wanted more from their relationship and was convinced marriage was right for them. Before they found each other, divorces, family tragedies, and for Matt, the Vietnam War, had caused them to retreat from the world. Matt, especially, had built invisible yet formidable barriers around himself to protect his soul from further abuse. He had been a prisoner of war in Hanoi for six years, shot down by a heat-seeking missile that slammed into the rear of his A-4 jet as it cruised off the coast of Haiphong. It was a miracle that his seat ejected on impact before the plane blew apart like an exploding star. He fell, in his parachute, into a chicken coop and the welcoming arms of the Viet Cong. Alex continued to be amazed by Matt's ability to think positively about his imprisonment. He often said flippantly, "If you can't take a joke, you shouldn't put on your flight suit." Behind the laughter, she wondered if he meant it.

Alex, too excited to concentrate, found herself rereading the same page of her novel. Her eyes kept returning to the turquoise water and the low cays she could see lying dark and flat in the distance.

Without warning, the temperature plummeted and the wind quickened. Alex looked up at the towering clouds that had begun to rumble across the sky. Goose bumps appeared on her arms and legs.

"Hey, Skipper," she yelled from the fore deck, "we'd better close the hatches. Looks like we're gonna get it."

Matt peeked out through the companionway. "I've already closed the windows. How about getting the forward hatch?"

Alex collected her towel, paperback book, and sunscreen bottle and padded barefoot to the stern. The azure sky was quickly losing its hue and becoming leaden. She shivered as she inhaled and contemplated the impending storm. The air smelled like rain.

While below decks, she went to the V-berth to close the upper hatch. The wind had begun to sing in the rigging and she heard canvas flapping as Matt lowered the mainsail. When she returned topside, she stepped onto the roof of the cabin and helped him tie the sail to the boom.

"Not a perfect job," he said with a grin after they had finished, "but it'll do."

Alex looked at his twinkling blue eyes and felt warm inside. Matt, noticing her tender gaze, smiled.

"Okay, crew," he said, "we'd better duck below and put on our foul weather gear. This looks like a pretty good blow and there's no fiddler's green nearby."

Alex knew that fiddler's green was pilot slang for alternate airport, or more simply, a safe haven. It was Matt's way of saying they were on their own.

"I'm on my way," she said over her shoulder.

CHAPTER THREE

Mission Harbor

The shrill ring of the telephone violated Tyrone's quiet bedroom. After a late night on the town and most of the early morning in bed with Leona, Tyrone could barely move his head. His tongue, furry and sour tasting, seemed to take up an inordinate amount of space in his mouth. Willie could take credit for this. Tyrone and Leona had consumed several of Willie's deadly drinks in rapid succession.

Willie's, a three-story pink house with verandahs, white gingerbread, and wooden floors, was the most popular night spot for the locals as well as the tourists who began trickling in for happy hour at four. By six o'clock, there wasn't a seat in the house, and the reggae band began playing. By eight, Willie's stiff drinks owned the customers and everyone behaved as if there was no tomorrow.

It was always entertaining for the locals to watch the tourists and try to identify who was who. The serious boaters were easy to recognize with their sturdy brown bodies, Land's End shorts, and scuffed Sperry Topsider deck shoes. They loved to talk, mostly about the weather, anchors, and where they could wash a load of clothes. The hotel people, usually on vacation for a week or two, were always a lively bunch preoccupied with food, drink, and finding their next bed partner. They were the first ones to belly up to the bar and order doubles. Boat talk in general bored them and they didn't mingle well with the serious sailors until they had finished their second drinks and had started on their third. Their pink bodies were usually clad in Neiman Marcus outfits, and more often than not they wore new deck shoes from L.L.Bean.

The previous night the usual gang had been there; Lester and Pearl, Woody and his new squeeze, Laura, Rodney and Michelle, and Marilyn, always alone. Later the coke had given Tyrone its usual kick. Now he had to pay his dues until his body regained its balance.

The phone continued to ring, insisting that someone answer it. He opened his eyes, wiped a thin film of saliva from his lips, and tried to put the room into focus.

"Shit, somebody better had died," he said as he fumbled beneath Leona's bikini underwear and a discarded pizza carton. Clumsy with sleep, he knocked the receiver off the hook and it fell just within his grasp. Before he could say hello, he heard loud squawking on the other end.

"Yeah," Tyrone said and cleared his throat.

"You stupid shit!" Danny shrieked on the other end. "Jesus H. Christ, do you know what you and that dickhead did?"

Before Tyrone could reply, Danny shouted, "You put the fuckin' stuff on the wrong boat!"

Tyrone shot upright, pivoted, and planted his feet on the floor.

"You're shittin' me."

"I wish. Listen, prick, you assholes really fucked up this time! Some dude from Miami, Miguel somebody or other, showed up at the dock this morning and the coke was not, I repeat, was not on the *Amour*. When I saw Z. last night he told me that you guys had glassed the bags in, but hell, I never dreamed you'd screwed it up. I didn't find out until a few minutes ago that the coke was on the wrong boat and that the boat you idiots put it on had been taken out of charter. It's fuckin' gone!

Why did I listen to Ariel and try and do something for that jerk cousin of hers? And you, I expected more from you."

"Now listen, man," Tyrone said as his mind raced. "We made a mistake, but I'll take care of it."

Subconsciously this negative turn of events did not surprise Tyrone because bad luck had dogged him all his life. For as long as he could remember his mama had struggled to feed and shelter her seven children by washing clothes and hanging them on sagging lines that crisscrossed their backyard. Her customers were tourists and wealthy women from uptown who wore shiny purple dresses and wide-brimmed hats to church on Sunday.

Tyrone was a big man, six foot three, two hundred and thirty pounds of solid muscle. He had begun developing his physique when he was eight years old beginning with weight lifting exercises using unopened vegetable cans. He had built up his body out of fear rather than pride. To be strong meant that it was less likely he'd be at the wrong end of a fist on a Saturday night. His recurring dream to have money and power was nurtured by hard times. All he remembered about his father was the rich, woody smell of bourbon. He often sat in bars in order to inhale his memory.

He had learned as a boy that the white, perfumed tourists always had money, lots of it. They often asked, "How much?" but it didn't really matter. They bought whatever they wanted anyway. When he was growing up, one of those tourist dollars would have been plenty. Now a million of them would never be enough.

"It was that sorry-ass, shit-for-brains, asshole, Z.," Tyrone said. "He swore to me that he was sure about which boat it was, honest to God. I tried to reach you, man, you know, to double check. Ariel will tell you that I called yesterday." Tyrone tried to swallow. "Jesus, Danny, Ariel said she didn't know where you'd gone or when you'd be back. I told her that if she saw you last night, you were to call me at my place after midnight. Just ask her."

"That stupid bitch."

"Listen, Z. swore that he knew which boat it was, honest to God," Tyrone said in a rush. Do you think that I would fuck around with you or any of those guys? Those are some mean dudes and I sure as hell don't want to get on their bad side."

"Yeah, yeah, you're breaking my heart. You have until tonight to fix things or we're all screwed. Got it?"

"I swear, I'll take care of everything," he said. "Don't worry."

"And you'd better call me the minute, the minute you get the coke back to the dock."

With a bang, Danny slammed down the receiver leaving Tyrone seated on the side of the bed with the angry hum of a dial tone in his ear. He had reassured Danny but how was he going to reassure himself? Behind him there was a sharp clicking noise and a rustling of sheets. He turned to see Leona sitting up in bed quietly smoking a cigarette. Her dark mascara, smudged around her eyes, made her look like a blond raccoon.

"What's wrong, baby?" she asked between puffs.

"You don't want to know," Tyrone said shaking his head.

He stood up and felt the acrid taste of bile rising in his throat. Leona studied his firm black body that glistened with nervous sweat.

"I, uh, have business to take care of," he said. "I, uh…"

"Sure, honey," Leona said, "it's cool."

CHAPTER FOUR

Bahama Bank

Matt motioned to Alex to point the boat into the wind as he prepared to hoist the main. She nodded, changed the heading, and Matt quickly hauled the sail almost to the top of the mast, then used the winch to raise it the last few inches. He finished by looping the line in a figure eight around the main halyard cleat and tying it off with an inverted twist.

Alex turned the boat away from the wind and made one final trim setting before locking the mainsheet. The boat picked up speed as Matt returned to the cockpit, loosened the port jib sheet, and looped the other sheet around the starboard winch. She concentrated on holding her heading and watched as Matt pulled the roller furling line. Slowly at first and then with increasing momentum, the white-and-green-bordered sail popped fully open.

"Shut down the motor," he said, "and I'll re-trim the sails."

The intrusive throb of the diesel engine was replaced by the softer flap of canvas and the steady swish of water beneath the bow. Matt made one final adjustment to the jib, set the mainsail to match it, then secured them. With all her sailcloth up, the boat came alive.

"Now we can do some sailing," Matt said. "We've had to motor here more than I expected. Maybe we bought the wrong kind of boat."

"Bite your tongue!"

"Here, I'll take the wheel," he said. "I want to see how she handles on this point of sail."

"Then I'll be lazy. Call me when you want a break."

Matt watched Alex nimbly move to the bow, her favorite spot on the boat. He admired her trim body which resembled that of a much younger woman. Although she was thirty-five, she had worked hard at staying fit and the words middle aged didn't suit her yet. Her exercise program had definitely paid off.

He had not planned to marry again, and, in fact, had promised himself that he would not. After his other attempt at matrimony, a dismal failure, he couldn't imagine exposing himself to that much pain again. The whole evolution had cost him dearly, both emotionally and financially. Alex had insisted that they get married after they had been together for a little over a year. She was old fashioned about honor and commitment and wasn't comfortable having him as just a roommate. Matt could barely remember how afraid he had been at the mere prospect of remarrying. He believed that the moment they said their wedding vows, their relationship, which he considered ideal, would begin to disintegrate.

He had known a lot of women, all kinds, and had been let down by most of them. Alex was, he finally decided, his last chance for companionship and love. "Trust me," she had said repeatedly, but hell it hadn't been easy to trust her. She had offered to sign a prenuptial agreement before the ceremony and although he secretly liked the idea, he felt their marriage would begin on shaky ground if he took her up on her offer. In spite of his fears, he had jumped off the matrimonial cliff knowing that there would be no turning back. He couldn't remember when he stopped being afraid, possibly around year five. She did not change and did not expect him to change. There it was, truth in advertising. Surprise.

Over the years he had never tired of looking at her or touching her. She was fine boned and slender with proportions that fit her five foot five frame. Her delicate face housed large brown eyes that were often more expressive than her words. Like most women, she occasionally fretted about some part of her anatomy, her breast size or her belly, but sometimes when he looked at her, he was awed by her beauty. He regarded her good looks as a nice plus but considered it unnecessary icing on the cake. Of all her qualities, he most admired her gentleness and innocence which somehow had survived life's harsh realities. She still remained childlike and passionate which made him feel hopeful and alive. He wanted no one else.

"Did you see that?" Alex yelled as she pointed over the port side of the boat. "The biggest manta ray I've ever seen, six feet at least. It was tremendous!"

Matt peered over the railing and saw the dark shadow of the black creature that had just cruised by.

Alex, dangling precariously from the pulpit, hoped for another glimpse of the animal. The bow rose and fell with the waves, and for a moment he was fearful she might fall overboard and be crushed by the boat.

"Hey up there, be careful."

"I am," she said with her eyes still fixed on the water.

Sometimes she behaved recklessly, but he attributed this largely to inexperience. She had never faced death and therefore didn't know what it looked like.

Having found such a good life with Alex, one of his greatest fears was that something might happen to her. If she was late on a rainy night, his imagination ran wild and he had to resist the powerful urge to jump in his car and race up and down the highway frantically searching for her. He envisaged the wrecked automobile wrapped around her body, and he was impotent, unable to help her. With each passing day he found himself becoming more parental where her safety was concerned. If he continued in this direction, he knew that in time she would begin to chafe against his loving bridle. He both loved and hated her vulnerability. Intellectually, he recognized that he had overcorrected and his love mechanism had gotten out of control. Emotionally, he knew he was a goner.

Alex returned to the stern of the boat and kissed him lightly on the lips before she went below to make her deluxe ham, cheese, onion, and tomato on French bread sandwiches. Because Matt gobbled up everything she served him on the boat, she swore he would enjoy a paper plate with mustard smeared on it.

Matt watched the top of her head as she moved back and forth in the tiny galley. In a few minutes she handed him a plate through the companionway.

"Looks good," he said as he took it from her. "Where's yours?"

"I'll be right up."

Topside, paper plates in laps, they munched on their sandwiches and drank cold Budweiser beer from the can. Behind them, the boat's wake left an ever-widening trail.

CHAPTER FIVE

Mission Harbor

Tyrone banged on Z.'s door for five long minutes before he finally appeared, disheveled and sheepish behind the ratty screen.

"So…" Tyrone said.

"Yeah, so."

For a moment both men stared at each other, neither moving nor speaking. Finally Tyrone said in a monotone, "Get your gear. We're going on a little boat trip."

Z. pushed open the door and motioned for Tyrone to enter.

"Come on in. I'll get my stuff."

Z. wandered to the back of the house leaving Tyrone pacing in the cluttered living room. The house reeked of sour wine and stale cigarettes. The furniture, old rental, was torn and faded.

Z. emerged from the hallway with a duffel bag in his hand.

"Well, I'm all set," he said in a voice that was barely audible.

Tyrone clenched his fists in the bottoms of his pockets as he struggled to control his anger. When he first heard about the screw-up, his inclination had been to kill Z. Even now his fingers twitched when he glanced at Z.'s scrawny neck with its bulbous Adam's apple.

What a dumb shit.

Z. fumbled with the straps on his bag.

"You aren't, uh, gonna hit me are you?"

Tyrone eyed him without expression and motioned for Z. to follow.

Z. dropped his bag, reached down to pick it up. "It's kind of funny if you think about it."

"Funny? You think this is funny?"

"Not really I guess."

Tyrone could not give in to his feelings. He knew that if he didn't keep a lid on them, Z.'s house would be a crime scene. There would be blood, lots of it. And police. Police. That wouldn't do. Z. would be dead or severely maimed, Danny would be pissed, the law would be after him, and he'd be on his own to recover the missing coke. Having Z. with him wasn't worth much, but he knew that he needed someone to help him retrieve the bags from the *Amani*.

On the way to the Seaside Marina, Tyrone told Z. what he had planned.

"Listen," Tyrone said as he eased his Chevy through the traffic, "I'll go to the marina office and find out who took the boat and where they went. You take the car and go to the store and get us some supplies, some beer and ice. Buy one of those Styrofoam ice chests. Get us some sandwich stuff, you know, lunch meat and bread, some mustard. While you're doing that, I'm going to rent us a motor boat, one with a cabin. I'll meet you at the dock when I get finished."

After Tyrone pulled up to the marina office, put the Chevy in park, and got out, Z. eased behind the wheel. Tyrone tilted and positioned his face within an inch of Z.'s. He still struggled with the irrepressible desire to strangle him.

"Do this right, man," he said through clenched teeth, then stepped back and motioned to Z. to go forward. The car roared off, black smoke billowing from its rusty tailpipe and strains of, "Don't Worry, Be Happy," broadcasting from the radio.

Once inside the office, Tyrone found himself face to face with a petite, somber woman clad in a tank top and pressed blue jeans. She had a square face with thin, tight lips and an aquiline nose that supported thick glasses. Tyrone thought she resembled an owl because she blinked repeatedly. On the left side of her top, she wore a plastic tag that said, My name is Sadie, How may I help you?

"I'm looking for some friends of mine, uh, Sadie," Tyrone said.

Blink. Blink.

"These friends, I was supposed to meet them and go sailing. Dumb-assed me, I missed my plane and had to take another. Of course, I couldn't reach them by phone. Now I see that the boat's gone, and they probably think I stood 'em up."

"What boat are they on?"

"The *Amani,* a sailboat. Blue stripe, white hull."

She fumbled through a sheaf of receipts and found one somewhere in the middle.

"Oh, yes, the Pearson 323 that came out of charter early this morning."

"Yeah, that's the one. Left this morning, huh?"

"Americans," Sadie mumbled, "a nice couple."

"Yeah, they're good people."

Sadie pursed her lips and tapped a pencil she was balancing between her fingers on the counter.

"Well, you know," Tyrone said, "I have a great idea. I just might rent a boat and try and catch up with them. I haven't seen them in over a year. Do you happen to know which way they went?"

She scowled.

"We're not supposed to talk about our customers, sir. Some people are funny about that. Besides, I could get in trouble with Mr. Penske."

At that moment the phone on the desk behind her began to jingle and she turned to answer it. Tyrone quickly scooped up the slip she had set down on the counter and read the words, *Amani*, Final payment, Deleted from Listing, Copy Given to Owner. *Shit, that's no help.*

After Sadie hung up the receiver, she turned around and faced him. For a moment she looked perplexed.

This woman gives new meaning to the expression, dumb broad. He gave her his best smile.

"Oh," she said with a little sigh.

"Well, how about it?" My friends would be really surprised if I turned up. Like you said, they're nice folks."

She furrowed her brow and tapped her pencil on the counter again. *Come on bitch!*

Finally, she expelled another little sigh and said, "Well, I guess it would be all right, but you have to promise not to tell anyone that I told you, okay?"

"Oh, sure, right, you can trust me."

"Well, they mentioned that they were going to sail to the northern cays, quote, away from it all, unquote. I do believe I heard them talking about Charter Cay as their first destination, you know, New Union Settlement."

"Oh, that's just great! I'm sure I can catch up with 'em there. Do you rent boats?"

"Oh, no, sir, they handle that next door."

Tyrone backed out of the office.

"You have really made my day, Sadie, and you've made my friends' day, too," he said grinning. He raised a palm in a farewell gesture.

"No problem," Sadie said and blinked.

CHAPTER SIX

New Union Settlement, Charter Cay, Bahamas

The harbor at New Union, with its sailboats bobbing from their anchors, resembled a postcard. Sailors of diverse ages and nationalities motored to the newly-built dinghy dock to plant their feet on solid ground and experience civilization again.

Alex climbed down the stern ladder of the sailboat, carefully stepped into their orange-red Zodiac dinghy, and positioned herself aft by the outboard motor. She watched Matt swing first one leg and then the other over the railing.

"We should buy at least two loaves of that homemade bread," she said, as he stepped down the ladder and into the dinghy. "We need one to eat with dinner tonight and one to cram in our mouths on the way back to the boat."

Alex squeezed the rubber primer bulb on the red gas tank directly in front of her feet. She thought for a moment before she set the choke on the outboard and moved the throttle to the start position.

"Make sure you're in neutral," Matt said.

"I am," she said, as she reached for the starting cord.

In a series of smooth coordinated movements, she pulled the cord, repositioned the throttle to idle when she heard the engine start, and quickly disengaged the choke.

Once underway, the Zodiac bounced up and down the choppy waves as Alex maneuvered the little boat through the crowded harbor and up to the dinghy dock.

"Careful, honey," Alex said as Matt pushed two inflatables out of their way in order for them to get closer to the dock ladder.

"We're okay. Just cut the motor and I'll pull us in."

Alex brought the engine back to idle before turning it off. Once on the dock, they stretched their legs and enjoyed the sensation of flat dry earth beneath their feet.

"Where do you want to go first?" she asked as they strolled down main street carrying their empty tote bags.

"First I need to run to the hardware store and get a few things for the boat; a new thermostat, fuses for the electrical system, and an alternator belt, just in case that old engine develops the kind of problems that I know how to fix."

"I think I'll pass on the hardware store. I'm going to stop at one of the shops they mentioned in our travel guide and buy some T-shirts and postcards. I am, after all, a typical tourist on vacation."

"Listen, dear girl," he said as he rested his arms on her shoulders, "there is nothing typical about you."

"Ah, how sweet," she said and patted his cheek. "Why don't I meet you in about thirty minutes?"

"Is that going to be enough time for you to look around?"

"Oh, sure. I don't want to load us down. I just want to get my Mom a T-shirt with something tacky written on it, something like *Bahama Mama*."

"You're kidding. For your mother?"

"Sure, why not? She'll love it. She can wear it to bingo."

"Okay, I'll see you here in thirty minutes," he said.

After a half hour of browsing in the By The Way Hut, Alex returned to the spot where they had parted to find Matt sipping a Diet Pepsi.

"Hey, big boy, where'd you get that?" she asked as she took the can from his hand and took a swig.

"From the grocery store up the street, the one called Harold's. I met the nicest people and there really is a Harold. He's an old guy that sits on a bench inside the store and greets the customers as they come in the door. Not only is it a grocery store, it's also a souvenir shop and an unofficial chamber of commerce for the Settlement. I'll have you know that I learned a lot about this place in twenty minutes."

Alex glanced behind her at the tiny sherbet-colored houses that lined the narrow main street.

"Such as?"

"Such as, New Union Settlement population is less than four hundred and fifty. It was settled by the Loyalists. And in case you've forgotten your American History 101, the Loyalists were the ones who remained faithful to the British. After the revolution, they left America with everything but their crops and settled in the Bahamas because the Islands were governed by the Crown. Let's see. Their economy is based on fishing and tourism."

"Who told you all this?"

"Harold. I think it's the canned lecture he gives every tourist who stops to chat for a minute."

"Well, you can be a tour guide if we run out of money," she said and gave him a lingering kiss on the cheek.

"I also found out that the favorite local drink is called a Goombay Smash. It's a mixture of dark rum, apricot brandy, and, uh, pineapple juice."

"Ah, one of those killer drinks. Better watch out. I might get wild and dance nude on the table."

"That I would like to see."

"Trust me, it wouldn't be a pretty sight."

Alex opened her bag and pulled out a pink and turquoise T-shirt with a hand-painted palm tree on the front and a slogan which boasted, *It's Better In The Bahamas.*

"No *Bahama Mama*, huh?"

"They didn't have one like that. Besides, Mom will like this one just as well. You know how she is, just happy to be remembered."

"Let's go back to Harold's and get a few things," Matt said. "Harold told me that the boat from the mainland had come in this morning and they are stocking the refrigerators with fresh stuff. 'Buy today,' Harold said, 'because tomorrow there will be slim pickin's,' or something to that effect."

"And what about the tons of canned food that I have stashed on the boat? I could open my own convenience store."

"Well, fresh is better and we can afford it."

"Okay, but let's don't forget the bread."

After loading their bags with produce, they stopped again at the hardware store to buy some block ice for the boat.

"Are we going to be able to carry all this?" she asked.

"We'll manage."

Alex waited outside while Matt bantered with a friendly female clerk and paid for the ice. She enjoyed watching him. He looked animated, almost youthful through the cloudy glass. When he stepped outside into the sunlight, Alex noticed a softness in his muscle tone that belied his boyish face.

As they carried their bags to the dinghy dock, Matt suddenly said, "Coconut rum."

"What?"

"Coconut rum. That's another ingredient in that exotic drink I told you about."

"I'm sold. But for now, let me at that bread."

The loaf, still warm from the oven, seemed to melt in their mouths.

"Don't think about the lard in this or the cholesterol," Alex said between bites. "Anything that tastes this good must be bad for you."

"Who was thinking about that?"

"I told you we'd need two loaves," she said as she tore off another piece.

***

On the boat that evening the wind blew from the north. The *Amani*, anchored on a windward shore, sat comfortably. While Alex hovered over the pots simmering on the alcohol stove, Matt sat at the navigation desk and studied a chart for the next day's cruise.

"Have we definitely decided to go to Jack Cay tomorrow?" he said.

"I suppose. We haven't seen it and it's nearby, isn't it? Janice raved about the west end of the Island, said it was a paradise. And isolated. I'd like that."

"No, wait," he said as he tapped his pencil on the chart, "we can't anchor there because the wind may still be out of the north. The swell from the Atlantic probably wraps around this point here and that would make it a rough anchorage."

He tapped his pencil again.

"Let's see. It's either the southern side of Jack Cay or an Island called Pine. We can get protection from the north and east wind in either of those places. The woman in the hardware stare said that they were both pretty spots. By the way, did you notice how the townspeople talked? I think it's the British influence."

"Yes, did you hear that man in the grocery store say hoysters for oysters?"

"Yeah, I did. Well, what will it be, madam? You are the real captain of this vessel."

"You love to say that, don't you?"

"Only because it's true."

"Okay, let's go to Pine Island. I read that it has a long secluded beach and the shelling is fabulous at low tide. I'd love it if you would just turn me loose and let me explore for hours. I'll take a thermos of water and walk until my legs give out or it gets dark, whichever comes first."

"Pine it is," he said and put down his pencil.

As Alex bent over to retrieve a pan, Matt walked up behind her and leaned into her backside.

"Hey, little girl, you sure you want dinner?" he said.

"I thought I did," she said and turned to embrace him, "but I can skip it if you have something else in mind."

She turned, leaned into him, and tickled his neck with her tongue. His skin tasted salty.

Matt stepped back, patted her bottom, and said, "Oh, I can wait for dessert."

While Alex prepared instant iced tea, he flopped on a quarter berth and inspected the interior of the *Amani*.

"You know, he said, "the Charter Service really took good care of the boat."

He laced his hands behind his head and leaned back.

"I thought we might end up with a hull and not much else." he said. "As it turns out, it looks all right."

"I think so," she said as she glanced about the cabin. "It isn't in bad shape. Nothing is wrong that a lot of scrubbing won't cure. I can make new curtains and redo the upholstery myself. And I'd love to work on the teak railings."

"The engine. That's another story. It looks like I'm going to have to replace it before too long. It's racked up a lot of hours. We can't trust it to go too far without some kind of problem."

"I'm surprised the Charter Service did some fiberglass work on the boat. Did you notice the odor when we first got on? I can still smell it. Stinky."

"Yeah, but I haven't seen anyplace that looks like it's been repaired. I'll rummage around later. Let's keep our fingers crossed that the boat hasn't been in an accident and the hull has been weakened. The YCS didn't mention anything, but I'm not sure that's something they would tell us about."

"Come on," she said, "let's go topside and eat. We can watch the sun set. We only get so many, you know."

"Amen to that."

After dinner they sat in the cockpit while Matt drank his coffee, black, and Alex sipped Courvoisier. The sun had long since dipped beneath the horizon and left them sitting in the coolness of the gray evening. Matt put down his empty cup and slipped an arm around her. She shivered.

"You cold?"

"A little. It's getting chilly."

She nestled closer to him and he inhaled her fragrance.

"You're beautiful, you know," he murmured as he nuzzled her hair.

"I'm glad you think so."

She turned and gently kissed his lips. He tasted the brandy.

"Let's go below," he said. "Time for bed."

Once inside, Matt inserted the screen in the companionway while Alex rinsed the cups. He watched her hurriedly wipe off the galley counter and metal sink. As always, he was eager to hold her. From the beginning no problem had ever been allowed between them and the physical pleasure they shared. If they had an argument, they checked it at the bedroom door. Early in their relationship they both demonstrated that neither was responsible for the other's sexual fulfillment, and by so doing, the giving was boundless. Without demands, they found it easy to please each other.

When she finished tidying up, he drew her to him and held her against his chest. He felt her heart fluttering like the wings of a small bird. He stepped back, looked into her eyes, then focused on her parted lips. The tension was already starting to build inside him. He gently pushed her against the quarter berth. She looked up at him but did not make a sound. It was obvious that she wanted him, that the years had not taken away the edge. Her dark eyes drew him closer. They began to slowly disrobe. After they were undressed, she pressed her mouth against his and explored its depths with her tongue. He responded by placing his hand on her breast and gently massaging her nipple. The sensation evoked a soft moan from her.

As always, her eagerness made him throb and a slow smile crossed his lips. She exhibited a wanton desire that he found irresistible. After years of making love to each other, they were experts in knowing how and where to touch. With one precise movement, they were joined. As his passion intensified, he measured his response and paced himself. Oblivious to all else, they moved until she shuddered and urged him on. Only then did he yield and allow his own release. In the moments before they parted, he felt as if they were drawing the same breath.

CHAPTER SEVEN

Mission Harbor

By the time Z. returned to the dock, it was five-thirty.

"Shit, man," Tyrone said as Z. handed him a bag of groceries. "I didn't know you were gonna' take all fuckin' afternoon to buy a few supplies. I was just about to go lookin' for you. What took you so long?"

"Well, you know, I had to go to a lot of places, and I ran into Buster and Pearl at the Easy Sail."

"What were you doin' at the Lounge?"

"Well, I went there, you know, to buy the ice, the block kind. That's the only place I know to get it. And Pearl said, 'Hey, man, sit down and take a load off your brains.' I couldn't say no. Besides, I knew you had a lot to do here and…"

"Well, asshole, you knew wrong. I have been standing around here with my mind in neutral and my thumb up my ass for hours. We were supposed to be back, you hear me, be back with the coke by tonight. As it is, we'll be lucky if we catch up with the sailboat before dark. I already had to call Danny and tell him that we wouldn't be at the dock until tomorrow morning. You know he was totally pissed."

Z. cringed and looked at him like a battered wife.

"Oh, Jesus, just hand me the stuff!" Tyrone said. "We need to get underway before sunset. I'm not going near White Cay Passage after dark, I'll tell you that. If the sea's rough, we'll get our butts kicked."

Z. handed the rest of the supplies to Tyrone and no more was said until the engine of the cabin cruiser roared to life and the boat was out of the slip and threading its way through Mission Harbor's congested basin.

"I get seasick real easy," Z. said as they rounded the tip of the Island and set up a course for their first checkpoint, Broad Bay, some twenty miles distant.

"I'm sorry to hear that," Tyrone said and smirked. "What a shame."

The powerful engine drove the boat at twenty knots and in an hour they were beyond Broad Bay and on their new heading to Charter Cay. The sun, now below the horizon, offered scant light for them to see by. Tyrone jammed the throttle forward and the twenty-eight foot hull bounded through the waves leaving its wake crashing on the shore as they rounded White Cay.

"It's gettin' dark," Z. said.

His face bore a greenish cast in the twilight.

"We'll be there in another hour so hold onto your groceries."

"I feel like shit."

"You look like shit, but then that's not unusual."

Z. gripped the railing and clenched his teeth as the boat pounded through the chop.

As Tyrone expected, the heavy sea outside White Cay slowed them down. At seven-thirty Tyrone throttled back and idled the engine into the anchorage off Charter Cay. There were over fifty boats, all makes and sizes, most of them bobbing from two anchors positioned forty-five degrees apart. Some were so close together that passing between them in the dark was risky, both for his propeller and their anchor lines.

"Fuck!" Tyrone yelled over the engine noise.

"What's wrong?" Z. asked.

"It's too dark to cruise around here. Soon it will be as black as the underside of a Mau-Mau's moo-moo. We won't be able to see for shit!"

"What are we gonna' do?"

"What else can we do? We're gonna' anchor this goddamn thing and spend the night."

"Stay here 'til morning?"

"No, idiot, we're going back to Mission Harbor and come back tomorrow. Of course we're gonna' stay here, asshole. First, I already told you I'm not going around White Cay in the dark, and second and more important, we have got to get that coke. I don't know about you but I'm not going back without it. Now get the anchor."

"Do we have an anchor?"

"Jesus, yes we have an anchor. It's in the anchor well, in that compartment on the bow. Up front," he said and pointed straight ahead. "Go up there and look. You'll see it. Take the flashlight."

"Okay, but don't rock the boat so much."

"Jesus Christ, Z., I don't make the waves!"

Z. groped his way to the bow and spotted the anchor well with the beam of his flashlight.

"I found it! Here it is!"

"So, get it out, asshole!"

Z. lifted the hatch and peered inside.

"There ain't nothin' in here 'cept some rope."

"What?"

"I said there ain't nothin' in here 'cept some rope."

Tyrone made a sharp U-turn and headed out of the anchorage beyond the lines where they could drift and he could go forward to see for himself. A safe distance from the congestion he looked inside the anchor well and confirmed his fear, no anchor. He could hardly blame Z. for this little screw-up. He'd been so pissed with him for being late that he had neglected to make a proper inventory before they departed.

"Now what?" Z. said.

"Well, we'll just have to tie up to the Government Dock over there, the one they use for Customs.

"Do you think that's a good idea?"

"I think it's the only idea, how's that?"

Tyrone returned to the cockpit, put the boat in forward gear, and made his way to the dock which barely had room for the cabin cruiser. Fortunately, it was lighted and he could tie up with the lines in the anchor well.

"Tomorrow we'll get an anchor in town, first thing," Tyrone said.

"We shouldn't need an anchor tomorrow, should we? I mean won't we catch up with those people and be back in Mission Harbor before dark?"

"I'm not going anywhere else on this boat without an anchor. What if the engine quits? We could drift out to sea. Besides, the way things have been going, we just might need it."

"Listen, bro, we as good as have 'em. You'll see."

"No we don't, asshole. And quit callin' me bro."

CHAPTER EIGHT

Pine Cay, Bahamas

Pine Cay, shaped like a wolf's head with a long slender neck, was easy to identify. Within two miles, Matt made out a dilapidated pier and high tan bluffs on the western end of the Island. Through binoculars he saw two boats gently swimming at anchor a hundred yards off the pier. On shore, the skeleton of a derelict boat rose from the sand. It looked like a good anchorage.

When the *Amani's* nose pointed two hundred yards off the bluffs and the depth finder registered eight feet, Alex padded forward and dropped the anchor.

After a few minutes Matt called, "Is it holding?"

Alex, who was bent over, straightened up and shrugged.

"Amazing," she said as she returned aft. "The bottom looks like sand, but it acts like a terrazzo floor. I've never seen anything like it. The anchor feels like it's going in and then it just skates."

"Don't worry about it, honey, Matt said as he shut down the engine and began searching for his snorkel and fins.

"I'll dive on the anchor like I did yesterday and make sure the flukes are at least pointed in the right direction.

"Have you seen my mask?"

"Yeah, I'll get it. I hung it on a peg next to the power cord."

After donning his diving gear, Matt slid into the cool water and slowly paddled fifty feet in front of the boat. Alex hovered on the bow searching the water for anything threatening and watched as Matt dove down to the anchor, resurfaced, then dove again.

"How's it look?" she hollered, but he didn't hear her and began swimming back.

"Well I wouldn't bet my life on it," he said as he climbed up the stern ladder. "If there's any bad weather headed our way, we're out 'a here."

"How far did the flukes go in?"

"They're down about four inches. I shoved as hard as I could, but it's just like you said, a hard floor with sand and a few tufts of turtle grass on top. As long as the weather stays like this, we don't have to worry about the anchor dragging. If the weather turns sour and we need to find shelter in a hurry, I know some places to hide out. We could go to Great Cay, which is one of the northern islands, or we could go back to Mission Harbor. Another option is the sound at Charter Cay and there's one more place that looks interesting, Robert's Cay. It's small and well protected. You're not concerned about the anchor right now are you?"

"Well, not really. I guess I don't need that much sleep."

"Relax. I'll keep an eye on it."

"Listen, honey, if you say it's okay and you're not bothered about it, then I won't give it another thought."

"That's my girl."

"How 'bout a cold beer?"

"You betcha. I'm thirsty."

Alex went below while Matt stowed the gear.

"Can you believe this place?" he said. "Isn't this a paradise?"

"What did you say?" she said as she came up with the beer and an unopened bag of pretzels.

"I said can you believe this place?"

"It is beautiful," she said as she gazed at the Island. "There were too many boats in the anchorage last night. It was disappointing. I was under the impression that these islands were still undiscovered."

"We wish," Matt said as he took a swig of beer. "Ah, that's good."

"I guess I had an image in my mind of us as Robinson and Mrs. Crusoe, alone and uninhibited."

Matt leered and said, "You didn't seem all that inhibited last night, Mrs. Crusoe."

"Not that kind of inhibited. I thought we could frolic in the buff, you know, walk the beach for miles and not see another living soul."

"There are places like that not too far from here, honey. I heard the northern cays are not as popular and are more isolated. And I'll tell you what, I'll make sure before this trip is over that we visit some of those places where we can be as wild and wanton as you like."

"Why don't we go to the beach now and look around?" she said.

Matt looked at her sparkling eyes and eager face. When she asked something of him, the word, no, vanished from his vocabulary.

She looked longingly at the Island and then back at him.

"I want to explore that wonderful shore on the ocean side. There are supposed to be a lot of good shells."

"Well, I can take you in the dinghy, but I'm not sure about leaving the boat unattended with the holding as crummy as it is. How 'bout if I drop you off and come back and get you later?"

"Great! Just let me put on my bathing suit and get my tote bag for shells, and a jug of water, and a snack and…"

"You do plan to come back, don't you?"

"Maybe, maybe not."

"You'd miss me," he said.

"You got that right."

The Zodiac dinghy's four-horse motor wasn't powerful enough to make it plane, but it easily delivered them to the beach. As the water depth descended, its clarity increased. There were countless starfish resting like enormous brown hands on the sea bottom. They hauled the dinghy far enough ashore to tie it to a tree and then found a well-traveled path across the Island. At the end of the trail they were not prepared for the splendor that awaited them. The beach at low tide revealed a broad white sandbar jutting far out into a basin that opened into the blue Atlantic. Flocks of sea gulls soared, landed, then became airborne when Alex and Matt passed by. The water farther out was shimmering aquamarine, and frothing waves thundered ashore on a barrier island. For a moment, they were dazzled.

Alex, noticing the birds, pointed out that they were obviously having a bird meeting. "See," she said, "they have one guy standing out front, He's in charge. Probably discussing the shortage of pilings."

Matt smiled and continued strolling behind her.

"Or he might be commenting," he said, "that things have taken a tern for the worse."

"O-o-h, that's so awful."

Alex buoyed at the sight of the long pristine beach that stretched for miles. A walking trip around the Island at low tide appeared to be possible but would require some wading. Several casuarina trees, their foundations eroded by relentless tides, lay on their sides, partially covered by sand. She would have to maneuver around them.

There were numerous areas along the shore dotted with colored shells, pink and yellow, many white. Alex oohed and ahhed like a child with a wad of money in Toys 'R Us.

"Well," Matt said as he glanced behind him, "I suppose I'd better go check the boat. You sure you'll be all right alone out here?"

Alex looked at him absently for a moment before rising from a squatting position with a shell in her hand. She glanced up and down the beach.

"Sure, I'll be fine. We did find a deserted beach. It's wonderful. Look, there aren't even any foot prints."

"Okay then," he said as he backed away from her, "check your watch. I have two o'clock."

"Me, too."

"I'll meet you on the beach where we left the dinghy at five."

"I'll be there even though I feel I could stay here forever. See you at five."

Matt waved and started back. Before he had taken but a few steps, he turned and said, "Now don't be late or I'll worry. And be careful."

Alex, already engrossed in her quest for shells, didn't hear him and continued up the beach with her bag lightly tapping against her hip. Matt smiled and shook his head.

On the sound side, Matt untied the dinghy and pushed it into the water. As he climbed aboard, he noticed a proliferation of sea urchins and hoped that one of them hadn't punctured the dinghy with a spine. On his way back to the sailboat, he saw that two other vessels had arrived in their absence. A thirty-seven foot Tayana sailboat and a small cabin cruiser had anchored near the *Amani*. As he passed in front of the Tayana, he observed a balding, middle-aged man crouched on the bow unsnarling a tangle of anchor line. He looked up and waved when Matt came by. With no one on deck, the other boat, the cabin cruiser, silently rode the waves like a ghost ship. As he motored by, Matt read the name on the stern, *The Happy Hour*, and inwardly groaned. *I'll bet that's a party boat, and we'll be up all night. We just can't escape from the noisy, inconsiderate people*, he thought with a scowl. Suddenly he laughed. *What's the matter with me? They haven't made a sound yet.*

Matt lounged in the cockpit and updated his ship's log. He noted the date, place, time, engine hours, and briefly described their day. When he finished making the entry, he drew a happy face and closed the book with a clap. With his hands laced behind his head, he stretched out his legs and studied the other boats. Now there was no one topside. A lone fly circled before it landed on Matt's knee. Absently he brushed it away.

The boats were all silently bobbing and swimming at anchor like nervous colts. He glanced at his watch. It was almost two-thirty. The sounds of lapping water and a hanging towel fluttering from the lifeline had a soothing affect on him. He felt his eyelids growing heavy. I guess I have time for a nap, he decided and went below. Lying in the V-berth, he rocked like a baby in a cradle. Concerned that he might oversleep, he set an alarm clock for four forty-five and closed his eyes.

CHAPTER NINE

Pine Cay

Z. slouched against the backrest of the quarter berth and lit a joint. The pungent smell of marijuana quickly permeated every corner of the small cabin.

"Hey, man," Z. said, "what'd I tell you? Piece 'a cake. We got the engine fixed, just like I said. Everything's gonna be fine."

Tyrone, who was peering through the window above Z.'s head said, "Don't be so sure about that."

He had yet to recover from the delay caused by a clogged fuel filter. His nerves felt like guitar strings that had been wound too tightly and inside he vibrated with tension. Tyrone could not help wondering how their absence was affecting Danny. At least he had been able to call and explain their delay, but Danny had sounded strange, distant. It was not what he said but the way he had said it. He did not yell and make threats, and that wasn't like Danny. His words were as flat and even as store-bought bread.

"The Boat Doctor fixed us right up," Z. said. "All we had to do was call 'em and there he was."

"Yeah, four hours later. Longest fuckin' four hours of my life."

"But he fixed it, right? That's all that matters."

"Yeah, yeah," Tyrone said, "for a hundred bucks. I got a receipt and that goddamn boat rental is gonna have to give me back my money. They ought 'a put better gas in the tanks, not that cheap crap. We would have caught up with the sailboat this morning if the engine had been running."

"A small setback, bro. We have 'em in our sights now. Why don't you just kick back. Chill, man."

"You know what, Z., you're brain dead. I'm sure of it. Do you have any idea what kind 'a shit we're in?"

"Oh, I know, Danny's pissed, but he'll get over it."

A wave of frustration washed over Tyrone and he turned away from the window.

"Have you seen the woman yet?" Z. said.

"Not yet."

Tyrone was thinking about Matt, who he had observed earlier. Z. was down to the last drag of a joint which he held pinched between his right thumb and forefinger.

"Sure you don't want a hit?" he said and offered it to Tyrone.

Tyrone shook his head.

"Not now. Not now."

Tyrone knew there was supposed to be a couple on the sailboat so he assumed that the woman was below decks or on the beach. He guessed that the man was in his late forties, early fifties. He looked trim, gray at the temples, about six feet tall. Tyrone had watched him while he sat in the cockpit and wrote in a book before disappearing below. Tyrone stepped over to the window again and scratched his arm.

"We've got to make a plan, Z."

"Yeah, that makes sense. Whatcha think?"

"Well, we've gotta get close to the sailboat, make sure there's only two people on board. I don't want any surprises."

Z. nodded.

"Let's pump up the dinghy. It has oars."

"We have a dinghy? Far out! Where is it?" Z. said.

"Under the your bunk. Lift up the cushions. Get all that shit out 'a there, and we'll take it topside."

Above decks they opened the rubber inflatable and attached a foot pump.

"Okay," Tyrone said, "step up and down on that foot pedal there until you can't pump anymore."

"Why do I have to do it?"

"Why not, asshole? You are absolutely the most worthless piece of…"

Z. sighed, raised a foot, and began stomping up and down on the lever. In less than a minute he was out of breath and gasping.

"You're just the picture of health, aren't you dirt bag? Hurry up!" Tyrone said.

"Jesus, man, I'm going as fast as I can. Why don't you take a turn."

Tyrone pushed Z. aside sending him backwards. Z. hit the deck with a thud and got up with a look of pained surprise.

"Hey, bro, take it easy."

Tyrone pumped hard and rhythmically and soon the gray inflatable had filled and taken shape. He removed the pump and capped the valve on the dinghy. After attaching a line to the bow, they hoisted the little boat over the side.

"I gotta take a leak," Z. said and unzipped his pants.

"Not outside, asshole. Too many people around. Civilized people don't wanna see your johnson. Use the head. We don't want everybody lookin' at us."

Tyrone followed Z. below. His worry had compounded like interest on an overdue loan, and he couldn't shake the nagging feeling that they were in more trouble than even he imagined. He did not have any experience in the drug business but recognized that they were probably in over their heads. He also knew that he lacked one necessary characteristic to be good in this game and that quality was ruthlessness. He could defend himself or protect someone else, but to be an aggressor was not his style. The truth of the matter was that for all the material deprivation he had endured as a child, his Mama had always loved him, and he knew it. It was not in him to hate. Unlike his peers, he possessed a gentleness that made him feel that he was lacking.

Before Z. finished in the head, Tyrone heard the sputter of a dinghy motor and peeked outside just as the man passed by the stern of the boat. He was making his way toward the beach on the eastern end of the Cay. Tyrone watched him grow smaller as the red dinghy drew nearer to the distant shore.

"Where are the binoculars?" he said.

"Hell, I don't know," Z. said.

"You had 'em last, asshole. Where did you put 'em?"

"Oh, yeah, right, I did. They're, uh, outside under the steering wheel."

Tyrone found the binoculars and focused them so that he could clearly see the man approaching a woman on the beach. She appeared to be carrying something in her arms, and the man took whatever it was from her and placed it in the dinghy. She then removed some kind of footwear from her feet and tossed them into the boat before helping the man lift the inflatable off the beach and into the water. In a few moments, she started the motor and guided the boat in his direction.

Z. lay back on one of the berths. Relaxed by the marijuana, he closed his eyes.

Five or six minutes later, Tyrone heard the hum of the small outboard as it once again passed by the stern, and he heard a woman's voice. She said, "I just couldn't believe it. I found some perfect specimens. I'll have to look them up in the shell book. The time went by just like that."

The man said something Tyrone couldn't make out. Then he heard the woman say, "It was so beautiful. And I didn't see another soul. I want to go back again tomorrow."

Once the couple was propelled out of hearing range, her voice became resonant as it was picked up and carried back to him on the wind. She must have laughed because Tyrone remembered his sister Maggie's laugh was very much the same. The sound reminded him of wind chimes tinkling softly in a summer breeze. Thinking of his sister brought his old home in Soundside to mind. He wished he was there now and not trying to get on board some stranger's boat. He wished he had never met Z., or Danny, for that matter. He should have taken his Mama's advice and gone to Nassau to work with his Uncle Isaac. Well, he thought, I can wish in one hand…

Tyrone watched the couple board the sailboat and briefly embrace. He found their affection for each other disturbing. Except for his Mama, honest love had eluded him.

When he glanced down at Z., he saw that he was asleep with his arms flung over his head. His nose whistled each time he inhaled.

CHAPTER TEN

Pine Cay

Alex, sitting across from Matt in the cockpit, reached inside her bag and pulled out one of her treasures. Beside her lay an opened shell book.

"Okay, check this one out," she said. "It's a Sunrise Tellin." She held up a pink and white shell that was neatly joined by a thin ligament.

Matt eyed it with polite interest but obviously did not share her enthusiasm for mollusks.

"Yeah, that's pretty."

"And you know if I had more time, I could have walked around the entire Island. I'll bet there are hundreds of shells on the other end."

She handed him another one.

"This is, uh, let me see," she said as she thumbed through the book. "It's an Eastern Turret. See how detailed it is? And nothing's broken."

Matt placed the shell next to the first one she had shown him.

"I have a lot but we can look at the rest later."

Matt nodded. He felt mildly relieved that he didn't have to pretend to be interested in the whole bag.

"You know, I'm a mess. I've got sand everywhere, and I do mean everywhere," she said as she put the shells back into her beach tote. "I'll get a couple towels and we can take a real Bahamian bath."

"How's that?"

"Pat told me that you can bathe in salt water with Joy dishwashing soap, so I brought some along. You can wash your hair with it, too. You'll have to put your bathing suit on, though. Too many boats around."

"Won't we be sticky from the salt water?"

"That's easy. After we get back in the boat, we make a dash for the shower and quickly rinse off with fresh water. That way our ship's supply will last longer."

"I'm game," Matt said as he stood up. "I'll put on my trunks."

Alex climbed out of the cabin with two towels and a bottle of Joy soap. Matt followed her up the companionway.

"Okay," she said as she put the things down near the ladder, "here I go!"

With a squeal, she dove over the side and came up laughing. Matt followed.

As directed by Alex, he lathered himself with Joy soap and rinsed off.

"Let's go for a swim," Matt said.

The chilly water became more comfortable after a few minutes. Alex trailed behind Matt as he swam ahead with strong even strokes. They paddled to the cabin cruiser, then turned and paddled back to their boat. Before they climbed the stern ladder, they each held onto a lower rung.

"I love you, you know," she told him and pushed a wayward lock of hair away from his brow.

"I love you, too," he said and drew her to him.

"Let's get out," she said and tapped his nose. "I'm cold."

She grasped another rung and climbed up the ladder.

"Now I'm freezing," she said and giggled.

"Hey, wait for me."

Matt followed her trail of water to the shower where he found her naked and trembling in the tiny cubicle.

"Hurry! Get in!" she said, then closed the folding door behind him.

"Come here," she said.

She looped her arms around his neck and pulled his face close to hers. Suddenly, a look of panic crossed his eyes and he stiffened.

"I, uh, can't stay in here," he said.

"What?"

"I, uh, ..."

Before he could explain, he began clawing at the door.

"Too close," he said as his bare back vanished into the main cabin.

Alex found him lying on the floor taking deep breaths.

"What is it?" she asked as she knelt beside him.

"I'm sorry. That hasn't happened in a long time."

"Is it because of...?"

Her brow knitted with concern.

"Yeah, but I'm better now."

"Want me to help you up?"

"No, I'll be all right in a minute. You go ahead."

"Okay, but call me if you need me."

After Alex finished her shower, Matt decided to rinse off in the stall by himself.

"Sure you'll be okay?"

"Well, if I'm not, I'll be out of there in a shot. I did fine last night. I think I just panicked because we were both in there and I felt trapped, like I couldn't get enough air."

Matt finished rinsing off while Alex prepared Dijon mustard and mayonnaise potato salad and fried a few pieces of canned ham. They had some fresh tomatoes from Harold's, which she sliced and liberally sprinkled with Italian dressing, salt and pepper.

Matt set the table with knives, forks, and napkins, and filled two large glasses with unsweetened iced tea. They sat down and began eating. The food was especially tasty. They were ravenous.

"I'm famished," she said before she stuffed a heaping fork of potato salad in her mouth.

"Me, too, but then as you have pointed out on numerous occasions, I usually am when I'm on boats."

"Try the tomatoes." she said as she nudged the plate toward him. "They're delicious."

They devoured everything she had prepared and after the dishes were washed, they took their coffee and brandy to the cockpit.

"Thanks for the good chow, ma," he told her and took a sip of black coffee.

"I'm glad you enjoyed it. I know I did. Weight Watchers here I come. I don't know what it is out here. The fresh air? The exercise? Being totally relaxed? Whatever it is, food always tastes yummy."

"All of the above," he said and took another sip of coffee.

"Do you, uh, feel better now?" she asked him and gently touched his shoulder.

"Sure, don't worry about it."

"We haven't talked much about prison," she said. "I always hesitate to ask you too many questions because I don't want to make things worse. You know, the bad memories and all."

"Oh, I don't mind talking about it. To be perfectly honest, most of the time I don't even think about it It's almost as if it happened to someone else, someone I used to know. I have a new life, our life, and the other is all behind me. Getting shot down goes with the territory when you're a military pilot. I don't feel cheated. I didn't feel cheated when I was in a cell in Hanoi. But before I got shot down I did think I was pretty tough. But they broke me. They broke almost all of us. Some just took longer than others."

He paused and took another sip of coffee.

Alex sighed and wondered if she was probing too much.

"Well, anyhow," he continued, "that's not what we're talking about. We're talking about my claustrophobia. They," Matt began and hesitated for a moment, "they used to put us upside down in a cement pipe in the ground and cover it up."

He swallowed hard and looked off into the distance.

Alex couldn't see how such a horrifying experience could be that far behind anyone.

"It was, uh, so black, and I couldn't breathe," he continued. "I didn't know each time if they were coming back. Hell, I messed all over myself and screamed until I was hoarse. I couldn't move because they tied my hands and feet. I…" he began and stopped. "Well, I survived. Now I don't have to face that anymore. I have the boat," he said as he patted the fiberglass seat, "and more importantly, I have you in my life."

CHAPTER ELEVEN

Pine Cay

"They're outside," Z. whispered like a child with a secret.

Tyrone looked at him and wondered at just what age Z.'s development had been arrested. Eight? Ten?

"Okay," Tyrone said, "I think we ought to just ease over there and say hello. See if they're alone."

The two men filed out of the cabin. Tyrone descended the ladder and positioned himself at the stern of the inflatable.

"Get the oars," he ordered Z.

"Where are they?"

"You've been stepping over them all day, stupid. They're lying on the port, uh, left side of the boat where you walk back and forth."

"Oh, yeah, here they are."

He handed one and then the other to Tyrone and started down the stern ladder. After placing a foot on the edge of the dinghy, Z. clung to the boat railing, afraid to let go.

"Get in, asshole."

"I'm comin'. I'm comin'. You know I hate the water."

"I cannot believe that anyone can be so dumb. You're scared to death of water but you live somewhere where you're fuckin' surrounded by it."

Z. suddenly released his grip and fell backwards into the dinghy.

"Jesus, you swamped us.! Now there's three inches of water in the bottom."

"I didn't mean to. I'm sorry. Okay?"

"So what's new? You're always sorry. Just sit still and shut the fuck up."

Tyrone began rowing towards Matt and Alex, who were watching from their cockpit. Tyrone's massive biceps swelled with every pull of the oars. From a distance, his face looked grim, angry. Z. hunkered low in the bow.

As they drew near the *Amani*, Tyrone's expression changed. He yelled out a hearty ahoy. His warm smile, like that of a used car salesman on his best day, was disarming. Alex was charmed and receptive. Matt, always on guard, was wary.

"Ahoy!" returned Alex as she raised a hand in greeting.

Tyrone rowed to the starboard side of the cockpit and grabbed the teak railing. His head bobbed up and down with the swell.

"We're your neighbors," Tyrone said. "On the boat right over there." He pointed behind him.

Alex smiled and said, "We know. We saw you board your dinghy."

"Well, yes," Tyrone said. "How goes it with you folks? Enjoying the Bahamas?"

Alex looked intently at Tyrone's even white teeth. She thought he had a remarkable face. His skin, shiny black, was taut over high cheekbones and a wide brow. His nose was delicate, almost lost between his full lips and large eyes. Still, he was handsome. He was wearing a gold loop earring in his left ear. The other one, the one who had not spoken, was wan and puny with road-map eyes. She noticed that he was constantly shifting them back and forth as if he were viewing an imaginary tennis match. His face was narrow, thin; his mouth weak. He couldn't settle on an expression. And he stank.

"My name is Alex Spencer, and this is my husband, Matt."

Matt leaned over the rail and extended his right hand to Tyrone.

"Nice to meet you," Tyrone said. "I'm, uh, Charles Woods, but my friends call me Charlie. And this is Jack Purdy."

Z. squirmed when everyone looked at him, licked his lips, and nodded in their direction.

"Nice boat you have," Tyrone said. "I couldn't help noticing the name when we came in. *Amani*, that's an unusual name. What's it mean?"

"We were told that it means 'peace' in Swahili," Alex said.

"I sure like it," Tyrone said. "Has a nice sound. What brings you folks to the Islands? Vacation?"

"Oh, it's a long story," Alex said, "but yes, we're on vacation."

"We've been planning to tour the Bahamas for several years," Matt said, "and this is our first opportunity. Is this your home?"

"Always," Tyrone said. "I'm from Soundside," he said and pointed west. "As soon as the sun goes down you can see the lights."

Alex smiled and looked in the direction he was pointing.

"How long you folks planning to stay at Pine Cay?" Tyrone said.

"Well," Matt replied slowly, "our plans aren't too definite. Like we said, we're on vacation and we want to hang loose. What brings you guys here?"

"Uh?" Tyrone said. "Well, uh…"

Before he could finish his sentence, Z. leaned forward and blurted out, "We're selling conch. We're conch divers, and we wanted to ask you if you'd like to buy some."

Tyrone stiffened and he cut his eyes at Z. *What the fuck is that asshole up to now?*

Z. shrank from his glare.

"Conch?" Alex said. "We've heard about conch. It's as popular in the Islands as hot dogs are in the States, isn't it? We saw tons of conch shells when we were at New Union Settlement. There were hundreds on the shore. How much do they cost?"

"Uh, three dollars each, m'am, "Z. said and cleared his throat.

"We'll take one just to try. If we like it, we'll buy some more. How's that?"

"Just a minute," Matt said. "I'll have to go below and get three dollars out of my wallet."

"Wait," Tyrone said quickly, "what Jack meant to say was that we sometimes dive for conch but we haven't been diving today and we don't have any right now. Fresh out. But when we get some, we'll bring 'em by your boat."

"Will you show us how to clean it?" Alex said. "I mean we'll do the work. You just tell us how to do it."

"Oh," Z. said, "it's very simple, really. The conch is in a shell and you have to tap a hole in the top part. Then you, uh, can get the conch out."

Tyrone glared at him.

"You can show us when you bring it to our boat," Alex said. "When do you think you'll have some? Honey, are we going to be here tomorrow?"

"Probably. I'll have to listen to the weather report, but yes, as far as I know, we'll be here."

Z. and Tyrone both nodded.

"Okay," Tyrone said, "guess we'd better get back to our boat. It's gettin' dark. Good to meet you."

Alex observed that Tyrone was a big man, powerful. The small inflatable looked like a child's toy beneath him. *Obviously he takes good care of his body. Must be all that diving.*

Matt raised a hand in farewell.

"Hope to see you folks again soon," Tyrone said.

"See ya," Z. said.

"Bye," Alex said. "Nice to meet you."

Tyrone maneuvered the inflatable away from the *Amani* and began rowing with long strokes toward *The Happy Hour.*

"They certainly were friendly, weren't they," Alex said, "but they're a strange pair. That skinny guy sure could use a serious scrubbing."

Something about them disturbed Matt.

"I'm pooped after another wonderful day in paradise," Alex said. "How 'bout let's go to bed early and cuddle up. We can read books and do crossword puzzles. Or if you like, I'll read to you. That always puts you to sleep."

"Yes," Matt said as he stretched his arms upward and yawned, "sounds good."

CHAPTER TWELVE

Pine Cay

"Get below!" Tyrone said.

"Jesus, man, what's your problem? I was just tryin' to help. What are you so pissed about?"

Tyrone, no longer able to control his anger, shoved Z. from behind, sending him sprawling.

"Hey, man, why'd you do that?" Z. said as he got up.

"Because, genius, you almost fucked up everything."

"How? Because I told them we were conch divers?"

"Yes, asshole. I don't need any more complications. I just wanted to get close enough to look them over, make sure they're alone on the boat, so that tomorrow while they're ashore we can make our move. We can go to their boat, chip out the coke, and be gone before they get back. We only need thirty minutes. If that dude gets suspicious, dynamite won't blow him out 'a there. And what's this conch diver shit? Do we look like conch divers? Have you ever been conch diving?"

"I have. I went with Danny once," Z. said and folded his arms across his chest.

"Conch divers, for Christ's sake!"

"Seemed like a good idea at the time. I wanted to help."

"You're too stupid to have ideas. The next time you get one, fight it. I'm supposed to do the thinking, not you. Got that? We're in a rented power boat. Do you think conch divers rent power boats? Do they carry inflatable rafts?"

"Well, I don't know. They might," Z. mumbled and hung his head.

"Just keep your big mouth shut! Shut! That dude may be old but he ain't stupid. I don't want him to think about us except that we're two good old Bahamian boys. Can you, just this once, do what I tell you ?"

"Yeah, sure," Z. said as he rubbed the small of his back. "That hurt, ya know."

"I meant for it to. And if you don't wise up, I'm gonna' do more than that. Understand?"

"Tough guy. Danny will put the hurt on you if you mess with me."

"Danny wouldn't find out. I'd take you out in deep water and toss you over the side. You wouldn't even be a ripple after the sharks got through with you."

Z. paled at the thought.

"Tomorrow morning they plan to go ashore. She had a bag of shells in the cockpit. And when they went by in their dinghy earlier, I heard her say she wanted to go back to the Island tomorrow. Well, we'll just wait until they hit the beach, then we'll row over and get the stash. Simple. Easy in, easy out."

"That's a good plan, bro. Oughta' work."

"It will work," Tyrone said through clenched teeth, if you just fuckin' do what I tell you!"

Z. flinched as if he had been struck.

"God knows what Danny must be thinking. We've got to get the job done tomorrow and get back to Mission Harbor. For all we know, those guys from Miami think we've run off with their dope and they're lookin' for us right now."

Tyrone looked at Z. with contempt. He was feeling less charitable toward him with each passing hour. On this night, their second on this miserable quest, tension bubbled up inside him and overflowed into the confines of the tiny cabin like an oil spill.

Z. settled back on the quarter berth and rolled a joint.

"Wanna' smoke?" he said.

Tyrone hesitated for a moment before accepting the reefer.

"I guess I need this," he said. "Hell, I may have two."

"That's the spirit. Kick back. Take it easy. It'll make you sleep like a baby."

***

When the wind picked up around midnight, Matt went forward to check the *Amani*'s position relative to the radio tower at Soundside. He watched as the cabin cruiser strained at its anchor and hoped that his neighbors were firmly tethered to the ocean floor.

***

The crew of *The Happy Hour*, mellowed and relaxed by the marijuana, slept soundly throughout the night. The next morning, the wind was blowing a steady fifteen knots out of the southeast, and Tyrone was awakened by the creak of the anchor line as it reached the end of its scope.

He sat up and rubbed his eyes. Z., still asleep in a quarter berth, lay curled up in fetal position. A thin bead of saliva trickled from one corner of his half-open mouth.

"Hey, asshole," Tyrone said, "get up."

Z. fluttered his eyelids a few times before he opened them.

"What?"

"I said get up," Tyrone said. "We've got to get ready to move. And make us a couple of sandwiches. I'm hungry."

"Sure, sure," Z. said. as he rose and scratched his greasy head. His hair had slipped from its rubberband and lay in matted clumps about his shoulders.

"Want some coffee?" Z. said. "I think we have some left."

"Yeah, but hurry up."

Tyrone stood up, stretched, and lost his balance. The boat was rolling with the heavy swell making conditions below almost intolerable. He grabbed a hand rail, peeked out the window, and looked in the direction of the *Amani.*

"What time is it?" he asked over his shoulder.

"It's, uh, eight-thirty or thereabouts," Z. said.

Tyrone wiped his eyes and looked through the glass. The *Amani* was not in sight. His heart skipped a beat. He rushed to the other window and looked out. The boat wasn't there! He bolted up the companionway steps to the cockpit and looked around.

"Jesus Christ," he said, "they're gone!"

"Gone? Gone?" Z. said. "What do you mean gone?"

"Gone, as in not here. They've fuckin' left!"

"This kind 'a screws things up, huh?" Z. said as he continued spreading mustard on the slices of white bread he had lined up on the galley counter.

Tyrone's eyes were wide like those of someone who had just witnessed an automobile accident with fatalities.

"Forget the sandwiches. Hurry up! Run forward and pull up the anchor."

Z. took a bite of bread and began to chew.

"We don't have time to eat?" he said.

Tyrone narrowed his eyes, glared, and started to speak.

Z. flinched.

"Never mind. I'm goin'. I'm goin'. Jesus."

Tyrone was certain that if he didn't bring the cocaine back to Mission Harbor by that night his worst nightmare would come true. He didn't know what those men from Miami would do, but he could well imagine. He'd heard the horror stories. He didn't want to kill that couple, certainly not that woman, but this just couldn't continue. His life depended on quick action. He wasn't about to die for them. It was just their tough luck that they got on the wrong boat.

He reached under a V-berth cushion and took out his 357 Magnum. For a second he looked at the long blue barrel then shoved it beneath the cushion before going aft to start the motor.

Tyrone realized that if he approached the man on the sailboat with a gun, the dude just might shoot him first. He had heard that tourists were gun happy, that they panicked easily if they felt threatened. Somehow he had to surprise them.

"Move it!" Tyrone said as he muscled the inflatable into the boat.

As they slowly powered out of the anchorage, Z. said, "Well now where are we goin'?"

Tyrone pulled away from the Island and looked east and west. He saw a number of sailboats headed toward Charter Cay. In the other direction, there were a few power boats and sailboats, their outlines fuzzy and small in the distance. A sport fishing boat roared by on the opposite side of the channel, leaving a thundering wake behind it.

"Goddammit!" Tyrone screamed and pounded the wheel. "I don't fuckin' believe this!"

He paused and tried to collect his thoughts. Okay, she said that she wanted to look for some more shells, but apparently they changed their minds about staying. Why? Tyrone looked up at the cloudy sky. Bad weather coming? Maybe they decided to move to a safer anchorage. If they want shelter, they will probably go back to New Union Settlement at Charter Cay because it's the nearest place. I don't think they would go to Soundside. She's too prissy. I can't see her pulling herself up that rickety ladder at the gasoline pumps. And there aren't any restaurants. No, they must have gone back to Charter Cay.

"How 'bout I get the binoculars out," Z. said.

"How 'bout you shutting up?"

Tyrone felt the wind freshen and saw the sky was indeed growing darker. Confident his assumptions were correct, he thrust the throttle forward and the boat surged eastward jolting Z. backwards onto the deck.

CHAPTER THIRTEEN

Robert's Cay, Bahamas

"Good sailing, Captain, Alex said. "It was wonderful to get up before dawn, raise the sails, and glide away from the anchorage. Pretty hot stuff. I didn't know you could do that."

Matt looked down at the compass and made a small correction in his heading.

"We couldn't have sailed out of there if we'd slept late. The wind is already shifting," he said as he glanced at the tell-tails. "Fortunately, at dawn it was easy to pop the jib and take up our heading. When I listened to the weather report out of Portsmouth last night, they said that a front was coming. If it continues on its current speed and direction, it will pass over our heads tomorrow night."

"Will there be a storm?"

"I don't think so. A lot of boats will run back to Charter Cay, but it isn't necessary. The report said that it would be a mild front with little rain. There will be the usual build up of southeast wind, a quick wind shift, and then it'll blow like hell out of the northwest for a day. That's why you had to get up so early, madam. We needed to take advantage of the southerly winds and get to Robert's Cay before the wind shift. We'll be farther along and protected from anything from the north."

"Are you suggesting, Captain, that I'd rather sleep than watch the sun rise?"

"Look over there," he said and pointed. "That's Robert's Bank. I've heard a lot of sailors don't realize how far out it extends and the next thing they know, they're hard aground. See the difference in the water color? It has a lighter hue, almost white, very distinctive. See it?"

Alex peered in the direction Matt was pointing and nodded.

"How about getting my chart and reading glasses?" Matt said.

Alex went below to retrieve Matt's glasses and chart.

"Here you go," she said when she returned.

Matt removed his sunglasses and put on his half-eye spectacles. Alex thought they made him look distinguished. He studied the chart before handing it to her.

"Now," he said, "based on time, distance, heading and speed, where do you think we are?"

Alex, sitting cross legged on the lazaret, held the chart in front of her, checked her watch, the knot meter, and their last position, and pointed to a place on the chart.

"Very good."

"I'm improving," Alex said with pride in her voice. "It really builds my confidence when I can do that. When I solo, I'll be prepared. I used to think it was magic when you could locate a channel marker in the dark. It's all so simple."

Matt took up a new heading of 320 degrees.

"Well, honey," he said, "as I thought, we'll have to start the engine and lower the main. I was hoping we could sail into the harbor, but the sea is too sloppy and the channel's pretty shallow.

Alex jumped up and went below to turn the engine ignition key before she lowered the main. While standing on the cabin top, she glanced over the boom and saw that the Robert's Cay entry was more circuitous than it appeared on the chart. Matt throttled the engine back to 1100 RPM's. Alex went forward and stood on the bow pulpit to scan the depths for shallow water and coral. In the cockpit, Matt watched the depth finder as it descended to three feet before it began rising again.

"Ah," said Matt, "I do believe we are going to make it in here without leaving half our bottom paint."

Once they had turned due north, Alex was surprised to see such a small inlet. The channel cut through to the Atlantic and only by anchoring to the east and creeping out of the channel by some twenty yards could they escape the raging current that flowed off their stern. There was one other boat nearby, tied to a bright red mooring ball. The boat, at least a forty-footer, had a light green hull with a narrow white stripe. On the port side, three black automobile tires dangled from its railing. It had two dingy white cabins that appeared to be homemade. They resembled something a child might build out of plywood, boxy and flat roofed. No one was on deck.

Matt pointed at another mooring ball that lay gently bobbing several yards beyond the bow.

"Go ahead and grab it," he said. "It says in the cruising guide that the owner doesn't mind if boaters use it when he's not."

Alex grabbed a boat hook and positioned herself forward on the port side. As Matt guided the boat to the ball, she hoisted the mooring line with a boat hook and wound it around a bow cleat. Once the boat stopped its forward movement, she undid the line and ran it through the port chock before cinching it. A stream of silt ran down the port gunnel.

"All set up there?"

"All set. Everything seems to be in good shape."

Alex watched as the line tightened, then creaked.

"Smooth landing," he said when she returned to the cockpit. "You've got to be the world's best crew."

"Sure, and I bet you have a fence you'd like me to white wash, Tom Sawyer."

Alex went below and turned off the circuit breakers for the auto pilot, depth finder/knot meter, and the VHF radio before she returned topside to straighten up. She handed the binoculars and Matt's glasses down to him. As she was about to go below-deck, a small power boat entered the channel and motored directly to the forty-foot boat moored a short distance from the *Amani*'s starboard side. Two men sitting in the power boat stared at her, but neither spoke nor smiled when she waved at them. She flushed at their lack of response and brushed her hair from her eyes.

Alex saw two men board the big boat and enter the aft cabin. Several minutes later another vessel, larger and newer, rounded the channel and made directly for the boat next door. A repeat of the earlier arrivals, four men stared at her but did not speak. This time she only half-smiled in their direction.

"Hey, Matt," she whispered, "six guys have just gotten on that big, homemade thing next to us."

"Yeah?"

"Yeah, and they're not very friendly. Do you think they're fisher-men?"

"Why are you whispering?"

"I don't want them to hear me talking about them."

"Honey, they can't hear you all the way over there."

After a few minutes, one of the men climbed into the larger power boat, pressed the starter and gunned the engine when it caught. He cast off from the forty-footer and motored a twenty yards to the nearby shore. From the trees on the Island, a group of women and children appeared and impa-tiently fidgeted at the water's edge while the power boat slowly made its way in their direction. When the bow gently touched the sand, they climbed aboard, one by one. The older girls held the babies and the younger children crawled forward and perched on the bow. Again the engine sputtered and mumbled as the power boat crept back to the big boat. The passengers, all sizes and ages, noisily invaded the forty-footer, and the quiet, lifeless hull became a bustling hub of activity. The men sat aft sipping beer and smoking cigarettes while the women cleaned fish on the bow and the children tussled amidships.

"Matt, can you believe that gang next door?"

"Believe what, babe?"

"That boat next to us," she whispered. "It's amazing."

Matt peeked through the companionway.

"Got crowded."

"Boy, did it. Do you think all of them live there?"

"Probably. You have to realize that many of these people live off the sea and have virtually no other skills except a knack for surviving."

"Man, I really would like to take a picture of them."

"Go ahead."

"I can't now. The sun's not right. Too many clouds. And besides, it wouldn't be polite. Those men are staring at us."

Matt looked out again.

"Well, honey, we're staring at them. They're probably just curious," he said.

"I suppose we look as interesting to them as they look to us."

"I would think so."

"I just wish they were a little friendlier," she said.

***

That night, Alex heard the hum of the generator on the forty-footer. When she looked out the window on the port side, she saw the vessel's muted outline and the occasional glow from inhaled cigarettes. The flickering dots reminded her of fireflies. In contrast, on the starboard side, the Cay blazed with harsh, bright lights.

"Matt," she said, "the Island is lit up like a football stadium."

"M-m-m, h-m-m, "he hummed as he completed another crossword.

"What's up there?"

"According to the cruising guide, a military tracking station."

"It must be huge. I've never seen so many lights. You know, this is really strange."

"What?"

"Well, on one side of us it's completely dark. All those people are crammed on that boat. On the other hand," she said as she looked out again, "the Island is well lighted, yet it looks deserted. I mean, it's, uh, kind of weird."

"Well," he said as he put down his puzzle book, "come here, woman, and I'll give you something else to think about."

CHAPTER FOURTEEN

New Union Settlement, Charter Cay

Earlier that day, Tyrone had eased the cabin cruiser alongside the Government Dock at New Union Settlement and watched as Z. frantically groped for a piling.

"Got it?" Tyrone said.

"Yeah, got it," Z. said with a groan as he bear hugged a piling, "but hurry up with a rope. I dropped mine."

After Tyrone tied the boat fore and aft, he changed his T-shirt.

"I'm going to the Government Building to use the phone," he said. "We better let Danny know that we've had another little setback and haven't run off with the coke. You stay put until I get back. And don't mess with anything. Just sit."

"Yeah, I hear you. Don't worry about me. I'm gonna eat a sandwich."

Tyrone checked his watch and was amazed to find that the trip back to New Union had been such a long and difficult one. The wind and waves had been on their bow all the way and they had really taken a pounding. Below decks was a shambles. It had taken them twice as long on the return trip to travel twenty-five miles.

Tyrone walked up main street to the pay phone outside the Post Office in the Government Building. He dialed the operator and was relieved when someone answered almost immediately, a rare occurrence in the Islands.

After the operator placed the call, Tyrone imagined the sound of the phone ringing inside Danny's apartment. In less than a minute, Ariel answered.

"We have a collect call for anyone from Tyrone Reed. Do you accept the charge?"

"Boy, do I ever," said Ariel.

"Ariel…"

"My God, Tyrone, where the hell are you? Danny's about nuts. Some guys were over here last night and they said some real bad things about you."

"Yeah, I'm sure, but listen…"

"And Danny tried to calm 'em down. He told 'em that he'd known you a long time and that you were one straight dude and that…"

"Yeah, listen, Ariel, I don't have much time. I need to speak to Danny."

"He's not here. He's, uh, with those men. I don't know where they went, but he seems pretty upset."

"Tell Danny, now this is important, tell Danny that we found the sail-boat, but we've had another little delay. More engine trouble. But I'll take care of everything. Tell him not to worry, that I won't let him down. The stuff is safe, got that?"

"Yeah, the stuff is safe. He's not to worry."

"We should be back no later than tomorrow night, maybe even by tonight. But with our, uh, engine problem, it may turn out to be tomorrow night. But I'll call him the second we pull up to the dock."

"Okay, Tyrone, but you'd better get back here soon. I've never seen Danny this way. Those men he's with, they're, uh, some really bad dudes. I can tell Danny's afraid of 'em."

"I'm sure. Well, I gotta go, but remember to tell Danny everything I said. My life depends on it. Danny's life might depend on it."

"Do you know what a Colombian necktie is, Tyrone?"

Tyrone was silent.

"Cuz' that's what they said they were gonna give you."

After a few seconds of heavy silence, Tyrone hung up the receiver. Before going back to the boat, he stopped by the hardware store and bought several charts of the area and a bag of ice. One of the clerks, a rotund woman with a perpetual grin, gave him an update on the weather. As she explained to Tyrone, yes, there was a front on the way, but it wouldn't be a problem until the following night. One good piece of news.

After looking for the sailboat at the Charter Cay anchorage, they stopped at the Charter Cay Shore Club for fuel. Tyrone pored over the charts while a young Bahamian pumped gasoline into the tank.

"How fast does a big sailboat go?" Tyrone asked the boy.

"Well, with all its sails up on a day like today, maybe five, six knots, I guess. Hard to say. Depends on how big it is, how many sails it has, lots of stuff."

Tyrone tried to convert that information into statute miles per hour, but his brain had seized. A feeling of dread, like a hungry cancer, had begun to consume his thoughts making it difficult for him to concentrate on anything.

After he guided the boat out Charter Cay's narrow channel, Tyrone gave the helm to Z. When they arrived at the eastern end of Jack Cay, he scanned the anchorage. There were five sailboats close to shore. He instructed Z. to turn in so he could get a better look at them.

"Is this close enough?" Z. said.

"Go in a little farther. There's one boat that looks like theirs, but I can't see the name. Goddamn sailboats all look alike to me."

Once Tyrone determined that the *Amani* wasn't in the anchorage, he pointed his finger west and motioned for Z. to change course. Z. nudged the throttle.

The back of Tyrone's neck felt like it had a stake driven in it. He moved his head from side to side in an effort to relieve the tension. *Calm. I must be calm.*

At the western end of Jack Cay, the sailboat wasn't on the sound side, but as they roared west, Tyrone motioned for Z. to slow down while he studied a chart. Sure enough, there was an anchorage on the ocean side of the Cay.

"There's another place to drop a hook," he told Z. "Go that way," he said and pointed to the Atlantic.

"Out there?"

"Yeah, asshole, we have to look. If it's not them then we'll come right back to the Bank. Now turn in and let me see the name on that boat over there," he said and pointed to a tall black mast.

Z. aimed the boat north before slowly making a wide arc into the anchorage at the western end of the Island.

"Shit," Tyrone said, "it's not them. Go back."

Z. made a U-turn and powered back to the long stretch of Bahama Bank. And so they continued heading west, motoring into each anchorage on the way. As the hours crept by, Tyrone became more agitated, and Z., for once, remained silent. By sunset, they had searched all the places that Tyrone considered possibilities.

"I'm not a sailor," Tyrone said, "but I know that a sailboat with a fuckin' little diesel engine doesn't go very fast. They have to be around here somewhere. I'll just have to go over the charts again."

Frantic, he studied the charts and noted the check marks which he had made by each anchorage they had searched. He rubbed his eyes and rotated his head.

"Surely those assholes wouldn't go out to sea!" he shouted at Z. "Where would they go?"

Z. shrugged his shoulders.

"Well, we'd better find some place to anchor for the night. It's too dark to go on. We'll have to start again at sunup."

CHAPTER FIFTEEN

Robert's Cay, Bahamas

"Matt, wake up! There's somebody outside!"

He opened his eyes and looked up at the sunlight streaming through the upper hatch. Outside, a propeller churned the water. He swung around in the V-berth and hurried to the main cabin to retrieve his Bermuda shorts. The boat sounded like it was circling. He ran his fingers through his hair and emerged topside through the companionway. Two men in a small runabout spotted him in the cockpit. Using short bursts of power, they carefully inched alongside the *Amani*.

Matt saw a beefy man, pie-faced and soft in the middle, standing behind the wheel. His nose, bulbous and red, stood out like a beacon. He wore a yellow sweatshirt that rode up on his belly, and long khaki shorts. The other man, younger and thinner, wore a blue baseball cap with Washington Redskins written across the front, a striped cotton short-sleeved shirt and gray running shorts. His eyes were concealed behind dark glasses. The driver waved at Matt when they made eye contact.

"Morning," said Matt, who squinted in the bright sunlight.

"You must have come in late yesterday," the helmsman said.

"Yeah, just before dark."

"I'm Ely Dunbar but my friends call me Shorty, and this is Fletcher Weyburn. We work up there at the Tracking Station," he said and glanced back at the complex on the hill.

"I'm Matt Spencer. Nice to meet you fellas."

"We make it a practice to greet all the boats that come in, sort of a two-man welcome wagon. We'd like you to join us for a drink this afternoon, that is, if you're going to be around that long."

"Thanks for the invitation. I can't speak for my wife, she's not up yet, but you can count on me. Any place in particular that I need to bring my dinghy?"

"Yeah, there's a dock just around there," Fletcher said and pointed behind him to the north. "It'll be casual," he added with a wink.

"That's good," Matt said. "Formal doesn't work out here."

"See you later then," Shorty said as Fletcher shoved their power boat away from the *Amani*. The men waved, headed toward the channel, and turned north before they disappeared around a point of land.

"Well, that was nice," said Alex, who had been eavesdropping below. "I think that would be fun. I wonder what they do up there."

"I read in the Guide that it's some kind of Missile Tracking Station. It's been on the Cay since the sixties. Ready for coffee, madam?" he said as he reached for the pot.

"The sooner the better. How'd you sleep?" she said and gave him a hug from behind.

"Great! Just great! Slept like a baby. I only got up once to check the mooring line. And you?"

"My usual night on the boat. Up down, up down. I can't seem to sleep an entire night out here. It's not that I'm afraid of anything. Concerned is more like it. I just feel that I need to keep watch until you get up. I know, don't say it. It's silly."

"It's ironic," he said smiling. "I can't sleep at home, and you can't sleep on the boat. We're certainly well matched."

"I can take a nap if I get sleepy. I do love the boat, and I'm having a wonderful time. Most of all, I enjoy being alone with you. No phone. No dogs barking. No noisy neighbors. Not too noisy, anyway. At first light, the group next door did the mirror image of what they did yesterday evening. All the women and children piled into a boat and one of the men delivered them to the shore."

Matt nodded as he filled the coffee pot with water and lit the stove. The raw smell of denatured alcohol quickly permeated the cabin.

"Now the women and children are back on the Island," she continued, "and the men have gone out on their boats. What a different life they have, from us, I mean."

"I haven't thought much about it," Matt said, "but I bet they're really very happy. They probably eat well enough and live peacefully among themselves."

"What about school, though? I don't suppose any of those children go to school. Some of them appear to be eight or nine, maybe older."

"They don't need school to do what they do. They fish, they play, they drink rum, they smoke. They love each other. We can't expect them to live by our standards."

"I guess not."

Alex peeked over Matt's shoulder and said, "You need to add a little more coffee."

"Hey, hold on now. Jesse's robbin' this train."

Alex looked at him with raised brows.

"Haven't I told you that joke about Jesse James robbing a trainload of passengers?"

"I don't remember. Every time I blink, it's a new day. Tell me again."

"Okay. See, there was this trainload of passengers in the old west. Jesse James stopped the train, boarded, and demanded that everyone fork over their jewelry and watches along with their gold. When he came to one well-dressed matron, who was wearing a heavy gold necklace that disappeared between her rather large jugs, he insisted that she remove it and give it to him. When she refused, he shoved his hand down her cleavage and pulled it out. A city slicker standing next to her said, 'Now Mr. James, I, sir, am a gentleman, and I must object to your rough treatment of this fine lady.' Before Jesse could say anything, the woman hit the man with her handbag and said, 'Mind your own business, mister. Jesse's robbin' this train.'"

Alex grinned.

"I wish I could remember all the jokes you tell me. They'd sure come in handy."

The cabin had begun to smell like coffee and less like alcohol. Alex slipped into the head to brush her teeth. In a few minutes she called out in a voice muffled by the folding door, "Hey, Jesse, is the coffee ready?"

Matt smiled as he filled a mug, stirred in a scant teaspoon of sugar, and brought it to her.

"Just right, I hope," he said.

"It always tastes good when you fix it, dear boy."

They sat down at the table and quietly sipped their coffee.

"It's nice to see the sun shining," she said.

"It shouldn't cloud up until later in the day. We can expect some higher winds tonight."

"I'll recheck the mooring line before we go to the Tracking Station, just to be on the safe side," she said.

Matt gazed at her and thought that she had never looked more radiant. Her dark eyes were clear and sparkling, her nose dotted with freckles.

"What time are we going up there?" she said as she poured herself another cup of coffee and offered him the pot in gesture.

"Yes, thanks. Let's say about three. I need to check the fuel filter for trash and I'll have to bleed the line. The engine tried to cut out a few times yesterday."

"I'll help," she said.

"We'll get started after we eat. Speaking of eating, what's for breakfast?"

Alex rummaged through the cupboard in the galley and found some canned brown bread. How about this and some bananas?"

"That's fine."

"Yuk, forget the bananas. Their time has come and gone. How about canned peaches instead?"

"Anything's okay."

At one o'clock, Alex climbed into the Zodiac dinghy before Matt. She felt attractive in her new beige shorts and emerald green tank top.

"Should we lock up the boat?" she said before Matt untied the dinghy line.

"I don't think we need to worry about that here, honey. In fact, if the truth be known, I think that we have less to worry about in the Islands than in the States, and that's a depressing thought."

"Okay, if you're sure. Feels funny, though. I'd hate for someone to steal our traveler's checks."

"Really," he assured her. "It's okay. There's no one around, and besides, the Bahamians don't steal from the tourists. If they did, people would quit coming here to vacation."

Their dinghy plowed through calm water until they rounded the western tip of the Island and were met with short choppy waves from the sea. They bumped along until they saw the runabout tied to the only dock in sight.

"This has gotta be the place," Matt said as he turned off the motor and allowed the dinghy to coast to the pilings.

Alex tossed her sandals on the wooden planks and awkwardly pulled herself onto the dock with both hands.

"Just call me Grace," she said over her shoulder.

Matt gave her the bow line which she held tightly until he stood beside her. After positioning the dinghy so that the tide and wind would not sweep it against the barnacles on the pilings, they made their way up a crude path which led them to concrete sidewalks at the top of the Cay. Alex found it strange that except for the sound of the ocean, it was deadly quiet. They passed by gun metal gray buildings that had been baked for years by summer sun and soaked by seasonal rains. The wind whistled forlornly among the eaves and the signs which read, *Abandon In Place, No Further Maintenance Required, No Trespassing*, made it clear that this was a forgotten place. Alex folded her arms across her chest as she walked.

"Isn't this eerie?" she said and reached for Matt's hand.

"Well, old and unused might better describe it."

"Say what you like," she said. "It's creepy to me. I wonder where we're supposed to go."

Following the walkway, they found themselves standing outside a building with an open door and without a *No Trespassing* sign tacked to it. A red hibiscus stood out brightly against its faded wall.

Matt rapped on the screen door with his knuckles.

From inside, they heard a low growl, and both Alex and Matt stepped back a few feet. Suddenly a barking German shepherd appeared at the door. Alex looked startled.

Behind the dog stood Shorty Dunbar.

"Oh, not to worry," he said, "she's a good girl. Hey there, now Ginger," he murmured. "It's okay, girl. It's okay."

The dog stopped barking and began to wag her tail and lick Shorty's fingertips.

"There now, what did I tell you? She's a good girl, her is," he said to the dog.

He pushed open the screen door and Alex and Matt entered the building. A rush of sights and smells flooded their senses; lifeless green paint, cracked linoleum, the strong smell of pine cleaner. They followed Shorty and Ginger down an unlit corridor.

"It's this way," Shorty said as he directed them to the left down another dark passage. "In here."

The hallway opened into a large room which obviously served double duty as a combination radio and relaxation room. Banks of short wave radios and other communication equipment were lined up at the far end. A long rectangular table occupied the center.

"You folks have a seat over here," Shorty said and motioned for Alex to sit down on one of the folding chairs at the table.

Fletcher Weyburn sat across from Alex nursing what appeared to be more than his first drink of the day. He nodded when they came in. Shorty sat in a chair at the head of the table and poured himself three fingers of vodka from one of the many liquor bottles that littered the table top. Some of the bottles were empty, others only partially consumed. Shorty took a hefty swallow and didn't flinch.

"I'm Alex Spencer," she said and looked at each of them.

"Of course you are," Shorty said.

Fletcher nodded at her. He had removed his sunglasses. His green eyes looked red and tired.

"So," Shorty said, "glad you folks could come up."

He hoisted his glass again.

"Well," Matt said and cleared his throat, "uh, how long you guys been up here?"

"Three years, one month, and eight days," Shorty said, "but who's counting?"

He chuckled and emptied his glass.

Matt repositioned his folding chair and the metal legs beneath him screeched across the floor.

Alex smiled and studied the dismal room. The dog had curled up on an easy chair next to the head of the table where Shorty sat.

"You like dogs?" Shorty said when he noticed Alex gazing at Ginger.

"Oh yes, if they don't bite."

"If they don't bite, ha ha," he giggled and said, "Ginger doesn't bite. She barks, but her doesn't bite, does her? In fact, my Ginger can sing?"

Before Alex could comment, Shorty fell to his knees in front of Ginger saying, "Okay now Ginger, sing! Sing for Daddy!"

Shorty surprised them when he began to howl like a wolf. Ginger licked his face and settled deeper into her chair.

"Ah, come on now, Ginger. We have company. Sing for Daddy."

Shorty began to howl again. Ginger finally came forth with a low ruff.

"No, I didn't say speak," Shorty said. "I want you to sing. Come on, sing, Ginger."

After several long minutes and no further contributions from Ginger, Shorty returned to his seat at the table and assured Alex that Ginger really could sing, but she was self conscious because she was unaccustomed to company.

"So, you guys have been here for over three years?" Matt said. "What exactly do you do?"

"Oh," replied Shorty, "we mostly stand by. This used to be a pretty active base, Air Force. It was a fully operational Command Missile Tracking Station back in the sixties. Over a hundred and fifty men were here back then, so I've been told. Then gradually, with the new satellites and all, they just sort of reduced the number."

"How many of you work here now?" Alex said.

"Two. Just the two of us. Me and old Fletch. That right, Fletch?"

Fletch nodded and tapped a cigarette from a Marlboro pack on the table.

"I see," Matt said, "so now the two of you run this place."

"Well," Shorty said, "I, uh, don't know if 'run' isn't stretching it a bit. We are just sort of here. We don't recover missiles, but we do serve as a navigation station for ships and airplanes. We make sure the equipment's working. Mostly we just stand by."

"How much communication do you have with the outside world?" Matt said. "Do you get to go back to the States from time to time?"

"The boss gives us a call every couple 'a weeks and we have some time off at Christmas and then two weeks during the year. They send somebody to fill in. It's not so bad, huh Fletch?"

Fletch chuckled and said, "Maybe not for an old fart like you, but me, I'm in my prime."

Alex noticed that Fletch's cheeks were flushed.

Shorty laughed and splashed some more vodka in his glass.

"There are tanks on the Island, just sitting, rusting. She might wanna see a tank," Shorty said and looked at Matt.

"Then you guys are Air Force?" Matt said.

"Us? Hell no," Shorty said. "We're private. We work for an airline company."

"Where are our manners?" Fletch said. "How 'bout a drink?"

"Oh, that would, uh, be nice," Alex said and looked at Matt.

He smiled at her and nodded.

"Well, you can find yourself some ice in the freezer," Shorty said. "In there."

He motioned behind him with a thrust of his head.

Before Alex could rise from her chair, Matt held up his hand and told her to stay put, that he'd get it. He wandered into the kitchen which adjoined the R and R room. Inside he found several oversized trunk-style freezers lining the walls. He started to return for more explicit instructions but decided instead that it would be easier to look for the ice himself. One by one he opened the freezer lids. He found enough frozen peas, turnip greens, lima beans and corn to stock a small grocery store. But no ice. Not a cube. He returned empty handed and shrugged his shoulders at Alex.

"Did you find the ice?" Fletch asked around a cigarette that he had clamped between his teeth.

"No, but that's okay," Matt said.

"It's right there," Shorty said and pointed at a refrigerator in the back of the R and R room. Matt smiled and opened the freezer portion of the refrigerator. There were several chunks of ice in a glass bowl inside the compartment and nothing else.

"Want a glass?" Shorty said. "There's one in the kitchen."

Matt, amused by the lack of hospitality, smiled to himself as he returned from the kitchen with a glass he had carefully washed and dried.

Fletch nudged a vodka bottle across the table in Alex's direction.

"If you don't like vodka," he said, "we have a lot 'a rum. You want rum?"

"No, no, vodka's fine," Alex said and poured herself a small shot.

"The lady's a light drinker," Fletch told Shorty and belched.

"How 'bout you? Shorty said. "Wanna wet your whistle?"

"No, thanks, I'm just fine," Matt said.

"Suit yourself," Shorty said as he dumped more vodka into his glass.

Matt noticed that Shorty's words had begun to have more syllables.

"You like lobster?" Shorty asked Alex.

Alex smiled and said, "Who doesn't?"

Before she could elaborate, Shorty wobbled into the kitchen and returned with two frozen lobsters that were unwrapped, freezer burned, and obviously caught some time during the preceding decade.

"Here," he said, and tossed them to her one at a time.

Alex caught one and dropped the other on the floor.

"Hey," Shorty giggled, "plenty more where those came from."

He returned to the kitchen and brought back two more.

"Here," he said again and pitched them in her direction.

Matt stood up and mumbled something about having to check the mooring line on the boat. Alex began to giggle and couldn't regain her composure. After she started laughing, Shorty began howling, then Fletch, and soon they all had tears streaming down their faces. Alex, in an effort to be polite, clasped the spiny lobsters to her chest.

"Oh, these are wonderful," she said to Shorty, "but no more, really. There's just the two of us. No, really, but thanks."

"There's one under the table," Matt whispered in her ear, "but don't pick it up. They'll find it later."

Alex and Matt made their way, unaccompanied, down the narrow corridors and out into the waning afternoon. Alex, who couldn't stop giggling, kept dropping the lobsters. Matt followed behind her and picked them up.

"Have you ever seen," Alex began, then broke into peals of laughter, "anything like that?"

Matt chuckled. "I must admit, that wasn't exactly what I had expected."

"They're a couple of odd balls," she said as she stumbled down the path, "but nice."

"Those poor guys," Matt said. "It must be awful to be stuck up there day after day. No wonder they drink."

"Yeah, and these lobsters must be a hundred years old. The fish will love them."

Once they were settled in the dinghy, Matt started the outboard and motored slowly toward the *Amani*. As they rounded a point of land, they saw that another boat had arrived and anchored not far upwind of them. Matt couldn't see the name on the stern but he recognized at once that their new neighbor was *The Happy Hour*.

"Matt, I think that's the same boat that anchored next to us at Pine Cay. I hope they have some conch this time. It would be wonderful to have something besides canned food. Aren't we lucky they showed up?"

CHAPTER SIXTEEN

Robert's Cay

"Oh, shit, they're back," Z. said. "Now we can't just run over there and get it."

Tyrone peeked out the window and saw the red dinghy round the western tip of the Island. The man aimed the inflatable at the stern of the sailboat. The woman sat near the bow. He noticed her green shirt, tanned skin, and shiny hair. He imagined her face fixed and cold and thought killing her would be a terrible but necessary waste.

"I think I have this figured out," Tyrone said. "There are some fishermen on the boat next door. I'm gonna buy a couple of conch from them. We're gonna take 'em over to the sailboat and sell them, like we said, to those goddamn people. Now you're sure that you can clean 'em so that you at least look like you know what you're doing?"

"Oh, yeah, sure. Like I told you, Danny showed me before. Shit, though, after cleaning one, you sure as hell don't wanna eat it. Even when it's fresh, it stinks like a two dollar whore."

"I know what it smells like and tastes like, moron," Tyrone said as he paced back and forth in the cabin. "I just want those people off that boat long enough for me to get aboard and chip out the stuff. You take them ashore in their dinghy. It has a motor. Go to the beach on the other side of the Island. While you're gone, and you need to take at least thirty minutes, I'll get aboard the boat. Simple. No hassle. Unless…"

"Unless what?"

Z. looked at him blankly.

"Forget it," Tyrone said. "I hope it doesn't come to that. This is their last chance. We're out 'a time. Fuck it. They're out 'a time."

"Okay by me, bro," Z. said. "Does this mean we're goin' home tonight?"

"You got that straight. I don't care how dark it is or how late it is. We're heading back. We've got no more time to fool around with this shit. I think everything will be okay if we show up at Mission Harbor tonight, with the coke."

"I don't know what you're worryin' about," Z. said. "Danny won't let nothin' happen to us."

"You still don't get it, do you, asshole?"

"Get what?"

"Never mind. Let's go."

CHAPTER SEVENTEEN

Robert's Cay

Matt watched as the two Bahamians they had met at Pine Cay stepped out of their cabin and muscled their inflatable raft into the water. After the skinny one fell backwards into the dinghy, they rowed to the wooden boat nearby and began talking with the fishermen who were lounging aft. Matt couldn't hear what they were saying, but an animated exchange concluded with loud guffaws, and then one of the men on the big boat handed something to the men from *The Happy Hour*. Occasionally the black man, the one who called himself Charlie, looked over his shoulder in the direction of the *Amani*. He couldn't see Matt, who was keeping an eye on them from below.

"Here come the guys," he told Alex, who had just finished bathing.

She wrapped herself in a thick pink towel and combed her wet hair straight back. Her skin, moist from the shower, smelled like herbal soap.

"Do you want me to get three dollars?" she said as she turned to slip on a clean pair of shorts and a T-shirt.

"Sure, my wallet's in the top drawer."

"Do you think one conch will be enough? I wonder how much edible meat you get from one of those things."

"Better bring me six dollars," Matt said, "in case they're small. I'll get two."

The guys appeared off the stern, grinning and eager to sell. Like hungry dogs anticipating a meal, they quivered.

"Hey, mon, we're back with the conch, just like we promised," the one who called himself Charlie said.

"Hello, Charlie, is it, and I apologize," Matt said, "but I can't remember your friend's name."

"Oh, that's Jack, Mr. Spencer. We saw your boat and thought what a surprise. Didn't we Jack? We said, 'There's that sailboat we saw the other day at Pine Island.'"

Z. bobbed his head up and down.

"Well, we brought you some conch, just like we promised," Tyrone said. "Here they are," he said as he held up two large, brown shells. "This is conch."

Alex, standing behind Matt, looked over his shoulder and commented, "They look a lot like big snails, don't they?"

"Oh, yeah, but they taste a whole lot better than those fancy snails you get in restaurants," Tyrone said with a show of teeth. "Yeah, the little rascals are hiding right inside."

Matt noticed that Charlie's eyes were flat and out of sync with his broad smile.

"How do you remove the shell?" Alex said. "And more important, how do you cook them?"

"Not so easy to get them out, m'am," Tyrone said, "and they are very messy to clean. They'll get your beautiful boat all mucked up. It's better to do it on the beach. And I have good news for you. Jack is an expert conch cleaner and he will take you and Mr. Spencer to the Island and clean them for you. He'll also tell you how to cook them, won't you Jack?"

"Oh, yeah," Z. said nodding. "Did you know, Mrs. Spencer, that we eat conch raw? It's supposed to make us, uh, more manly, if you know what I mean. And they are yummy to eat. So good," he said and rubbed his belly in wide circles.

Matt, listening to the exchange, felt troubled. Something was definitely wrong. He didn't know about these men, who seemed terribly eager for a six dollar sale. Their cabin cruiser was not the sort of boat fishermen would own. The thick gold chains that dangled from Charlie's neck suggested that whatever business these men were in must be lucrative. Matt studied them while Alex commented on the beauty of the Islands. The skinny guy, Jack, seemed especially nervous. He repeatedly licked his lips and avoided eye contact.

"I'll tell you something that would taste good with the conch," Tyrone said. "Something my Mama used to make."

"What's that?" Alex said.

"Pigeon peas and rice."

Alex waited for him to continue.

"First you fry a little bacon up nice 'n crisp and save the grease. You can eat the bacon if you want. You add some onion to the hot grease and cook it until it turns light brown. Then you add some thyme and a small can of tomato paste and cook it a little while. Let's see, you, uh, drain a can of pigeon peas, add them to the onion and stuff and pour in a few cups of water. When everything begins to boil, you, uh, gotta be careful not to burn it. Yeah, when everything begins to boil, you dump in a couple of cups of rice, white, brown, whatever you got. You let this boil awhile and when it's all done, I'm talkin' good."

"Sounds delicious," Alex said. "The next time we go to the grocery store, I'll buy some of those, pigeon peas, was it?"

"Right, pigeon peas. Well, when can you folks be ready to go to the beach?"

"Well, I, uh, just took a shower," Alex said with a note of apology in her voice.

"Don't you worry about gettin' dirty, m'am," Tyrone said. "No m'am, Z. will do all the work for you."

"I thought his name was Jack," Matt said.

Tyrone gulped and snickered.

"Oh, his name is Jack. It is Jack, but my nickname for him is Z., sort of a private joke. He doesn't like other people to call him that, do you Jack?"

Z. shook his head.

"Now how about you folks take your dinghy cause ours doesn't have a motor. Mr. Spencer, you can steer your boat and just go around the corner over there," Tyrone said and pointed west, "and beyond there a little ways is a beautiful beach and Jack will clean the conch for you. How's that?"

Alex looked at Matt, but before she could speak, Matt raised a hand and said, "No, we really appreciate it, guys, but we'd better stay put. We're, uh, expecting a call on the radio from some friends who are look-ing for us. Actually, they could be arriving at any moment."

Tyrone looked stricken.

"You mean," Tyrone said, "that you don't want to buy the conch?"

"Oh, no, we'll buy the conch," Matt said, "but we need to wait for our friends to get here."

Alex looked at Matt with a question in her eyes. His glance told her to be silent.

Tyrone looked from Matt to Alex and back again.

"But…" he stammered.

"No, Charlie, we really do appreciate your kind offer," Matt said, but we need to stay close to our radio. Here's six dollars for the conch."

Tyrone's jaw tightened and for a brief moment he and Matt looked directly at each other. Neither man's gaze wavered, and Matt saw some-thing dangerous in Tyrone's expression. There was an uncomfortable break in the conversation. Alex heard a baby crying on the forty-footer.

"Well," Tyrone said, "all right, if that's the way you want to do it. We gotta go. Here's your conch."

Matt gave him six dollars in Bahamian currency.

"We'll enjoy it, I'm sure," Alex said.

Tyrone and Z., silent as they cast off, rowed back to the cabin cruiser.

"Matt, what…"

"Just a minute," Matt said as he waited for the two men to be out of earshot. "Something's wrong," he told her. "I'm not sure what those guys are up to but I do know we need to leave here as soon as possible and head back to Charter Cay where there are people and maybe police at the Settlement."

"What's wrong? They seem very nice."

"They're nice all right, too nice. Too eager. Don't you see, they want us off our boat. Why? And that Charlie guy, if his name is Charlie, first told us his friend's name is Jack and then he called him Z. They said they were divers but they got the conch from the men on the boat next door, I'm sure of it," he said, remembering that he had observed something pass from one of the fishermen to Charlie just before the two appeared alongside the *Amani*. "It just doesn't figure. They're both so nervous they're trembling. And they're a little too slick. They may need a bath, but they look like city boys to me."

"Maybe they want to steal the boat," she said.

"That's possible. That big guy, Charlie, he behaves like a desperate man. Did you see the way he looked at me when I told him we were going to stay put? I thought he was going to climb into the cockpit and grab me by the throat."

Alex took Matt's hand and pulled him down into the cabin.

"Matt you're scaring me. What should we do?" she said.

"I don't know if they will bother us anymore now that they think we have friends on the way. That is, if they believed me. I wonder how responsive the Bahamian police are. We could call them on the radio but what would we say? Some suspicious-looking characters claiming to be fishermen sold us some conch."

"Well, let's just go," she said. "Let's just untie the mooring line and start back to Charter Cay."

"It's getting late," he reminded her as he glanced outside, "and we can't move the boat at night. These waters don't offer the safe cruising conditions that we have in the States. There are few markers and those that are standing are unlighted for the most part. There is shoaling that isn't noted on the charts. And the bottom has coral heads that would shred the boat's fiberglass hull in a matter of minutes. No, honey, we have to stay put until first light."

She shivered, hugged herself, and bottled her emotions in the middle of her throat.

"Don't worry," he said as he drew her to him. "We have guns and I know how to use them. You can, too, if it comes to that."

"You know how I feel about guns," she said.

"Listen," he said as he clasped her shoulders, "we'll do what we have to do."

"Let's call the guys at the Tracking Station," she said. "Maybe they can help us. We should at least tell someone."

"That's an idea but the gang was well on their way to getting blitzed when we left and who knows what condition they'll be in by now. You're probably right, though. Can't hurt to try."

Matt turned on the VHF radio and positioned the dial on Channel 16 with maximum range.

"Robert's Cay Station, Robert's Cay Station, this is the sailing vessel, *Amani*, over."

The radio, heavy with static, crackled and hissed. Matt turned down the squelch and repeated his call.

"Robert's Cay Station, this is the sailing vessel, *Amani*, over."

Shorty came up.

"*Amonty, Amonty*, this is Robert's Cay Station. Do you have channel seventy-two? Over."

"That's a roger," Matt said before he switched the dial to channel seventy-two.

"Amonty, Amonty," Shorty said in a dull voice that trailed off.

Matt waited for him to unkey his microphone and then said, "Listen, Shorty, this is probably nothing, but there are a couple guys who have shown up at two different islands where we have anchored in the last two days. They claim to be conch divers, but, well, they haven't done anything, but we have the distinct impression that they want us off our boat. We're not sure what they're after. We, uh, just wanted to let you know. Over."

"Are you talking about that big fishing boat that's tied up at the mooring ball because if you are, they're okay."

Silence.

Matt keyed his mike.

"That's a negative. We're talking about a small cabin cruiser called *The Happy Hour*. I repeat, *The Happy Hour*. There are two Bahamians on board, one black, one white. Over."

"I'd have to eyeball it to say if I knew 'em or not, but you say they're on a cabin cruiser called *The Happy Hour*? There's a charter out of Mission Harbor with that name. It's been in and out 'a here a few times. Could be the same one."

"You mean these guys are on a rental? Over."

"Well, if it's the same boat out of Mission Harbor, I would say they are. Now of course there could be another boat with that name."

There was a round of static followed by dead air space.

"That bit of news just makes me more uneasy," Matt said, breaking the silence. "I'm sure conch divers don't use rental boats. How should we contact the Bahamian police if these guys get more aggressive? Over."

"The Bahamian police? Good luck. Those guys are hard to get on the wire and when you do they're tough to deal with. They're all on the take, drug money, you know, and you can't expect any help from them.

In this part of the world, my friend, you are on your own. Every man for himself, so to speak. Kind 'a like the old west."

Silence.

"Thanks for the info," Matt said. "If things turn sour, you may find you have company for the night. Over."

"Sure, come on up if you like. Old Fletch's not feeling so hot. Too much Johnny Black. Me, I'm up and drinking coffee. One of us has to stand by. Ginger and me would be glad to have you. Isn't that right, Ginger?"

"Well, I'd rather stay with my boat unless things get out of hand, but I don't want my wife involved in anything dangerous. Over."

Silence.

"Shorty, you still up?"

The radio crackled and hissed. To conserve battery power, Matt turned off the set.

"At least he sounds halfway sober," Alex said. "That's some comfort. Maybe we should lock up and dinghy to the Island. At least at the Tracking Station we have light and two other, well, one other able-bodied person. I don't think they would bother us up there."

"Don't bet on it."

"Matt, stop it. You're scaring me."

"I'm sorry, babe," he said and wrapped his arms around her. He held her against his chest and felt her heart pounding. "I may be over-reacting, but I'll be damned if we're going to abandon this boat. Besides, this is probably just a routine attempt to rip off some tourists. Now that they know we're not going to cooperate, they'll probably look for another victim."

"I've heard stories about piracy," Alex said, "but usually it's told by a friend of a friend of a friend. You know what I mean, third hand."

Matt rubbed his upper lip and felt his neck stiffening. He didn't want Alex to know how terribly vulnerable they were. If those guys were on drugs and dangerous, they wouldn't be deterred by a simple "no" or a dark look. They would come back and be more aggressive next time.

"Get my thirty-eight from the shelf on my side of the V-berth," he told her.

Matt liked revolvers. He knew that they were considered as out of date as flint-lock muskets by those who carried a weapon in their daily lives. He was aware that automatics could hold twice the ammunition and shoot faster and more accurately than a revolver. Inserting a clip of fresh ammo into an automatic is easy and quick. The revolver on the other hand, takes fifteen or twenty seconds to reload, longer when you're under pressure.

For all the virtues of an automatic, Matt had never seen one that didn't jam, catch a round crossways in the feeding mechanism, or try to re-digest one of its spent shells. Matt believed that if an automatic is used regularly, its reliability went up, but if you don't use it often there can be problems at the worst possible moment. In contrast, except in the rare case of bad ammunition, wet or outdated bullets, he had never seen a revolver fail to fire. For self defense, Matt concluded that he wanted to buy a gun, shoot it a few times, clean and load it, and put it away knowing that if one's life depended on it, all of the bullets would come out of the barrel without a hitch. In most self-defense situations, Matt knew that if he needed to shoot, it would be frantically and within six feet of the target. If half a dozen bullets wouldn't do the job, then nothing would.

Alex went forward to retrieve the gun. Matt saw that the sun had set, the sky had darkened, and the wind had picked up a couple of knots. He decided to go forward to check the mooring line. As he made his way up the port side, he looked at the cabin cruiser some twenty-five yards upwind of the Amani. All its lights were off and no one was on deck. He noticed the waves careening around the western tip of Robert's Cay bringing white caps into the anchorage. He made a mental note to check the weather on his single-side-band receiver at nine p.m. when there would be another report out of Portsmouth.

"Matt," Alex called. "Honey."

"I'll be right there, babe."

The air had chilled and he had begun to feel wary and tense in a way reminiscent of combat. He didn't want to alarm Alex unnecessarily but neither did he want to expose them to danger because he refused to recognize it.

"God," he said to himself and rubbed the back of his neck.

"Matt."

"Coming."

CHAPTER EIGHTEEN

Roberts Cay

"I have to kill them," Tyrone said softly.

"What?" Z. said as he rifled through their remaining supply of food.

"I said that I have to kill them, that couple. They leave me no choice."

"Wow! Far out!"

"And it isn't my fault. Jesus Christ, I've done everything I can to keep from hurting anyone."

Tyrone had begun to rearrange his thoughts so that in his mind the Spencer's weren't real people. He tried to imagine that they were sophisticated robots or spies or aliens disguised as human beings. Killing something like that would be easy, just like in the movies.

The halyards on the *Amani* had begun to clang against its metal mast. To Tyrone, it sounded like an alarm.

"You know none of this would have happened if you hadn't picked the wrong boat."

Z. stood with his back to Tyrone while he continued to rummage in the small bags he had set on the galley counter.

"Hell" Tyrone said, "if they'd gone ashore at Pine Cay like they said, we'd been on that sailboat and out 'a there in thirty minutes. They'd a come back and we'd 'a just been gone."

"You hungry?" Z. said over his shoulder.

"And if that goddamn engine hadn't fucked up, we'd 'a caught up with 'em quicker, you know, that first day."

Tyrone picked up his magnum and began to turn it over in his hands. He studied the long smooth barrel.

"Ah, here's something," Z. said. "Now where did I put that can opener?"

"Or if they had gone to the beach with you to clean the conch. Easy in. Easy out. Nobody would 'a had to get hurt. But no, that cocksucker wouldn't leave his boat. And the way he looked at me. I felt like he was fuckin' readin' my mind."

Z., eating pork and beans directly from the can, discovered a soggy piece of fatback. He stabbed it with his fork, lifted it out of the can, and eyed it suspiciously.

"Christ" Tyrone said as he stood up, "if the queen had balls, she'd be king. I gotta do what I gotta do."

"What are you really gonna do?" Z. said without taking his eyes off the meat balanced at the end of his fork.

"Do? I'll tell you what we're gonna do. We're gonna wait for it to get a little darker and then we're gonna fuckin' go over to that fuckin' sailboat and blow their fuckin' brains out."

Z. tasted the fatback with the tip of his tongue.

"And I won't ever forget that this is your fault, asshole. Never!"

"Ah, so it's come down to that," Z. said. "I was just waiting. So now I'm the enemy or something."

Tyrone's stomach churned .

Z. removed the meat from the fork with his teeth.

"So, we'll be out 'a here tonight?" he said after he chewed and swallowed.

"We have to be."

"You know," Z. said, "we could have a nice time with that woman before you kill her. She's a looker. Nice tits."

"I would expect you to think of pussy at a time like this, but I've got a news flash for you, dickface. We're gonna be on that boat like lightening. Flash we hit, boom we shoot, and then we haul ass with the coke."

Z. scraped around the bottom of the pork and beans can with his fork.

"Hey, how about gettin' me a spoon," Z. said.

"Get it yourself, asshole."

CHAPTER NINETEEN

Roberts Cay

When darkness shrouded the anchorage, Matt went below decks. Alex had thrown together some sandwiches for dinner, but neither of them had much appetite. Every few minutes Matt would get up, turn off the cabin light, and check for any activity on the cabin cruiser. Each time he looked, he saw the faint outline of *The Happy Hour* as it silently rode the waves. Inside his head a battle raged. Was he just being paranoid and frightening Alex unnecessarily or were these guys a real threat to them?

Matt picked up the thirty-eight from the navigation table, pressed the release lever, and swung open the cylinder. He carefully dropped all six bullets in his hand and checked them for corrosion. Before reinserting them into the cylinder, he looked down the barrel to see if there were any obstructions. Once the bullets were back in the cylinder, he closed the chamber and wiggled it to be sure it was locked. When he set the gun on the desk top, Alex jumped.

"I've gotta get a grip," she said as she cleared the uneaten sandwiches and iced tea glasses from the table. I can't believe how jittery I am."

"You have reason to be. Nothing about those characters adds up and we should be concerned."

"Do you think they want to steal the boat?" she said.

"I don't know if they're after the boat. They don't look like they would be very good sailors. That skinny guy, whatever his name is, can hardly walk around the deck without tripping over his feet. I think that if anything, they're after our money, the electronics, or both."

Alex fussed about the cabin, straightening the cans of applesauce and lima beans and folding and unfolding dish towels. Matt wanted to be prepared for the nine o'clock weather forecast. He got out his single-side-band receiver and set it on the dining table. The wind had shifted 180 degrees and the boat had pivoted at its mooring. The anchorage was becoming uncomfortable.

"I'd better go forward and put chafing gear on that mooring line," he told her. "Can't hurt. Turn off the cabin light soon. We need to conserve our battery power."

"Okay, just a minute. Here's a flashlight," she said and handed it to him.

"Thanks."

He leaned over and nuzzled the top of her head.

"It's going to be all right," he assured her. "Really."

She looked at him wide eyed and nodded without conviction.

As he held onto the lifeline and clutched his way to the bow, he glanced at the cabin cruiser and noticed that something was different about it. He stared for a moment but wasn't sure what it was.

Crouched on the fore deck, Matt wrapped the mooring line with some canvas and tied it with a couple pieces of cord. It had already begun to stretch and groan against the strain. He watched it for a while before making his way aft. Amidships, he paused and peered into the darkness.

Something is different. What? The longer he stared at the outline of the cabin cruiser the fuzzier it became. He glanced down and looked up again. *God, their dinghy's gone! Did they haul it on board? If not, where the hell are they?* He looked around. There was no sign of anyone on the forty-footer next door, no glow of cigarettes. Even their noisy generator was mute. If the fishermen's two power boats had not been tied to its stern, Matt would have thought that no one was aboard. *Maybe their dinghy is on the starboard side of the big boat. No, that wouldn't make sense. It would be almost impossible to board from anywhere other than the stern.*

He rushed to the cabin and called to Alex in a hushed voice. "Where are you?"

"I'm here," she whispered.

"I want you to get the hatches," he told her.

"Why? What's the matter?"

"Get the hatches and help me close up the boat."

"Is it going to rain?"

"Yes."

Alex hurriedly inserted the companionway hatchboards and shut the windows.

"Get the stick from the American flag, you know, the pole, and give it to me," he said.

Alex removed a cushion that covered one of the port storage areas and retrieved the flagpole.

"Here," she said as she handed it to him.

He jammed the pole between the leading edge of the hatch and the fixed edge of the cabin top.

"There," he said, "now no one can open this from the outside."

"Oh, God, Matt!"

"Now, Alex, I want you to be calm. I need you to stay together. It's probably nothing, but those guys may have left their boat and I don't know what they're up to. They could have lifted their dinghy on board but I can't be sure."

"Matt…"

He heard a catch in her throat.

"Do you think…"

"I don't know what to think. I'd better get my shotgun out of the hanging locker. And we'd better turn off the galley light."

"Here," he said as he handed her the flashlight, "close all the curtains while I double check the hatches."

The flashlight beamed brightly in the tiny cabin. Alex's fingers trembled as she fumbled with the curtains on the port side.

"We're probably going to laugh about this one day," she said in a voice that didn't resemble her own.

Matt didn't speak for a moment, then said, "I hope so."

In a few minutes, the cabin became warm and close. Matt peeled off his shirt.

"Bring that flashlight over here to the locker," he said.

Shoving aside the foul weather gear, he reached for his twelve-gauge that was leaning against the back wall.

"I got it," he said with a groan. "The shells are in my drawer."

"They used to be, honey. I moved them to the bottom of the locker to give you more drawer space."

"Not a good place, babe. It gets awfully damp in there and the box will disintegrate pretty quickly."

He stooped and fumbled in the bottom of the narrow closet.

"Aim that light a little lower," he said.

The cardboard box containing the shells felt soft and pliable when he found it with his fingertips. As he lifted it, one end broke open and several shells tumbled out.

"Damn!"

"I'm sorry honey, I…"

"Hold that light over here," he said as he began picking up the shells. "God, this locker stinks. Fiberglass."

"That must be where they did some work on the boat."

"H-m-m…"

"What's the matter?"

"I could be mistaken but I think this closet was bigger than this when we picked it up at the factory. Aim the light over here."

"I've never really looked in there so I don't know," she said and coughed.

"Hold the light still," he said as he began to run his hands along the new fiberglass at the back of the locker. "This is really strange. It feels like something... Let me have that flashlight."

Matt aimed the beam directly at the wall and saw the smooth new fiberglass and fresh paint reflected in the light. He could think of no logical reason for another wall to have been added nor could he imagine any kind of accident or collision which would damage this precise area. He stood up and went to another storage compartment which housed his tools, opened one of the boxes, and took out a chisel and hammer. When he returned to the hanging locker, he squatted and handed her the flashlight. Using the tools, he began to chip and pry at the new fiberglass. It was slow going at first but after several desperate minutes, he was able to chop out a six-inch hole. With his fingers, he clawed at the sides of the opening and crammed his hand inside.

"There's something in here."

"What is it?"

"I don't know. I just," he said and groaned, "about have it."

He wormed his hand backwards and came up holding a plastic-wrapped package. He had cut his knuckles on the rough edges of the fiberglass and blood trickled down his arm. Matt didn't hear Alex saying, "What is it? What is it?" All he could see was the bag; all he could hear was a roar in his ears. With trembling hands, he removed the package from its storage bag and peeled away the plastic wrap.

"What is it?" Alex kept saying. "What?"

He held his breath as he pulled the top of the bag apart and looked inside. It contained a fine white powder. He rubbed some of it between his fingers and sniffed it. The substance smelled a little like ether.

"Drugs," he said flatly. "They're after drugs."

"Are you sure? Where did it come from?"

"I don't know. "It's probably heroin or cocaine or something like that. And we can guess who put it here. I don't know why, but I know who. This isn't all. There's more behind that wall. And they want it."

"Well, let's just give it to them."

"It's not that simple. You see, babe, we know. We know about their drugs. We know what they look like. We mean trouble to them. We're a liability. They might think they have to get rid of us and sink the boat."

"Oh, no, Matt!"

"Turn off the flashlight."

"Your hand?"

"It's okay."

She extinguished the light and they sat in the dark, not speaking. Matt heard her breathing, quick and shallow. The wind, blowing out of the northwest, moaned in the rigging. He felt the cabin closing in around him and inhaled deeply with measured breaths.

"I'm gonna have to open one of the windows in the head," he told her. I can't…"

He unlatched a window, inhaled the moist night air.

"What are we going to do?" Alex asked when he returned.

"I don't know just yet. We have to think."

They sat still while their minds raced to make some sense out of what was happening to them. Alex broke the silence.

"I have an idea."

"What?"

"We could hide the bags on the Island and show those guys that we don't have them on board. You know, then if they want the stuff, they would have to do as we say. And they couldn't do anything to us because if they did, they'd never find the drugs on their own. They might not want to risk losing whatever it is. They'd have no choice but to cooperate. You say we just can't give it to them because of what they might do, so we won't."

Matt rubbed his chin as he considered her suggestion.

"Actually, that makes good sense. If we hide the bags, we have a bargaining chip. Just might work," he said nodding. "Let's do it."

"Now what?"

"Help me get the rest of it out of the locker. We'd better hurry. God knows what those guys are up to."

"Please hold me a minute," she said softly. "Just a minute."

Alex rested her head on his shoulder and leaned into him, trembling. He stroked her hair for a moment.

"There," he said and gently pushed her away. "We have to hurry."

"Okay, what do you want me to do?"

"Hold the flashlight while I make a bigger opening."

Matt feverishly chipped and hacked out the remaining packages, twenty altogether. Alex's hands shook as she stacked the powder-filled bags on the dinette table.

"I wonder what all this is worth?" he said.

"Probably a lot, maybe thousands. Let's triple-bag the stuff in those freezer things we planned to put fish in, you know, the jumbos."

Alex pulled out a box of extra-large freezer bags which they quickly filled and sealed.

"I can't believe this is happening," she said.

"It's happening."

"We're going to be okay, aren't we Matt?"

"Check to make sure they're closed," he said as they worked. "I don't want water to seep inside and spoil the goods."

Alex silently examined each package. When they finished, Matt grabbed a heavy-duty trash bag and stuffed the packages inside.

"Get me a sail bag," he said. "I'll put everything inside it."

Alex felt the wind buffet the boat and shivered.

"Now I'm going to hide this somewhere on the Island, and I don't want you to know where it is."

"Matt…"

"I think that the less you know, the safer you'll be. I'm going to take this ashore. I won't be long. You'll be okay after you put the pole in place. No one will be able to get in."

"But I want to go with you."

"I know, babe," he said and drew her to him, "but this is the best way. I can move faster by myself. I don't want to have to worry about you. Really, I'll do better by myself."

"But..."

"I'm going to climb out the hatch and then you put the pole back. I'll leave you the thirty-eight."

"But Matt..."

"Listen, dammit," he said as he gripped her shoulders, "we don't have time for this. I have to get the bags ashore. I promise I'll be back before you know it, in a half hour or less."

She nodded.

"That's my girl. Now I won't be long. Remember, put the pole back as soon as I close the hatch."

"I will."

"And you'd better turn off that light."

He gave her a brief hug and lifted the heavy sack with all twenty bags. "Okay, I'm off."

He removed the pole, slid back the companionway hatch, and peeked outside.

"Matt," she whispered, "your knife?"

"I have it, and I'm taking the shotgun."

He hoisted the sailbag over the hatchboards and dropped it in the cockpit. Without glancing back, he climbed out of the cabin and quickly slid the hatchcover in place. Alex reinserted the pole and extinguished the cabin light. To bolster her courage, she picked up the thirty-eight. Once seated at the table, she switched off the flashlight and sat trembling in the dark. She had no sense of time. The wind and waves tossed the boat about like a toy. She imagined that rolling down a hill in a tin can would not feel much worse. Quaking, she tried to swallow. Her mouth felt arid, her throat tight. Unable to muster the inner strength to rise and get herself a drink of water from the galley, she remained fixed with her back molded against the seat rest. *Hurry Matt!* She listened. The steady clang of the halyards signaled an increase in the wind. When she turned on the flashlight to check her watch, she saw that only ten minutes had elapsed, barely enough time for Matt to make it to the Island and drag the dinghy up on the beach. She licked her dry lips.

Then she heard it. The sound was muffled, but she heard something over the wind and waves. Footsteps. Topside. The fiberglass cabin creaked with each footfall. She cringed and held onto the gun butt with both hands. She thought she heard a voice carried on the wind. It sounded almost like a sigh. Her teeth began to chatter. Holding the gun rigidly in front of her, she stared into the darkness.

CHAPTER TWENTY

Robert's Cay

The Tracking Station lights on the hill blazed, illuminating the compound like a mall parking lot. Matt wheezed as he hoisted the sack over his shoulder and proceeded up a twisted path that began at the beach. At some point, he knew that he would have to leave the trail and make his way through the knotty brush until he found a suitable hiding place. The casuarina branches convulsed in the wind; surf battered the Atlantic side of the Island. He wouldn't allow himself to think about Alex. *She'll be okay. I just have to hurry!*

Thirty yards up, he veered to the right and encountered dense underbrush that thwarted his passage and scored his bare legs. The bag rested heavily on his left shoulder, the one he had broken when he ejected from his airplane over Vietnam. He shifted the weight to his right and groaned. *This is unbelievable.* He shook his head. *Why did they put drugs on our boat? Why our boat? They must have been following us since we left Mission Harbor.*

When he came to an isolated pine in a small clearing, he dropped the load, knelt down, and brushed pine needles and twigs aside. Fortunately, the ground was loamy and he was able to make a two-foot hole using his hands. As he dug deeper, though, the soil became harder, almost impenetrable. He groped for a piece of wood and found a thick branch that served his purpose. *I've gotta hurry. Get back.* It took him a long time, an eternity, to hollow out a crater deep enough to cover the sack.

I should have brought something to dig with. Got to calm down, think.

When he finished covering the bag with sand and pine straw, he spread brush and debris on top to further conceal it. On the opposite side of the tree he made an X on the bark with his knife. It was just a scratch, but he was certain that he would recognize it in the daylight.

As he made his way back to the trail, he counted his steps, *twenty-one, twenty-two, twenty-three.* Relief washed over him when he found the well-traveled footpath and paused to carve a notch on another tree. Afterwards, he turned and bolted. Halfway down the trail, he thought he heard a sound over the wind and crashing surf. It was muffled, sort of a pop. He ran faster. Again there was the same sound, only this time there were several reports in rapid succession.

"Oh, God, he thought as he raced toward the shore. *That sounds like gunfire!*

Matt's feet could not propel him fast enough. He felt like a man moving underwater as he untied the dinghy and shoved it into the rough sea. Because his legs trembled so badly, he thought for a moment that he wouldn't be able to lift them over the side and into the inflatable. His body responded to danger as it had in Hanoi when the Viet Cong half carried, half dragged him to the infamous torture chamber, otherwise known as the Green Knobby Room. Panic bubbled up his throat and threatened to choke him. He sobbed.

As the dinghy plunged through the ragged chop, he clutched the twelve-gauge. I'm a good shot, he reassured himself, and with this, I can hit what I need to. He thought he heard the dull throb of an engine somewhere near the channel entrance.

The *Amani* gradually took shape in the gloom. It wandered at its mooring, and this movement, coupled with his weak legs, made it difficult for him to board. Mustering all his strength, he hoisted himself over the stern rail and called out.

"Alex, it's me!"

Silence.

Head down, shoulders bent, he approached the companionway and found the hatch boards lying on top of the starboard lazaret.

"Alex!"

He heard waves slapping the hull and the wind tugging at the sail cover. He waited with his twelve-gauge pointed at the companionway. Because his hands had begun to quake, he gripped the gun like a vise. Overwhelmed by his concern for Alex, he leaped into the cabin and groped for a light. The air below still felt warm. Matt saw that Alex wasn't there. No one was on the boat. He quickly examined the companionway hatch and found a hole the size of a fist had been blown through it. This opening had enabled someone to reach in, remove the flag pole and hatch boards, and enter.

And I told her she'd be safe. Oh, God.

He felt something sticky beneath his feet and kneeled down to see what it was. It appeared that something had spilled on the floor. He fumbled for his flashlight and aimed its beam on the teak boards. To his horror, he saw blood, fresh, bright blood. Lots of it.

"Alex," he whispered. "Alex."

He stood up, turned off the cabin light, and crept up the steps. Crouched in the cockpit, he peeked over the stern rail and looked toward the cabin cruiser. He stared until he was dizzy. It was so dark and windy his eyes kept watering. He wiped them, blinked. There was no way around it. *The Happy Hour* was gone. And Alex was gone.

Matt stood up, looked to the heavens, and emitted a raging cry that was swallowed up by the wind, the waves, and the impassive night sky.

CHAPTER TWENTY-ONE

Bahama Bank

"Goddamn bitch shot me!" Z. said again.

"Shut up!" Tyrone yelled over the engine noise. "Just shut the fuck up and make sure she stays put!"

He glanced below. Z. had lost a lot of blood. Crimson droplets trailed from the cockpit into the cabin and pooled on the starboard bunk where Z. slumped against the backrest.

"I'm gonna fuckin' die!" he said.

Alex, still unconscious, lay sprawled face down on the cabin floor. Clotted blood had begun to dry on the back of her head and mat her hair. Tyrone ran the boat wide open now that they had exited Robert's Cay Channel and crossed into open water.

Good thing we draw so little, otherwise we would've never gotten out of there in the dark.

He looked down at the compass to make sure he was following to the letter the directions given to him over the radio.

Jesus, this has been a total screw-up since the beginning. From start to finish.

He squinted and plunged the boat through the murky sea with reck-less abandon.

Danny had called them on the radio after they had returned from the aborted conch mission and ordered Tyrone to get the coke, now, and to meet him at Sandy Cay by midnight.

At least I have the woman. The woman will explain everything, say it wasn't my fault. She'll tell Danny where the cocaine is. Danny will have to believe me. What a fuckin' disaster! Nothing has worked out. Not a god-damn thing.

When he saw the dinghy leave the sailboat, he had assumed that the man and woman were both heading for the Tracking Station on the hill. He was certain he had seen the silhouette of two figures in the little boat. Earlier that evening they had listened in while the man, Spencer, talked to someone at the Station over the VHF. It sounded like the guy was really concerned about his wife. Tyrone thought that once they left the *Amani,* he and Z. could hop aboard, get the coke, and haul ass. Shit, it wasn't hard to blast a hole in the hatch, reach in, and shove the stick aside. They had rushed down the stairs and started groping for a light switch, Z. on one side of the boat, he on the other. Z. had been babbling about something, as usual. Then, holy shit, there was a shot and then another. Z. yelped like a dog that had been side swiped by a car and began thrashing about the cabin. The gun kept firing until he heard the telltale click of an empty chamber. Then Tyrone had reached blindly until he found someone and grabbed that someone by the hair. It was the woman. She was crazed. It was like trying to hold onto a deranged cat. She clawed his face and tried to get away from him. Tyrone touched his fingers to the dried blood on his cheek. In the darkness, he could not see her face but he knew he was holding her head. He hammered it against the wall until he felt her relax and go limp. When he released his grip, she tumbled to the floor and didn't move.

Z. was somewhere in the cabin sobbing and muttering something about his mama. Tyrone swore when he couldn't locate a light switch.

Then, to his relief, he found one over the sink in the galley and turned it on. A soft glow shone over the three-burner stove and metal sink. The rest of the cabin was visible but hard to see. Tyrone felt around for another switch and found one by the navigation station. Once he turned it on, he could see clearly. The woman lay unconscious and bleeding. Z. held a bloody left shoulder.

"She's killed me," Z. had said. "Bitch!"

Tyrone quickly examined Z.'s shoulder and ordered him to be quiet and sit still. He grabbed a handful of paper towels from the galley and had Z. press them tightly against his wound. He found a flashlight on the floor and snapped it on. The hanging locker was open with one door banging like a loose shutter in the wind. He opened both doors and aimed the light inside. His heart beat wildly, and for a second, he ceased to breath. The plywood wall had been hollowed out and the stash was gone.

This is too much, too much, he had thought. *We're dead.*

Frantic, he had searched the entire boat, pulling open drawers and looking in storage compartments concealed by foam cushions. Then it occurred to him that who he had seen leaving the cabin earlier had been the man and the coke. He took it to the Island, that son of a bitch. Maybe to the Tracking Station. *Jesus.*

Tyrone throttled back and focused the flashlight beam on the coordinates he had jotted down, then checked his watch. Almost midnight. The woman hadn't stirred and he wondered if maybe he had slammed her head against the wall a little too hard. He needed her alive.

Z. had finally stopped whimpering and the only sound Tyrone heard was the gurgle and sputter of the engine as they slowly entered the channel at Sandy Cay. When he looked ahead, he saw a huge power boat, fifty feet or more in length, anchored a hundred or so yards away. All its lights were glowing yellow and bright in what otherwise appeared to be a black void. He swallowed hard and tried to form an expression of confidence. He did not want Danny or any of those guys to see how desperately frightened he was. He had no way of knowing what they were going to do or how they would react to this most recent downturn of events. *Four days and no fuckin' coke.*

Two men, like specters, waited silently on the port side of the motor yacht. Danny appeared at the stern but did not speak. In fact, no one said a word.

CHAPTER TWENTY-TWO

Robert's Cay

What now? Where have they taken Alex? And why?

Matt paced forward and aft in the cabin. Three steps forward, three steps back. *Hanoi all over again. Alone. They might as well have put me back in solitary.* His neck and shoulders ached.

Okay, think. He took a deep breath. *I still have a bargaining chip, the drugs. They won't hurt Alex as long as I have their heroin or whatever it is.* "They wouldn't," he said and rubbed his eyes with the heels of his hands.

"Okay," he said. "Options?" "What are my options?" *Number one, I can wait until morning. Shit, I have to wait until morning in any event. I'll never get out of the channel in the dark. I'd run aground and might not be able to get off.* "Okay," he said. *Wait until morning. Sunrise. No, just before, when the sky is gray. I'll be able to see well enough. Gotta check the tide tables, though. Okay, I can call the guys at the Station. But what good would that do? Besides, I don't want those assholes who took Alex to know what I'm up to. What, what if they didn't take her anywhere? What if she's dead, thrown over the side?*

He rushed to the cockpit, searched the choppy water for some sign of her. Except for the lights on the hill, there was only black sky and the mournful sound of the constant wind. He returned to the cabin.

I could… Let me see. "Okay," he said and pounded a fist on the galley counter. *I could go to Mission Harbor to the Bahamian Police. There must be some kind of law. Kidnapping tourists cannot be okay with them. So Shorty said they wouldn't help. He could be mistaken. Maybe I should search every cove, every cay. God, a sailboat is no match for speed next to a power boat. Not this one anyway. They could be anywhere by sunup. Will they come to me? Maybe. Yes. They have to.*

The *Amani* bucked as the wind freshened out of the north. Matt paced, stopping only to peer outside to see if by some miracle the cabin cruiser had returned. Beads of sweat meandered down his spine, and his eyes burned from searching the darkness, from straining to see that which was not there.

As he roamed the cabin, he located bullet holes in a number of places. Above the stove in the galley. Behind the starboard bunk. Two in the ceiling. One lodged in a stair step. Five. He counted the holes again and again. From the blood, it was clear that one shot connected. But who got shot? Alex? He picked up his flashlight, turned it on, and crawled on his knees across the floor leaving streaks of clotted blood behind him. *So much blood. But whose?* He searched the boat by inches; V-berth, head, wet-locker, galley, storage compartments, lazarets, anchor well. He wasn't certain what he was looking for. Evidence maybe. Evidence that would tell him that Alex was alive and well. He found none.

He checked his watch. It was a little after midnight. Matt rummaged through his sailing books, dumped them on the floor and the quarter berths. *Tide tables, tide tables.* When he found the tables for the Abacos and Northern Bahamas, he determined that high tide would be at nine a.m. That would be important when he exited the shallow channel.

"What to do?" he muttered and ran his fingers through his hair. It felt sticky from the damp salt air.

"I have to think."

This isn't Hanoi. I have choices. I'm not tied up. I have weapons. I have their goddamn drugs. If I'm not here when they come back, they might think that I've run off, left Alex, taken their stash. They'd kill her.

His only option suddenly became clear to him. Wait. He had to sit and wait for them. They must come to him.

"They want to fight? I'm ready!"

The words sounded hollow inside the empty cabin, and behind his bravado, even he wasn't convinced.

Steely dawn appeared at six-thirty. The wind had begun to settle and blow ten knots out of the north. Matt checked his twelve-gauge. He had a formidable weapon and plenty of ammunition. At six forty-five, he hunched down in the cockpit and waited for the light to come.

They'll be back. They have to come back.

CHAPTER TWENTY-THREE

Sandy Cay, Bahamas

"My name is Jorge. Do you know what the name means in English?"

Tyrone did not break eye contact with the stocky, olive-skinned man standing a few feet away from him. He shook his head.

The man, compact and muscular, had unwavering brown eyes. Dressed in white slacks and a light green knit shirt, he seemed out of place on a boat. His hair, long and wavy, was pulled back tightly in a pony tail. His English, though almost flawless, still revealed his Spanish origin.

"Jorge means George, my friend. And you are called Tee-rone. Now, Tee-rone," he said as he paused to light a cigarette, "we seem to have a little problem." He inserted the lighter in his right pants pocket. "My friends and I, we have been very patient."

Danny, standing next to Tyrone, bobbed his head up and down. Tyrone would not have been surprised if Danny had shouted, "amen, brother."

"Do you know what our little problem is, Tee-rone?"

"I know what it is if you'll just let me…"

"Shut up!" Jorge said. "Just answer yes or no."

"Yes," Tyrone whispered and locked his jaws.

Jorge smiled, shook his head, and continued.

"Yes, we must solve this little problem without further delay. You see, we had some drugs flown to Mission Harbor from Columbia."

Jorge's eyes now resembled those of a fish.

"We paid good money to have them brought in. We made an agreement with some businessmen to have the drugs hidden on a sailboat that was to deliver the cocaine to the U.S. When our man goes to pick up the boat, do you know what he finds?"

Tyrone swallowed and said, "Yes, sir, I do."

Jorge continued.

"Not only was the boat gone, but the cocaine, our property, was missing as well. Can you imagine?"

Where is all this leading? If they would only let me explain. They have to let me tell my side!

Tyrone did not avert his gaze from Jorge, who roamed about the cabin puffing on his cigarette. Although Jorge's body appeared muscular and compact, he moved, surprisingly, with the grace of a dancer. The other men, the two who were topside when they first arrived, were still above decks. One other, an older man, sat quietly playing solitaire and did not look up from his game. Z. remained outside. Sweat had formed across Danny's upper lip and hung there, precariously. His face, grim and mask-like, followed Jorge.

"Now I'm a patient man," Jorge said. "I don't like a lot of fuss. I take life easy, don't I Pablo?" he said to the man playing cards. "I talked to these businessmen. I'm a businessman, myself. I said, you know sometimes things happen. You know like that bumper sticker you see in Miami, *Sheet Happens*."

Jorge looked directly at Danny.

"I told one of these businessmen that I would wait one day, take it easy, but then I said, I want my property."

Danny shuffled his feet, looked down at the floor.

"Now this businessman assured me, my friend, that my property was safe and would be returned within twenty-four hours. Do you know how long it has been since that time?"

Tyrone nodded.

"Of course you do," Jorge said. "Ninety-six hours, and I find that even though I am a patient man, I am getting, how you say, uncomfortable with the situation. I'm feeling just a little foolish, like perhaps you think I am stupid."

Jorge looked down at the man playing cards and said, *"Miralos sufriendo."*

The man glanced up at Jorge and grinned. Danny smiled stiffly in response to this baring of teeth. Tyrone thought his face would crack if he tried to join in.

"And so, my friend, we have been looking for you and your *compañero.* Finally, my patience, even my patience, has worn out. Is there anything I've said so far that you do not understand?"

"No, sir," Tyrone replied in a whisper.

"So I say to you now, I want my property."

Jorge fiddled with the heavy gold chains draped around his thick neck.

"It's, uh…"

"Where is it?"

"When we left Mission Harbor," Tyrone began, "we…"

"I don't care anything about that. I don't want your life history. Get to the point."

Danny winced.

"The man, he, the American has it," Tyrone stammered. "The man on the sailboat, her husband," he said and glanced at the hallway where Alex had been taken.

"I see," Jorge said and furrowed his brow. "And you couldn't take the cocaine from this man? Why not?"

"Well, I, uh, we didn't want to make a scene. There were always other people around and when I would get ready to do it, something would always go wrong."

"Tsk, tsk, you poor boy. Why didn't you just shoot them and take the drugs? You didn't have to make a spectacle. It goes like this. You wait until dark. You go to their boat and engage them in conversation. You pull out your gun. You do have one, don't you?"

"Yes, sir."

"You shoot them. You get the drugs. See, no fuss. It's done. *Listo.*"

"Well," Tyrone said and gulped, "I didn't think I had to, uh, kill them. They got off the boat often enough and I assumed that I could get on board and get the coke before they returned. They…"

"But you didn't, did you?"

"No, but…"

"Maybe you had other plans for our property?"

"Oh, no way, no, absolutely…"

"Maybe you thought you could trick us into believing the drugs were put on the wrong boat. How do I know you didn't plan the whole thing?"

"I'm here now aren't I? Would I have come if I wanted to make off with your coke?"

"You're here," Jorge said scowling, "because we were right behind you and something went wrong with your plan.

"I could have killed them both at any time. I…"

"You could have but you didn't, did you? Once more, where is our cocaine?"

"I'm not exactly sure. The man, he has the coke. He took it off the sailboat, put it somewhere on Robert's Cay, I think. Had to. It wasn't on board. I swear to God!"

Jorge said to the man playing cards, *"Pablo, el jura por Dios."*

Pablo smirked and reshuffled the deck. The cards were rigid and shiny. Tyrone saw a discarded cellophane wrapper and an empty box on the edge of the table on which the man was dealing his next hand. The box, colored red, white, and blue, had "Bicycle Rider Back Playing Cards" written on it.

"So this is how it is," Jorge said. "The man, her husband, has the cocaine at Robert's Cay. We have his woman here. He rubbed his chin thoughtfully. "It's very simple."

"Yes," Tyrone said, "he will give us the coke if we give him back his wife. Make an exchange. I'm sure."

"I don't believe a man like you can be sure about anything, Tee-rone."

Jorge smiled and closed his eyes for a moment. When he opened them and looked at Tyrone, they were glistening.

"Yes, my friend, it is quite simple. But I must tell you that you and your friends are in the wrong business. I mean," he said, "that in this business, there is no room for mistakes." Jorge suddenly called out, *"Juan, tu y Alberto vengan a buscar a estos bastardos."*

Tyrone turned when he heard the cabin door open. Two men entered the main salon.

"I hope you'll let me explain everything," Tyrone said in a rush.

"Explain? What's to explain? You and your friends are obviously in the wrong business. You're better suited for waiting tables or fishing. You've made a mistake, several mistakes."

"But," Tyrone said quickly, "I know how this must look, but it wasn't my fault. That Z., what a fuck-up, right from the start. He's the one who picked the wrong boat. Isn't that right, Danny? Right Danny?"

Danny's eyes were a picture of terror.

Tyrone trembled. Fear, black and heavy, overwhelmed him, making it difficult to breathe.

Jorge held up the palm of a hand and shook his head.

"There is nothing to discuss," he said. "I know what needs to be done. It was all a mistake. You meant well. These things happen. Juan, Alberto, let's get underway."

The men nodded and grinned.

Tyrone and Danny looked at each other with raised eyebrows.

Topside, someone started the powerful inboard engines and engaged the anchor windless. Tyrone exhaled, relieved that the ordeal was finally over.

CHAPTER TWENTY-FOUR

Robert's Cay, Bahamas

The sun rose, hot and brilliant in the cloudless sky. Crouching in the cockpit for hours had made Matt's knees ache. He stood up and peered over the cabin top. The sea gulls overhead flapped down to take a look at him but after finding nothing of interest, sharply angled up and away. The boat people, as he had now come to think of them, had been up before first light and performed their daily ritual of one man patiently waiting while the rambunctious children scrambled aboard one of the power boats at the stern of the forty footer. When the young ones were situated on the bow, the buxom mamas and their babies followed. In the meantime, the other men moved about the cockpit with purpose preparing their fishing lines and organizing their gear. Occasionally they would glance in his direction but would quickly look away when they saw him looking back.

Surely they know something has happened here, Matt thought. They must have heard the gun shots. *Can they help me?*

Behind him, the rumble of an outboard motor caught his attention and he looked around to see the fishermen departing for the day.

"Hey," Matt yelled waving his arms.

The helmsman hesitated for a moment but after speaking with the others on board, turned the bow in Matt's direction.

"You call us, mon?" the driver shouted over the engine noise.

"Yes, please, I need to talk with you for a moment. Could you turn off that thing?"

"Sure, mon," the man said and cut the engine.

Matt tossed them a line so their boat wouldn't drift away with the current.

"Do you know what happened here last night?" Matt said

"No, mon."

"Some men, two men, well, my wife, someone has taken my wife. I—"

"We don't see nothing, mon," another man said.

They all nodded.

"You saw her, I'm sure. She waved to you."

"We see her the other day, but don't know nothing about somebody taking her."

"There was another boat, a cabin cruiser, with a black man and a white man on it, Bahamians, I think. You spoke with them. They took her. Their boat is gone."

"We see the boat gone, mon, but we don't know nothing about it."

Matt fingered the bitter end of the line he was holding and tried to think of some way to reach these men.

"Okay, but if you see that boat called *The Happy Hour*, I will give you a thousand American dollars if you tell me where it is. Would you do that?"

The men looked at each other and all shook their heads no.

"We can't help you, mon," said one of the fishermen seated near the bow. "These are bad men messing with you, and they could hurt us. We are sorry about your woman. It's a bad thing what they do but we have woman of our own. And children. We don't want no trouble."

"I'll give you anything I have. My boat…"

"We don't want your trouble, mon."

The black Bahamian at the helm pulled the engine cord and restarted the outboard. Like a huge mixer, it sputtered and churned their boat away from him. Matt watched as a man seated at the stern turned his head and looked back at him as the boat powered toward the channel. He pantomimed his apology by shrugging his shoulders and shaking his head. Matt saw him mouth the word, "Sorry." And then they were off, leaving only the boat's wake fanning out behind them.

Matt sat down on the cold fiberglass seat and tried to collect his thoughts.

I'm not good at waiting. In Hanoi, in the cell, I wasn't good at it. If I hadn't been allowed some movement, I wouldn't have made it until our release. He rubbed his chin and felt new stubble. Inside his head, the old demons were clawing to get out.

I can't just sit here. They're may be watching me right now, waiting. The only thing I have going for me is that I have their dope and they don't have a clue where it is. And they have Alex. At least Alex doesn't know where I hid the stuff. Surely she can convince them.

Matt decided to disregard Shorty's advice and call the Bahamian police. He switched on both batteries and set the VHF switch to the on position. Using the hailing channel, channel sixteen, he pressed the button on the microphone and said, "Bahama Police, Bahama Police, this is the sailing vessel, *Amani*, over."

He unkeyed the mike and waited. No reply. The police either couldn't hear him from this distance or they weren't interested. He didn't know which.

He fidgeted, shifted from one foot to the other. Then he repeated his call. Silence. Minutes passed. A full grown heron startled him when it flapped by the stern and flew toward the nearby shore.

"Let me see," he said to himself. *Maybe I need to hail the police on another channel.* He rifled through his collection of cruising books until he found the guide to the Islands. Trembling, he scanned the index until he located the special helps portion.

"Yes, yes," he said, "page fifty-five."

Turning to the page, he read that in an emergency one should call BASRA, the Bahama Air Sea Rescue Auxiliary. BASRA, the guide said, works with the United States Coast Guard and has a network of radio men on all the major Islands.

"Yes, that's it," he said.

He keyed the mike again and this time hailed, "BASRA, New Union, BASRA, New Union, this is the sailing vessel, *Amani*, over."

After gently setting the microphone on his navigation desk he paced about the cabin. Like a prairie dog, he poked his head up through the companionway hoping that somehow this was all a bad dream, that *The Happy Hour* would be anchored nearby, and Alex would be on the bow checking the mooring line.

A deep voice broke the radio silence.

"Sailing vessel, *Amani*, this is BASRA, New Union, over."

Matt grabbed the mike and replied, "This is the sailing vessel, *Amani*, over."

"Yes, *Amani*, switch to channel six eight, over."

"That's a roger, BASRA."

"*Amani*, this is BASRA, New Union."

"Yes, thank God you heard me. We're in trouble. My wife, she…" Matt paused to find his voice "Well, it's a long story and I'm not sure this is something that we should discuss over the radio but I don't have any other choice. You see, we, uh, found some illegal drugs hidden on our boat. Some Bahamians put them there. We don't know when or why. But they've taken my wife, Alex. I, uh, I'm here alone, and I don't know how to find them. I've got to find them! Will you help me?"

"We read you loud and clear *Amani*. What's your name, captain?"

"Spencer."

"Full name, please."

"Matthew John Spencer."

"Mr. Spencer, give us your location."

"I'm moored at Robert's Cay adjacent to the Tracking Station."

"Any others on board?"

"No, like I said, just me."

"We request that you stay where you are until we communicate with you further. We have a boat in your area that should be there within the hour."

"I won't go anywhere. I'm so relieved that help is on the way. This is a nightmare, unbelievable. My wife, she…"

"We'll be in touch."

"I'll stand by on channel sixteen."

"That will be fine, captain."

"This is the sailing vessel, *Amani*, switching back to sixteen."

He replaced the microphone in its holder and reset the VHF channel. *Shorty was mistaken. Thank God they're going to help me.*

Matt waited until the sun was high and there was still no sign of a BASRA boat. He checked his watch every five minutes and felt a knot of suspicion beginning to grow.

Shorty said they were all on the take. Maybe I was wrong to contact them. Maybe I wasn't talking to BASRA at all. Surely they would have been here by now, that is if they were coming. He looked at his watch. Almost twelve thirty.

I have to do something! Maybe I should move ashore, watch the boat from there. That way whoever shows up won't get the drop on me. I'll see them first. Jesus, someone has to come looking for the stuff. That's it. I'll move to the Island.

He gathered together his shotgun, binoculars, a jug of drinking water, his diving knife, and stuffed the small items into one of the tote bags that he and Alex used for grocery shopping. *Sunglasses. I'll need those.* He wished he had his 30-30 Winchester Carbine which could shoot long range. As a boy he had his first gun at six and was a deadly marksman by the time he was eight. Although he no longer hunted, he was comfortable with a gun in his hand. These days his forays into the woods were for companionship and communion with the outdoors.

I'll leave the hatches out so they can see that I'm not on board. I hope to God they don't sink her.

When the inflatable hit shallow water, he climbed out and muscled the dinghy with its Johnson outboard up the beach and behind some casuarina trees. He heard the sounds of a baby crying and a dog yapping somewhere on the Island. Nearby, he heard children's laughter.

Such normalcy in the middle of all this madness.

He checked his watch and noted that it was already one o'clock. Still no sign of BASRA or anyone else. This only served to magnify his anxiety.

Surely they'll bring her soon. They must.

He squatted behind some thatch palms and waited. The drone of a honey bee momentarily captured his attention. Then he heard children's voices. "Walter's it! Walter's it!" they called. The minutes weighed heavy. He rotated his head from side to side. The second hand on his watch pirouetted in slow motion. Surf pounded on the other side of the Cay. And nothing. No one. When he stood up and stretched, his stiff knees cracked at the joints.

By three p.m., he was bleary-eyed and fearing the onset of a full-blown panic attack like the ones he used to have in Hanoi when torture was imminent. He tried to breath rhythmically, in and out, in and out.

At three-thirty, he choked with impatience. At four p.m., he decided to hike up the hill to the Tracking Station. He hoped that Shorty and Fletch could help him but he wasn't sure what they would be able to do. He didn't want to leave his lookout. His eyes were riveted on the *Amani* as she rode the slender line tied to her mooring. The sailboat was the last place he had seen Alex, and he felt that if he kept looking at it, she would appear. To remove his gaze would be like letting go.

After taking one last lingering look at the *Amani* and the empty channel, he skirted the beach and made his way to the Station above. As before, he found the decaying buildings with their boarded windows and warning signs. He shivered even though the air felt warm and muggy. Once he located the building, he pounded on the unlocked screen door with a fist.

"Hey!" he yelled as he hammered on the wooden frame. "Shorty! Fletch!"

His voice reverberated down the gloomy hall.

"Shorty!" Fletch! It's me, Spencer! I need help!"

Surf. Radio noise.

Matt, uneasy and fearful, clutched his twelve-gauge. He wondered where the singing dog was, Ginger, wasn't that her name?

"Here, Ginger," he called through the screen door.

From the back of the building, he heard a low growl.

"Ginger, come here girl."

In a moment, he heard Ginger's sharp nails clicking on the brittle linoleum. She came to him eagerly with her bushy tail beating a greeting. Cautious, Matt pulled open the door and stepped inside. Ginger jumped up and planted her front paws squarely in the middle of his chest.

"That's a good girl," he whispered as she licked his face. "Some watchdog you are. Where's Shorty?"

He pushed her away and scanned the unlighted hallway.

"Let's go girl," he said.

Ginger trotted down the corridor ahead of him and disappeared. Matt followed, his gun cocked. In the back of the building he heard the crackle and hum of radios. He crept down the hall stepping lightly. *No voices.* The hair on the back of his neck began to rise. Swallowing was out of the question. He paused at the end of the corridor, quickly glanced back and forth, before he slid left around the corner and continued on his way to the radio room.

He found the room dark and musty, its blinds closed. The radios glowed hot along the far wall emitting red pinpoints of light. Otherwise, it was deadly quiet, and he realized that he could be walking into a trap. He hesitated at the threshold.

I have no choice. I have to find them. In two quick movements he turned on the overhead light and lunged behind the long metal table with his gun in front of him. The overhead neon light flickered on, bathing the room in fluorescence. *There they are.* Both men were seated at the table with their heads resting on their arms like kindergarten children taking a nap.

Ginger hopped up from her chair and padded over to him. His knees felt so weak that he wasn't sure he could stand up. The dog nuzzled his face.

"That's enough girl." *What the…*

CHAPTER TWENTY-FIVE

Atlantic Ocean

Alex regained consciousness in the spacious salon of a boat. Massive engines hummed and pulsed somewhere beneath her. When she moved, slivers of pain skyrocketed inside her skull. Her mouth, cotton dry, tasted of old blood.

She raised her head in increments and gazed around the room. Two easy chairs upholstered in dark green velvet were directly across from her. She lay on the floor, her back resting against a wall. Vibrations from the engine traveled up and down her aching spine. A plush oriental rug partially covered the varnished mahogany floor on which she sat. Between the chairs perched a glossy round table with a finely-etched crystal lamp on top.

Two men stood with their backs to her. One, who had rounded shoulders, appeared tall and lean. Shaggy gray hair spilled over his collar. His blue jeans, soft and faded, hung loosely on his hips; his deck shoes were worn unevenly on the heels. Another man, shorter and heavier, murmured to his companion. *Who are these men? Where's Matt?* They turned and looked at her.

"Well, it's about time. The beauty awakens. Except she isn't such a beauty right now, is she Pablo?"

"Who are you and where is my husband?"

"Yes, your husband," the shorter man said, "that's what we'd like to know."

"He's not here?"

"If he were here would we ask you where he was?"

Alex studied the stocky man who stood before her with his hands on his waist and his elbows flared at his sides. As he moved closer, she saw that he was a brute with round and heavy-lidded eyes. His neck, massive as a small tree stump, was encircled by several gold chains. Although his hands were thick-knuckled and bruised, his nails were neatly manicured and painted with clear polish. In contrast to the man standing next to him, his clothes were meticulously clean and neat. Full fleshy lips punctuated his mouth. She smelled the Aramis cologne he was wearing.

"You have no right to hold me here."

Both men smirked.

"Kidnapping is against the law. You have to take me back to my husband."

"We don't have to do anything," said the man who was doing all the talking. "I'm asking the questions here. You just answer and maybe you won't get hurt."

He paused a moment to allow Alex to consider his last statement.

"What is your name?" he said.

"Alex Spencer. I'm a U.S. citizen and you're making a big mistake."

"Alex. That's not a name for a woman. Why do you have a man's name?"

"It's short for Alexandra. You have to…"

"Ah, I see. Well, Alexandra Spencer, your husband has something we want. All he has to do is give it to us and I'll return you to him. Do you know what I'm talking about?"

"Yes, your white powder, your drugs. If you take me to my husband, he'll hand it over to you."

"Are you certain of that? Your husband has enough cocaine to live comfortably for a very long time. Will he return our property or will he desert you so he can enjoy the next few years as a rich man?"

"My husband would never leave me, not for any amount of money."

A drop of blood trickled down her chin.

"Nasty cut on your lip, Señora," said the other man, who hadn't spoken until now. "It is amazing what even the slightest beating can do to a pretty face."

Trying to determine what was going to happen next, Alex looked alternately at each of them. *My God are they going to kill me?* Blood pounded her temples and she wondered if her head injury was serious. It was obvious to her that these men were ruthless, without a shred of compassion. *I'm alive only because they want their cocaine. How can I get out of this?*

"So," the man who seemed to be in charge continued, "why don't you tell us where your husband has hidden our cocaine. We know that he removed it from your boat and took it to the Island."

"This is against the law. You have no right…"

The stocky man moved toward her, extended a hand, and ordered her to stand. Ignoring his gesture, she rose unsteadily to her feet. Without a hint of what was to come, he backhanded her. Knocked backwards, she fell against the wall. The room grew dim for a moment and her head began to bleed again.

"Now I repeat. Where has your husband hidden our cocaine?"

God, they're going to kill me.

"I don't know. He didn't want me to know. He took it to the Island, left me on the boat to wait for him. Those other men, the ones who were following us, pretending to be fishermen, must have seen my husband go ashore alone. Ask them. Ask them if they saw him take our dinghy to the Island. Alone!"

"We have."

"And?"

"Shut up. I'm in charge here."

Alex began to tremble. Her heart beat like the hooves of a runaway horse. *How can this be happening to me? To us?*

Someone tapped on the cabin door and a young man entered.

After a brief exchange in Spanish, the man retreated, closing the door behind him.

Alex fought her tears and couldn't stop shaking.

"We are going to stop the boat now, Señora, and drift for a while. I don't think you are telling me everything, but you will."

"I'm telling the truth!"

"That remains to be seen."

Alex stifled a sob.

The stocky man stepped closer to her.

"*Yo me llamo* Jorge Gaucha. That man over there is Pablo Romero or I should say, Dr. Romero."

"You don't have to do this. My husband will give you your cocaine. We don't want it!"

"Remove your clothes, Señora."

"What?"

"You heard me."

"My clothes. Why?"

"Don't make me repeat myself."

Alex cringed and clutched her tank top.

"I will not."

"Miguel," Jorge said over his shoulder to someone who was standing beyond her view in the hallway, "the Señora needs some assistance."

A drab, middle-aged man stepped into the room and moved toward her.

"Wait! Wait! I'll do it!"

Alex slowly pulled up her tank top and set it down beside her. Tears of humiliation and anger slid down her cheeks. She undid the button on her shorts and unzipped them.

"*Apurate!*" Jorge said. "Get on with it!"

She pushed down her shorts and stepped out of them.

"Everything," Jorge said.

She reached behind her back to unfasten her bra, slipped the straps off her shoulders and dropped it on the floor. Desperately searching for a means of escape, she looked around the room.

"Go on!" Jorge said.

She pulled down her white bikini panties and stepped out of them. There were goose bumps on her arms and legs; her cheeks burned. Nothing in her past had prepared her for this abasement.

"Now, Miguel, tie the Senora's hands behind her back," Jorge said as he handed him a two-foot length of rope.

In a split second, Alex lunged for the door. Although she took them by surprise, she wasn't fast enough and someone grabbed her by the hair. She struggled to escape but it was hopeless. They laughed.

Pulled backwards, her hands bound, she was shoved into a chair.

"Now I will give you one more chance to tell the truth. Where have you and your husband put our cocaine?"

"My God, I've told you everything I know. Why won't you believe me? My husband hid the bags. He didn't tell me where. Why are you doing this? Just ask him. If you will take me to him, he'll give you what you want."

"Oh," Jorge said after he lit a cigarette, "if only I could be certain about that." He snapped his lighter shut. "If you tell me where the cocaine is, then I won't have to worry about some foolish thing your husband might do."

"What do you mean?"

"He has a gun, doesn't he?"

Alex didn't reply. Her feelings, like a kaleidoscope, shifted from fear to anger to humiliation to fear.

"Of course he does, Señora. All gringos have guns. So if I can find out what I need to know, we can avoid needless killing. Think about that. He will be safe and you will remain alive."

"Listen, I would tell you if I knew, but I don't. You have to believe me."

"Oh, you're mistaken about that. You know, Señora, we aren't like those other men, the ones who were following you. They aren't very bright and they have a conscience. They can feel remorse. We, on the other hand, don't give a shit whether you live or die. You are nothing to us. Do you get my point?"

They're going to kill me.

"How can I convince you that I'm telling the truth?"

Jorge snorted and looked at Dr. Romero.

"Go get him," Jorge said to Miguel.

Get who? Matt?

Miguel returned in a few minutes with three other men, Tyrone, and two Alex had not seen before. Tyrone's hands were tied behind his back, his ankles loosely bound. He looked at her, started to speak. One of the men pinched the back of his neck and said, "Silencio!"

"You remember this man?" Jorge asked her.

"Yes, the man from the cabin cruiser, the fisherman, the…"

"This is a very stupid man who has made a lot of mistakes."

"It wasn't my fault," Tyrone said. "Don't hurt me, please."

"Shut your mouth!" someone said.

Alex looked at Jorge and Dr. Romero.

What are they going to do?

"This man has one purpose in life now," Jorge said, "and that is to serve as a horrible example."

Tyrone's lips quivered and he began to whimper.

"You don't have to harm anyone," Alex said. "Please, I beg you."

"If you say one more word, bitch, unless I ask you…" Jorge said.

Alex shrank into the chair as penetrating fear swallowed her whole.

"On your knees," Jorge said to Tyrone.

Jorge's round eyes were moist with excitement and spittle had formed at the corners of his lips.

This is all a game to him.

"Now Señora, I am going to kill this man if you don't tell me where my cocaine is."

"Please, this isn't necessary," she said. "If I knew, don't you think I would tell you?"

"I'm not sure about that," Jorge said after he lit another cigarette and inhaled. "It's just as well."

His words came out in puffs of smoke.

"I want you to understand me."

Alex's throat constricted. She choked, began to tremble.

"Now I think you have her attention," Dr. Romero said to Jorge.

"You," Jorge said to Tyrone, "have run out of luck. She isn't going to save your life."

It all happened very quickly. Tyrone screamed. The men held him while Jorge thrust a plastic bag over his head and cinched it tightly at the bottom.

Alex wanted to look away but could not. She stared at Tyrone's wild eyes and gaping mouth. He fought them, twisting and turning, but could not overpower four determined men. Alex watched, horrified, as the plastic hood expanded and contracted. Tyrone's eyes bulged. He convulsed, swayed.

Alex prayed that it would be over quickly. The man was suffering, in agony. His death came slowly. An eternity.

Please, please stop!

She finally looked away, sobbed.

A dull thud sounded when Tyrone's body hit the floor.

"Not bad," Jorge said. "He went a full five minutes, six seconds. Is that the record?"

"No," Dr. Romero said, "remember that other one, the gringo, you know, from Tampa."

"Did he go longer than that?"

"You said five minutes, eight seconds. Remember?"

"That's right."

Alex pressed her face into the back of the chair.

"What do you want to do with her?" she heard someone ask.

"I haven't decided yet," Jorge said. "Miguel, lock the bitch in a cabin."

CHAPTER TWENTY-SIX

Robert's Cay

Matt was relieved to find both men were merely hung over and taking a nap. For a brief moment, he had thought they were dead.

"Shorty, wake up!" he said and jostled his shoulder.

"What? What is it?"

At first, Shorty seemed disoriented and did not appear to know who he was. After he rubbed his eyes and focused on Matt for a few seconds, a look of recognition crossed his face.

"Spencer."

Fletch raised his head, stretched. "What's up?" he said. "What's the matter?"

"They took Alex! They took my wife!"

Shorty and Fletch looked at each other, then at Matt.

"Whoa, slow down. Who is they? Took her where?" Shorty said.

"We found some drugs hidden on our boat, heroin or cocaine. Last night. I found it in the hanging wet locker, bags of the stuff. I, uh," he gasped for breath before continuing. "I took it off the boat, to the Island. When I came back, she was gone. They were gone."

"You mean to tell me that there were drugs on your boat and you didn't know it?" Fletch said.

"Yes, fiberglassed inside the wet locker. I don't know why they put the stuff on our boat, but I know who took Alex. Those men I asked Shorty about, the ones on that boat, *The Happy Hour*. I knew there was something strange about them, but it just doesn't figure. Why our boat? We smelled some new fiberglass when we left Mission Harbor. I thought there had been some minor repair. We, uh… There it was, big as life, twenty bags in all."

Fletch whistled. "We're talkin' big bucks and heavy dudes here."

Matt looked at him and scowled.

"I don't give a damn about the money or those people, whoever they are. I just want my wife back."

"Of course you do," Shorty said as he patted Matt's shoulder. Let's settle down and talk about this."

Matt's nerves quivered like rubber bands that had been twisted to the breaking point. He wondered if he could sit still, even for a minute. Doubt about his decision to leave his lookout on the beach fueled his anxiety.

"Come on," Shorty said as he pulled one of the metal chairs away from the table.

Matt sat down stiffly, still clutching the shotgun.

"Why don't you, uh, put that thing on the floor," Fletch said.

"Oh, yeah," Matt said and lay the gun down beside him.

Shorty returned from the kitchen with half a glass of dark liquid, whisky it turned out, and pressed it into Matt's hand.

"Drink," he said, "then we'll talk."

Matt took a big swallow and coughed.

"Damn, can you believe this shit?" Fletch said.

"I believe it," Matt said. "They've got Alex. Jesus."

Shorty sat down with his own drink clamped between both hands.

"Something has to be done, of course," he said, "but your wife's sur-vival depends on how you handle this. You have to be careful, think about every move you make."

"I called the police earlier," Matt said. "This morning. The BASRA at New Union Settlement."

"That was a waste of time," Shorty said with a smirk. "I told you about those assholes. They're all on the take out here."

"But they said they would help me."

"When were they going to help?" Fletch said.

"This morning, I thought. I don't know. They still might come."

"Listen," Shorty said, "don't hold your breath waitin' for 'em. Remember what I said before. Frontier stuff out here. No law. Your gun is your law. I know they don't tell you any of this in those fancy travel guides. It's all tropical islands, coconuts, and sunshine. The Bahamas Chamber of Commerce can't exactly advertise that the drug dealers are running the show. It would be bad for business. And next to drug deal-ing, tourism is the second biggest source of revenue in the Islands."

"But," Matt said, "they seemed…"

"How do you know it was the BASRA?" Fletch said as he shoved away from the table and stood up.

"I, uh, have no way of being certain, of course."

"In all probability, it was the drug boys. I'm sure they appreciated the call," Shorty said and took a drink from his glass. "Now they know exactly where you are and that you're alone."

"This is insane," Matt said.

"Yes," Shorty said, "insane, but there isn't anyone you can count on out here except yourself, and the sooner you wrap your mind around that idea, the sooner you can get down to the business of getting your wife back."

"She was such a pretty little thing," Fletch said as he came back into the room.

"Christ, she's not dead," Matt said.

"No, son, of course not," Shorty said softly.

Matt looked at Shorty's face and saw pock marks reflected in the harsh fluorescent light. His childhood had probably been a difficult one. His flushed, beefy face reported a long history of whiskey and cigarettes. His brown eyes, mapped with a spider's web of blood vessels, were kind. Matt saw a gentleness in Shorty's eyes that loneliness and hard times had not erased.

"There must be someone we can call," Matt said. "The military? Maybe the U. S. Coast Guard?"

"Useless," said Fletch, who had returned to the table with a Coors beer in his hand. "The military is far too busy to concern themselves with a couple of tourists who've gotten themselves tangled up with drug dealers, especially outside the jurisdiction of the United States. The Coast Guard works with the local BASRA, but the BASRA receives the distress calls and uses their judgment concerning outside assistance. If you were some politically-connected, rich dude with a fancy yacht foundering on a reef, well, then, you might get some action. But this business, drugs, forget it. The BASRA won't interfere. They ain't gonna call nobody."

Shorty inhaled some of his drink before wiping his mouth with the back of his hand.

"This is nasty business," Shorty said as he shook his head. "Nasty."

"Okay," Matt said, "I get the picture. It's up to me. Do you have any suggestions as to how I might get my wife back safely?"

"Safely?" Shorty said. "Concentrate on the 'get back' part. The truth might be too hard for you to stomach right now."

"What is the truth?"

"Do you really want to know or would you rather feel better?" Shorty said.

"The truth."

"These are the worst, most unfeeling sons of bitches you will ever have the misfortune to meet. They only care about money and power.

Violence is a way of life with them. They get off on it. They don't like your face, they shoot you. They want your woman, they disembowel you and toss you over the side of a boat. You walk funny, they'll stab you in the back. They…"

"I get the point. What you're saying is that they are going to hurt Alex no matter what I do."

Shorty nodded and waited for the grim news to sink in before continuing.

Matt jumped up and paced about the room. He couldn't stop thinking about Alex and what they might be doing to her. He clenched and unclenched his fists. He thought he might scream.

"Sit down, son. I'm not finished," Shorty said.

Matt returned to his chair.

"Okay," Shorty said, "so now you know the bad news, so let's talk about what you should do."

"But Alex…"

"Listen, Spencer," Shorty said, grasping Matt's arm, "concentrate on how to get her back and try not to think about what they are doing to her, It will make you crazy, and you won't be able to do what you need to do."

Matt drained his glass and set it down on the table with a bang.

"Okay," he said, "let's talk."

"We have guns," Fletch said, "and you can stay here with us if you like. So far they haven't messed with us. Probably think we're military and don't want to stir up a hornet's nest."

"The ball's in their court," Shorty said. "Your best course of action, as I see it, is rather straight forward. You wait for them to make the first move."

"I've never been good at waiting for somebody else to do something," Matt said.

"Well, you'd better get good at it," Fletch said, "because until they make contact with you, you have to sit tight. If you leave, they'll think you've run off with their goodies, and your wife will be shark bait for sure."

"What Fletch is sayin' is true," Shorty said. "They'll make you an offer on their schedule. They like to play games. When they contact you, you can decide how you want to go. In the meantime, we'll be here. I don't think they'll kill her as long as you have their drugs and as long as they don't catch you."

"I know all about that," Matt said. "Better than you know."

"Okay, for now we can offer you weapons, a place to hide, and advice," Shorty said. "I don't believe it would serve any useful purpose for Fletch and me to sit down on the beach with you lookin' like we're poised for World War Three. No, we've all got to play it cool."

"High Noon," Fletch mumbled.

"In fact," Shorty continued, "our presence may only complicate matters. Your goal right now is to negotiate, play the game."

"I appreciate your frankness," Matt said as he picked up his twelve-gauge and stood up. "I expect they'll be looking for me."

"You can bet your sweet ass they'll be looking for you," Fletch said.

"Okay," Shorty said, "let's take a look at our arsenal."

CHAPTER TWENTY-SEVEN

Atlantic Ocean

Alex opened her eyes, turned her head, and tried to focus on the ceiling. *I've been asleep. How long?* She smelled salt air and felt her lungs inflating and collapsing. *I'm alive.*

The powerful engines throbbed below decks, propelling the yacht to a destination unknown to her. Outside the open cabin door, she heard the murmur of voices.

I've survived so far, but what will they do next? Why won't they take me to Matt? Thinking about Jorge and his men was like contemplating one's worst nightmare. Only this one was real. *And that poor man, Tyrone, what a horrible way to die.* She shivered. Her throat, dry and sore from straining, craved water. *Water. Oh, for a sip of water.* She was uncertain about what she should do, feign unconsciousness and perhaps delay further brutality, or let them know that she was awake? *Oh, Matt, where are you?*

"The woman is stirring," she heard someone say.

No use pretending now, she thought as she struggled to sit up. Her hands were still bound behind her back.

"So the little bird that will not sing has opened her eyes and discovered that she is still in this world and not the next. She probably didn't know whether or not we would kill her in her sleep. This time she woke up. How fortunate for her," Jorge said as he leaned over her. She smelled whiskey on his sour breath.

"Get her up," she heard Dr. Romero say from the doorway. Miguel, the faded, quiet man she had seen earlier, appeared above her and seized her by the shoulders. She moaned when he hoisted her to her feet and dragged her to a chair in the main salon.

"Could I please have some water," she said. "I'm so…thirsty."

"Of course, of course," Jorge said and motioned to the right with his head. Miguel left the room and returned in a moment with a glass of clear liquid. She heard the ice cubes clinking against the sides of the glass.

"I feel sick to my stomach," Alex said.

"Of course you do," murmured the Doctor. "Witnessing an execution has that effect on some people. Ah, there isn't anything as refreshing as a cold glass of water. Settles the nerve, makes one feel alive. Don't you think so, Jorge?"

"Oh, Sí, Sí."

"Imagine," Dr. Romero said, "water that is so clean and pure that outside the glass, it would look like air."

"And cold," added Jorge, "icy as a mountain stream."

Alex tried to lick her lips, but her tongue felt like something that belonged on an old shoe.

"Some water, please."

Jorge took the glass from Miguel's hand and brought it to her. She leaned forward in anticipation of that first long drink. He held the glass within inches of her lips. She leaned forward again. He pulled the glass back another inch. She looked up at him and saw that he was smiling.

"The water…"

"Oh, yes, the water," he said and walked away with the glass in his hand. "If you want water, first you have to tell us where your husband hid our cocaine. Then we will give you all the water you want."

Alex fell back.

"God," she said, "you don't get it, do you? I don't know! I don't know! How can I prove it to you? What can I say? Don't you think I would tell you if I knew?"

"I'm not certain, Señora," Jorge said. "If you love your husband, and it appears that you do, you might do anything to protect him, maybe even die. Now, once more, where is our cocaine? Tell us and the water is yours." He held up the glass for her to see. "Afterwards, we'll take you to your husband. I promise."

Alex stared at Jorge. She could lie, of course, but it wouldn't be long before he found out the truth. And what about Matt? They might kill him if they decided they no longer needed him.

"I wish we had more time to enjoy this little game, Alexandra, but unfortunately, we have other business to attend to," Jorge said. "Besides, I think you just might be telling the truth."

Alex tried to swallow but she couldn't find a drop of moisture in her mouth. Her throat felt like it had been packed in gauze.

"We could give her a dose of something," Dr. Romero said and grinned. He extracted a pair of reading glasses from his shirt pocket, put them on, and looked over the rims at her. She saw errant hairs protruding from his ears and nostrils and his teeth were yellow with remnants of his last meal wedged between them. There was nothing antiseptic about him.

"It would be entertaining, but she might die, and we need her alive, for now," Jorge said.

"Don't dismiss the idea right away," Dr. Romero said. "I have lots of goodies in my bag. This one, for example," he said as he reached inside and came up with a small bottle. "The label says proloxin." He spelled the word for her. "Do you know what this does?"

Alex shook her head.

"It paralyzes you, Señora. Completely. Then we could do anything we want to you and you couldn't resist. We could invite all the men on the boat, and there are several, to touch you, violate you in any way they choose, and we would all watch."

"Now that you mention it, that would be amusing and might put me in a better mood," Jorge said.

"No," Alex said in a whisper."

"Oh, you don't like that idea," Dr. Romero said as he returned the bottle to the case. "Well, now, let me see."

He plucked at his chin, smiled.

"Here is another remarkable drug. It is called apomorphine. Do you know this drug?"

"No," Alex said. "I don't know anything about drugs."

Both men burst into laughter. Miguel remained expressionless.

"Apomorphine," Dr. Romero continued, "induces continuous vomiting for sometimes as much as an hour."

She shuddered.

God, please, please save me from these people.

"That one's a little messy," Jorge said from across the room.

"All right, let me see what else I have in my little bag of tricks. Oh yes, one of my favorites. This one is called anectine. You know, it is hard to pronounce some of these words. My English isn't so good. How am I doing?"

Alex did not reply.

"So let me see, where was I? Oh yes, anectine. It comes from curare, by the way. What does it do? It stops your breathing. Sometimes you can't breath for a little while and then, depending on the dosage, well, sometimes you just stop breathing altogether. I especially like this one. How about you, Jorge?"

"You know, I have always liked that one. I enjoy watching their eyes bulge and seeing them turn so many beautiful colors, like a human rainbow. It is so...very...stimulating."

"If you have any decency, you won't hurt me. I've told you everything I know."

Jorge came toward her. Although his mouth was smiling, his eyes were cold. She cringed.

He knelt down, placed a hand around her throat. With his right thumb, he stroked her windpipe. "If I find out you have lied to me, Señora Spencer, I will personally take care of you. The man's death you witnessed earlier will seem merciful by comparison to what I will do to you. It won't be pretty or quick. Comprende?"

Alex had lost her voice. She nodded against his thumb. He shoved her head to the side and walked away.

Jorge motioned for Dr. Romero to follow him across the room where they stopped and huddled several feet away. She heard whispers but couldn't make out what they were saying. She felt hopeful. Jorge had said they still needed her alive.

After they finished conferring, Jorge turned and narrowed his eyes at her. She looked back at him, tried to mask her fear.

"Get her out of here," he said to Miguel.

CHAPTER TWENTY-EIGHT

Robert's Cay

Twilight. Matt waited on the west side of the Island, well hidden behind a dense stand of palmettos. From this vantage point, he had a clear view of the anchorage. Physically and mentally uncomfortable, it was difficult for him to sit perfectly still for such a long time. He was painfully aware of his arthritic knees and stiff neck. The *Amani* gently bobbed at its mooring.

Our dream, Matt thought. *Why? Why us?*

He stood up, stretched, and felt all of his forty-eight years. Memories of prison and Hanoi swept over him, pervading his thoughts with old fears and phantoms. Terror did not grip him. For the moment, that had passed, leaving only a grim realization of what a desperate situation they were in.

It isn't hopeless. I am armed. I am free. I can fight back this time.

In prison he had been physically captive like all the other pilots who had plummeted from the sky. But the Viet Cong had never succeeded in capturing their minds and hearts. They were able to fight them moment by moment in little ways. Misinformation, hidden gestures before the

159

visiting media or Red Cross, feigned acquiescence, secret communication, all were their weapons. This time he had some leverage. He had
their damn drugs and a Winchester twelve-gauge riot gun.

Crouched with his back against the bark of an Australian pine, he
closed his eyes and listened to the curly-tailed lizards scurry across the
dry underbrush. The boat people were conducting their nightly ritual.
He heard a woman's shrill voice and then only the sounds of the night
creatures and rustling casuarinas interrupted the silence.

Now in almost total darkness, the *Amani*, barely visible, drifted. An
abandoned ship, she appeared to be waiting for someone or something
to return to her. Finding it difficult to keep his eyes open, Matt blinked.
His stomach rumbled, reminding him that he needed sustenance. He
rubbed his stubbled cheeks and pressed his fingertips to his eyes.

The blazing lights of the compound behind him were a comforting
sight. He swigged water from the gallon jug he had brought from the boat.

*I don't understand. Where the hell are they? Why are they holding Alex?
And the police? Could Shorty be wrong about them? No, no, if they were
going to show up, they'd be here by now. God, Alex has to be all right. She
can't tell them anything. They'll figure that out in a heartbeat. Jesus, please
don't let them hurt her.*

"Alex," he whispered and felt a rush of anguish.

In his weary state, he began to ponder what he would do if they did-
n't return soon.

*I can't leave. Surely if they come for their dope and I'm not here, they
will think that I'm more interested in saving my own neck, that I've
deserted her.*

The mosquitoes and no-see-ums found him shortly after dark, arriving by stealth with the adeptness of a Marine Commando Unit. They
attacked his bare skin and burrowed into his scalp. His body itched as
angry welts erupted on his exposed arms and neck. His thin t-shirt
offered scant protection. Frustrated, he cursed and slapped at the
marauders, stood up, paced, and scolded himself for leaving the insect

repellent on the boat.

Hell, how was I to know that those bastards wouldn't come right back to get their precious stuff?

As the hours crept by, Matt finally had to admit that he needed some sleep and something to eat. He recognized that he was no longer thinking coherently. Only a moment before he was remembering his grandmother's coconut pie recipe.

"Shit," he said under his breath as he rubbed the bites on his arms.

Abandoning his gear, he set off for the Tracking Station on the hill and was barely able to climb the rise. As the compound lights grew brighter, his spirits lifted a bit. A clean bed and company awaited him.

Shorty and Fletch may have some new ideas about how we can get out of this.

Passing through the courtyard, he was surrounded by the shabby, dilapidated buildings. In spite of their dreary faces, they were a welcome sight.

It will be good to eat, see Shorty and Fletch. Rest.

The hum and crackle of the radios greeted him at the door. Peering through the screen, he saw light glowing at the end of the corridor.

"Shorty! Fletch!" he called as he pulled the door toward him. "Hey, it's me, Spencer!"

He eased inside, letting the screen door thump dully behind him.

"Shorty!"

He passed through the entry and started down the hall.

God, I'm hungry.

The lights went out. The compound, ablaze like Dodger Stadium only moments before, was now an ominous black void. Matt crouched and listened. The radios were off. He heard the surf thundering on the shore; his body felt hot and cold in rapid succession. He stood still, paralyzed in the corridor, debating whether he should flee or continue down the dark hall before him.

Suppose the guys are in trouble.

Matt began to regress to another time and place, another war. He cocked his twelve-gauge and was comforted by the clacking sound as the shell was jacked into the chamber. Again he agonized about whether to go or stay, press on or retreat. He thought about Shorty and Fletch, kind and understanding, offering their help.

Do I really have a choice?

Repeating his previous entry into the building, he tiptoed down the dark corridor and positioned himself at the end of the hall.

Maybe a freak power failure? Sure.

His body was tense, so much so he could feel the muscles contracting on his shoulders. The air was warm. He held his breath, tried not to make a sound.

Steeling himself at the end of the corridor, he turned left toward the radio room. Unchecked, his demons clawed their way out of his subconscious.

Toward what? Who will be there? Is this the Green Knobby Room, the room where they pull your arms together until your elbows touch the back of your head? The room where they hoist you to the ceiling by your dislocated shoulders and leave you there, sometimes for days! Run! The Rat, your old interrogator, is waiting at the end of the hall. The Rat, the one who can make you offer your mother in exchange for a sip of water or release from the ropes.

No! No! This isn't Vietnam. This isn't Hanoi. I'm free!

Run! Save yourself!

His legs started to buckle.

"No!" he thought, then realized he had said it aloud. The word ricocheted down the hall like a bullet. No sounds emanated from the R and R room.

In this maze, the main power switch could be anywhere.

He moved like a blind man, sliding his left hand before him along the damp wall. He realized that should his hand touch another's, he would have to fall back, fire.

But what if it is Shorty or Fletch? No, they'd be banging around, groping in the dark for a flashlight, cursing, muttering to themselves.

He considered his choices and decided they were limited. To run or go; standing in the doorway was not a viable option.

Think. See the room. Remember the metal chairs, where they sit, and the cabinets that line the walls. And the desk, yes, in the far corner next to the old refrigerator, littered with papers and old coffee cups and the remnants of half-eaten snacks.

With halting steps, he inched through the dusky gloom. When his foot bumped an aluminum chair, the jolt traveled up his shin like a dull shock. He stopped and listened, poised to react. He comforted himself with the thought that if he could not see, than neither could anyone else.

He waited a moment, exhaled, then cautiously moved on. His breathing sounded loud, harsh in the quiet room. He squatted and waved a hand under the table. Only chair legs and dead air space lay beneath it.

Have to find a flashlight.

He felt his way along until he found the desk in the corner next to the refrigerator. His fingers touched soft ashes and several cold cigarette butts in an ash tray. He lightly danced his fingertips across the loose papers strewn on top until his hand nudged a coffee mug. He dipped a finger inside.

Warm. Someone has been drinking from this cup, and not too long ago.

Before continuing his search, he paused, strained to hear any sound other than his own ragged breathing. Nothing.

He slowly pulled open the top drawer and rummaged inside. His fingers identified pens, pencils, a pack of opened cigarettes, a pad of paper, glasses, unopened gum. He quietly slid the drawer back in place. The next drawer, to the left, was filled with some kind of booklets, the size of a small spiral binder. He closed the drawer and moved on. The bottom drawer held an assortment of items: a small cylinder, probably a thermos jug, sheets of paper, and…

A flashight!

He grasped the cold metal in his hand and removed it from the drawer.

Please, please work.

Hesitantly, he slid the switch forward. A dull glow shined through the cloudy glass.

Better than nothing, but just barely.

The faint light was only useful in a small area, but he was grateful to have it. Expecting to find someone lurking in the unlighted room, he raised the gun in front of him and searched it a section at a time. He found no one but recognized that with the building's many hallways and spaces, hiding would be an easy task. He jumped when he heard a noise coming from the kitchen and suddenly realized that his light was a liability. Someone watching could easily follow his movements.

God, I'm not thinking straight.

He quickly snapped it off and once again found himself enveloped in darkness.

The kitchen was easier to traverse with its equipment and fixtures lining the walls. There was no table. He fumbled his way along. It had been over a decade but the fear, the anger, the instinct to survive, had all come back to him.

If only I could get my hands on one of those bastards. I'd make him tell me where Alex is. I could...

He paused, listened. Silence. He moved on until he arrived at the refrigerator, the one that stood next to the double sink. He turned on the flashlight and gently opened the door. Inside was the assortment of food that he expected to find: moldy cheddar cheese, a partial six-pack of Coors beer, two packages of bologna, and a large jar of French's mustard with the lid screwed on lopsided.

God, what am I doing?

He shut the door and leaned against it.

Where are Shorty and Fletch?

He felt lightheaded. As the minutes ticked by, he was confused about what he was looking for and what he should be doing. He desperately wanted to find the men alive and well, to determine the whereabouts of the drug boys, but somehow this seemed futile in the unlighted building. There were a million places to hide. And he was so very tired. His muscles ached from the tension.

Maybe I'm the one who should be hiding.

He took two steps, slipped, hit the linoleum with a resounding smack, and lay there dazed, not moving. He was flat on his back; his right hand gripped the flashlight. When he fell, the twelve-gauge had flown from his grasp and clattered to the floor.

He got up slowly, awkwardly, clutching the flashlight.

The gun, where?

He explored the area around his feet. There was something. He knelt down, aimed the beam, and raked a finger through a substance pooled at the bottom of one of the freezers. It was dark and thick, and there was plenty of it. He sniffed his finger.

Blood.

He focused the light on the freezer beside the puddle. Bloody footprints. Red streaks pointed to the lid.

Don't let this be what I think it is.

With a trembling hand, he opened the chest and aimed the fading beam. Inside were disjointed arms and legs, a torso, a head.

He slammed the lid, dropped the flashlight and backed across the room. His spine connected with another freezer. He whirled, stumbled, fell to his knees.

Oh, God! Shorty and Fletch. Dead!

It was all stored in his brain for eternity, a detailed picture of body parts, captured by his mind's eye in less than a second. Hunched on all fours, he vomited, began to dry heave.

After a few minutes he rose, trembling, and picked up the flashlight. He found the shotgun and snatched it off the floor. Tense, motionless, he stood, listened. Silence.

The smell of blood was strong, everywhere. *Why didn't I notice it before?* His stomach churned; he swallowed bile. Matt extinguished the flashlight at the kitchen door and fled.

CHAPTER TWENTY-NINE

Morgan Cay

Alex blinked her eyes to keep them open. She did not know how long she had been asleep, but outside the sky was inky, dotted with stars. They had stopped moving. She heard tidewater lapping at the boat's hull.

Still bound at the wrists, she was prodded from the boat to a wooden dock. The fifty-two-foot yacht, Eva, had shut down its engines only minutes before, and Miguel, grim and silent, had untied her hands and helped her dress. She could not remember when she had last eaten or had something to drink.

On the well-lighted pier, she spotted two heavyset men carrying formidable-looking weapons. Lean Dobermans, vigilant and poised for command, stood beside them. Both men and dogs alike eyed her curiously.

Jorge stepped out of the cabin looking rested and clean shaven. He had changed into gray knit pants and a mauve short sleeved shirt. He was humming.

"*Ola! Que pasa?*" he called to the men as he climbed onto the dock.

One of the guards, the one nearest the boat, spoke in hushed tones to Jorge, who nodded and glanced toward a dirt road which lay beyond the parking area.

"Sí, Sí," she heard Jorge say.

"Yes what?" Alex wondered.

She sank down on the rough wood and rested her head on her knees. Food no longer interested her, but that came as no surprise. Stress had always diminished her appetite. She just wanted to drink a gallon of water and to sleep. Escape.

After Dr. Romero joined them, Jorge untied her hands and motioned for her to follow him and the Doctor to a car parked nearby. Miguel did not accompany them.

Lying down on the back seat she closed her eyes. *Is Matt all right? What is he thinking?* The ride was bumpy. *How will this end? I have to get away, find Matt.*

She groaned, sat up, and looked out the window. En route they drove near an airstrip. She heard the roar of engines and noticed colored lights twinkling through the trees.

"How do you like our little Island so far?" Dr. Romero said over his shoulder.

She did not reply and continued to stare out the window. Jorge said something to him in Spanish and both men laughed. She felt a savage anger, one she had never known before. She wanted to hurt them in the same way they had hurt her, through torture and humiliation. *Something slow and painful would be nice.* Finding out that she was capable of violent thoughts stunned her.

When they came to a fork in the road, Jorge turned left and continued up a shell driveway that lead to a three-story house. All the windows looked like framed yellow pictures against the night sky.

Jorge and the Doctor each held her by an elbow and half pushed, half lifted her up a series of steps to a spacious verandah. She noticed rattan chairs with plump cushions resting on the seats and an oval glass table with a bouquet of fresh flowers on it.

The front door opened and a tidy-looking woman who wore her hair pulled back tightly in a bun nodded at them. Her mouth resembled a thin red line.

"So, you bring the woman," she said as she inspected Alex with her eyes.

"How goes it, Consuelo?" the Doctor said.

"Well enough," she said. "It is late. Bring her this way."

They waited for several minutes in a dimly-lit foyer until a man came down the stairs. He was wearing faded blue jeans and a soft blue denim shirt unbuttoned to his breastbone. Well toned, he obviously lifted weights. He had dark, penetrating, brown eyes. The unidentified man held out smooth slim fingers and shook hands with each of the men. After a brief exchange in Spanish, he focused his attention on Alex.

"Well, Señora," he said softly, "I understand that you have been having a difficult time. For that, I apologize. I hate to see a lovely woman abused but unfortunately, sometimes in my business it is necessary."

"You men have no right to do this. You're... This is criminal."

"Please," he said and gestured, "let's sit down."

Consuelo ushered them into an adjoining room where Alex fell into an arm chair. Jorge and the Doctor perched on a painted beechwood sofa. The man remained standing.

"I am Raoul Chavez," he told her. "You have something that belongs to me and I want it back."

"I feel like I'm having a nightmare and I can't wake up," Alex said. "This is all so... Why are you people doing this?"

"You've heard of wrong time, wrong place?" Raoul said.

"The United States government will..."

"Leave me alone with her for a minute," Jorge said.

Raoul raised an open hand. "Not necessary yet. She isn't going anywhere."

"I've told you everything I know. This isn't complicated. If you take me to my husband he'll give you what you want."

"That remains to be seen. This is an unusual situation," Raoul said. "I need to consider it."

"Consuelo."

"Señor?"

"Take her upstairs. To the front bedroom."

"As you wish."

"You're making a big mistake," Alex said.

Raoul smiled at her, dismissed her with a wave of a hand.

"We will discuss that issue later."

CHAPTER THIRTY

Robert's Cay

Matt cursed the darkness each time he encountered an obstacle as he hurried from the radio room.

Can't risk using the flashlight.

He hastened down a long corridor that lead him toward the opposite end of the building.

God, it would be wonderful to be able to see for just a minute. He paused every few steps, listened. His muscles protested as he moved; his eyes ached from trying to identify shapes in the murky gloom. He heard a bush clawing the side of the building and the murmur of the casuarina trees.

Matt would not allow his mind to focus on Alex and what might be happening to her. He remembered Shorty's advice, "Get her back, then worry about what they did to her."

He's right, of course. I can't think about what those animals might be doing to her or I'll go nuts.

There was a dull thud inside his chest, and for a moment, as he stood thinking of her in the dark hallway, the anguish was almost more than he could bear. He swallowed the pain whole and continued.

Shorty and Fletch, dead. Why?

His fingers found smooth-surfaced doors with cool knobs. They stood like sentries, challenged Matt to open them. His demons were loose, out of control.

You must cooperate with the camp authorities, Pen. If you do not, you are violating the laws of the camp and you will be severely poonished.

At the end of the hall, he came to a glass door, pushed against it and found that it wouldn't budge.

God, now I have to go back the way I came, leave by the other door. No telling who's behind me. You know who's behind you, Pen.

Weary, he rested against the door jamb and closed his eyes.

You have the bad attitude, Pen, and it must be corrected.

He stood there for several moments until a noise from the opposite end of the hall startled him. He raised his gun. Silence.

You are being evasive, Pen.

There it was again, a click. Then nothing. Perspiration drenched his shirt; he trembled.

I'm hearing noises…everywhere.

Another click. He waited, flattened against the wall. He could fire into the darkness, but what if he missed? He would be firing wild.

If it isn't anything, if they're anywhere on the Island, they'll hear the blast, find me. Think! I can break the glass. Do something!

His right index finger found the shotgun's safety button, engaged it. Using the gun butt, he smashed at the glass panel and felt a spray of glass as it hit home. Once he began, he struck like a man possessed. When the door finally shattered, he crawled through the jagged opening and bolted.

The outbuildings which had looked so foreboding when he and Alex first saw them were now a welcome refuge. He dashed around to the back of a vacant storage facility and sprinted through an open doorway. Once inside, he pressed his back against the wall and slid to the floor.

I cannot go any further, he thought as he closed his eyes. I'm too damn old for this. Just as he had felt in prison, he wished that he was a tougher man.

You are the blackest creeminol, Pen.

He was so keyed up he wondered if he would be able to sleep, but when he finally let go of consciousness, he had nightmares. He twitched and moaned as his dreams were invaded by severed heads, corpses with vacant eyes and Vietnamese interrogators with false smiles.

CHAPTER THIRTY-ONE

Morgan Cay

Alex awoke on top of a queen-sized bed in a sunny bedroom. A comforter, plump and soft beneath her, felt warm against her cheek.

I'm still here. That means they haven't found the cocaine. If they believe that I don't know anything, they still need Matt to give them their drugs.

She raised on an elbow and noticed a dark stain where she had been lying. *Blood.* When she touched the back of her head, she felt matted hair.

As she gazed about the room, she saw that delicate lace curtains framed the windows and an ornate print boudoir chair occupied one corner. A hand-carved dressing table with a round mirror and bench seat were positioned across from the end of the bed. A bouquet of yellow mums sat on an antique-looking chest of drawers in front of the windows.

She eased herself into a sitting position by increments and continued to survey the room. When she encountered her image in the dressing table mirror, the pale stricken face that looked back at her did not resemble her own.

A sun dress, sales tag dangling, lay across the back of the chair. Towels and undergarments were stacked on the seat. Further scrutiny revealed a door in one corner opened into an adjoining room where white tiles gleamed on the floor. *A bathroom.* She moved to the edge of the bed.

Using one hand to keep her balance, she made her way to the faucet where she gulped water from the spigot. The cool water refreshed her while she drank, but as soon as she had consumed her fill, her stomach churned. Feeling faint, she pressed her forehead against the cool wall tiles and waited for the queasiness to subside. When she felt less nauseous, she returned to the bedroom where she pulled back a drape and looked out. A shell path lead from the house to the woods beyond. Through the pines, glints of bright sunshine winked on the water.

When she attempted to open the windows, she discovered they had all been nailed shut. When she tried the door, she found it locked and unyielding. She beat on it with her fist.

"Hey, unlock this door!"

No response on the other side. She pounded the wood with both fists.

"Hey, somebody!"

She clasped the knob, rattled the door.

"I want to see…"

What was his name?

"I want to see the boss, the owner, Señor …"

She beat on the door again. Heard footsteps. A key in the lock. As the door swung open, she stepped back. A man in his twenties, tan and muscular, wearing camouflage pants and a faded brown T-shirt stood before her. He held a nasty-looking gun.

"Señora, I am only going to tell you once, so I want you to listen very, very carefully. If you knock on this door one more time, make any noise at all, I am going to tie you to the bed, cut off a piece of your body, and stuff it in your mouth. Comprende?"

Alex stepped back.

"I, uh, yes."

He turned, slammed the door, and locked it.

Shaking, she sat down on the end of the bed and picked at the comforter.

What can I do? I'm trapped until they let me out.

The thought of bathing appealed to her. She returned to the bathroom where she removed her soiled clothing. The shower stall was clean, pristine white. She turned the handles on the faucets and stepped behind the sliding glass doors. The spray hit her skin like needles as she stood beneath it, swaying and drinking water. All her life she had worked hard at keeping her emotional house in order, and now, thrust among strangers and violence, she wasn't sure who she was anymore. Alex felt as if she had been transported to another dimension.

After several minutes, she used a bar of soap and washed every inch of her body. When she finished, she scrubbed again. She preferred to stand behind the sliding doors while the warm water cascaded over her until Matt came for her or until she awakened from the nightmare. When the water ran cold, she turned it off and stepped out dripping from the stall. The bathroom mirror had fogged; she wiped it in a circular motion with her towel. When she peered into the glass, she looked more like her old self. She had never been hit before, certainly had never been knocked unconscious, and she wondered if there might be some lingering damage.

A new toothbrush in its wrapper lay on the bathroom vanity along with a tube of Crest Toothpaste. Methodically, she brushed her teeth and gargled, and found comfort in the familiar ritual.

Wrapping a towel around her, she sat down at the dressing table and brushed her hair. Using a hand mirror, she tilted her head and angled to see the cut, but regardless of how she positioned herself, she couldn't get a clear view of the wound. The bleeding seemed to have stopped. She now looked like a different person than the one she had glimpsed in the mirror before her shower. Somewhat revitalized, her face, freckled and tanned, looked back at her like an old friend. The small cut on her lip had already begun to heal.

She removed the sales tag and donned the sun dress. Because she couldn't find any sandals or shoes, she remained barefoot.

Very clever not to give me any shoes. It would be painful to flee across shell and coral on tender feet.

She eased into the boudoir chair and closed her eyes. A fan twirled over the bed, neatly slicing the air with its sharp flat blades. A brass clock on one of the bedside tables ticked. She heard planes flying overhead. Voices in the house, male and female, reverberated.

What next?

She fell asleep, and when she opened her eyes, the room was cloaked in darkness. Glassware and cutlery clinked somewhere below. Food smells wafted up the stairs and made her salivate.

Creaking stairs alerted her that someone was coming. She stiffened. A key turned in the lock before the door slowly opened. A woman stood at the threshold, silhouetted by the bright light behind her. Alex watched her fumble for a wall switch just before brilliant light flooded the room. Alex blinked.

"Oh, I see that you have taken you bath and put on the clean clothes. That is good," Consuelo said. "You so dirty, like the *cerdo*. I thought I might have scrub you myself. Aiyaiyai, *Yo no guise hacerlo.*"

Alex started to speak.

"*Ahora*," Consuelo said as she turned on lamps and extinguished the overhead light. "The time it is for you to eat. Señor Chavez says me set the place at table. You come."

"Wait a minute. What is going to happen to my husband and me?"

"Come, Señora."

"Where is my husband?"

"Señora, you speak to Señor Chavez, no to me. I no know why you here or where you husband go. My job clean house, cook food."

"But…"

"Por favor, Señora, you to come."

Alex, still feeling a little dizzy, clung to the banister as she descended the stairs. The tantalizing aroma of food lured her to the dining room where a long candle-lit table had been laid out with sterling silver place settings for two on a white linen table cloth. A dozen red roses high-lighted the center.

Consuelo entered the room and motioned to her to sit down. Apparently she was to be the only guest.

Everything seems so civilized. How can I sit here while God knows what is happening to Matt?

Shadows from the lighted candles danced on the walls. The aroma of fresh baked bread slipped beneath the cracks around a swinging door at the opposite end of the room.

After sitting alone for several minutes, she began to feel uncomfort-able and foolish.

Could this be another one of their tricks, another effort to find out if I know more? How clever these people are. Of course they realize that I'm starving. I'm supposed to sit here and drool while they whip up all kinds of delicious concoctions in the kitchen. They'll offer me food after I tell them what they want to know. No talk. No food.

Alex started to get up from her chair when she heard the sound of soft footsteps. The man she had seen come down the stairs the preced-ing night appeared beside her. Once again he greeted her.

"In case you don't remember my name, Señora, I am Raoul Chavez, the owner of Morgan Cay and your host."

Alex said nothing.

He took his place at the opposite end of the table. The man who sat across from her leaned back in his chair and scrutinized her. His eyes, brown and clear, twinkled in the candlelight. A lock of hair fell across his forehead; he brushed it aside. A full mustache covered most of his upper lip.

"Where is my husband?" Alex said. "Why are you doing this to me? To us?"

"So many questions, Señora, and before dinner. In time."

"In time? How can I calmly sit here when you've kidnapped me and God knows what has happened to my husband. You…"

"This isn't the United States, Señora. This is Morgan Cay and in case you haven't figured it out, here I am law. There is no democracy, no bill of rights."

"Why are you keeping me here?"

"Evidently you will not stop asking me these questions until I tell you so for my own peace of mind and your continued good health I will answer. First of all, your husband has something that belongs to me. Second I have something that belongs to him. When he returns my property, I will release you. In the meantime, you will be my guest. It is quite simple."

"My husband will never hand over your cocaine unless I am brought to him at the same time. He's too smart to do it any other way."

"I must admit," Raoul said as he leaned his elbows on the table, "that this poses an interesting problem. I will not be blackmailed."

"It seems to me that you are the one who is the blackmailer here."

"Your husband will do as I wish, Señora, and not the reverse. Is that clear?"

Alex was silent.

Chavez looked at her for a moment before jangling a silver dinner bell. A boy about fifteen entered the room carrying a silver tray.

"First we are having oysters and some caviar," Raoul said. After tasting the roe, he said, "It's beluga."

Alex looked puzzled. She had never eaten caviar and didn't know anything about it.

"Beluga, you know, sturgeon."

After the boy left the room, Raoul raised his glass and said, "A toast to beautiful women, and that includes you, Mrs. Spencer. You are quite lovely."

He took a sip and returned his glass to the table.

Alex did not raise her glass.

"Drink," he said and motioned with his hand.

She took a small sip.

"Do you like the wine? It's my favorite. Montrachet, Chateau Des Herbeux, a white burgundy."

Alex remained silent.

Raoul dipped into his caviar and began to eat. He continued to watch her while he chewed. She returned his gaze but did not eat.

"What? What? he said. "You don't like oysters or caviar?"

"It's not that, I, uh…"

"Oh, I see," he said and laughed. "You think… Oh my dear Señora, that's very funny. Please feel free to eat my food. You are my guest. I don't poison my company or my prisoners at my table."

He patted his lips with his napkin.

Alex began eating. The oysters, chilled, firm, and fresh, had a slightly salty taste. She found them exquisite. She ate one and then another. Chavez watched her with shining eyes and an occasional smile.

CHAPTER THIRTY-TWO

Morgan Cay

Raoul, impressed by Alex's wholesome good looks, admired her silky hair and full lips, her small straight nose. He found her eyes, large and dark, to be her most stunning feature. They were gentle eyes suffused with innocence. She certainly couldn't hide behind them.

He enjoyed watching her devour her dinner, hesitantly at first, and then with passion. Between bites she glanced across the table at him but remained mute. He sensed that she was afraid of him, of what he could do to her.

She trembles. How wonderful.

"Do you like the French truffle casserole? It is one of my favorites."

"It's fine."

"I'm glad."

Raoul was amazed to find himself so captivated by this American, this woman who had stumbled into his life. Women were not a problem for him, never had been, not before he rose to power in the Cartel and definitely not after. These days, women competed for his attention, fought over him, and of late, this game had grown tiresome and repetitive. Where was the challenge? The excitement? He prided himself on being cultured and well read, both qualities he found lacking in most of the females he encountered.

After a dessert of white-chocolate mousse with fresh strawberries, they lingered at the table and sipped cognac from crystal snifters. The woman exerted great effort to remain poised. She manifested defiance and terror at the same time.

What a delightful contradiction.

He took a last sip of cognac and rose from his chair. As he walked toward her, she watched him with wary eyes, her body tense.

"Come, you need sleep," he said and helped her to her feet. "Return to your room upstairs and rest. I will see that the door remains unlocked in case you wish to come down and talk to me later. I'm usually up very late."

"I want to talk with you now. Clearly you are the boss here. I can see that you're a man of reason. Won't you help me?"

"I am the boss, yes, that is true," he said and pushed her along by her elbow. "As far as my being a man of reason, my enemies might challenge you on that one."

"I just want to go back to my husband. I'm sure your men told you what happened, I mean about the drugs. We had nothing to do with the cocaine being placed on our boat. We don't care anything about drugs or drug money, honestly. We just want to go back to our lives. Please, won't you take me to my husband? He'll give you your cocaine and we'll be off. And we won't tell anyone what happened, not a soul. You have my word."

Raoul paused at the foot of the stairs and looked down at her.

"Your telling anyone about me or my business, Señora, is the least of my concerns. You will do exactly what I tell you and so will your husband. If not, who's to say what might happen."

"But," Alex stammered, tears welling up in her eyes, "this shouldn't be so complicated." Alex clutched his arm and said, "you must take me to my husband at Robert's Cay."

"No, Señora, now go to your room," Raoul said and nudged her toward the stairs.

"Please, won't you let me go back to my husband?"

Raoul raised his eyebrows.

"What am I saying to you that you don't understand, Señora?"

CHAPTER THIRTY-THREE

Morgan Cay

Jorge tapped his fingers together while he waited for Raoul to join him. He was seated in a velvet griffin armchair, a valuable antique, but an uncomfortable piece of furniture on which to rest one's haunches. Raoul expected visits to his office to be devoted to business, and the chairs in the room, with the exception of Raoul's leather desk chair, reflected this.

Jorge lit a cigarette and exhaled the smoke in small puffs. His rounded lips pulsed cloudy rings that widened and vanished as they drifted away. The passage of time suggested that Raoul must be enjoying his dinner with the woman.

That American bitch. So high and mighty.

Secretly he wondered if he had failed Raoul this time. He considered himself an expert in torture, both physical and mental. Information was not long withheld from him. He still harbored some doubt about the woman.

Does she know more than she let on? Is she holding back, protecting her husband? Does she love him enough to die for him?

He found that last thought disturbing. In rare moments when brutal honestly crept into his thoughts, he recognized that no one had ever loved him enough to undergo even the slightest inconvenience in his behalf, not even his own mother. He sighed and ground his cigarette butt into a crystal ashtray.

The bitch's husband will pay. I'll see to it personally.

He planned to enjoy the contest for awhile, terrorize the American into submission. Killing him too quickly would spoil the fun. Besides, since Raoul had chosen to take the woman under his roof, he had to wait and see what he wanted done with her. In the meantime, the cat and mouse game entertained him.

The floor creaked, the office door swung open, and Raoul appeared, flushed from pleasure or wine, carrying a snifter of cognac. Jorge sprang to his feet.

"*El Jefe, hola!* How goes it with the American bitch? Did she say anything else about the cocaine?"

"Sit down," Raoul said and motioned to him to resume his seat.

Jorge sank into his chair and watched as Raoul sat down behind his desk.

"That bitch, as you call her, what a delightful change. She didn't take off her panties and ask if I wanted dessert. She didn't try to convince me that I needed her to make me happy."

"Oh, they're all alike, those high class whores," Jorge said as he lit another cigarette. "Those sluts, they grow up having everything their way. They hang back because that's how they get what they want. They politely seduce a man. The result is the same. Whores to the last one."

"Tsk, tsk, such anger against one little woman, Jorge, or is it all women?"

"That cunt suffered plenty. She doesn't know anything, I'm certain."

"Perhaps."

"Now what about the husband and the coke? Shall I continue my little game or..."

"Yes, that matter needs to be taken care of. I want to keep the woman for a while, but you must recover the cocaine. I realize it's small change, only twenty pounds, a meager amount, but you know how I feel. No one, absolutely no one is allowed to take anything from me. It would set a bad precedent. And besides, I can't exactly write off the loss on my taxes." Raoul laughed.

"I would have killed that whore on the boat. You know, I should have. We don't need her."

"But you didn't, and now I have plans for her. She amuses me."

"Maybe I will require her to make an exchange."

"*El Christo*, I can't believe my ears."

Raoul sipped his cognac.

"Use your imagination, my friend. How difficult can it be? Catch him. Use your devious and painful methods to extract the information from him. Then kill him and feed him to the fish, like all the others."

"Of course, El Jefe, but…"

"Is there a problem?"

"No, of course not, El Jefe, I will take care of the matter. I'll take Jesus and Luis. We'll use one of the Whalers and…"

"Spare me the details, Jorge," Raoul said, raising a palm. "Get the cocaine. Kill the man. Understand?"

"Sí, El Jefe, as you wish."

Jorge lingered in front of Raoul's desk.

"Yes?" said Raoul, who had shifted his attention to a letter on his desk.

"The woman…" Jorge said.

"What about her?"

"May I… Will you let me have her when you've finished with her?"

Raoul looked up at him, studied Jorge's face.

"Another one, huh?"

"Yes, I… You know what it means to me."

"How many times are you going to murder your mother?"

"I have told you before. I didn't murder my mother."

"She was strangled to death. You were there. No one else. Why do you deny it?"

"It was an accident. I only wanted to teach her a lesson, frighten her."

"Evidently, you succeeded."

"The woman?"

"As long as it isn't like the last time. That one almost got away."

"No, that won't happen again."

"When I'm finished with her, she is yours."

"*Gracias, El Jefe.*"

"I have work to do."

"Your cocaine will be returned soon."

"Good night, Jorge."

CHAPTER THIRTY-FOUR

Morgan Cay

The house, hushed and dark, did not reveal what might be prowling just outside the bedroom door. Alex, still wearing her dress, got up from the bed and stood on the plush Oriental rug. The fibers felt cool and soft between her toes. She stood motionless, waited.

Stepping lightly, she made her way to the bedroom door where she paused and pressed her ear against the wood. Only silence on the other side. She turned the brass door knob and heard the faint sound of the latch bolt sliding inside the strike plate. Holding her breath, she pulled the door toward her and peeked through a narrow crack. The hallway appeared vacant. She opened it farther, then slipped outside, gently closing the door behind her.

In spite of her inability to see clearly, she managed to make her way down the stairs without making a sound. She stopped often, fearful she might encounter someone. Any noise she made would no doubt be magnified and bring her captors running.

As she passed Raoul's office, she saw light glowing at the bottom of the closed door. She paused for a moment, strained to hear sounds from within. Tiptoeing to the front of the house, she found the entry door unbolted.

Warm, damp air filled her lungs when she stepped outside onto the porch. The sky held a sliver of moon which provided scant illumination for her to see.

They must not have expected that I would attempt to escape.

Briefly elated, she sobered when she realized that standing outside the house did not represent escape. She still had to make her way to the boat dock, where, hopefully, she would hijack one of the boats and flee into open water. If she could get off the Island undetected, when the sun came up she would hail a passing boater to help her find Matt. The hard part lay directly ahead.

When her bare feet stepped onto the hard ground, she winced. There were countless pointed objects the size of golf balls scattered everywhere. She squatted and picked one up. Too dark to examine closely, she guessed that it must be some kind of seed or cone.

I can't think about the pain, she thought as she tossed it aside. I have to close my mind and hurry. Someone might check to see if I'm in my room, and if they find I've gone, they will send those Dobermans after me.

Winding her way among the trees she stumbled over unseen branches and shrubs. On one tumble she lunged against a broken tree branch and gasped when a long sharp splinter pierced the palm of her left hand. It felt like a toothpick had been jammed underneath the skin, and the tender flesh throbbed from the shock. She ignored it and continued in the direction where she thought the dock might be.

To the east, the airport glowed, and the roar of small airplane engines disturbed the night. Though she had slept and eaten, she found her strength rapidly diminishing. Her lungs labored; her legs trembled. Thoughts of Matt kept her in motion, but part of her desperately wanted to surrender and return to the slumbering house which offered the appearance of safety.

She had no sense of time. It seemed that hours had elapsed when in fact it could have been only minutes. Her feet, bruised and bleeding, evoked a wince with each step.

The noise from the airport grew louder; the twinkling runway lights looked brighter. She stopped, tried to remember how the airport had appeared from the window of the car.

On my right. Now it's on the left. Okay, think. I must be heading toward the dock. How big can this Island be? If only I could walk along the beach, but then someone might see me.

In spite of her exhaustion and fear, joy bubbled up inside her with each agonizing step.

They didn't think that I would run away, certainly not barefooted and unarmed. And tomorrow, oh, how I'd love to see their faces.

After what seemed like hours, Alex paused when she heard the familiar sound of a sputtering motorboat engine. Jubilant, she almost shouted. Then she saw lights, down low, a couple hundred yards to her right. Cautious, she crouched and darted from tree to tree.

She heard voices from the parking area as a knot of men sauntered by. They were smoking and talking, carrying guns, and obviously patrolling the grounds. She didn't see any dogs.

Again, Alex, elated and frightened, felt her emotions rise and fall. The dock was well lighted. Once she stepped out of the woods, she would stand out like a blackberry in a bowl of milk. She leaned into a tree, felt the rough bark against her cheek.

I've come so far.

As she waited to sprint to the dock, from behind a sweaty arm encircled her neck and jerked her backward. The stench of stale cigarettes flooded her nostrils.

"Going for the little walk, Señora," a man said in a husky voice.

She gagged from the pressure against her throat.

"What you think, American stupid bitch, that we *imbeciles!*"

She choked, struggled to pull the man's arm away. He tightened his grip, wrapped his other arm around her. A callused hand slid down the front of her dress and began to knead her right breast. He panted in her ear.

"How you like?" he said.

She couldn't breathe.

"It would be the good lesson for you."

Absolute terror gripped her. She tried to scream but couldn't find her voice. Alex's adrenaline kicked in. She jabbed him in the stomach with a quick thrust of her elbow. Stunned, he grunted, released his hold, and grabbed her by the back of the neck.

"*Hija de puta!*" he said.

The guards, who had passed by only moments before, turned and sprinted toward the commotion. They pointed flashlight beams in the direction of the scuffle. A brief exchange in Spanish ensued before the man let her go, and Alex, choking and hacking, fell to her knees.

Hot tears welled up in her eyes but she quickly looked down. She thought it would be much worse if they saw her cry.

CHAPTER THIRTY-FIVE

Robert's Cay

Matt awakened shortly after dawn in a vacant, dusty building with sunlight fanning through the cracks in the boarded windows. He groaned to his feet and peeked around the open door. Except for a flock of gulls strutting aimlessly in front of the main building, the courtyard looked deserted.

He checked his watch and noted that it was a little after seven.

Did I sleep too long?

He gazed at the bleak buildings, and a graphic picture of Shorty and Fletch's dismembered bodies flashed across his mind's eye. He shuddered.

Where are those pricks?

He heard the gulls and the sea, his heartbeat, and nothing more.

I'd better check the anchorage, see if there are any new boats. Those assholes can't walk on water.

Crouching, he slipped out the door and jogged to the beach with his shotgun in hand. His muscles ached as he ran, a painful reminder of how old and tired he felt.

No doubt about it, combat is a young man's game.

Seeing the tracking Station's runabout tied up at the dock made his heart soar. With a power boat, he could follow and he could search. *Escape.* A closer scrutiny revealed that the engine was not simply disabled. It was missing. He sighed and his shoulders drooped.

The boat people, passing the time on the east end of the Island, seemed unaware of his presence. He noticed a child standing within calling range. The boy, about eight years old, was urinating in the sand and watching his stream with interest. His smooth, black skin glistened with perspiration. Matt called to him from behind a tree.

"P-s-s-t! Hey! Over here!"

The child, engrossed in relieving himself, didn't hear him at first. Finally he looked in Matt's direction.

"Hey, you, come here a minute," Matt said.

The boy's eyes widened; he took a few steps backward.

"Who's there?"

Matt stepped into view and motioned for the boy to come closer. "It's okay, I won't hurt you. I just want to ask you a couple questions."

The boy glanced at the other children, who were swimming in shallow water just off the beach, and eyed Matt warily.

"Listen, I have money," Matt said. "I'll give you an American quarter, twenty-five cents, if you just answer a couple questions for me."

The boy seemed torn between greed and an innate fear of strangers, particularly white ones who hid in the bushes. He hesitated for a moment before he took a small step toward Matt.

"What do you want to know?" he asked, lingering just beyond Matt's reach.

"Are there men on this Island, strangers?"

"There is one man," the boy said.

"Where is he?"

"Right here," he said with a crooked grin. "Right here."

"What?"

"He is you. Now give me my quarter."

"No, no, wait a minute. Let me put it this way. Are there any other strangers, other than me, on this Island?"

"There were two men yesterday. They came in a boat that landed on the other side of the Island."

The boy pointed north.

"Have they gone?"

"Their boat is gone."

"When did they leave?"

"I don't know. We come to the beach for the day and go back to our boat at night. That one," the boy said and turned toward the forty-footer. "Those men come in the day but they did not see me. They are bad men, I think. That's what my mama say. They stole the motor on the big boat that belongs to the white men who live up there," he said and pointed behind Matt.

"A woman, did they have a woman with them? A white woman?"

"No, I didn't see a white woman. Now give me my quarter."

Matt dug in his pocket and found a few coins, two American quarters, and a Bahamian dollar bill. He extended his hand with the two quarters. The boy snatched them and sprinted up the beach. Matt felt both relieved and filled with dread at the same time.

Why would they leave without their drugs? Why didn't they talk to me before they killed Shorty and Fletch? Did the guys fight with them? Why'd they cut them up? Why wasn't Alex with them?

His head and shoulders throbbed.

Time to go back to the Station, find food.

He remembered the body parts in the freezer and felt queasy.

It doesn't matter. I have to eat, make a plan, figure out what the hell I'm going to do to get us out of this mess.

Once he arrived at the main building, he hesitated, not as much from fear as from revulsion. In order to find food, he had to return to the kitchen with it's adjoining larder. He knew that he could go to the *Amani* for provisions, but once on board, he would be vulnerable if attacked.

Not a good idea.

He knew what he had to do.

Besides, I have to see if any of those radios can be made operable. The Amani's radio only has a range of twenty-five miles, and that's on a good day. The radios at the Station operate by power and it's out. But maybe not permanently. First I'll eat and then I'll look for the fuse box or a battery-operated radio with a wider range.

Inside the dreary building, the silence unnerved him. Matt wanted to believe that except for the boat people, he was alone on the Island; but nothing had gone the way he had anticipated. He had expected a simple exchange, the drugs for Alex, and then the two of them would run like hell. But no one had even attempted to approach him.

Why?

And what about Alex? He trembled when he thought of her with men who have no conscience or compassion. Who…

The stench of death permeated the air. Matt opened the venetian blinds allowing bright sunlight to flood the radio room. He felt safer than he had the preceding night when he had fumbled his way in and out of the building in utter darkness. He made a mental note to search for essentials, a good flashlight, ammunition.

The larder, stocked for hurricanes and power outages, offered a wide array of boxed and canned food. Absently, he grabbed a can of Delmonte green beans and a small can of Spam. In one of the kitchen drawers, he found a can opener. When he turned on the faucet at the sink, air banged up the pipes and droplets sputtered from the tap.

Ah, they've cut off the water, too.

In the pantry he found a tall can of Donald Duck orange juice. He took that, along with his beans and potted meat, and settled at the littered table in the radio room. At first he was only conscious of the odor of blood, but once he opened the cans, the food aroma flooded his nostrils. Matt, sitting some fifteen feet from the decaying bodies inside the freezer, devoured his cold meal.

When he finished, he wiped his fingers on his shirt and stood up. From the windows, he saw only a small portion of the Island. The beach appeared absent of all life, save the gulls who had migrated to the nearby shore.

Now I must search in earnest.

Methodically, he checked all the radios and found them intact. Matt had expected no less since they had been operating just before the power went out. His search took him to a small bunk room at the opposite end of the building where he discovered what had once been a fuse box. Someone had done a nice job on it.

While rummaging through the countless drawers in the building, he located a battery-operated spotlight that actually worked and found an arsenal. A supply of bottled water sat neatly stacked in a room near the kitchen.

Catching a glimpse of himself in a bathroom mirror, his haunted, red eyes stunned him. His beard had already begun to grow, and, disbelieving that the image in the mirror belonged to him, he rubbed his cheeks.

How long has it been since they took Alex? Two days?

Having eaten, he felt somewhat renewed His spirits, though by no means buoyant, were better than they had been. He still had hope and he kept telling himself that there would be a successful conclusion to this nightmare. He would get Alex back. Alive.

Immersed in his thoughts, he almost didn't hear the slow click behind him. A bolt of terror shot through him. He whirled and aimed his gun. Ginger took another tentative step and hesitated.

"God, Ginger."

The dog stood up on her back legs and pressed her front paws on his chest. Matt laughed until tears streamed down his cheeks.

Chapter Thirty-six

Robert's Cay

"What do you make of it?" Jeremy said as he lowered his binoculars.

"Beats me," Dwight said as he reached for the Steiner glasses and pressed them to his eyes. "Could be he's here to make a drug deal. He hasn't returned to his boat in almost two days and yesterday a couple of Raoul's boys showed up on the beach."

"Maybe it's a done deal and he's just not in a hurry to leave the sunny beaches."

"Maybe, maybe not."

"Well, our job is clear," Jeremy said. "We're supposed to observe and report and make our meeting with Driggers on the fifth. We can't get mixed up in any kind of a drug bust, no matter how tempting it is."

Dwight lowered the binoculars and stared at Robert's Cay in the distance. How odd, he thought, that a retired American Naval Officer and former Vietnam prisoner of war is involved with the worst kind of scum. It just doesn't figure.

Jeremy stood up, adjusted the string in his baggy surfer trunks. "I'm going to get my fishing rod. Want me to get yours?"

"Forget the rod. Bring me a beer."

"In a sec," Jeremy said before he went inside the cabin.

"Hey," Dwight called, "bring me that other bag of chips too."

Jeremy rolled his eyes. He wanted to suggest that Dwight's big belly didn't need another beer and a bag of chips, but he thought better of it.

The boat, a thirty-two footer, had been getting smaller with each passing day. There were times when both men had to call time out and retreat to opposite ends of the ship to cool off. This was, according to Jeremy, the worst kind of shit duty.

"Here we are," he moaned, "in paradise with no women, stuck at one monotonous anchorage after another."

Sand and water, sand and water. The head had malfunctioned and stank up the cabin, and neither man could claim any culinary skill. Shit duty.

Jeremy returned with his fishing rod and a beer.

"Thanks, my good man," Dwight said with a nod as he took the Budweiser. "No chips?"

"Forgot 'em. I'll get 'em in a minute."

"Ah, never mind. Beer'll do." Dwight opened the can and took a swig. "So, here we are," he said. "Another shitty day in paradise. What do you think Spencer will be up to today?"

Earlier the preceding day Dwight had transmitted a coded inquiry to the DEA office in Miami concerning the boat, *Amani*. In short order a message had been sent back stating that the *Amani*, a documented vessel, belonged to none other than Commander Matthew J. Spencer, who had been a prisoner of war in Vietnam for six years. He had no criminal record, had not even received a speeding ticket. He was well known and respected as a Naval Officer and a patriot, both during and after the war. Using the description provided by the DEA, it was clear that this was none other than Commander Spencer in the flesh. He was reported to be married to one Alexandra Jane Spencer, but neither agent had observed him with anyone, male or female. When Raoul's operators appeared on the beach and vanished into the Tracking Station compound, the agents were unable to discern the purpose of their visit to the Island.

Dwight had suggested that they go ashore and explore the Cay like typical tourists, but Jeremy had objected.

"Our directive is to meet Driggers, show up at the regular meeting place, exchange information. Nothing more."

Although Agent Driggers had not appeared as scheduled the preceding month, it was hoped that this time would be different and contact would be made. Because Drigger's had not communicated with the Administration in six weeks, it was feared that his cover had been blown and he had been murdered by Raoul and his boys. Steps had already been taken to minimize the damage in case Driggers had given everything up.

In the meantime, the two agents were there to observe and report, to be unobtrusive, to blend in with other tourists. Jeremy thought too much snooping would be dangerous. They were supposed to be burned-out yuppies on vacation.

Dwight put down his beer and stretched. Jeremy glanced at Dwight's bathing suit and looked away. He hated the bright orange and white striped bikini that barely covered his enormous crotch. A long line of curly red hair emerged from the waistband and traveled lushly up to his belly button. A roll of fat overflowed around his waist making him look like he was wearing a bicycle inner tube. Everything about Dwight was beefy and thick.

Dwight, noticing Jeremy's expression, looked at him with a question in his eyes. Fearing that Dwight might somehow be able to read his thoughts, Jeremy coughed and baited his hook with a piece of conch. Standing clear of Dwight, he flicked his wrist and cast the line out thirty feet, where it slowly descended into the sparkling blue water.

"Damn I hope Driggers is okay," Dwight said. "He and I go way back, before Quantico."

"Let's hope for the best. He's probably in Colombia right now, fuckin' broads and smokin' fat cigars with Raoul's boys."

"God, I hope so."

"I wish I had some live shrimp," Jeremy said.

"Yeah?"

"I'd like to try some of that bone fishing that's supposed to be so hot out here. Bradley, you know, that guy from Atlanta who came down a few months back, he told me about it." He reeled in a few feet of line. "Yeah, he said that bone fishing is suppose to be where it's at. I should probably dinghy over to the flats by the Island over there and see if I can catch one."

"What's so special about 'em?"

"The thrill. They say they're damn good fighters. Bradley told me you can catch 'em by wading but fishing from a small boat is better. You get into say one, two feet of water and look for their tails. Apparently they eat stuff off the bottom and their tails are visible while they're chowin' down. He said they were real nervous fuckers, easily spooked. But if you can cast up-current of 'em and let the bait drift back, you have a good chance of hooking up with one."

Dwight finished his beer and crushed the empty can.

"Bradley said with a little practice you can get good at casting sideways and not scare 'em. As he put it, 'They're touchy fish.' Once a bonefish strikes, you have to set the goddamn hook right away or you'll lose your bait. If he can't get off, he said that son-of-a-bitch will put up one hell of a fight."

"Can you eat 'em?"

"Naw, they're just for sport."

"I'm liking them better all the time," Dwight said.

There was a telltale tug on Jeremy's line and he began reeling. Dwight watched as he hoisted a wriggling fish into the boat.

"Look," Jeremy said as he held up a sixteen-inch blue-striped grunt. "Caught another one of those suckers. Good eats tonight."

Dwight nodded and tried not to think about how much he hated fish.

CHAPTER THIRTY-SEVEN

Robert's Cay

Ginger followed so closely on Matt's heels that he tripped, and then she disappeared. He had poured a half gallon of water into a bowl from one of the bottled jugs, emptied a can of dog food onto a dinner plate, and repeatedly offered them to her. Thus far, Ginger had not attempted to eat or drink but merely sniffed, whined, and backed away.

The morning had been productive. He had located some useful items that would serve him well in an emergency.

God, what can those bastards be up to? Why in the hell don't they just bring Alex to the Island and ask for their damn drugs?

Because they had murdered Shorty and Fletch, Matt surmised that they intended to wear him down, catch him, torture the information out of him, and kill him. If they had wanted to make a straight-forward exchange, they would have already done so. His mind worked overtime, battled to keep his Hanoi demons in check.

During the morning he had explored every one of the compound's vacant buildings and hidden several weapons. He was thinking more clearly. The sound of the rolling surf had soothed his nerves, and the normalcy of locating essentials had calmed him.

At least I have their damn drugs, which must be worth something. They won't just walk away. They're going to have to deal with me sometime. But they cannot, cannot be allowed to catch me; otherwise, I will be vulnerable to whatever torture they come up with, and I can be broken, like I was in Hanoi.

After a nap and an hour wasted trying to fix the fuse box, he saw that night was drawing down, signaling the end of yet another day at Robert's Cay and another day without Alex. He would not allow himself to consciously think of her, but sometimes, when he least expected it, an image of Alex would interrupt his thoughts like a flasher and leave him gaping. "Oh, God," he often said, but stopped at that point. He did not want to confront his worst fears by articulating them.

As the sun's rays diminished, Matt huddled just inside the open doorway of the room that had sheltered him the preceding night. He watched sandpipers tiptoe along the water's edge as a slice of yellow moon appeared in the starry sky. For the first time in fifteen years, he craved a cigarette.

When darkness fell, he was tense but more confident than he had been the night before.

Now they are the prey and I'm the hunter.

Ginger had returned and sat by Matt's feet.

Because of the waning light, he did not see the power boat at first, but the sputter of its outboard motor alerted him. There it was, a small run-about, no more than twenty feet, nosing its way to shore. Matt stepped back, and Ginger, startled by his sudden furtiveness, bolted around the corner of the building.

His eyes fixed on the gray shore, Matt observed two men wrestle the boat to higher ground and another plant a bow anchor deep in the sand. They were at least a hundred yards away, making it impossible for him to hear their voices. Although he had bolstered his confidence by telling himself that he had the upper hand, he recognized that the game plan, for the most part, belonged to them. He ran when they turned and headed in his direction.

Clutching his shotgun, he hid inside one of the unoccupied buildings as the threesome, clad in dark clothing, fanned out in the courtyard. One man vanished inside the main building while the other two ran in opposite directions in the compound. It appeared that they were going to conduct a thorough search for him.

Okay, here we go. Here we go...

After a long silence, he heard a noise in an adjacent building. A door's rusty hinges complained as it was thrust inward. His heart began to pick up beats, steadily rising from light taps to a heavy drum roll. His throat tightened; a bead of sweat trickled down his spine.

I hope I can surprise them. If not, I'm screwed.

Then came the slap of running feet on the cement walk outside his hiding place. The footfalls stopped in front of the doorway. Matt held his breath.

The knob rattled just before the door swung open. A figure hesitated at the threshold before he stepped inside. Scantily silhouetted by the moonlight, he seemed to be fumbling with something. Matt did not hear the telltale click of a flashlight but its narrow beam suddenly blinked at him from the doorway. He ducked just as a thread of light slid past his head.

The man stepped inside and continued illuminating each corner and along the floor. Matt heard the unmistakable sound of a hammer being cocked. Sensing that he was about to be discovered, Matt jumped up and fired his twelve-gauge. The force of the blast slammed the gun butt against Matt's shoulder and thrust the intruder backward onto the walkway. Trembling, Matt darted outside, jumped over the body sprawled on the sidewalk, and sprinted to another building. Once inside, he stood panting, his back pressed against a wall for support.

An ominous hush blanketed the yard for several minutes, at least until a man dashed from the main building. Matt watched him as he crouched and scurried across the courtyard.

One down and two to go, unless they make it clear they want to deal. Otherwise…

The man who had jogged to the far end of the courtyard when the trio first arrived was nowhere to be seen. His conspicuous absence added to Matt's tension. His eyes ached from probing the darkness for some sign of him.

Matt saw a furtive movement in the courtyard. A man darted to the main building and entered. Given a choice at that moment, Matt might have fled. The *Amani* was a means of escape. He imagined himself crashing through the pines, frantically swimming to the mooring.

Matt huddled in a room with yellowed newspapers strewn among stacks of discarded desks and broken wooden chairs. Had he not been there previously when the sun was high and the room well lighted, he would not have been able to navigate the quarters so skillfully in the dark.

Again he heard footsteps, cautious, furtive, followed by the door slowly swinging open. Fresh air flowed into the room, rustling the newspapers on the floor just inside the entrance. Matt remained motionless, careful not to make a sound. This intruder did not brandish a light but stood silently with his head cocked. Matt heard him breathing. After a few seconds, the man stepped forward, then yelled. Matt sprang from behind a desk and fired. The assailant managed only one wild shot in Matt's direction just before the buckshot hit him.

Earlier that day, Matt had noticed a crawl space between the floor and the ground. He had sawed a hole through the wooden floor, one wide enough for a man's body to fall through, and covered the opening with newspapers. When Matt had galloped inside the building, he had been careful to leap widely across the threshold.

Now it's just him and me.

The air, though somewhat cooler since the sun had set, still felt warm and oppressive. Unlike the night before, Matt was grateful for the obscurity which enabled him to move from one building to another cloaked in darkness. He wasn't certain the last man was in the main building, but that was his best guess.

Matt circled around the back, slipped through the broken glass door where he had fled the preceding night. He grimaced at the sound of shards crunching beneath his feet. With a blind man's eye, he saw the hallway as it appeared in daylight and remembered how many doors opened on each side. His feet were leaden, reluctant to carry him toward the last attacker who awaited to ambush him somewhere within the unlighted building. The walls he touched were damp; the air he breathed, heavy and foul. Unable to see what lay ahead, Matt felt as if he were inching down the throat of a hideous beast. He crept toward the radio room counting each door as he passed. Just beyond the last door, someone jabbed what felt like a gun barrel against his back and ordered him to halt.

"Gringo, I suggest you stop or I'll be forced to kill you where you stand."

Matt closed his eyes, hesitated before he said through clenched teeth, "Yes, and if you do, you can kiss your precious drugs good bye."

Out of the corner of his eye, Matt saw the glow of a light.

"Drop your weapon!"

Matt paused, released the twelve-gauge.

He was ordered to move straight ahead and shoved toward the radio room.

I can't let this happen. Not again. I'd rather die.

Matt pivoted, charged, connected with his left shoulder. The light clattered to the floor and went out. In the narrow hallway they slammed each other against doors and walls. Their grunts were magnified inside the empty corridor. The battle, though frenzied, was brief. Matt felt the man's hot breath on his face just before he was kneed in the groin, struck on the head, and rendered unconscious.

CHAPTER THIRTY-EIGHT

Robert's Cay

"What the hell?" Dwight said.

Using binoculars, he had observed the arrival of a small power boat which had beached on the northern shore of Robert's Cay. Three figures had disembarked and made their way to the Tracking Station compound where they disappeared from his field of vision. Shortly thereafter, Jeremy and he had heard what sounded like a gunshot. At seven forty-five, they heard more reports. Both of the agents had remained topside while they attempted to capture a glimpse of the activity on the Cay.

"There seems to be some kind of misunderstanding, wouldn't you say? I wonder if they've killed Spencer," Jeremy said.

"Could be."

"I must say, the bad boys save us a lot of trouble by killing each other."

"You got that straight."

"Think we ought to call this in?"

"I suppose. We'd better let the boss know what we've run into. Trouble is, we don't really know ourselves. We're speculating. We could ask those men at the Tracking Station but everybody and his mother would hear us on the radio. I guess we could just call them to see if they're still alive."

"I'll try to raise 'em," Jeremy said before he stepped inside the cabin. After a few minutes he returned, shrugged his shoulders. "No answer. What do you think?"

"I think somebody's in trouble up to his eyeballs but we can't do anything about it. We'd blow our cover."

"Well, I'll call the boss and tell him what's up, or what we think is up," Jeremy said.

"What say we take a little dinghy ride tomorrow morning, check out the carnage," Dwight said.

"I guess, so as long as we're casual about it. Can't hurt to play tourist and have a look around. Keep your eyes open and let me know if you see anything."

Jeremy went below to call the Miami office while Dwight continued scanning the beach. He was glad he was not the American who was somewhere on the Island with the threesome from the power boat.

He's probably dead by now. The dude is way out of his league.

CHAPTER THIRTY-NINE

Morgan Cay

Raoul stood up to greet Pablo Martinez and Eduardo Ocha, who had just arrived from Miami.

"El Jefe," Eduardo said as he walked into Raoul's open arms, "it's good to see you. And you're looking so well."

"Sí, prosperity agrees with you," Pablo said as he waited to embrace Raoul.

The two visitors sat down in the armchairs in front of Raoul's desk. Raoul laced his hands and rested them on the desk top. Pablo was red-faced and bleary-eyed, his sparse gray hair porcupine from wind gusts. He looked at Raoul from beneath bushy brows.

"So, all is well?" Eduardo said as he set his eel-skin briefcase across his knees.

"*Muy bien*," Raoul said as he reached for a silver box and lifted the lid to offer a cigar to his guests.

"*Gracias*," the men said as each removed a long Havana cigar from the box. Raoul took one for himself, ran it beneath his nose.

"Talk to me," Raoul said.

"Business is good," Eduardo said. "The Americans cannot live without their cocaine. The demand is steady. We supply. Capitalism at its finest. As you predicted, we can undermine them from within. We don't need armies. Ah, such fools. They're committing suicide."

"What we've known all along," Raoul said after he finished lighting his cigar. "We should thank Fidel. Without him we could not have organized so quickly."

Eduardo extracted several documents from his briefcase and looked at Raoul through thick lenses. "Although sales are down a bit, the quarterly figures still look good, El Jefe. This year the Cartel has received thirty-two point four billion dollars from the United States. Fourteen billion came from the sale of cocaine; seven point four billion from marijuana; nine point eight four billion from heroin; and one point forty-four from other drugs. We still control seventy-five to eighty percent of the market."

"How far down are we?" Raoul said.

"Year before last, we received forty-one point twenty-eight billion; last year, thirty-nine billion point eighty-four."

"This continuing decline concerns me," Raoul said as he leaned back in his chair. "How do you account for it?"

"Many reasons, El Jefe," Eduardo said. "First of all, there is a glut on the market. We've got to dry up the supply, manipulate the price higher. Second, the Bogota Cartel has eased in on our territory."

"Your recommendations?"

"As I said, it's time to hold back so we can demand a higher price. We must also interrupt their shipments whenever and wherever we can."

"I suggest that we infiltrate the Bogota Cartel on a grander scale. We need more inside men to inform us if we are to effectively undermine their operation," Pablo said.

"I agree," Eduardo said. "I also think that we need to get a better foothold in the Tokyo Cartel. Yakamura is losing control. He's busy watching his back right now. We should take advantage. He's vulnerable."

"Yes, always go for the soft underbelly," Raoul said, nodding.

"And," Eduardo said, "the Mexicans have been marketing their black tar heroin very cheaply. They are selling in twenty-two U. S. cities, and quite successfully, I might add. Approximately eighty pounds is distributed monthly, worth more than seven million. This heroin is highly desired because they are selling it at such a high level of purity, and, as you know, this drug is most addictive."

"How are they bringing it into the country?" Raoul said.

"Well, El Jefe," Eduardo said, "they are using young girls and men in their sixties, who travel alone. They carry one to two pounds concealed in their waistbands or in the back of boom box radios."

"Clever," Raoul said as he tapped his cigar ashes into the crystal ashtray on his desk. "I'll call a special meeting this month so we can address these issues."

"That is good, El Jefe," Pablo said.

Eduardo nodded.

"Forgive me, would you like a drink?" Raoul said as he pressed a button beneath his desk.

"Sí, pisco, would be nice," Eduardo said.

"Beer for me," Pablo said.

A willowy Spanish woman opened the door to the office and peeked inside.

"Sí, Señor Chavez, you called?"

"Yes, Margarita, some drinks for me and my guests. A pisco for Señor Ocha and a Heineken for Señor Martinez. Another cognac for me. Open another bottle of Hennessy."

"Sí, Señor."

The servant girl gently shut the door behind her.

"Is that Consuelo's daughter?" Pablo said.

"Sí," Raoul said. "She is a fine young woman now."

"A lovely girl," Eduardo said. "She will be marrying soon?"

"Yes, my driver, Manuel. The wedding is in three months. You're welcome to come if you wish."

"I would like to deflower the girl myself," Pablo said with a smirk.

Raoul narrowed his eyes. "Please, gentlemen, let's focus on the business at hand."

Pablo cleared his throat, sat up straighter in his chair. "I apologize, El Jefe. I forget my manners."

"*No te preocupes,*" Raoul said with a wave of his hand. "Let's continue."

"As you know there has been much trouble at home," Eduardo said. "The Americans have put a lot of pressure on our government to have us arrested and our operation dismantled. All and all, we have made a good fight. I thought it might interest you to know that in the last year, 240 judicial employees, twenty-five of whom were Supreme Court Judges, have been assassinated. Three candidates in the last presidential race were eliminated. We have also killed twenty-three journalists and have bombed two leading newspapers."

"It should be clear that we will not be stopped," Raoul said. "If need be, we will escalate the violence. I am not opposed to killing babies if it serves our purpose."

"Remember that traitor, that journalist, de Munos?" Pablo said.

"Of course," Raoul said. "That idiot who won't quit while he's ahead."

"We don't have to worry about him anymore," Eduardo said.

"That's right," Pablo said and snickered. "He won't be writing any more columns."

Raoul raised his eyebrows.

"Gonzalez shot him yesterday, in the Latin section of Queens, in New York, in a restaurant. I wish I'd been there to see that bastard get blown away with Gonzalez's 9mm semiautomatic. Kaboom! Kaboom!" Eduardo said and laughed.

"Gonzalez, the invisible man, walked in and out. And, of course, nobody saw a thing," Pablo said.

"Excellent news," Raoul said as he put out his cigar.

"Well," Eduardo said as he leafed through the papers in his lap, "where was I? Oh, yes, I have deposited another five million dollars into your Luxembourg account and two million in your bank in the Caymans. I'll have a new total of your assets and their location in writing to you by the end of this month. Suffice it to say you are a very wealthy man. The Americans are frantic to find out what you have but the bank's secrecy laws protect you."

"We do have some bad news," Pablo said.

"Yes?" Raoul said.

There was a light tap at the door and Margarita entered carrying a tray of drinks. The glasses clinked against each other as she walked across the room.

"Senors," she said as she lowered the tray within their reach, "your drinks."

"*Muchas gracias, Señorita,*" Eduardo said.

"*Sí, gracias,*" Pablo said.

Margarita placed a napkin on the desk before carefully setting down a snifter of cognac in front of Raoul.

"Will there be anything else, Señor Chavez?"

"*No es nada,*" he said and smiled at her.

"You have only to call," she said with her head bowed.

"*Gracias,* Margarita, that will be all."

After she left the room, Pablo remarked, "What a beauty."

Raoul looked at him and frowned before he said, "The bad news?"

"Yes," Eduardo said. "The bad news is that over seventy of our inside employees at Kennedy International Airport have been arrested for smuggling. As you know, this has been a very successful operation for us. Our people have been diverting our marked packages to domestic flights and using their licenses to bypass Customs. We have our best attorney at work on the matter and because of technicalities, mostly errors on the part of the arresting officers, we should be able to get most of them off. We can put them to work in other airports."

"The good news," Pablo said, "is that we have at least forty more employees at J.F.K. who will take up the slack. There will be little interruption in business."

"How were they discovered?" Raoul said.

"There was a spy, an agent of the Custom's Service who infiltrated the operation. He posed as a baggage handler. Some of our people talked a little to freely," Eduardo said.

"I want him and his family executed," Raoul said quietly. "Wife, children, parents. Everyone."

"As you wish, El Jefe. I'll see to it," Eduardo said.

"Anything else?" Raoul said.

"That American politician's body has been found and identified," Pablo said. We…"

"I said I wanted him to disappear. Permanently," Raoul said.

Raoul frowned, rubbed his chin.

"Jose put his body in the trunk and pushed his car into a water-filled gravel pit, thirty feet deep. The body was underwater for nine days. Who would have thought…" Eduardo said.

"Somebody should have. What happened?" Raoul said.

"They shouldn't have been able to get prints, not after nine days. Jose had cut off his head, buried it in another state. No dental record ID if you don't have a head," Eduardo said.

"Get to the point," Raoul said, tapping an index finger on the desk top.

"Some hot-shot pathologist in Birmingham," Pablo said, "somehow removed the skin from the stiff's hands, sent it to someone, another pathologist in Alabama somewhere. Word has it the second guy used a pair of rubber gloves, slipped them over the skin, and was able to make some impressions."

"Got his prints," Raoul said.

"Amazing stuff what those pathologists can do," Eduardo said.

"Make sure this information is shared with Gonzalez and the others. Next time they need to cut off the hands and feet as well, discard them elsewhere."

The men were silent for a few minutes.

"Well," Eduardo said, "our chemists have finally perfected smokable heroin and it should do for heroin what crack has done for cocaine. We will have a whole new, and, I might add, lucrative market. Even as we speak it is being distributed."

"That should turn things around," Raoul said.

"Something else, El Jefe," Pablo said. "You will like this. The former nuns from Quito are proving to be good mules. They strap packets of cocaine to their legs and waddle right through Miami Customs. So far they have made twenty trips averaging one point two million street value each. They use different passports each time, of course, and thus far no one has gotten suspicious. As you pointed out when we began, who is going to strip search a nun?"

Raoul reared back in his chair and laughed.

"More drinks, gentlemen?"

CHAPTER FORTY

Robert's Cay

Matt opened his eyes and saw nothing.

Dark, black. Where am I?

A putrid odor flooded his nostrils. Beneath him, he felt things, some hard, some flaccid. Raising his hands, his fingertips encountered a rigid, damp surface.

Can't breathe.

Soft things squirmed on his skin, tickled his exposed neck and arms. He remained motionless.

Subconsciously, he knew where he lay, but he couldn't face the horror all at once. His mind protected him, let reality slowly seep in. He contemplated his predicament like one adrift in shark-infested waters.

Interminable seconds passed.

Air. Need air.

Inside his head the burning truth began to take form and shape, assume a life of its own. He moved.

Beneath him, he knew, were body parts.

Probably what's left of Shorty and Fletch. The stench? They are decaying. The tickling sensation? Maggots. Total darkness? I'm in the freezer. Trapped!

A scream exploded from his throat as he shoved against the lid.

Open! Open! God, help me! Open!

He couldn't make it budge. Not a fraction of an inch. His cries became dull inside the chest as he struggled to escape. The metal top, as unyielding as a coffin lid buried six feet below ground, wouldn't give. He felt faint.

Got to get out! Can't breathe! Can't move!

His conscious mind wanted to abandon him, go somewhere safe. He hung on to his sanity by a thread of hope.

They won't let me die. They can't. Unless, oh, God, unless they found the bags and don't need me anymore.

Minutes passed. An eternity. His lungs worked to sustain him. His hands, bruised and bleeding, pushed and clawed at the lid. His head throbbed.

Got to get out! Get out! Get out!

When unconsciousness and death seemed imminent, the freezer door opened and fresh, cool air washed over him. He sat up, gulped in as much oxygen as his lungs could hold.

"So, my friend," a man said from a few feet away, "you don't like keeping company with the dead. And I don't blame you. Rather a messy business."

Matt looked in the direction of the voice but could not see beyond the darkness.

"I will release you now but for how long? That depends on you."

Matt continued sucking in air, savoring each breath. A maggot nosed his neck until he slapped it away and climbed out of the compartment. His legs wobbled as he clung to the rim of the freezer.

"Oh, my, you don't look so good," the unidentified man said as he fixed a beam of light on Matt's face. "Just a little pale, I think."

Matt collected his thoughts as he stood gasping.

"This way, gringo! Come on! In here!"

Surprised he could still walk, Matt stumbled into the R & R room.

"There," the man said as he aimed the light beam at a chair, "sit down."

Matt fell into one of the metal chairs and placed his hands on the table in front of him.

"So," Matt said and cleared his throat, "what now?"

"Yes, my friend, what now?"

"My wife, where is she? Is she all right?"

"The American woman? Very pretty."

Matt tensed; his fingers twitched.

"You will see your wife after you show me where our cocaine is."

Matt contemplated for a minute before he said, "Here's the deal. You bring my wife to me, alive and well, and I will show you where I've hidden the bags."

"Gringo, you're a fool and in no position to make demands. How would you like to rejoin your friends in the freezer?"

"This can be a simple exchange, my wife for your cocaine. I don't understand why you people are making this so difficult. You're all fucking nuts."

"It's not that simple. If you don't cooperate, here and now, something unpleasant may happen to your wife. It is not for me to decide. I am supposed to return with you and the coke. You are to meet El Jefe. He will decide about your woman."

"That's a goddamn crock of shit. I'm as good as dead the minute you find those bags and you know it, so let's cut the crap."

"I can see that I didn't leave you in the compartment long enough. Maybe you need to get back in for a while longer."

"You'll have to kill me first because I'm not going to climb into that fucking freezer like a fucking good little boy."

"Listen, gringo, I have no quarrel with you. I have my orders. I am supposed to return with you and the cocaine. I have no choice. Do you understand?"

"Absolutely."

Pen, if you cooperate, you will be given the lenient and humane treatment.

"If I show up without the cocaine, I will be disgraced, possibly executed. I am in, shall we say, a difficult position."

"Somehow I can't get real worked up about that."

The man stepped behind Matt and said, "Put your hands behind your back."

Matt hesitated.

"Put your hands behind your back I said!"

Matt crossed his hands behind him, felt the cold metal chair touch his forearms and a cord wound around his wrists.

Matt snapped his head backward throwing the man off balance. The chair overturned, clattered to the floor. He shook off the binding, hurled himself at the hard, stocky body that reeked of cologne and perspiration. They thrashed about the room crashing into chairs, the table, through the open kitchen door and onto the linoleum. Matt felt the man's teeth sink into his right arm. He gouged the man's eyes, yanked his hair. Finally, Matt climbed on top of him and choked him so thoroughly that he ceased moving. Matt fell away and lay on his back, panting. The respite was brief. The man coughed, began to revive. Matt crawled across the floor and groped outside the kitchen door for the flashlight that had been knocked over when the struggle began. Finding it in a corner, he picked it up and panned the room. The man's automatic lay underneath an overturned chair, where it had fallen during the fight. Matt scooped it up and pointed the light at the prone figure that lay gasping on the kitchen floor.

"On your feet!" Matt said.

The man looked bewildered.

"Up! Now!"

The man sat up, rubbed his throat.

"I said, get up, asshole!"

The man rose and proceeded to straighten and brush off his clothes and shoes and rearrange his hair. As the stranger preened, Matt watched him with amazement.

CHAPTER FORTY-ONE

Morgan Cay

"We have a new warehouse in the panhandle of Florida, somewhere off highway 98," Eduardo said. "A perfect front. We…"

The sounds of heavy footfalls and a woman's high-pitched voice resonated outside the office before the door burst open. Eduardo and Pablo turned to peer around their chairs. Raoul looked toward the door with a question in his eyes as Jorge barged into the room and rushed to his desk.

"El Jefe," he said panting.

"What?" Raoul said quietly.

"Things, uh, didn't go as planned."

Jorge paused for a moment, his chest heaving, and tried to catch his breath.

"The American…"

"Is he dead?" Raoul said.

"No, not yet, but Luis is dead and maybe Jesus. I know the American shot Luis. I saw his body. We didn't expect…"

"You didn't expect what?"

"We, uh, didn't count on the gringo to be so... I thought he would throw himself at my feet after we butchered the two men at the Station and didn't contact him as he probably expected. He's had some time to become anxious about his wife, soften up. But no, he hides, he shoots, he..."

"You mean," Raoul said standing up, "that one simple-minded, pampered American can outwit you?"

Jorge stared at a tic that appeared on the right side of Raoul's face.

"I tell you, El Jefe, this man is loco. He doesn't behave with caution. He..."

With a wave of his hand, Raoul gestured for Jorge to be silent.

"Gentlemen," Raoul said to Eduardo and Pablo, "I apologize for this interruption, but more pressing business forces me to end our meeting. Please allow Margarita to show you to your rooms."

"No matter, El Jefe," Eduardo said. "It grows late and I'm not as young as I used to be. The sheets will feel good."

"*Sí, buenas noches,*" Pablo said.

"*Buenas nochas.* We'll continue our discussion tomorrow."

After Eduardo and Pablo closed the door behind them, Raoul stood with his hands on his hips and stared at Jorge. Jorge glanced down at the floor.

"So, Jorge," Raoul said sitting down, "what am I to do? Can I no longer trust you with the simplest task?"

"No, no, El Jefe, of course you can trust me. Have we not been friends since we were boys in Medellin?"

"I cannot allow friendship to interfere with business. You know that."

"Of course..."

"Until now, I have placed my complete confidence in you. Now I am not so sure that you are able to do your job. Is it the crack that you've come to love so much? How addicted are you? Enough to affect your work?"

"No, El Jefe, I have everything under control. I hardly ever use it now."

"Listen closely, Jorge, because I am not going to repeat myself. You will kill the American and bring me the cocaine without further delay. Is that clear?"

"Perfectly clear, El Jefe. I already have a good plan."

"I hope you do, Jorge, because my patience is wearing thin, and my confidence in you is eroding."

"I will take care of the matter. You should not concern yourself."

"I don't intend to. See that the job is done. I want my cocaine and I want the gringo dead. It's quite simple."

"Yes, El Jefe."

"And Jorge…"

"Yes?"

"What is that putrid smell on you?"

"It's a long story."

"No details, please."

CHAPTER FORTY-TWO

Robert's Cay

Sunlight filtered into the room where Matt lay sprawled across a yellowed mattress. Ginger lifted her head, cocked her ears, and looked in his direction when he sat up and rubbed his eyes. Sleep had come in the early morning after fatigue had gotten the upper hand.

"Hungry, girl?"

Ginger eased up, rested on her hindquarters, and stretched her front legs. She made a whimpering sound in her throat when he started for the door.

"I know just how you feel."

After shifting the file cabinet that he had muscled in front of the door the preceding night, he went down the hall to the bathroom to relieve himself. The only sounds he heard were those he generated. Ginger sat by the commode and stared up at him with soulful brown eyes. His thoughts held more questions than answers.

Why don't they bring Alex to the Island? Could she be... When are they coming back?

He had explored the entire complex and located several good hiding places. Matt knew that it would be foolish to go anywhere near the site where he had buried the cocaine. They might be watching him, and he couldn't afford to lose his leverage.

After splashing water on his face, he fed Ginger, drank half a can of warm orange juice and downed a package of Planter's salted peanuts. Peering through the windows, he saw no sign of life other than the gulls promenading outside the screen door.

Leaving by the front, he made his way to the first man he had shot. The body lay on its back, its startled eyes fixed skyward. Matt searched the man's pockets and came up empty. No ID, not even a wallet. The man was young, no more than nineteen or twenty, and wore several gold chains and a top-of-the-line Rolex watch. Flies hummed about the man's body and feasted inside his gaping chest. Matt hauled the corpse by its heels to an empty cistern and dropped the remains inside with an echoing thud.

The second body lay slumped over in a Mexican siesta position. Matt thought a sombrero would have rounded out the picture nicely. The close-range blast from the twelve gauge had almost disemboweled him. He, too, was young and wearing expensive jewelry. Matt carried the dead man over his shoulder to the cistern where he deposited the body and took off down the path through the trees to the beach below. The *Amani*, still at her mooring, drifted in the light air. She seemed to be waiting for life to return to her.

Would it ever?

The children, playing farther up the beach, looked at him when he appeared on the shore and beckoned to them. They remained distant, wary of him, and whispered to each other.

"Hey!" he called and motioned with his hand.

The Bahamian boy, the one who had spoken to him the day before, said something to the group before breaking away and slowly walking in Matt's direction.

"What do you want?" the boy called from a safe distance.

"More information."

"What's that on your shirt?"

Matt looked down at the corpses' blood on his T-shirt.

"Nothing. I cut myself shaving."

"You have money?"

Matt fumbled in his pockets and found only a bill and a few coins.

"I have a dollar and three pennies."

"All right," the boy said, moving closer.

"Have you seen any strangers, other than myself, on the Island this morning?"

"Yes, I have."

Matt stiffened. After last night, nothing would surprise him.

"When did you see them? How many? Where are they now?"

"That's a lot of questions," the kid said. "How much money did you say you have?"

"I gave you my best offer."

The boy rubbed his forehead and looked off in the distance.

"Okay, there are two men, white men, who've been staying on a big boat on the other side of the Island. They're behind you right now, coming up the beach."

Matt turned and saw two men in bright bathing suits strolling together along the shore. One was overweight and panting. Sunlight glistened on his hairy arms and shoulders. He had on a gaudy orange and white suit and wore pink and yellow, amphibious shoes dotted with tar. His companion, leaner and shorter, sported a close-cropped, conservative haircut and was clad in baggy, lime-green surfing trunks. The two gave him a cursory glance before they stopped to inspect a sea shell. Matt backed away leaving the boy standing on the beach.

The men squatted and picked up a few shells before they resumed their stroll. The lean one had long delicate feet that barely left an imprint in the sand. The heavyset fellow, all fuzz and bulk, etched trenches behind him as he plodded along.

Matt peeked at them from behind a tree as his heartbeats accelerated to a rapid thumpa, thumpa, thumpa. He watched and listened.

They look like tourists. Can that be? Ordinary tourists?

They stopped not far from where Matt had melted into the pines, looked in his direction, and murmured to each other. Matt, unable to hear what they were saying, stood motionless, poised to fight or flee.

When the strangers turned and started up the path to the compound, Matt raced through the trees ahead of them and hid behind one of the outbuildings near the end of the trail. They appeared within Matt's view a few minutes later. Obviously, they weren't in a hurry.

And, if they're assassins, they don't seem to be anxious to take care of business.

The chunky one spoke to his companion, who stepped away and positioned himself in front of one of the abandoned buildings. Matt noticed that the heavyset man carried a camera which dangled from a thin black strap around his neck. He held it up and suggested that the other man pose for a picture. The younger man ceased laughing and struck a solemn pose, standing stiffly with his hands at his sides. Frozen in time for a fleeting second, the camera blinked and captured his wooden image on film.

Tourists. They must be. But can I trust them? And will they be able to help?

They appeared unarmed, unless the younger one had a gun hidden in one of the pockets of his baggy trunks. They resumed their stroll, stopping from time to time to look at a plant or gaze at a dilapidated building. Matt followed just out of sight hoping to get within hearing range.

"…an oleander that…native to this area," Matt finally heard one of them say. "There…varieties…" The words, disjointed as they were, suggested that these were true, honest-to-God tourists, who only had an interest in Bahamian flora and fauna. Matt trembled as he resisted the temptation to run to them and blurt out all that had transpired. His time in Southeast Asia had taught him that things are seldom what they seem. A young girl begging for a chocolate bar might have a bomb tied to her back. For Ho Chi Minh, she would give her life and take many American soldiers with her. The interrogators, when assuming a more devious approach, would offer tea and meat in hopes the prisoner would weaken and tell them what they wanted to know. They hid behind a mask of kindness while planning all the while to pull your arms backwards until your shoulder blades touched and then hoist you in the ropes.

No, I must be very careful. Last night didn't work for them so maybe today they are trying a different method. It would be an ingenious move.

The men looked at the bloodstained sidewalk when they passed by. They stood over it for a moment, whispered to each other. The two glanced toward the main building, casually sauntered to the doorway, and stopped. The heavyset man tapped lightly on the door frame and stepped back. When there was no answer, he leaned forward, formed a sun-visor with his hands, and spoke into the screen.

"Hello!" he called. "Anybody home?"

Matt waited.

"Hello!" he said again.

The two talked for a moment, then turned and looked around. They shuffled their feet. The younger one stepped forward and banged on the door with his fist.

"Yoo-hoo!" he called. "Anybody home?"

The younger man thrust his hands in his pockets and positioned his weight on one foot.

After another brief conference, they headed toward the path that brought them up from the beach. As the two ambled down the trail, they stopped to study a stunted thatch palm and point at a curly-tailed lizard that scampered in front of them. As they neared the beach, they paused and looked behind them. When they turned around, Matt stood a few feet away with his shotgun pointed at them.

"Hold it," he said.

"Whoa," the younger one said, raising a palm.

"Turn around and put your hands behind your head."

"Sure, sure, whatever you say," the heavyset fellow said.

"If you intend to rob us," his companion said, "you're out of luck. We don't have any money with us."

"Turn around," Matt said. "Now."

Matt crouched and patted the younger one's pockets. One contained a bottle of sunscreen lotion.

"Okay," Matt said, "you can face me now."

They pivoted and looked at him. Although startled when they first saw him, neither looked terribly alarmed, and that disturbed Matt.

A tourist would be frightened. These guys are as blank-faced as seasoned poker players.

"Now, who are you and what are you doing here?" Matt said.

"We might ask you the same thing," the younger one said.

"Except I have the gun, and I'm asking the questions," Matt said.

We're on vacation," the older, heavyset man said. "Here to escape the hustle and bustle of Miami, get away from the traffic, the stress, the muggings."

Matt didn't smile at the man's feeble attempt to lighten the situation.

"This isn't a mugging," Matt said. "I just need to know who you are and what brings you here."

"He told you," the younger man said, "we're…"

"I know what he told me," Matt said. "It's just that I'm not sure I can believe you. You see, I…" he said and paused.

"Hey, buddy, you in some kind of trouble?" the older man said. "If so, maybe we can help."

Matt looked directly at the man's eyes.

"How can I be sure that you're who you say you are?"

"We have ID on our boat," the heavyset man said and pointed east. "It isn't far. We could get it for you if it would make you feel any better."

Matt agonized. Dare he trust them?

"All right, one of you," Matt said and pointed to the heavyset man, "you, go to your boat and bring back some ID. Your friend and I will wait for you at the Tracking Station."

The strangers looked at each other, and the husky man said, "Well, I'll hurry so we can clear things up."

"Go ahead, but be quick about it," Matt said.

Matt and the other man watched as the red-haired fellow stumbled down the path before Matt motioned to his companion to lead the way up the trail to the compound. Without speaking, they walked toward the Station. Matt checked his watch and estimated that it should take the big boy no more than thirty minutes to dinghy to his boat, retrieve their ID, and return to the compound. He had not decided what he would do if the man didn't come back.

"You're an American," the stranger said as he sat down on a step outside one of the buildings.

"Yeah," Matt said.

"You here on a boat?"

"Yeah," Matt said and raked a hand through his hair.

"Is that blood on your shirt?"

"I…never mind."

"Are you alone?"

"Why do you want to know?"

"No reason in particular, just making conversation."

"Be quiet. I'm trying to think. We can talk later, after your friend gets back. I should say if he gets back."

"Oh, he'll come back. He's a stand-up guy."

"You better hope so."

"There are two men who work here," the man said and pointed to the main building.

"How do you know that?"

We've been here before. We come this way every year, sort of an annual hiatus from work."

"Good for you."

"You're awfully uptight. Won't you tell me what's wrong?"

"No. Can't you shut the fuck up for a minute?"

"Yeah, sure. Fine."

In exactly thirty-five minutes, the red-haired man appeared at the top of the hill, his chest heaving, his face flushed.

"Here," he said waving two wallets in the air.

Matt motioned for him to sit on the step next to his buddy and said, "Toss 'em over."

The man complied and looked with raised eyebrows at his companion. The younger man shook his head.

Matt opened the first wallet and read the name on the Florida driver's license.

"You are Harold D. Ludlow?"

"Yeah," replied the red-haired man. "From Ocala, Florida, originally. I recently moved to Miami. I…"

"And you," Matt said, peering at the younger man, "you are Joseph P. Driver?"

"That's me, in flesh."

"What the P. stand for?"

"Piedmont. Piedmont after my great Uncle. It's a family curse."

Matt examined each wallet carefully not certain what he was looking for. He knew that he could not be absolutely sure about them no matter what he found. Both wallets contained social security cards, voter registration cards, library cards, copies of their birth certificates, several business cards, Visa cards, American Express cards, and pictures of twenty-something women. There were differing amounts of cash, but no more than a hundred dollars contained in each.

"That's funny," Matt said and looked at them. "You both have the same kind of ID in your wallets."

"We're close, you know, roommates," the one called Harold said. "We travel in the same circles. Been together a long time. We're just pals, though." he said and winked. "We both have regular girlfriends."

The other man grinned at his buddy's reference to their sexual predilection.

Matt tossed them their wallets.

"You don't want the money?" said the younger man, the one who had identified himself as Joseph Driver.

"No, Mr. Driver, if that's your real name. And I don't know why, but something doesn't feel right about you two."

Matt sighed and looked away for a moment.

"In any event," he said, looking back at them, "I have to trust someone, and you guys are the only game in town. The Bahamian police are, evidently, unresponsive to tourists in distress. You may not believe what I am about to say, but I'm running out of ideas and out of time. Let me tell you what happened to me, that is, to us."

Matt spent almost a half hour relating what had occurred over the last few days while both men listened and occasionally nodded. When Matt finished, they asked him to step away so they could confer privately for a moment. Matt decided that he had come this far and had no choice but to trust them.

Leaving them to discuss the matter, Matt headed for the beach to look around. He had been distracted with the two tourists for some time, and it would have been easy for a boat bearing bad tidings to come ashore without his knowing it. He felt relieved after talking with them even though he still had some misgivings.

They don't respond in a normal way. They weren't especially alarmed at having a shotgun thrust in their faces. Maybe I didn't look that threatening. Maybe this happens all the time in Miami. If they're hit men, they've had ample opportunity to do whatever it is they were hired to do.

The beach appeared lifeless except for a few sandpipers meandering along the shoreline. Although the sky was partly sunny, he noticed dark clouds forming in the west. From the path, the two men strode toward Matt with their brows lowered and their lips tight.

"Hey," Jeremy called to Matt. "Let's talk."

Matt met them halfway and as a trio, they strolled.

"We've made a decision," Jeremy said, placing his hand on Matt's shoulder.

Matt winced.

"What's the matter?" Jeremy said. "Are you hurt?"

"It's a little present from that guy I told you about. Actually, he bit me. It's nothing, really. Just sore. You were saying?"

"We've made a decision, one that could get us into a lot of trouble, but we do sympathize with your situation. You see…"

"You see," Dwight said, "we're undercover agents for the U. S. Drug Enforcement Administration."

Now it all made sense. Their manner, their response to him, their matching ID's.

"Agents," Matt said. "I see. Then you can help me?"

"Well, we can and we can't," Jeremy said. "We're here to do a surveillance job, nothing more. We're not supposed to do anything that will jeopardize our cover."

"That's right," Dwight said, "what we're doing is pretty important. These men who are making your life so miserable are small fish, piranha, if you will. We have bigger game in mind. We're reporting on drug activity, the names of the boats involved, and," the man confided in a hushed tone, "we're looking for Raoul Chavez, a high-powered drug lord from Colombia. We think he's back on Morgan Cay, an Island he owns and operates out of when he's in this part of the world."

"We have orders to be as inconspicuous as possible," Jeremy said. "That's why we move from Island to Island, so we really do look like tourists. The drug guys have patrols. They know which boat is anchored where and for how long. They keep up with our movements, probably better than we keep up with theirs. We watch. They watch. It's all part of the game."

"Yeah," Dwight said, "we pose as tourists and they pose as human beings."

"We're gonna pull anchor in a little while and move closer to Morgan Cay. We'll fish and swim, keep our eyes open," Jeremy said.

"Do you communicate with the DEA?"

"Yeah, sure," Jeremy said.

"Get me some help," Matt said. "Call in. Tell them that I'm an American citizen, whose wife has been kidnapped. God, I've already killed two men, and there are two more bodies in the main building."

The agents looked at each other and kicked the sand.

"Spencer, you aren't getting it," Dwight said. "We're not even supposed to be talking to you. We've already broken a dozen rules by revealing who we are and why we're here. How can we call in and report that we've revealed who we are and that we're helping you with an emergency?"

"An emergency? That's a tidy, civilized way to put it."

"Listen," Dwight said, "I don't know how to say this nicely so I'll just spit it out. You see, there are more lives at stake here than yours and your wife's. We can't endanger our mission or the lives of other agents. Besides, you're not even considered our responsibility once you leave U. S. soil."

"Hell, we're not gonna desert you," Jeremy said. "We are, after all, here, and trained for this sort of thing. You tag along with us and we'll help you get your wife back. We just have to come up with a viable plan that will save your butt and not blow our cover."

"You understand our predicament, don't you?" Dwight said.

"Jesus," Matt said, "I'm in the fucking Twilight Zone! I'm less than a hundred miles from the U. S. and no one, no police, no fucking DEA agents, will help me. God, you've got to know what kind of thugs I'm dealing with. The kindest thing I can say about them is that they're creative."

"That's another thing." Jeremy said. "There are three of us and hundreds of them. We've gotta be practical and careful. That doesn't mean we can't be effective."

"Hang with us," Dwight said. "We'll help you work this out."

"Yeah, we'll put our heads together and come up with something," Jeremy said.

Matt looked at the darkening clouds. Somewhere beyond his view, a violent storm was brewing. He wanted to rail at the heavens, curse God and everyone, for allowing the one person who he needed and loved to be taken from him. He felt as powerless to stop the bizarre chain of events that was unfolding as he was to halt the thunderstorm marching directly toward them.

CHAPTER FORTY-THREE

Morgan Cay

Jorge stood under the hot shower and slowly turned in a circle as the hot jets worked their magic. He had washed every inch of his body, rinsed and then scrubbed again. He couldn't escape the stench of rotting flesh. It seemed to have permeated the pores of his skin.

Damn that American for making me lie on top of a dead man! The filth! Those insects!

He picked up a stiff brush and began scouring the backs of his arms and legs.

Getting clean is not my worst problem. No, El Jefe is very angry with me, disappointed. I must make amends, and soon. I admit it, the gringo got the better of me this time, but I'll go back and kill him myself.

He began washing his hair.

At least I didn't deliver the gringo's ridiculous note. That bastard. He just wanted me to look foolish in El Jefe's eyes.

Although Jorge knew the message that Matt had given him for Raoul was shredded and its pieces scattered on the bottom of the Atlantic, the words were forever branded in his mind. It had read, "A simple exchange. Send a man next time."

I know, Jorge thought, I'll take Roberto and Juan with me. We'll put the gringo back in the freezer. The bodies will be especially ripe. I'll sit outside, listen to him scream. Later, when he stops crying, I'll open the lid, revive him. Yes, I'll bring him back from the dead, give him hope that his life will be spared, then slam it shut again and relive those wonderful moments. Jorge closed his eyes, sighed. I can prolong his agony indefinitely. He'll lose his mind before he loses his life. At the end, he'll tell me anything, beg me to kill him, like the others. And the gringo's wife, that whore, El Jefe will eventually grow weary of her, turn her over to me. It is just a matter of time. With my two hands I will define pain for her.

He imagined Alex's face, her pale slender neck. His fingers twitched in anticipation. He could almost feel the silk scarf in his hands.

Jorge stepped out of the shower and stood before the fogged mirror. When the glass cleared, he proceeded to examine his eyelids, his nose hair, and parted his lips to inspect his gums and teeth.

He lacked sleep and his eyes ached. When he entered his bedroom, he sat on the edge of the bed and opened a drawer in the night stand. Inside was a plastic bag filled with cocaine. He withdrew it, cradled it in his hand for a moment. Using a razor blade and a small hand mirror he carefully arranged the white powder into two slender lines one eighth of an inch wide and one inch long. He hesitated for a moment, prolonged the anticipation. He leaned over and inhaled the blow through a narrow glass tube.

He felt the first rush within three minutes but the full impact of the coke did not hit him until fifteen minutes later when it flooded his circulatory system. The neurons in his brain were stimulated again and again giving rise to intense physical pleasure. He no longer felt tired or hungry or afraid and was in total control of himself. Jorge felt perfect and unconquerable.

In less than an hour he would crash and have to return to the well to renew his euphoria. Later, when he tried to sleep, he would have to take

Quaaludes. In the meantime, he was pumped up and ready to kill. He left the house whistling. Jorge had a plan.

CHAPTER FORTY-FOUR

Morgan Cay

Raoul stood on the porch steps and waved good-bye to Eduardo and Pablo. He watched as Manuel opened the automobile trunk and tossed their overnight bags inside. Eduardo clutched his briefcase and carried it with him when he climbed into the back seat of the car. Pablo turned and raised his hand in farewell before Manuel closed the Lexus door and walked around to the driver's side. Consuelo, standing on the porch behind Raoul, waved to Manuel as they pulled away.

"Something for you, Señor?" she said.

"Sí, coffee. I'll take it out here."

Consuelo entered the house just as Margarita stepped outside. The two women exchanged glances.

"Good morning, Señor Chavez. You are well?" Margarita said.

"What? Oh, Sí," Raoul said.

"Alfredo wishes a word with you."

"Yes?" Where is he?"

"He waits out back. Shall I send him to you?"

"Sí, gracias."

Alfredo Gonzalez, wearing soiled army fatigues and carrying a Red Chinese AKA-47, climbed the steps to stand in front of Raoul.

"El Jefe, I'm sorry to disturb you but you told me to report the Senora's movements. I would have spoken to you earlier but you were meeting with the Senors."

"What about the Señora?"

"She left the house last night and tried to escape. She went to the boat dock."

"And you followed her?"

"Of course. It was a little past two. I knew that she could not get away. Where could she go? She did not know I was behind her."

"Well," Raoul said as he tapped a forefinger to his lips, "interesting that she thought we would not be watching her. Hopefully she has learned a valuable and painful lesson."

"We brought her back to the house."

"Was she…molested by anyone?"

"No, but she would have been had I not intervened. You know how… We weren't sure about your feelings on the matter so we left her alone."

"For now, I don't want her touched. Make sure everyone understands that."

"Of course, El Jefe."

"How did it go when you captured her?"

"She struggled, but not for long. It was most amusing. She was very weak, her feet were bleeding."

"I see. Gracias, Alfredo. A good job. Get some rest. Who will keep an eye on her while you are absent?"

"Diego. He's already out back."

"Very well. Take some time. You'll be needed later."

"Sí, El Jefe."

Raoul looked down, studied his clasped hands.

So, she tests. That's good. I admire courage.

Consuelo returned with black coffee and placed a cup and saucer on a glass-topped rattan table next to Raoul's chair.

"Tell Margarita to bring the woman to me," he said.

"As you wish, Señor."

Raoul sipped his coffee and listened to the birds chirp. On this rare occasion there was not a steady hum of airplane engines. He savored the quiet.

Alex, unsteady on her injured feet, came to the porch. She sat down across from Raoul as he motioned for her to do so and looked at him from behind heavy eyelids.

"So, Señora, you weren't tired last night and decided to take a little walk. That's good. Exercise is excellent for the body. And you are safe here, except for the dogs, of course. I assume that you didn't have an unfortunate encounter with my dogs last night?"

"Not the four-legged kind."

"Look at you. Such a mess. I hate to see a lovely woman in such a bad state."

"My looks are unimportant. I want to go back to my husband. I don't understand what you want from me. I've told you everything I know."

"I'm not certain what I want from you. How's that? But until I decide, I suggest that you stay in my good graces. If I were to turn you over to Jorge, you would soon wish you were dead. Your husband would never want to touch you again, I can assure you. Do you understand what I'm saying?"

"Yes."

"You are a beautiful woman, Alexandra. You interest me."

Alex's eyes flashed.

"I don't want to interest you. I, uh…"

"Say what's on your mind," he said as he finished his coffee. "Say it now. I'll permit it this time."

"God, where do I begin? I don't know what's with you people. You are like actors in a play pretending to be something you're not. You act civilized, yet you deal in drugs and murder. You're…you're beyond contempt. You're despicable. Monsters…"

Raoul leaned back and laughed.

"First of all, my dear Alexandra," he said after he regained his composure, "what do you know about drugs? Have you tried them?"

"No, and I haven't shot myself in the head to find out if it's fatal either."

"Take cocaine, for example. One snort and you are a changed human being. You're more confident and strong. You don't get tired. And, I might add, the sex is the best you will ever have. It would be the most exquisite thirty minutes of your life."

"You sound like a typical street thug."

"When was the last time you met a street thug?"

"You know what I mean. You're a…"

"Don't press your luck or I might tie off one of your arms and inject a little something in a vein. You'd thank me later, of course, but I prefer your company in its natural state for the moment."

Alex's eyes widened.

"As for our being beyond contempt, don't you think you Americans have drugs and murder? Such hypocrites! What about the poor people who are so oppressed and neglected? They have nothing. I have committed no crimes any worse than those perpetrated by your own people, and I'm not talking about drug pushers and the pimps. I'm thinking about your illustrious politicians. Is there a more sleazy, degenerate bunch of people anywhere? Where do you think all their power and money comes from? Their meager salaries? Ha!"

"Alexandra, I don't sell cocaine simply for the money. I have a greater plan. I want to flood the United States with drugs and accomplish what armies cannot. I will undermine your entire system and your country will crumble from within. I intend to let you Americans kill yourselves. You want to commit suicide? I'm happy to oblige you. One day there will be a new government, one that raises the poor to equality, and I will be in charge. Like your former esteemed President said, a new world order."

"Obviously, you're no different than those disgusting, power-hungry men you speak of."

"Perhaps, but I don't pretend to be anything other than what I am. And, I do care what happens to the poor. I know that I can be instrumental in making life better for them."

"How will life be better for them if they're so whacked out on drugs they will abandon or sell their own children for a fix?"

"Would you like some coffee? It's very good."

"Don't you see that if things go your way, you'll have a nation full of whacked-out, irresponsible addicts?"

"Will I? I intend to legalize drugs and educate the people as to their proper use. They'll be taught their limits. Drugs and medical care will be readily available to everyone."

"You're out of your mind. First of all, just say that you succeed in your plan and legalize drugs. What about the down side? What kind of citizens will you have when they have to be high to function? What kind of business leaders, teachers, clergy, and administrators will you have? They won't give a damn about anything but their habit."

"I disagree. I have faith that the masses can be enlightened."

"Addiction has no limits. It overrides reason. There's a saying I once heard that applies to drinking, but it is applicable here. The man takes a drink; the drink takes a drink; the drink takes the man. Substitute the word, drink, for the word drug."

"Have you finished your lecture?"

"Am I getting anywhere?"

"Don't be absurd. I have already thought about this many times, and I am convinced that I am right. You don't want any coffee?"

"No. I want to be with my husband. Now. I want to leave this Island as soon as possible and never see it again. I…"

"Save your breath, Alexandra. For now, you're not going anywhere. Return to your room until I send for you. I'll have Consuelo bring you something to eat and drink, fresh clothing. Clean yourself up. If you do not, I will have some of my men do it for you. Comprende?"

"You're disgusting," she said and stood up.

"Watch what you say to me, Alexandra. You need me to stay alive. Do you understand?"

"I'm tired."

"Go to your room and stay there until I send for you."

CHAPTER FORTY-FIVE

Robert's Cay

"You need to come with us," Jeremy said. "Don't you see, we can get you to Morgan Cay where they are probably holding your wife."

"No," Matt said as he shook his head. I'd better wait here until they get back. They're going to have to talk to me some time."

"Has it occurred to you," Jeremy said as he placed his hand on Matt's shoulder, "that you're screwed? They'll kill anyone that gets involved in their business, however innocent. They don't give a shit about that piss ant little bit of cocaine you have stashed somewhere. They're more concerned with saving their precious reputation and punishing you. Don't misunderstand. They'd like to get their drugs back, but more importantly, they want to send a message to anyone else who might interfere with their business."

"That's probably true," Dwight said. "Those dudes are rollin' and I do mean rollin' in dough. It's beyond our comprehension. Your best chance to get your wife back is to go to Morgan Cay and get her. Jeremy and I have talked it over and we have an idea."

"Yeah," Jeremy said, "we can anchor just off the Island and pretend we're having engine trouble."

"Hell, we can disable the engine for real if it becomes necessary. And if they get nosy we can show them the problem and humbly apologize for anchoring so close to their private Cay. I don't think they would shoot us for that," Dwight said.

"Naw," Jeremy said, "happens all the time. We haven't heard of any tourists on disabled boats disappearing. Those who do vanish without a trace usually are involved with drugs or have had the misfortune to come upon a drug exchange in progress."

"I don't know," Matt said. "What if they come back and I'm not here?"

"Listen," Jeremy said, "there's no telling what they'll try next. Being locked in a freezer with a corpse will be hard to top but I'm sure they're planning something equally unpleasant."

"Consider this," Dwight said, "once you get to Morgan Cay you might be able to talk to Raoul himself, or maybe you could swim to the Island, rescue your wife, and be back at the boat before they realize she's missing. They won't be expecting you to do anything as bold and reckless as that. And we'll help you, won't we Joseph?"

"Are your names really Harold and Joseph?"

"No," Jeremy said, "but those are the only names that you need to know. And remember, no matter what happens, we're counting on you not to mention anything about us. Got that?"

"I know the drill," Matt said.

"So what if they come back and you're gone," Jeremy said. "Big deal. Your boat will still be here. You might piss them off but they still need your wife as long as you're the only one who knows where their coke is."

"You have a point there," Matt said.

I can't jeopardize Alex's safety, but they need her to get the cocaine from me. It seems like a reasonable idea. This waiting is making me crazy, and, hell, I'm a sitting duck.

"So, what's it gonna be? You comin' with us?" Jeremy said.

"I suppose it makes sense. I want to be in the driver's seat for a change. I have felt so damn impotent. Goddamit, I have to do something."

"That 'a boy," Dwight said as he clasped Matt's arm. "Let's get movin.'"

"Wait," Matt said. "I have to go back to the Station and put out some dog food and water."

"What?" Jeremy said.

"That's another story. I'll meet you guys on the beach in fifteen minutes."

Matt jogged back to the compound and opened several cans of dog food and emptied two jugs of water into a large aluminum pot. Although he called her, Ginger failed to appear.

Gathering together a few essentials, his shotgun, sunglasses, knife, and wallet, he exited the building through the back door. He found the agents digging trails in the sand with their toes.

The dinghy ride to their boat was rocky. The wind and tide, acting as opposing forces, had kicked up three to four foot seas.

When Matt saw their power boat, he thought it looked rather small.

"Here's home," Dwight said.

"What's the name of your boat?"

"*Fishy Business*," Jeremy said.

"How appropriate," Matt said.

CHAPTER FORTY-SIX

Morgan Cay

Alex turned over on her back and looked up at the ceiling. A small black bug was inching from the center to the corner near the bathroom. She rolled over on her side and flinched when she saw Raoul sitting in a chair next to the bed. She wondered how long he had been waiting there, watching her.

"Rested?" he said.

"What do you want?"

"Want? I want to talk with you."

"What about?"

"Your future."

"I'm glad to hear that I have one," she said, sitting up. Alex raked her hand through her hair, looked away.

"I'm convinced that you don't know where my cocaine is hidden," he said, "and, well, there is plenty more where that came from."

A warning bell sounded in her head and her chest tightened.

"Your drugs must be worth a lot of money," Alex said as she eased over to the edge of the bed. "Surely."

"It's an insignificant amount," he said as he examined his manicured nails. "I have more money than I could possibly spend in a hundred life times. As you have probably surmised, the drug business is profitable."

Alex shook her head. Raoul seemed relaxed as he looked at her with his dark eyes.

"I was born in a town called Rio Negro in Colombia," he said. "It's a beautiful place, in the mountains. My father was a poor farmer who worked very hard just to survive. When I was only a boy I used to sell gravestones to help feed the family. Now I have a fleet of airplanes and over two hundred apartments in Miami. I also have a ranch in Bogota," he said. "It's a cattle ranch with over five thousand head. I will retire there one day."

This man thrives on his own importance. I must use this to my advantage. Maybe I can convince him that I can be trusted and that will enable me to escape.

"How big is your ranch?"

"Over twenty thousand acres. Can you imagine?"

"No, I can't. I'm impressed."

"The ranch has over three hundred champion horses."

"Amazing," said Alex, who walked to the dressing table and sat down. She turned on a lamp and looked at her reflection in the mirror. Her image appeared ghostly pale. She began to brush her hair.

"The ranch is truly a paradise, a haven. I am loved in Colombia. The people are my family, my children."

Alex nodded and continued brushing.

"And your relatives, where do they live?" Raoul said.

"My mother lives in Pensacola, Florida. My father, he, uh, died several years ago. And my husband, of course, we…"

"Yes, your husband," Raoul said rising. "Which brings me to the real reason I want to talk with you. I…" he said and stopped behind her. She watched him in the mirror, her eyes wide.

"I don't know how to tell you this, Alexandra, but, well, your husband…"

"What about him?" she said and stood up to face him. "What?"

"There is no easy way to tell you this, but the truth is your husband is, uh, dead."

Alex's knees buckled; she grabbed Raoul's arm to steady herself.

"How? When?"

Raoul held her by an elbow, guided her to the bed.

"Sit down," he murmured. "Let me get you a drink of water."

She heard water running from the tap in the bathroom sink and when he returned with a half-filled glass, she refused it.

"Your husband was foolish. He tried to leave the Island with the cocaine. My men had no choice. They…"

"Of course not," she said as her eyes flooded with tears. "He would have exchanged the cocaine for me! For me! There was no other way. I told you!"

Raoul's face became distant, his words muted.

"…gave them no choice," she heard him say from somewhere far away. "He…a gun."

"Leave me alone," she said. "Get out!"

"Of course, Alexandra. I…terrible shock…probably don't believe me, but…sorry for you." He patted her shoulder. "…will go now…talk later."

"Leave me alone."

"Of course."

She heard the door click shut after him.

Matt dead? It can't be true. Matt can't die. He's forever. He's all I have.

She would not give in to the feeling of hopelessness that clutched at her.

Could this be another cruel trick? A lie? But for what purpose? Raoul said the cocaine didn't matter. He said he believed that she did not know where his drugs were hidden. Would he lie to her about Matt? If so, why? Why?

She crawled beneath the covers and curled up in a tight ball. The house dissolved around her before she disappeared into safer world. She closed her eyes to everything.

CHAPTER FORTY-SEVEN

Robert's Cay

Jeremy gunned the Mercury engine before easing the throttle back to idle.

"I'll bet that goddamn anchor has gone to China," Dwight yelled over his shoulder.

"You can handle it," Jeremy said.

Dwight gripped the anchor line, pulled it in several lengths at a time, then waited for the boat to move forward. Each time he gathered in a few feet, the boat crept closer to the point where the plow was buried. The rough line chafed his palms.

"How's it comin'?" he heard Jeremy call from the stern.

"Almost got it up," he said, groaning, as he cinched down a bight on the cleat. The boat overrode it then snapped taught causing the bow to dip.

"Shit!" Dwight said, "we're gonna to have to run over this sucker and then pull it up. I told you it was in deep."

Jeremy thrust the throttle forward. The boat surged. When the bow passed over the anchor, the boat hesitated before it bobbed free. Dwight quickly gathered in the line and hoisted the plow topside. He signaled a thumbs up to Jeremy, who turned the boat toward the channel. As they departed the anchorage, Dwight looked back at Robert's Cay and thought grimly about the bodies at the Tracking Station. He also thought about Matt, who was below, and wondered what would become of him. He wasn't too optimistic about his rescue mission.

I'd better not tell him that she's probably dead, or worse. Much, much worse.

It was relief to escape from the Cay. The Island's tropical charm had been overshadowed by a pall of violence and death. Jeremy powered the boat due west toward Morgan Cay so they could continue their surveillance and the man below could attempt to save his wife. Dwight held on tightly as the boat skipped across the waves.

CHAPTER FORTY-EIGHT

Robert's Cay

Jorge, three men, and a woman arrived at the Cay well after sunset. The sea bucked and rolled making it difficult to control the boat as they nosed the bow ashore.

After climbing down the stern ladder, they found themselves in cold, ankle-deep water. In the darkness, their feet left a shimmering trail of phosphorus as they shuffled to higher ground.

"You know the plan," Jorge said. "You cannot show a light to that son of a bitch. You cannot make a sound. Be as quiet and deadly as a snake. He will shoot you if he gets a chance. Just find him and report back to me. I will talk to him myself. If you have to say anything at all, tell him that his wife is with us. That's why Maria has come. She looks like the gringo's wife. All you have to do, Maria, is stand still and say nothing. He'll see you and think that we are ready to make the exchange. Instead I will… Well, never mind."

"Now, Roberto, you follow me. Juan, you search on the south and east sides of the compound. Pablo, you look on the north and west.

Remember, do not shoot him. We must find out where he has hidden the cocaine."

"Yes," they all said and nodded.

I won't let that bastard get the best of me again, Jorge thought.

"We know what needs to be done," Juan said. "We'll meet you outside the radio building if we do not find the American."

The men dispersed.

"Find him!" Jorge hissed after them. "Maria, you follow me."

The men scurried toward the gloomy compound, weaving their way in and out of the buildings. Jorge and Maria went to the back of the main building where Jorge peered through the broken glass door. He waited breathlessly, listened.

Juan and Pablo were enjoying the hunt. Earlier they had injected themselves with thirty milligrams of speed and were now feeling both invisible and indestructible. Their hearts pounded with excitement and the methamphetamine that coursed through their veins.

Roberto waited for five minutes to elapse after Jorge entered the radio building. As he approached the broken glass door he heard a gunshot. He crouched, tightened his hold on his gun.

"Jorge," he called through the door, *"que pasa?"*

Jorge muttered something too low for Roberto to hear.

"Nada, nada," Jorge said from the dark hallway. "Come in and bring your light."

Roberto slipped between the broken panels and withdrew his flashlight from his belt.

"Turn on your light," Jorge said, "and shine it this way."

Roberto switched on the flashlight and cast the beam in the direction of Jorge's voice. It stood out like a beacon in the black void that surrounded them.

"Here," Jorge said. "Over here."

Roberto's light located Jorge's face.

"What is it? Did you shoot him?"

"Aim your light over here," Jorge said and cast his eyes downward.

Roberto slid the narrow beam down the center of Jorge's body and focused it on a pile of fur at his feet.

"I'll be," Jorge said, "a fucking dog. Scared the shit out of me. Jumped right at me in the dark."

Roberto laughed. "Jorge, we had better get this guy before you accidentally shoot your nuts off."

"Shut up, you idiot. If Juan and Pablo don't find that bastard, I want the lights back on. You'll have to fix the wires."

"I will if I can."

"I want that man," Jorge said. "Do you hear me?"

CHAPTER FORTY-NINE

Morgan Cay

Alex awakened with bad dreams still turning inside her head. The details lingered for a moment making it difficult for her to rejoin the world of the living. There were voices downstairs, the aroma of food cooking. A door slammed somewhere in the house.

If Matt is dead, why is Raoul keeping me alive? Surely with all his money and power he can have almost any woman he wants. Can Matt really be dead?

She couldn't imagine her life without Matt, the one man in her life who had healed her, who had encouraged her to become her own person. He had inspired her to be more of a thinker than a feeler. Although she had grown spiritually and intellectually since she had met Matt, she considered herself to be a kite and Matt the one who held the string. Would she fly away if he let go?

How can I escape? Raoul seems protective of me, but what will happen when whatever motivates him no longer exists? Will I be shot and thrown into the ocean, or worse, will he turn me over to that horrible creature, Jorge, who will do God knows what to me?

Matt has told me so little about his captivity, she thought, and there has been much about his past that I did not understand before. Now I am beginning to feel the full impact of being held, of not knowing what each moment will bring, of being at the mercy of captors.

Perhaps I should try to get better acquainted with the women in the house. They are, after all, women, who should be sympathetic to my plight. They seem devoted to Raoul, but I wonder how deep their loyalty runs. Consuelo is withdrawn, and Margarita, well, I haven't seen her enough to make a judgment.

She thought about Matt again and wondered if they had really shot him. Could they have captured him, forced him to tell where he had hidden the bags? That would explain Raoul's changed attitude. He might not care what I know or whether or not I'm telling the truth because he's already gotten what he wants. Matt has always said that anyone could be persuaded to talk, that it was just a matter of time. And if Raoul's lying to me, for what purpose? So I won't try and run away?

She found a clean dress and underclothes in the closet but still no shoes. Her hand throbbed from the embedded splinter and her feet burned from her thwarted escape attempt. Like the other garment, the new dress was made of cotton. It was simple in design yet finely made. She pulled it over her head and sat down at the dressing table to search for a pair of tweezers. Inside the bottom drawer among the nail clippers, emery boards, and nail polish, she found a sharp pair.

She was shocked to see how swollen and angry the flat of her hand had become. The palm was three times the size of her other one. Steeling herself, she gouged an opening and released the infection that had built up inside. Carefully she probed for the dark tip of the splinter that eluded her again and again. Finally, she was able to grip the end and extract the piece of wood from her hand. Beads of sweat formed on her upper lip and she felt light headed for a moment. After cleaning the wound in the bathroom sink, she washed her hands and began to search in the medicine cabinet for a bandage.

"What you look for?" Consuelo said.

Alex jumped. She had not heard her enter the room.

"I'm trying to find some Band-Aids or some gauze and adhesive tape for my hand."

"In the closet on top of shelf," Consuelo said as she brushed past her. "I get."

When she returned with gauze and adhesive strips, she said, "Here, Señora, me help you.

"Thank you," she said as Consuelo affixed the tape. "Gracias."

"It nothing. You wash youself?"

"Yes, but I can't find any shoes."

"None to be."

"I see. Well at least I'm not pregnant."

"I beg the pardon, Señora?"

"A little joke."

"It almost time for the dinner. You must go to table."

"Consuelo, have you worked for Señor Chavez for very long?"

"Sí, many years. He my family."

"What kind of man is he?"

"Wonderful man, good to people. He feed the poor, help other have better lives. He pride of country. He pay for new roads, the street lights, build thousands homes for people. He make clinics of health for who not can pay the doctor."

"I see. And you know about the drugs that he sells? And this doesn't bother you? That he's responsible for many deaths, that is."

"You mean the gringos?"

"Not just Americans. People from many countries."

"In Colombia, we have the coca for long time. Long time. It not kill us. We know how live with it. The Americans not know how handle it. They need be teaching. Also, you killing youselves. This good."

"Good? Why do you hate us so much?"

"You gringos take, take, take. You try make other countries do you say. I am said the poor in U. S. have the much suffering."

"What about all the good things that the United States does? Billions of dollars are spent helping other countries."

"You governors buying other countries, Señora. They want countries do as they tell. The Americans, they not fool us."

"But you really don't know us, do you Consuelo?"

"And you really not know the Señor, do you Señora?"

"Not really, but what I see horrifies me."

"You no understand, Señora."

"In some ways perhaps…"

"Enough speaking. Go to table. You not keep Señor waiting."

Alex nodded and started down the stairs.

CHAPTER FIFTY

Morgan Cay

Thunder rumbled across the sky and the wind quickened. The *Fishy Business* hobby horsed at anchor a quarter mile off Morgan Cay. Below decks, the men closed the hatches in preparation for the squall line that would soon be passing overhead.

"So far so good," Jeremy said. "We've been anchored for three hours and no one has come out to investigate. They can't be too concerned about us."

"They'll probably be along shortly," Dwight said as he popped open a warm can of Budweiser beer. "That is, if the weather doesn't get any worse."

Matt picked up a pair of binoculars and carried them to the cockpit.

"Hey, Spencer," Dwight said, "don't let them see you looking at the Island through those. That's just the sort of thing that will get us in trouble. We don't want to appear too curious."

"I need to get the lay of the land before dark," Matt said.

"Sure," Dwight said, "but don't be so obvious about it. We have some night vision glasses you can use after dark."

"You know they have 'em, too," Jeremy said. "That wouldn't be a good idea either."

"Good point," Dwight said before he took a slug of beer.

Matt returned to the cabin and peered out the windows on the port side.

"See anything?" Jeremy said as he rolled up some charts and snapped rubber bands around them.

"Not too much. Beach and trees, a fair-sized dock. The binoculars would help but I'll just have to find out what's what when I go ashore."

"When are you planning to make your move?" Jeremy said as he slid the rolled charts into a teak holder mounted on the ceiling of the cabin.

"Tonight, after dark. As you pointed out, they won't be expecting me, and I can't wait another night to find Alex. There's no telling what they're doing to her."

"You do realize," Dwight said, "that she may not even be alive."

"Yes, I've considered that, but I have to find out for myself."

Matt turned away when he felt tears well in his eyes.

"We know quite a bit about the Island," Dwight said. "Let us give you a briefing and then maybe we can make some suggestions."

Matt sat down at the dining table across from Dwight while Jeremy got a blank piece of paper and a pencil.

"Let me draw you a map," Dwight said as Jeremy sat down at the table and slid the sheet across to him. "What you can see from where we are is, of course, the south side of Morgan Cay," Dwight said as he sketched. "There's a dock on this side. To the east is an airport, and, I might add, it's usually busy. On the west side, here, there are three or four houses where some of the guards and their whores live. Further north there is a rambling, one-story house that's used for Raoul's classier prisoners. His house is also on the north side, near the beach. It's a three-story job, very fancy. On the eastern side of the Island there is a restaurant, laundry, liquor store, you know, all those necessities for the men. There are also more quarters over here for the domestic help."

"I didn't know all that," Jeremy said. "How come you know the setup better than I do?"

"I've been paying attention in class," Dwight said, grinning.

Jeremy scowled at him.

"In any event," Dwight continued, "if you come ashore at the west end, you can make your way to the out houses. I like that, out houses. Full of shit," he said and chuckled. "If she's alive, they're probably holding her in one of them. And that's just a wild guess. The Island is more complex now that Chavez has driven out the previous owners and redeveloped it. There are dogs, guards, and elaborate alarm systems. Your chances are, I'd say, one in a thousand that you'll be able to go ashore without detection."

"I have no choice," Matt said as he stood up. "And I do have the element of surprise, which greatly improves the odds."

"That's true," Jeremy said as he wadded up the paper with the diagram of the Cay. "My heart goes out to you, buddy." With the crumpled paper in hand he walked to the stern of the boat and shredded it over the side. "Boy, it's really starting to blow out there," he said when he returned. The boat had begun to wallow in the heavy seas.

"You get seasick?" Dwight asked Matt.

"I usually do the first couple of days of any voyage, but then I don't have to deal with it again until the next trip."

"Lucky guy. Anytime I have to stay below for a long time I end up tossing my cookies."

"The lights on the Island are coming on," Jeremy said. "You guys want some chow?"

"You'd better eat something, Spencer," Dwight said. "It may be your last meal."

"Jesus, Dwight," Jeremy said, "why don't you discourage the guy? Last meal."

"No, no, asshole, I meant his last meal for a while. He needs his strength."

Over a dinner of canned Beanie Weenies and warm beer, Dwight watched Matt methodically chew each bite.

"Not hungry, huh?" Dwight said. "Can't say I blame you for losin' your appetite."

"Would you be hungry?" Jeremy said.

"Let's talk about your best course of action," Dwight said. "It seems to me that if you can remain undetected after you go ashore, and if you find your wife and get her away from whatever guard she's under, and if you get back to our boat by sunrise, then you ought to be able to pull it off."

"If, if, if," Jeremy said. "Christ, don't you think he knows what he has to do?"

"What the fuck is your problem?" Dwight said, frowning.

"You're becoming a pain in the ass," Jeremy said to Dwight as he tossed his paper plate into a garbage pail in the galley.

"I do care what happens to you," Dwight told Matt, "more than you know. I'd be willing to go with you if you think I can help."

"I can't ask you to do that," Matt said.

"What?" Jeremy said. "You go with him? Have you lost your goddamn mind? What about our orders to be unobtrusive? You'll fuck up our whole mission and probably get us all killed in the process."

"I'm sick of orders," Dwight said, standing up. "I want to do something worthwhile for a change. What if Karen was the one being held on that Island, Jeremy? Wouldn't you like a little help getting her back?"

Jeremy pictured his girlfriend, Karen, for a moment and nodded.

"Yep, now that I think of it," Dwight said as he moved away from the table, "I'm going with Spencer. If we're not back by dawn you pull anchor and haul butt out 'a here."

"Are you out of your fucking mind, Dwight?" Jeremy said. "Listen to me. You're gonna screw everything up. Our meeting with you-know-who is in a few days and what about our surveillance?"

"Think about Karen, Jeremy. Think about what we've been doing the last few years, sitting on our butts with our thumbs up our asses and our minds in neutral. Face it, kid, we've been put out to pasture and just don't know it. No guts, no glory, my man."

"We should at least check with the boss."

"Sure, sure," Dwight said. "He's gonna say its okay for one of us to go ashore and visit Mr. Chavez, himself. I can just hear it now. "Of course, boys, go ahead, but be real careful and not blow your cover.""

Jeremy paced about the small cabin, shoving his hands in and out of his pockets. Dwight was beginning to feel good about himself for the first time since he could remember. Matt, lost in his own thoughts, was oblivious to the debate between the two men. In his mind, he had crawled ashore, and, like a poacher, was slipping through the woods.

Suddenly a flash of lightening pierced the darkness and thunder cracked a few seconds later. They all jumped.

"Jesus, that was close," Jeremy said.

"Scare ya?" Dwight said.

"Shut the fuck up," Jeremy said. "You're being a real asshole."

"I've never seen this side of you, bud. What's the matter with you? Why can't you understand that I'm tired of sitting at the light and revving my engine. We're always waiting and watching, waiting and watching. I want to do something, make a difference. That's why I joined the team. We haven't done jack in the last four years. I'd love to see Raoul's face when he finds out that someone has waltzed in and rescued a captive right out from under his nose. Think about it."

"All right, all right, I see your point," Jeremy said and nodded. "Maybe I should go with Spencer."

"You? What? I'm the one who should go," Dwight said. "It was my fucking idea."

"We have to stick together, man, like always," Jeremy said. "Besides, I've never wimped out in my life. Let's even the playing field and draw for it. I'll put a few pieces of folded paper in this bowl here," he said as he pulled one from the galley cupboard, "and I'll put an X on one. We'll each draw until one of us gets the marked paper. The unlucky guy with the X goes with Spencer."

Matt, unaware of what had transpired, was perplexed when he saw Dwight and Jeremy ceremoniously taking folded pieces of paper from a bowl.

"What are you guys doing?" he said.

"Wait a sec," Dwight said as he watched Jeremy unwrap his third piece of paper.

Jeremy looked at Dwight and held up the paper marked with an X.

"Jesus, Jeremy," Dwight said. "Goddamn, it was my idea. I should be the one."

"We're a team, right?" Jeremy said.

"Right, but…"

"No buts, Dwight. We're in this together, all of us," he said and looked at Matt.

"We'll have to swim ashore," Jeremy said to Matt.

"That's okay by me," Matt said. "I didn't think Harold or Dwight or whatever his name is was going to drive us up to the dock."

Jeremy didn't smile; instead, he looked out the window at the first drops of rain that had begun to fall.

CHAPTER FIFTY-ONE

Morgan Cay

Jorge rushed from the dock to his house where he began disrobing the second he closed the door behind him. Once undressed, he wadded his clothes in a bundle and threw them in a corner of the bathroom. When he turned on the shower, the sound of the water splattering on the porcelain calmed him a bit.

Son of a bitch! Son of a bitch! he thought as he twirled beneath the spray. The gringo is gone, but how? Where did he go?

They had searched Robert's Cay and the sailboat moored just off-shore and came up empty. It is possible, Jorge thought, that the American simply eluded them, but that was unlikely. The Island is small and there are only so many places to hide.

He lathered the soap between his palms and furiously rubbed his neck and chest.

How? How could the man just vanish? Obviously, someone helped him. But who? And why?

The steam rose from the shower in billowing clouds and settled in a film over the bathroom. Jorge scrubbed his anus and crotch, carefully handling his genitals with gentle fingers.

That must be it. He has help. From the American government? No, they would not concern themselves. Could it have been the Island people? Impossible. They wouldn't dare. Tourists? Maybe.

Squatting in the stall, Jorge lathered between each toe. As the warm water cascaded over him he leaned into it. Yes, that has to be it, he thought. Tourists. I must find out which boats have been anchored at Robert's Cay the last few days. That should be easy enough to determine.

Having planned his next move, he felt his anxiety dissipating, his mind settling. Of course, he thought as he stepped from the shower and reached for a towel, the man has help and is no longer on the Island. But where would he go and how far away from his wife would he travel? Surely he is anxious about her and wonders what we will conclude. He certainly doesn't want us to think that he has taken our cocaine and run away. That would mean certain death for his wife. Unless he has decided that he no longer cares about her. H-m-m. He shook his head. No, that little bitch has been prized. I can tell. He won't leave the Bahamas. I'd bet my life on it.

Jorge swallowed hard at this last thought. He may be betting his life on it. Raoul would not be pleased by yet another failure. He began to dress.

The gringo's disappearance is indeed a serious setback.

Jorge knew what would help him get through this difficult time. Opening a drawer in a chest next to the bed, he reached inside for his private paradise. Because he had recently awakened to find blood stains on his pillow, he had switched over to free basing. By smoking pure cocaine, his damaged mucous membranes would get a much needed rest and the nosebleeds would cease. On top of the chest was a beaker, a small torch, a bottle of ether, and a water pipe containing several layers of stainless steel screens. Beside these, he placed the bag of cocaine.

Eager for his first hit, Jorge's fingers shook as he extracted a little less than twenty-five milligrams from the bag and mixed it with water and ammonium hydroxide. He separated the cocaine base from the water by using ether. In anticipation, his mouth flooded with saliva and his heart began to pick up a few beats. He placed the freebase on the top screen of the pipe, melted it to an oil, and then heated it slowly with the torch. He leaned over the table and inhaled through the stem in the pipe. In a matter of seconds he felt an intense rush of pleasure.

His heart pounding, he lay back on the bed and pressed the flat of a hand against a breastbone. He was in ecstasy.

Oh, Jesus, this is incredible.

Later, as he finished dressing, he noticed that his clothes were beginning to lose their shape and hang loosely on his frame. He would have to buy new shirts and pants the next time he went to Miami. Jorge realized that he should eat more, but food wasn't very appealing these days. After he slipped on his shoes, he had a strong urge to undress and bathe again. Lately his skin had begun to crawl and itch.

I must make my contacts right away, he thought as he hurried from his room. Contemplating his image in the hall mirror, he licked his palms, smoothed his hair with each hand, and stepped away to admire himself. His dilated pupils stared back at him. With a new sense of purpose, he bounded down the porch steps and out into the stormy night.

CHAPTER FIFTY-TWO

Morgan Cay

Alex ate little of the lobster ragout and foie gras and did not touch the salad and cheese plate before her. Raoul sipped his wine and studied her while she fidgeted in her seat, looked down at her food, and twirled her wine glass.

"Am I making you ill at ease?" he said.

"Of course. Isn't that your intent? Why do you keep staring at me?"

"You're a beautiful woman and an intelligent one. You intrigue me."

"I'm a married woman, who you have kidnapped. I don't think we have much of a future together."

"That's for me to decide. First of all, you are no longer married. Remember, you're a widow now."

"I don't believe you," she said and swallowed the lump in her throat.

"You doubt my word?" he said. "You require evidence?"

"Let's face it," she said and looked at him squarely, "you don't exactly represent law and order. Lying should come easy to someone like you."

"What would be my purpose in lying to you?"

"I haven't figured that out yet. Surely you aren't so interested in me that you feel the need to lie."

"Think what you like. I dreaded telling you that your husband was dead. I knew that it would be a devastating blow. Now I see that I need not have concerned myself since you choose not to believe me."

Her eyes filled with tears and she looked down at her plate for a few seconds. When she looked up, she took a deep breath and said, "My feelings are my business. And besides, I don't trust anything you say. Matt is too smart to get captured. I have absolute and complete confidence in him."

"That must make you feel very secure. I have to say, I admire your loyalty, however misguided."

Consuelo entered the dining room with a bottle of wine wrapped in a white cloth and carefully filled their glasses.

"Would you like some passion-fruit sorbet, Señor?" she said as she began removing the dinner plates.

"I think not," Raoul said and looked at Alex with raised eyebrows.

Alex shook her head.

"Coffee, perhaps?" Consuelo said.

"The wine is all we need," Raoul said.

Alex sat quietly and listened to the patter of rain on the roof. The soft drumming was interrupted by a distant roll of thunder. Lost in thought about Matt, she gazed at the clear liquid in her glass.

Raoul pushed back his chair and stretched his legs.

"I love the rain," he said.

Alex wondered where Matt was, what he was thinking. She would not accept that he was dead. It was too horrible to contemplate.

"You know," Raoul said as he folded his arms across his chest, "I could make love to you if I wished."

Startled from her reverie, Alex looked across the table at him. No doubt about it, he was a striking man with dark flashing eyes and classic features. If this was another time, another place, if he were a different sort of person, and especially, if she didn't love Matt so much, then she might be moved to encourage him. Instead she remained cold and unyielding.

"But, I am a patient man. I would enjoy you so much more if you came to me freely."

Alex continued to be astounded by the man's tremendous ego.

"You mean you think you can kidnap me, kill my husband, and expect me to hurl myself into bed with you? Amazing!"

Raoul laughed and took a sip of wine.

"You certainly are brave, Alexandra. I really appreciate that about you. I am so weary of everyone saying yes to me. 'Yes, Señor Chavez, of course, Señor Chavez.' It has become tiresome."

"Do they have a choice if they want to keep on living?"

"I suppose not, but nevertheless, it is a bore at times. You, on the other hand, are refreshing."

"And when you no longer find me refreshing, what then?"

"Who knows? In the meantime, you should enjoy yourself. He put down his wine glass. What would you like now, a brandy, perhaps?"

Alex finished her wine and folded her hands in her lap.

"I would like to be with my husband, but instead I'll have to settle for returning to my prison upstairs."

"Ah, that disappoints me, of course. It is early yet. But I understand. Tomorrow is another day and who knows what might happen."

She stood up and set her dinner napkin on the table. Raoul rose, walked toward her end of the table. He did not speak but looked at her with his smoldering black eyes. She stepped back. He continued moving in her direction, slowly, but with purpose. She turned. He grabbed a wrist and pulled her to him. She smelled wine on his breath, his cologne. Raoul wrapped his arms around her. She struggled to push him away. He laughed, held her tightly. His lips lightly brushed her neck. She trembled, started to speak, then decided to remain silent.

"I want you," he said. "There's something about you. I can't explain it. You…" He kissed her throat, began to explore her with his hands.

Alex felt the searing heat of his skin, the downy hair on his arms, the hardness of his body as he leaned into her. The dining room, the flickering candles, began to blend and dissolve. His breath felt like a whisper on her cheek. A whimper escaped from her lips. He smiled, continued moving his hands over her, touching her.

"You said you wouldn't force me."

"Did I say that?"

She again tried to pull away from him. He was stronger and very determined.

"You did, you said, you…"

"How does it feel to be so desired?" he murmured in her ear.

"You…"

"Alexandra, I haven't felt this way in a long time, years."

His fingers, like hot coals, began unzipping her dress, stroking her bare skin.

I have to stop him.

She turned her cheek, tried to avoid his kiss, but he held her head, forced her mouth against his. She whimpered again, trembled. His tongue touched her teeth, parted them. His kiss was warm, passionate, promising. When the hand that held her neck relaxed for a moment, she turned her head.

"Please, you said…"

When he cupped her chin in his hands, his eyes were filled with longing. Hesitantly, she returned his gaze and was jolted by a primitive yearning that frightened her. Raoul was powerful, strong, and decidedly handsome. For a moment, she imagined herself lying naked beneath him, caressing him, moving… He half-smiled, slid a hand down her back. Her cheeks flushed.

"You said…"

"Yes, I did," he said and released her. His eyes were blazing.

Alex cleared her throat, turned.

"Another time," he said as she started toward the door. "But don't make me wait too long, Alexandra. I enjoy the game, but only to a point."

She hurried upstairs to the bedroom and leaned against the door as if she were being pursued. Confused and afraid of her emotions, she realized that she was not only running from him but from herself as well.

How can I be attracted to that man, that criminal? Thank goodness I didn't respond. I can't be judged by what I think, can I? No one ever has to know.

She fell across the bed, squeezed a pillow to her chest, and pressed her face against it. Outside, the rain intensified and the casuarina trees shuddered and swayed in the powerful wind that whistled through their branches. Alex wished that she could lock the door from the inside.

To lock him out or lock me in?

CHAPTER FIFTY-THREE

Morgan Cay

The *Fishy Business* pointed into the wind and bucked against the oncoming sea. Her bow swung to the full extreme of her port anchor line, shuddered, then traveled to the full extent of her starboard. Alive with sounds, wind shrieked like banshees in her rigging, and raindrops pummeled her deck. Below, Matt and Jeremy prepared to go ashore.

"Jesus, what a night," Jeremy said, as he finished zipping the top to his wet suit "I sure hope you're a good swimmer, Spencer."

Matt glanced at his watch and noted that it was a little before nine. He felt numb inside.

"Now listen," Dwight said, "you guys need to make landfall at the west end and get by the guards. The dogs shouldn't be much trouble in this weather. Like I told you, once you go inland, you'll come to three houses. These are living quarters. Further in is the guest house."

Jeremy nodded and said to Matt, "Stick with me, bud. I can show you where to go."

"The rain is a definite plus," Dwight said. "They won't be expecting visitors on a night like this. They'll probably be hunkered down, shootin' up dope, or bangin' their old ladies. I'll expect you guys no later than sunup. If you're not back by then, well… Just don't make me leave without you."

"We know. We know," Jeremy said, as he picked up his diving knife and strapped it to his right leg.

"Don't forget to check the anchors often," Matt said "Take some bearings. The boat's really taking a pounding and the wind has shifted. You're on a lee shore."

"Right," Dwight said.

"Well, I guess this is it," Matt said as they prepared to go.

"I hope you're a good swimmer," Jeremy said again. "Long way to the beach. Got your snorkel?"

"Right here," Matt said.

"Ready?" Jeremy said.

"As I'll ever be," Matt said, as he stepped outside into the rain. "See you on the beach."

"Good luck, guys," Dwight said before he shut the door behind them.

Camouflaged by their black wet suits, the men were virtually invisible. First one and then the other slipped over the stern and into the murky sea. Matt shuddered as he felt the icy water invade his wet suit and envelope him. He adjusted his mask before he pressed the snorkel between his lips and began to swim toward the beach. At first, he made irregular strokes, but after a few minutes, he fell into a rhythm and every muscle and tendon moved with precision.

Halfway to the beach, he treaded water and searched for Jeremy. The rain, falling like darts, made it impossible for him to see anything. Forty-five minutes later, Matt realized he was being swept out to sea by a rip tide. He remembered what he had learned in Navy survival school; swim parallel to the beach until you are out of the rip tide, then swim in. He did so, but found he was still being pulled away from the Island, carried by a powerful current. His heartbeat accelerated as he felt his muscles giving way.

Don't panic. Just go toward the beach.

After what seemed an interminable length of time, the Cay loomed through the rain a hundred yards off to his right. Angling toward the beach, he stroked harder and willed himself on until the ocean floor touched the bottom of his feet. From all sides, the confused sea buffeted him. He reached beneath the water and removed first one fin, then the other, and pushed his mask back on his head. Checking for his knife, he reached down and found it still strapped to his leg.

On shore, he dropped to his knees and took long, deep breaths. The rain had slackened, making it easier for him to see. He scanned the beach for some sign of Jeremy.

Jesus, I hope he didn't drown out there.

He pulled a miniature waterproof light from inside his wet suit and focused its tiny beam on his watch. It was almost eleven.

Two hours. We've been swimming out there for two goddamn hours.

Again he peered into the darkness. Nothing.

Dwight's sketch remained clear in his mind. Without Jeremy, he was, as always, on his own. Somehow he couldn't imagine that it would ever be any other way.

High on the beach behind a piece of driftwood, he hid his fins, mask, and snorkel, but kept on his thick booties to protect his feet from the sharp undergrowth beneath the pines. In the distance, he saw bright lights glowing in the windows of the *Fishy Business*. He imagined Dwight anxiously eyeing his watch and checking the anchors.

He sat down on the driftwood to wait for Jeremy. As planned, whoever arrived first was to stay put on the west end of the Island until the other one showed up. He checked his watch again. It was eleven fifteen. Matt stood up and wandered near the trees. He had to avoid detection at all costs. So far, he had not seen or heard anyone.

When another line of storm clouds rolled in, he sought refuge beneath the casuarinas. Concerned about Jeremy's absence, he wondered if he should deviate from the plan and run east to look for him. As Matt considered his next move, a jagged finger of lightening pierced the night sky and struck just offshore. Simultaneously, there was an earsplitting crack of thunder. Matt hoped that Jeremy was safely out of the water and on his way to this end of the beach.

The wet suit was a blessing. Without it, he would have been thoroughly chilled The rain, falling in sheets, was relentless and inescapable.

At midnight, he concluded that something had happened to Jeremy. He had waited for an hour, plenty of time for him to make his way to this end of the Island if he had made it ashore. There was nothing left for him to do but proceed alone.

Using the small compass attached to his wrist watch, Matt headed inland away from the sea and the comforting lights of the *Fishy Business*.

CHAPTER FIFTY-FOUR

Morgan Cay

Alex awoke at midnight, fully clothed and lying on top of the covers. She sat up and listened. A loud noise had awakened her, thunder perhaps, or a door slamming. She got out of bed and went to the bathroom where she splashed cold water on her face. When she returned to the bedroom, she thought she heard voices downstairs. She pressed an ear against the door. Yes, she was certain. There were men talking below. She opened the door a few inches. They were speaking Spanish, and she could only make out a word here and there. Then she heard a door close and the conversation became muffled.

She desperately wanted to know what was going on. It was late and a dreadful night for a meeting. Alex turned off the light and tiptoed down the stairs. The voices grew louder as she neared the first floor. There were three voices, all male.

A step creaked beneath her foot. She paused, breathless, fearful she might be discovered. After a moment, she moved farther down, straining all the while to hear what was being discussed in Raoul's office.

The voices became animated. Raoul said something in English now. Yes, she clearly recognized his voice. Another man spoke in a voice that was vaguely familiar. She could only hear bits and pieces of their conversation. They all began to speak English.

"Son of a bitch," someone said.

"No, this is good," she heard Raoul say. "It couldn't have worked out better. And you will be well paid, as usual. Take this. I'm sure you can put it to good use."

There was a brief silence followed by, "As always, Señor Chavez, you are a generous man."

Alex pressed her ear against the office door. Behind her, in the darkness, she thought she heard a footstep and quickly glanced over her shoulder. When she turned around, she only saw the empty foyer and the unlighted rooms beyond.

The voices grew louder. She heard shuffling steps on the other side of the door. They were coming her way. She searched for a hiding place.

God, where can I go?

The doorknob turned, and the office door opened an inch and then stopped as someone paused at the threshold. A second before the men came out of the office, she found a three-foot door that opened into a storage compartment beneath the stairs. With her heart pounding, she crawled inside and shut the door just as the men stepped out into the hallway.

"Gracias, Señor Chavez," one of them said.

"There is plenty more where that came from," Raoul said. "You are important to us."

"I hope so," a man said. "I'll be in touch."

She heard the heavy front door open, the sound of rain hitting the steps outside, and then a solid thump when the door closed. Alex trembled inside the cubbyhole and wondered how she was going to return to her room undetected. Raoul and the other man began speaking quietly in Spanish. They walked back into his office and closed the door. She remembered the remaining man's voice but could not place it.

Opening the compartment an inch at a time, she peeked out. There were pools of water on the hardwood floor between the office door and the entry. She eased through the small door, walked softly around the stairwell, and sprinted up the stairs without making a sound.

Once inside the bedroom she trembled with relief. She did not know what would have happened had she been discovered but something told her it was best that she had not.

That voice, where have I heard it? So familiar.

She sat down at the dressing table and stared in the mirror at her frightened eyes. Then she remembered.

Of course, the man from the boat , the one who enjoyed hurting her so much, the one who suffocated the Bahamian called Tyrone. Jorge!

It was his voice that she heard. He is the man downstairs with Raoul. The color drained from her face and she pressed a knuckle between her teeth.

CHAPTER FIFTY-FIVE

Morgan Cay

Matt felt well concealed, almost transparent, as he moved inland through the pines. He checked the iridescent numbers on his pocket compass as he proceeded north toward the houses which had been described to him. As Dwight said, the first of three cottages soon appeared. He remembered that these were living quarters for Raoul's men.

Matt scurried to the first lighted window and peeked inside. Two men sat at a table playing cards while sounds of heavy metal screeched from a portable tape player nearby. Matt stood on tiptoe for a better view just as a tall, anemic-looking blond entered the room. She approached one of the men, leaned down and nuzzled his neck. He said something in her ear which made her smile. Matt quickly ducked when she glanced in his direction, uncertain as to whether or not his face could be seen from within.

Over the din of the rain and the rock cords, Matt heard something behind him. A heavy truck with its lights blazing lumbered past him and continued up the road. Matt ran to the corner of the house and watched as the tail lights, like two red eyes, blinked when the truck rounded a curve and disappeared.

Matt's best guess, Alex wasn't here. He hastened to the next house which stood unlighted and gloomy with rainwater dripping from its eaves. An air of emptiness clung to it. He realized it would be pointless to look through the windows, so he slipped up the porch steps and pressed an ear against the front door. Silence. He lightly touched the knob, grasped it, and trembled when he felt it turn. His hand quaking, he opened the door an inch at a time and listened for sounds from within. Once inside, he quickly closed the door behind him.

The room was cluttered with chairs, a coffee table, and an overstuffed couch, their colors and substance muted by the darkness. Matt crept to the first door which appeared off to his right, leading, he assumed, to a hallway or kitchen.

His wet suit, most welcome in the cold rain, had become a liability. Perspiration, flowing freely, spilled over his eyes and blurred his vision. He reached for his knife, eased it from the sheath on his leg. Although the knob turned smoothly, the warped wood resisted his initial attempt to separate it from the frame. He grunted and pushed until the door burst open with a noisy crack.

Peering into the void beyond, he discerned no object, no sound, no person. He eased his pocket flashlight from his wet suit and turned the head. A pinprick of light streaked from the end. Before him lay a dark hallway. He moved down the corridor shielding the light. As he shuffled along, his booties squished on the hardwood floor. He found a dingy bathroom, two bedrooms with unmade beds, and soiled clothes strewn about.

God, I hope I don't run into one of those assholes like I did at Robert's Cay. I might not be so lucky this time. At least they aren't expecting me.

A complete search of the house further revealed a kitchen with dirty dishes piled high in the sink and an empty milk carton on a stained dining table. Matt stood at the counter and looked out the window. Rain beat like tom toms on the roof of the cistern next to the house. The thunder and lightening had ceased.

Retracing his steps, he closed the front door behind him and moved to the next cottage. Finding no one within, he stepped outside and checked his watch.

Two a.m. It's late, but I'm surprised that I haven't seen any guards. No dogs. This is easier than I expected. Maybe too easy. Hell, who knows? I just might pull this off.

The guest quarters were closer to the sea. A sprawling house with a wide porch and many windows, it looked homey and inviting. Matt had to resist feeling overconfident. Things were going well. He thought about Alex and tried to block her image from his mind. He pictured brutal men beating and raping her, erased that picture, and pressed on. He swallowed the knot in his throat and focused on the task at hand, to find Alex and get her safely off the Island. He would worry about the rest later.

Again, he was relieved to find an unlocked door. Security did not appear to be one of their concerns. He crept inside and gently closed the door behind him. The room, dark like the others, had a damp, musty smell. He looked around, tried to distinguish the shapes.

As in the other houses, there was an abundance of furniture and lamps. He saw, too, that this place contained something that the others had not.

Jesus, I've really walked into it this time.

In rapid succession a bright overhead light came on and a group of men yelled in unison, "Surprise!"

Matt stood before them, speechless. They broke into raucous laughter, slapped their sides. Someone looking in would think that his closest and dearest friends had gathered to honor him with a celebration.

One of the men stepped out of the group, extended a hand. He was almost too pretty to be a man.

"Forgive my dark humor," he said with an even smile. "I have been anxious to meet you."

Matt remained standing with his back to the door, ignored the man's hand. He quickly surveyed the room for a means of escape. Was there still time to turn and bolt? A way out?

"Don't even think about it," said the man, who had lowered his arm. "I have men surrounding the house and running would be futile. Besides," he continued, "you and I have important business to discuss."

Realizing it was pointless to flee, Matt's body didn't move. His mind, though, took a trip of its own. The years melted away, carried him back to a place he had never wanted to be again.

Matthew John Spencer, Lt. Commander. 579821. 8 February 1935.

Yes, we know all about the Geneva Convention, but this is not a declared war. You are an aggressor. You will be treated by the laws of this country, not the laws of Switzerland.

CHAPTER FIFTY-SIX

Morgan Cay

Alex padded across the rug and pressed her face against a window. Unable to see out with the light behind her, her image was clearly visible to anyone who might be looking in. There wasn't a sound except the rain strumming on the roof. She sighed, closed the curtains.

Something is going on. Could it have anything to do with Matt? And that man, that stranger who was in Raoul's office, who was he and what brought him here on a night like this? What about Jorge? I'm sure he's never up to any good.

Alex roamed about the room. It wasn't her nature to wait for life to unfold around her. She preferred to determine her own destiny. So far, she had only been an unwilling player in this frightful drama. Her previous escape attempt had been futile, doomed from the beginning, but why shouldn't she try again? Raoul had not threatened her, had not locked her door. Dare she continue to test him? When she saw him last, at dinner, it was apparent that he was growing impatient with her. She could still feel his hands, hot and urgent, moving over her body.

A gust of wind buffeted the house, rattled the panes. Alex entwined her arms across her chest and continued pacing. The more she thought about making another run for it, the more she trembled. The very idea terrified her, and yet, what other choice did she have? Sooner or later Raoul would force himself upon her, or worse, abandon her to Jorge. She shuddered. And what about Matt? Was he alive or dead?

I have to run, she decided.

On a night like this I'll be harder to see, and the dogs might not be able to follow my scent in the rain.

Alex opened the closet and was dismayed to find it empty. She had hoped clean clothes would be there and she could layer them over the dress she was wearing. The extra bulk, she thought, might keep her a little warmer.

In any event I'll be drenched and I'm not sure anything will make a difference.

After shaping pillows and towels to resemble her sleeping form, she covered them with the comforter and turned off the lamp by the bed. When she opened the door, she saw the shadowy stairwell. Peeking over the banister, she glimpsed a soft light coming from Raoul's office below.

He's still up. And Jorge?

Holding her breath, Alex started down the stairs. As she descended, she heard the wood groan beneath her feet. She moved slowly, pausing occasionally to listen for footfalls or voices.

At the landing, Alex saw Raoul's office door to the left was ajar. She imagined him sitting at his desk, listening to her tread, waiting for her.

If he hears me, I'll pretend I want some company. His inflated ego won't ask any questions.

It occurred to her that she needed a weapon. If she had a gun she could deal with Raoul's men and she would have a better chance of escaping. Alex felt certain that Raoul must have one somewhere in his office. She stood at the threshold, strained to hear any sound from within. Through the opening in the door, she glimpsed part of a bookcase packed with leather-bound books. After a few tense minutes, she braced herself and looked inside. Finding the room vacant made her weak with relief.

Quietly closing the door behind her, Alex quickly glanced around. A mahogany desk occupied the back of the office. A shiny gold pen and several sheets of paper stacked neatly in one corner rested on top. She smelled Raoul's cologne and cigar smoke.

A circular, inlaid, marble-top table stood across from the desk. An exquisite piece of furniture. She imagined that it must be priceless. Along both walls, hand-carved bookshelves held expensive-looking editions of Shakespeare's works as well as volumes on the subjects of mathematics and chemistry. There were also works by Longfellow, Dickens, and Keats. One entire shelf was devoted to Adolph Hitler and The Third Reich. This is no ordinary thug, she thought as her fingertips lightly touched the book bindings.

Alex recalled Consuelo's adoration for Raoul and realized that she, too, felt something for the man. Thus far, he had not harmed her, merely tried to seduce her. Then she remembered the untold numbers destroyed by the drugs Raoul was instrumental in distributing. She thought about the children whose lives were shattered. And she thought about Matt.

Dear, sweet Matt.

Alex shifted her attention to the desk.

Surely Raoul has a gun somewhere.

She slid open the top drawer, shuffled through papers that listed dates and figures. She noticed the scarcity of the desk's contents. The other drawers contained boxes marked, "Havana Gold," a plotter, a ruler, a protractor, several sharpened pencils and some writing tablets.

Where's the damn gun?

Again, she opened the top drawer in the center of the desk and removed all the papers. She searched the back of the drawer with her hand. There were more pens, a roll of tape, then, success, she felt the cold steel of a pistol.

Of course, he would always have a weapon handy.

Alex slid it toward her, lifted it by the butt. It was an automatic, unlike the revolver Matt had taught her to fire. She had never liked guns but recognized their usefulness. Matt had convinced her that she should learn to shoot one.

What was it they called them? Equalizers?

She gripped it like the hand of an old friend.

Just as she started to leave the room, she heard the patter of rain grow louder, then quieter, as the front door opened and closed. In spite of her bravado, she did not want to get caught in Raoul's office with his gun in her hand. Frantic, she looked for a place to hide. There were no closets, no heavy drapes, no back door.

Where to go? Underneath the desk. It's my only hope.

Alex quickly shoved the papers inside the drawer and closed it. Terrified she was about to be discovered, she almost dropped the automatic when she ducked beneath the desk. She heard muffled footfalls that became more distinct with each step. Alex squeezed her eyes shut, wished she were anywhere other than on that Island, in that house, under that desk. If anyone, if Raoul sat down, it would all be over. She would have to shoot him. If she did, the others would come running and her fate would be decided. She chastised herself for lingering in the office.

At least I have a weapon. But do I have the courage to use it?

Someone approached the front of the desk. She cringed, prayed. Papers rustled on the desktop. Someone hummed, tapped a foot. Then silence. Dreadful silence.

Does he know I'm here? Did I make a mistake, leave something out?

The humming resumed, faded. She heard footfalls that became fainter as someone walked away. There was another sound, a sharp click, just as the door closed. She listened until all she heard was her own ragged breathing. For several moments, she remained curled up in a ball beneath the desk, paralyzed by fear. Finally, she took a deep breath and climbed out.

Okay, she thought, so far so good. Now, to get out of here without being seen.

Will this gun work if it gets wet?

Careful not to make the slightest sound, she held the automatic by her side and tried not to consider the dangers beyond the house. If she succeeded in escaping the grounds undetected, she would attempt once more to get to the dock, flee from there. Raoul's men were probably everywhere, watching, waiting for her. She would have to be invisible and silent.

Without a sound, she opened the office door and peeked around it. There were more puddles of water standing near the entry. After taking a deep breath, she rushed to the front door, opened it, and stepped out onto the porch.

Outside, she smelled wet earth as she hesitated on the verandah and waited for her eyes to adjust to the darkness.

Where are Raoul's men? Where? Where? Where?

She scanned the perimeter of the yard, listened for the sound of a dog's bark or a man's voice.

Emboldened by the gun in her hand, Alex slipped off the porch and out into the stormy night. Cold before the first drop of rain hit her, she trembled. In a few minutes, she was drenched and shivering. This time, she decided, I'll follow the lane and hide in the woods when a car comes.

The jagged road lacerated her soles, but Alex found her feet traveled better on the broken shells, dirt, and lime rock than they did stumbling over branches and through the underbrush. She hurried, seeking refuge in the forest only when a turn prevented her from seeing oncoming headlights. Before long, she was gasping and clutching her side.

Within a half mile, she noticed a lighted house off to her right, crawled into a thicket, and painfully made her way over brittle shrubs. When she was directly across from it, she saw dark figures standing outside. Alex assumed they were men because of the low voices she heard murmuring across the road.

Afraid they might see her, she burrowed deeper into the brush and continued crawling on her hands and knees until she felt safely hidden from their view. She had knotted her dress in front in order to travel in this awkward manner. The gun, now soaked, had sand inside its barrel.

How much abuse can this thing take before it won't fire?

Hearing the men's voices had jolted her like an electric shock and left her tingling. Until then, she had felt brave, almost confident. Her knees were bleeding when she stood up and made her way back to the road. Because her legs had become heavy and weak, Alex had to will herself forward.

Rounding a curve, she saw three more houses on her right. Only one was lighted.

Again she left the road and returned to her crawling posture. Her hands and knees throbbed but she continued in this manner until she was far away from the cottages and their inhabitants. Although she was bitterly cold and frightened, Alex felt somewhat optimistic about eluding Raoul and his men. After all, she had come at least a mile, maybe more, and no one seemed to be following her.

Of course, I thought that last time.

She turned around and looked. Behind her, the Bahama pines swayed, whispered in the wind. The shells on the road, slick with rain, glistened in the moonlight. Alex saw no one.

Her mind raced ahead. She imagined herself taking a power boat and heading out. The seas would be high and she would not be able to see the brittle coral that could quickly shred a boat's fiberglass hull and sink it.

"I have to think," Alex whispered.

Oh, God, what should I do now? If I manage to get away by boat, it will be hours before sunup and I could just as easily die out there.

She realized that she had not thought things through. It would be reckless, no, suicidal, to try and escape during a storm. A calm, moonlit night was one thing, but a rainy night in unforgiving waters was another. In spite of her progress, she sobbed.

God, now what?

Alex expected her absence would be noticed at any moment, and the Island would soon swarm with vicious dogs and ruthless men, all intent on tracking her down. And Raoul would probably be angry, so angry that he would let Jorge take her.

Why not? What am I to Raoul?

Well, I'll get to the dock she decided, and then I will see what I will see.

Alex clutched the gun to her chest and trudged up the road toward the lights twinkling through the trees.

CHAPTER FIFTY-SEVEN

Morgan Cay

Matt stood in the center of the room with his hands bound behind his back. He feared the loss of his freedom almost as much as any pain they could subject him to. Captivity, he knew, was his worst enemy. His demons triumphed for a moment. He saw the Green Knobby Room with its rough, pea-green walls and felt the cold cement beneath his feet. He looked for the ropes.

Most of the men had vacated the premises leaving the brawny little man, who Matt well remembered from Robert's Cay; a man identified as Raoul Chavez; and another man they referred to as Miguel, who stood by what appeared to be a kitchen door. Matt struggled to stay in the here and now, focus on the little man parading before him.

"So we meet again," he said.

His ego has been badly bruised and he wants his pound of flesh, Matt thought.

Raoul appeared calmer, more in control. He spoke excellent English with barely an accent. His clothes, expensive and tailored, fit him perfectly. Matt observed that Raoul's fingers were manicured and pale, not the hands of a working man. Matt surmised that he was the boss Dwight had told him about and the one whom he should address.

"Sit down," Raoul said as he shoved a chair in Matt's direction.

Matt backed into the chair and sat up straight without averting his eyes from the drug lord, who held his and Alex's lives in his hands.

"So," Raoul said, "I understand you have something that belongs to me."

"Yes, and I believe you have my wife."

There was a flicker across the man's dark eyes, very brief, but undoubtedly it meant something.

"I don't have your wife."

Matt licked his lips, looked down for a moment, struggled to keep his emotions in check.

That son-of-a-bitch has Alex and he doesn't intend to give her up. Either that, or she's dead.

"I was told by that man…"

"Forgive my bad manners. I didn't realize the two of you had not been formally introduced. Jorge this is Mr. Spencer. Mr. Spencer, I present Jorge Gaucha."

"Bastardo!" Jorge said.

Raoul raised his left hand and Jorge clamped his lips together.

"Later," he said over his shoulder, "should it become necessary. Now where were we? Oh yes, you have something that belongs to me and I intend to get it back one way or the other. I've allowed this to go on too long, this game you have been playing."

"I haven't been playing any game. You have my wife. I have your drugs. A simple exchange is all I have in mind. It's all I've ever had in mind."

"Not so simple. Your wife is no longer on the Island."

"Where is she?"

"She went with some tourists, who were anchored nearby. I let her go because she was of no use to me."

Matt doubted that Raoul had released Alex. Why would he? He had everything to gain by keeping her.

He's lying. Why?

"Now that we have put that little matter to rest, let's get back to the business at hand, my cocaine."

Raoul walked toward Matt. His movements, like a cat's, were fluid and graceful.

"If you do not tell me what I want to know, I will be forced to turn you over to Jorge, who, as you can see, doesn't seem to like you very much. I am certain he can extract the information from you. What's more, he will enjoy doing so."

Matt looked beyond Raoul at Jorge. Spittle had gathered at the corners of his tight lips.

Salivating like Pavlov's dogs, the little shit.

"Do you understand what I'm saying, Mr. Spencer?" Raoul said as he yanked Matt's hair. "Do you understand?"

"I understand better than you know," Matt replied through clenched teeth, "and you'd better understand me. If you don't bring my wife to me, you can forget about your goddamn cocaine."

"Jorge," Raoul said as he released Matt's hair and spun around, "he's all yours. Come to my office when you have the information I require."

As Raoul made his way to the front door, Miguel ran forward with a yellow slicker on his arm.

"El Jefe, your coat," he said and assisted Raoul with his rain jacket.

"You're a fool, Mr. Spencer," Raoul said as he turned the door knob. "Do you want to die a long and painful death?"

"I want my wife," Matt said.

Raoul slammed the door behind him and a picture hanging over the couch crashed to the floor. Afterwards, inside the house was as hushed as the grave; outside, several men laughed.

Jorge, flushed and trembling, circled him. Matt knew the drill; only the players had changed.

"Miguel, remove Mr. Spencer's wet suit."

The man averted his eyes as he approached Matt.

"Hurry up!" Jorge said. "Be quick about it!"

Miguel's demeanor was apologetic. Matt wondered how such a gentle soul had found himself employed by such a brute.

Fear, no doubt, and a poor family somewhere in South America.

"Quickly!" Jorge said.

Matt feared the worst. In Vietnam, the VC had never abused the men sexually. That was strictly taboo. The prisoners were always grateful they hadn't been forced to suffer that particular brand of humiliation. Revulsion welled up inside him when he thought of Jorge touching him, penetrating him. For a moment he was almost overcome with nausea. After several awkward minutes, Matt stood naked, his hands and feet bound.

"Get on your knees."

You are an air pirate.

"Matthew John Spencer, 579821, 8 February 1935."

"What's that shit?" Jorge said before he stepped forward and with one swift movement connected with an upper thrust to Matt's groin that sent him to the floor writhing.

"That's better," Jorge said, although Matt was too busy retching to hear him.

Unchecked, Jorge released the anger that until now he had been forced to suppress. He beat Matt with a length of pipe, cursing him all the while. Again and again he slammed the lead piece across Matt's back and buttocks. Matt heard him say something in Spanish but the pain was so sharp, so penetrating, that he couldn't concentrate on anything else. Blood flowed across his back and ran down his sides. Each time he struggled to get up, Jorge attacked with greater force and Matt soon realized that he was better off on the floor.

This is okay. I can take this. I can...

Another blow muddled his thoughts.

"Matthew John Spencer, 579821."

Jorge kicked him in the chest, and Matt fell over on his back and looked up at him through blurry eyes. Even though the room was swimming, he saw Jorge's grin.

"Did you come, you little shit?" Matt said.

Without replying, Jorge kicked him in the face and blood spurted from Matt's nose.

"Keep talking, gringo. I live for this. My methods may seem primitive but they are most effective."

He booted Matt again, this time in the ribs. Matt felt bones crack inside his chest. The searing pain pierced him like a knife. Matt shook his head, struggled to remain conscious. Jorge kicked him in the stomach. The bile rose in Matt's throat. He heaved and lay still.

As quickly as the onset had begun, it stopped. Jorge disappeared into the back of the house. Matt heard a toilet flush and the sound of running water. Jorge reappeared, wiping his hands on a towel.

"Now, Spencer, let's talk," he said as he fell into a chair across from Matt.

Matt rested the back of his head against the bottom of a couch and tried to focus his eyes.

"So that's how it's going to be? How delightful. Usually I have better tools on hand, but I have never met a man I could not bring around to my way of thinking. Some take longer, that is true, but the result is always the same."

You must cooperate with the camp authorities, Pen.

Matt swallowed the blood running down the back of his throat and gagged. This time he was determined not to give in. He could not allow himself to be broken.

"Not ready to talk yet?"

Without warning, Jorge leaped from his chair and began bludgeoning him with the pipe again. He aimed for the delicate places where he could inflict the most pain and expend the least energy. The room became a kaleidoscope. Matt rolled over, tried to crawl away.

"Oh, that's good. Try to escape from me. Slither like a snake. Oh, yes, I like that."

Matt couldn't find any air. He gasped.

Is this it? Alex...

Instantly the world became dark and silent and painless.

CHAPTER FIFTY-EIGHT

Morgan Cay

Alex boarded a power boat, opened the salon door, and eased inside. Shrouded by darkness, she could see very little. The head smell was strong, the air laden with the aroma of mildew and must.

Groping her way aft, she searched every cabin and determined that she was alone. With a sigh, she sank to the carpeted floor.

Okay, progress. I am out of the house. I am on a boat. Now all I have to do is wait for dawn and figure out how to run this thing.

Alex had never piloted a large power boat but was optimistic that she could manage the basics.

How difficult can it be? At least I can try. What other choice do I have? Once I make a run for it, they'll have to catch me. If I can just get away from the dock and into open water, I'll have a chance.

A heavy weariness settled upon her. The frightening journey, the constant pumping of adrenaline, her concern for Matt, had left her weak and trembling. She closed her eyes, briefly, and lost consciousness. I should find someplace to hide she thought when she stirred.

Gathering her strength, she stood up and stumbled to the first door on the starboard side. A cabin with an unmade bunk lay behind it. Like the last reveler on a Saturday night, she crawled on top of the berth and sprawled out. Alex realized that sleeping for even a few minutes was a dangerous luxury, one she might not be able to afford. Her absence could be discovered at any moment and then the alarm would sound. After that, she was certain the men and dogs would come for her.

Alex turned over, looked up at the ceiling, and listened to the waves splashing beneath the dock. The ship's lines creaked with every pull, and the boat fenders groaned as they were crushed against the pilings. Above the din of the storm, she heard men's voices. She sat up, wary, anticipating the worst. Peeking out the window, Alex saw two men wearing bright yellow slickers strolling along the dock. They were both looking down to avoid the raindrops.

"American...Jorge..." she heard one of them say. "Dead meat," the other one said. "What the hell did he think he was going to do, barge in here like fucking John Wayne?"

One of the men, obviously Spanish, spoke broken English. Alex couldn't make out what he was saying. She strained to understand him.

"...guest house," someone said. "The boss will get it all, the bitch and the coke. I guess we'll have to cart off the stiff in the morning."

"Of course. Jorge will be finished with him by then."

The men continued past the boat. Alex's heart thumped wildly.

Who were they talking about? Matt? Guest house? Where is a guest house? Could Matt be there? God, is he somewhere on the Island? Who else could they have been talking about?

"Oh, God, oh, God," she said as she rolled off the bunk.

What should I do?

Alex stumbled to the salon door. After creeping outside, she crouched in the cockpit and surveyed the dock. The parking area was empty except for two vehicles that were within a hundred yards.

She climbed off the boat and onto the planks. The men who had strolled by only moments before had dissolved into the mist and gloom of the night. The dock appeared to be empty. She hunkered down and ran to the nearest vehicle, a gray van.

Like a sprinter, she dashed to the driver's side, grabbed the door handle, pulled open the door, and jumped in. Once inside, she lay down, and mentally chastised herself for slamming the door. Alex listened, expecting voices and footsteps. When no one came running, she exhaled, sat up, and felt for the ignition.

"Damn," she whispered, "no key!"

She lifted the door handle and slipped out of the van. After looking about, she dashed to the next vehicle, a rusty, two-door sedan. Finding that it, too, was unlocked, she opened the door and hopped inside.

Oh, thank God, a key.

Alex felt several dangling from the ignition switch.

Please don't let anyone see me.

She mashed the clutch, turned the key, and pushed gently on the gas. The engine started. With a quick thrust, she put the gear shift into reverse and backed the sedan away from the dock. Once she began moving forward, Alex turned on the windshield wipers and low beams. The car's motor hummed and the wipers rhythmically arced as she made her way up the twisted road toward Raoul's house. She glanced in the rear view mirror to see if she was being followed. Careful not to draw attention to herself, she drove slowly. Because it was so late, Alex did not expect many people would be moving about.

When she came to the three houses which appeared on her left, Alex stopped for a moment to look at them. They were all dark, quiet.

Nothing happening here. Where is the guest house?

Remembering the lone house where the men had been assembled, she shifted the engine into first and proceeded. She intended to drive beyond the house, leave the sedan, and backtrack.

If this isn't the guest house, I'll just have to keep looking.

As planned, she crept by the fourth house, which was partially lighted, and drove a quarter of a mile. She parked the car and got out. Images of Matt interrupted her thoughts like isolated pictures flashed on a movie screen. She clutched the gun as she sprinted back.

I know Matt isn't dead. Raoul lied. They all lie. Raoul wanted me to think Matt was dead for some selfish reason of his own. But what if it isn't Matt? What if it's someone else? Oh, God, what should I do then?

The house had a back door and someone stood outside it smoking a cigarette. Alex eyed what appeared to be a man's silhouette from behind a bush. When he finished his cigarette, he flicked the smoldering butt into the yard, turned, and went inside. The glass panes in the door rattled when it shut. She waited to see if anyone else was going to appear.

After a few minutes, Alex darted to the lighted side of the house and stood on tiptoe in a futile effort to peek in the window. She was too short and only the top of her head reached the sill.

Alex heard a man's loud voice emanating from within. It sounded like Jorge's. *Oh, Lord, this must be the place! Think Alex. Think!*

If she ran in brandishing the gun, there might be several men inside who would either kill or capture her.

Alex roamed the circumference of the house searching for something to stand on, a box, a lawn chair, anything. At last she found an old tire lying on the ground in the backyard. Filled with rainwater and cumbersome to lift, she struggled to raise it upright and roll it to the dark end of the house. After she angled it underneath a window, she jammed the gun inside her bodice. Holding onto the sill with her fingers, she stepped on top of the tire. On the first attempt, she fell sideways and landed on her right hip. A riveting pain shot through her and she gasped. Her injured palm throbbed from the effort.

Once again she positioned the tire and stood on it. This time she managed to maintain her balance. Fearing that her trembling legs might give way beneath her, she carefully pushed up and against the window. Inch by inch, it lifted. Finally she saw there was room for her to wriggle through. She had shinnied inside her own house when she was a child and this did not seem that different.

Except this isn't like losing your key.

The bulky gun made it difficult for her to maneuver through the opening so she reluctantly dropped it over the sill and heard a dull thump when it hit the floor. Afraid that someone might have heard the noise, she held her breath and waited. When no one appeared, she continued.

Pulling herself up with her hands and walking up the wall of the house with her toes, she managed to thrust her body through the space between the window and the sill. When she fell inside, she expected some sleeping person to shriek because she had landed on him. Fortunately, the room was uninhabited. After searching the floor with her fingertips, she found the gun and scooped it up.

Alex tiptoed to the door, turned the knob, and opened it. The hallway outside was in shadow but the rooms beyond were brightly lit. Alex heard Jorge's mocking voice followed by his shrill laughter. She cringed against the wall and listened. She remembered Tyrone, the plastic bag cinched tightly around his neck, his frantic eyes, his...

Who was the man on the back porch? Raoul? Where was that man? Is that who Jorge is talking to? And Matt, where is he?

And then all became deadly quiet. Exhausted by her emotional roller coaster ride, Alex needed time to make sense out of what had happened, what was happening, but there was no time. Alex had to do something.

Think, Alex. Think!

She fingered the chamber on the gun.

Why did Jorge stop talking?

The stillness was broken by muffled thuds and low groans that echoed down the corridor.

What is Jorge doing? Beating someone? Could it be Matt?

Unable to restrain herself or consider the consequences, Alex rushed down the hall toward the light and the sounds of torture. Without hesitating, she dashed into the room and pointed the gun at Jorge. He stood with his back to her. Not wearing a shirt, his upper body glistened with perspiration. His skin had a yellow cast under the garish overhead light. On the floor lay a body, someone too bloody to identify at first glance.

Who is it? That broken and mangled body cannot be Matt's.

"Stop," she said, "or I'll shoot!"

Jorge whirled and faced her. Clearly stunned to see her, his furry brows arched over his eyes. For a moment, they both remained frozen in place. Then Jorge's expression changed from one of surprise to contempt.

"Oh, it's the Señora. And what do you have there, Señora Spencer?"

"As you can see, a gun. It's loaded, and I know how to use it. Step back. Put your hands behind your head and don't move."

"Of course, Señora, whatever you say," he said and raised his hands.

Alex knelt beside the body on the floor, touched it.

Can this be?

Recognition filled her with horror and relief.

Oh, God, it's Matt.

"Matt, honey, what has he done to you?"

Jorge moved toward her and Alex motioned him back with the gun barrel. She had never been so close to shooting someone and clung to her humanity by a thread of conscience.

"Don't try that again or I'll kill you. Believe me, you son-of-a-bitch, I want to kill you."

"No, no," Jorge said as he glanced behind him, "I'm not moving."

"You in the other room," Alex said, "come in here or I'll shoot this man."

Miguel stepped out from the kitchen and observed the scene before him.

"*Quitale la pistola!*" Jorge said to him.

Miguel looked at Alex and then at Jorge before he shook his head. He stood still and rigid, as if his feet were nailed to the floor.

"You're a dead man," Jorge said to Miguel. "If the woman doesn't kill you, I will."

Desperate to help Matt, Alex turned to Miguel and said, "Please, some water and towels, clean ones. Hurry!"

Without hesitating, Miguel trotted down the hall, presumably to a bathroom, and returned with two towels and a glass of water.

"Here, Señora," he said and set them on a nearby table.

"Sit down," she said to Miguel and began to wipe Matt's face. She gently cleaned the blood from his nose and around his mouth. He moaned. Alex feared that she was hurting him.

"You bastard!" she said to Jorge. "You goddamn fucking bastard!"

She glanced from Matt to Jorge to Miguel. Finding it difficult to attend to Matt and watch both men, she ordered Jorge to lie face down on the floor with his hands behind his head. Showing her a twisted grin, he squatted and stretched out.

The towels were quickly stained red with Matt's blood. Alex could not stop her tears. She ached to see Matt in so much pain, maybe dying.

"More rags," she said to Miguel. "Hurry!"

"The others will be coming soon, Señora," Jorge said. "You cannot get away. Remember, this is an island. A very small one. If you give me the gun I'll forget this ever happened. I will help you and your husband escape."

"Shut up!"

"Don't be a fool. I can save you both. We can make a deal."

"No deals, you bastard."

Alex stood up, tried to decide what to do. She bounced from one foot to the other.

How can we get away? Can Matt be moved without inflicting further injury?

She glanced at Miguel. He was sitting with his arms crossed, watching her without expression. He had gentle eyes. She remembered him from the boat, "Eva," the yacht that had brought her to Raoul's Island.

Preoccupied for a moment, Alex didn't notice Jorge's hand snake out until his fingers wrapped around her ankle. Caught off guard, she fell backwards with a loud thud and smacked her head on the hardwood floor. Although dazed, Alex still grasped the automatic. Jorge rocketed to his feet and stood over her. His eyes, wild and angry, signaled his intentions. He was going to kill them both. She pointed the gun and fired three times. One of the bullets caught him in the neck; the others missed their mark. Stunned, Jorge clutched his throat and dropped to his knees. Like a geyser, bright red blood spewed from the wound and spilled down his chest and shoulder. No longer filled with scorn, he looked at Alex with wonder as his life's blood drained from his body. In a few minutes, he collapsed and lay still.

Miguel did not move. He smiled at her, a subtle, half smile.

"You hated him, too," Alex said. "Of course."

Turning her attention to Matt, she saw that he was regaining consciousness and appeared to recognize her.

"Alex," he said and attempted to sit up. A spasm of coughing wracked his chest; blood gurgled in his throat.

"Matt, my dearest," she said and touched him lightly with her fingertips. Alex desperately wanted to hold him but feared that by doing so she would inflict further damage to his battered body.

"Listen," she said to Miguel, "you've got to help me. You've got to!"

"Yes, Señora, but you have to take me with you. If I stay here, they will blame me for Jorge's death, for letting you escape, for everything. They would rather I sacrifice myself than allow those things to happen."

"We have to get my husband to the dock. I have a car. If we work together, we have a chance. We can leave by boat. No one knows I've run away or else they would be here by now. They will find out soon enough, though, so we have to get moving."

"I will do as you ask, Señora, but you must promise to take me to the U. S."

'Yes, yes, of course. You have my word. Do I have yours?"

"Sí, Señora.

"I hope that you aren't lying to me or it will all be over for us. All of us. Comprende?"

"Sí, Señora."

"Okay, the car is parked up the road near Raoul's house, about a quarter of a mile, on the left. The keys are in it. Get it and bring it to the back door. Then come in and help me carry my husband outside."

For a few seconds, Miguel paused, studied her. She didn't understand the meaning of his gaze but prayed that he was a man of his word.

I have no choice except to trust him..

"Please hurry!" she said.

Miguel whirled and left the house, slamming the back door behind him.

"Hurry," she whispered after him.

Kneeling beside Matt, Alex could barely see through her tears. He was gravely injured and she didn't know what to do. When she touched his cheek, he looked up at her through swollen and bloody eyelids.

"Leave me," he said before he drifted off again.

"Sh-sh-sh, don't talk now. Later. We've got to get you out of here."

CHAPTER FIFTY-NINE

Morgan Cay

Raoul sat at his desk absently tapping his pen on the desk top.

Something isn't right. What?

It was unbelievably bold and reckless for the American to come to the Island, but no harm was done, he thought. I was forewarned, and the gringo walked right into my trap. I will never forget the look on Spencer's face when the lights came on and they all yelled, "surprise!" Absolutely priceless.

Raoul recognized that Matt was an unusual man, and a brave one. Not many men would die for their wives. Raoul admired Spencer's devotion to Alex. Loyalty, freely given, was rare and highly regarded in the drug business, where nine out of ten times money and fear determined who could be trusted. If rewards and intimidation did not persuade a man, you found out who was important to him and you terrorized them. When all else failed, the man's love for his family, his soft underbelly, always brought him around. Sooner or later, they all came around.

Raoul sipped his cognac. When he put down his glass, he shrugged. His shoulder muscles were tight and quivering like horses' flanks. He leaned back in his chair, picked up the snifter again, and stared up at the ceiling.

That woman is up there, oblivious to the night and the violence that is occurring even now as I sit at my desk.

He resisted the powerful urge to climb the stairs and take her forcefully. Raoul hungered for her in a way that he found disturbing, yet exhilarating. He rocked his head from side to side. He needed some release from the pressure that had been building inside him. Being the boss of a thriving drug enterprise carried as many headaches if not more than any major corporation. He had to deal with the legitimate as well as the illegal aspects of the business. The belief that he was the cement that held everything in place gave him another burden.

I know that when I die someone else will climb over my corpse and assume my position, but who? No one in the Cartel is prepared for such a responsibility. Well I'm not planning to die anytime soon so I will think about that later. My fortune is growing, and I am safe here in the Islands and in Colombia. I have been able to make a positive difference at home. He sighed. *The Americans continue to want the drugs, demand them. If I don't supply them, someone else will step in to fill the void.*

He stretched his arms and allowed his thoughts to return to Alex.

She is so beautiful and innocent, an extraordinary find these days. She doesn't realize how lovely she is.

He longed for her and struggled to keep his feelings in check. He wanted to caress her, taste her warm moist places. His desire for her was taking on a life of its own.

I must wait for her, for that exquisite moment when she surrenders to me. I want to feel that ultimate power, possess her. I can always call for another woman. Luisa would be nice. All I need to do is summon her and she will come running. She adores me and knows how to please a man. But hell, I don't want to be pleased. I miss the fire of the old days and that woman upstairs makes me feel passionate, alive.

Raoul stood up and paced behind his desk. Accustomed to staying awake for long periods of time, the late hour was not a stranger to him. Most of the time he relied upon a pint of cognac and sex in order to sleep.

That gringo coming to the Island, that was a small thing, a rather an interesting move, but that woman, she is another matter.

Thoughts of Alex had begun to interfere with his usual calm interior. Normally he could compartmentalize his thoughts, but visions of her were interrupting them. Raoul felt foolish.

With one gulp, he finished the cognac and held the snifter before him. Suddenly, he slammed the empty glass on the desk and stood perfectly still. The quiet of the house surrounded him. He imagined Alex lying in bed, warm and naked. He thought of her silky smooth skin and dark eyes, her creamy thighs opening to him, welcoming him. His fingertips burned.

That's it, dammit!

He wrenched open the office door and climbed the stairs two at a time. The game didn't matter anymore or that lovemaking would be better if she came to him of her own free will. He needed her, wanted her, and that was all there was to it. Period.

Without hesitating, Raoul shoved open the bedroom door and entered. Whether she liked it or not, he intended to possess her.

CHAPTER SIXTY

Morgan Cay

Although pale and weak, once the blood had stopped seeping from his nose and mouth, Matt looked slightly better. Alex had brought him a glass of whiskey from a bottle she found in a cabinet, and he had taken a sip. She wasn't sure if the alcohol was a good idea, but she was desperate to find some relief for him.

Briefly leaving Matt, she checked the clock in the kitchen. Miguel had been gone for over twenty minutes, and Alex had estimated that it should take him no longer than ten to retrieve the car and return to the house.

Matt moaned as he drifted in and out of consciousness. She realized that on her own she could not help him. Without Miguel, there was little she could do. Silently, she prayed that he would return and they would be able to escape before Raoul discovered her absence. Now that she had killed Jorge, there was no telling what he would do to her and Matt.

These are the craziest people. Why didn't they just take me to Matt and get their cocaine? Why all this?

Matt winced, struggled to sit up.

"Stay down. I don't want you to move until you have to. Please, Matt, you're badly hurt and moving might make it worse."

"I told you, get away," he whispered. "Hurry. Make it to the beach. Swim for the boat."

"What boat?"

"Boat."

"Matt, what boat?"

"West side of Island, waiting."

"Who's waiting, Matt?"

"Man."

Alex's heart skipped a beat.

"You mean there's a boat just off shore and someone is waiting for you, someone who'll help us?"

"Yes," he said and coughed up a clot of blood.

"Go now."

"Quiet," she said as she placed her fingers on his lips. "I signed on for the duration, remember, so I'm not leaving without you. Save your breath."

When she ran to the kitchen to check the time again, she heard the low hum of an engine outside. She held the gun in front of her with both hands and waited. She knew that it could be Miguel and it could also be Raoul and his men, who had been summoned by Miguel. She took a deep breath and rushed to the back door.

CHAPTER SIXTY-ONE

Morgan Cay

Dwight felt seasick and anxious. At two a.m., he had noticed the Morgan Cay lights growing larger and brighter off the stern. He found the anchors had lost their grip on the ocean floor and the *Fishy Business* was literally backing into the Island. The thought of their boat careening into Raoul's private Cay struck him as rather funny. Scary but funny.

Jeremy lay sacked out in the V-berth. He had returned to the boat, exhausted, and reported that he couldn't find Spencer and had almost drowned in the raging sea. After hearing his account, Dwight was amazed that Jeremy had survived.

He splashed cold water on his face and chewed another Bonine motion sickness tablet. Earlier, he had vomited over the side and now only mild nausea and weakness lingered. He rummaged through the cupboards for some soda crackers. Sometimes munching something dry and salty afforded him some relief. He wished he had remembered to renew his prescription for Scopolamine ear patches before they embarked on this stake out. They seemed to be the most effective in combating his sea sickness.

Dwight heard Jeremy pumping the head.

"You up, buddy?" he said.

"Yeah, yeah," Jeremy said as he came into the main cabin and slumped into a seat at the dining table.

"What do you think?" Dwight said as he checked his watch. "It's almost dawn."

"I think the poor bastard has either drowned or is now the guest of Señor Chavez. In any event, there's nothing we can do for him now."

"I feel awful," Dwight said.

"I can see that. Did you take that sea sick stuff?"

"I'm not talking about me. I'm thinking about Spencer. I wish we could have helped him. All we've done is deliver him to the devil."

"Look, like I said before, it isn't our fault. We did what we could. Shit, we stuck our necks out for the guy. As it is, we need to think about ourselves and get the hell out 'a here, pronto."

"I want to wait until sunup," Dwight said as he heated a pot of coffee on the stove. Fumes from the burning alcohol wafted through the cabin.

"You gonna' be able to drink that?"

"I'm sure as hell gonna' try. I barfed my guts up a couple hours ago and now I'm dehydrated."

"You need water," Jeremy said.

"I gotta have some coffee. I haven't had any sleep and I need a jolt."

"Suit yourself."

The *Fishy Business* strained at the one anchor line Dwight had been able to reset. Jeremy peered out the cabin door and checked bearings with a hand-held compass.

"We aren't dragging anymore are we?" Dwight said.

"Doesn't look that way."

After several minutes, the coffee began to boil and Dwight lowered the flame.

"Want some?" he said and held up the pot.

"Yeah, I could use a cup."

Dwight filled two mugs and sat down at the table with Jeremy.

"I feel so bad." Dwight said.

"You look like shit."

"No, I feel bad about Spencer. I wish I had gone with him."

"And you think you could have made it?"

"I'm a stronger swimmer than you, and I just might of."

"Well I think you would have had your hands full and might have drowned yourself. I don't think the poor sap even got to the Island. The current, God, it was hellacious."

"Maybe, but all I know is that he was a man with a noble purpose, and a man with a noble purpose often achieves the impossible."

"You're not going to start that 'Impossible Dream' shit are you?" Jeremy said with a yawn, "because if you are, I'm going back to bed."

"No, I'm not, but I do want to wait until sunup before we haul butt, you know, just in case."

"Jesus, Dwight, you're nuts. Just suppose Spencer made it to the Cay and Raoul caught him and he spilled his guts? Don't you think they'll be after us at first light? He'll have blown our cover."

"Maybe, maybe not. I don't think that he would tell them about us. He's not that type."

"What type is that? Brave? Honorable? A war hero? Christ, Dwight, the guy is just a man. He puts on his pants one leg at a time, just like we do."

"Yeah, I suppose, but if he got caught, and I hope to God he didn't, he'll talk about his wife, the drugs, but probably not about us."

"For Christ's sake, they're gonna want to know how he got to the fucking Island. What's he gonna say? He swam from Robert's Cay? Hitched a ride with a passing tourist? Shit, Dwight, sometimes I think you're going senile on me."

"I don't think he'll put us at risk," Dwight said as he tugged at an eyebrow. "He won't."

"And you're willing to bet our lives on your instincts about a man you hardly know?"

"Yeah, I am."

"I give up. Let's just sit here until they come and get us, and we can go out in that blaze of glory you're always talking about. What the hell."

"Relax. We'll just sit still. If by some miracle Spencer made it and found his wife, I want to be here, like we said. But right after sunrise, I promise, we're out 'a here."

"Why don't you get some sleep. I can check the anchor and keep an eye out for Spencer or Raoul's boys, whoever gets here first."

"You're right. I think I'll lie down for a few minutes. That Bonine made me a little drowsy. Damn, I wish I had brought my patches."

"Go to bed, Dwight."

"Wake me in an hour. It's four-thirty now."

"Oh, don't worry. I'll get you up."

Dwight crawled into the V-berth, and once horizontal, felt his nausea further subside. The coffee he had downed, though, burned inside his stomach like a hot fist and he hoped that he wouldn't have to hang his head over the side again.

CHAPTER SIXTY-TWO

Morgan Cay

Alex almost embraced Miguel when he returned alone.

"I have the car, Señora."

"Thank God, you're back. Let's hurry. We don't have much time."

Miguel lifted Matt by his arms and Alex held onto his legs. Together they carried him out the door and down the steps. Matt's eyes were swollen shut, and he couldn't stay upright without their support.

Getting Matt into the passenger seat was painful and difficult for him. Once he cried out, and the sound pierced Alex's heart like a blade. She had found a man's bathrobe in one of the bedroom closets, and when they had situated him in the car, she draped it over him.

Miguel spoke English, but when he got flustered, he lapsed into Spanish, and Alex couldn't understand him. While Miguel drove, Alex crouched in the back. The sedan bumped over the pitted road, and the steady purr of the car's engine interrupted the early-morning stillness. As they neared the dock, Alex peeked out the window and saw two men leaning against a van.

"Miguel, quick, get out and speak to them. Tell them that Raoul has asked you to go somewhere."

"What should I say, Señora?"

"Tell them, uh, that you have to dump Matt's body."

"Sí, Señora," he said as he climbed out of the car.

Alex watched Miguel as he approached the men. One of them waved, shouted something in Spanish. She couldn't hear their conversation. They were too far away, and the wind was still gusty. The halyards on a lone sailboat tied to the dock clanged like an alarm bell. Alex lay on the floor in the back and waited for Miguel to return.

Please, please hurry!

After a few minutes, he came back to the car and opened the passenger door.

"Señora, I told them what you said," he whispered, "but as you can see, they are still standing there and will notice the Señor when I get him out of the car. What if he moves or makes a noise? They will see he is not dead. Jorge always makes them dead. They will…"

"I thought about that. Oh no," she said suddenly, "those men, they're coming this way. Tell them that you don't need any help."

Miguel called to the men, *"Todo esta bien."*

They nodded and wandered back to the van.

"God, that was close," Alex said after she exhaled.

Matt moaned, and his head lolled sideways.

"We have to hurry, Miguel. Which boat can we take?"

"There is a Whaler at the end of the dock. I've used it many times."

"Good. That'll work. Get back in and drive the car as close to the boat as you can."

Miguel climbed in and slammed the door. After a quick wave to the men, he turned the wheel and headed down the dock where the smaller boats were tied. He inched the sedan forward until the car's front bumper touched a piling.

"This is all we go, Señora."

"All right, now listen. Even though it may be painful for him, I want you to carry my husband over your shoulder and put him in the boat. Be as gentle as you can. I'll follow after you get aboard and start the engine. We can't let those men see me, or they'll come after us."

"Sí, Señora, but this won't be so good for the Señor."

"I know, I know, but we have no choice. I can't help you while those men are watching."

"I understand."

Miguel got out of the car and went around to the passenger side. With Alex assisting from the back, Miguel rolled Matt over his shoulder. Matt groaned, mumbled something unintelligible.

"Go! Go!" she said.

Miguel, though slight in build, managed to stagger with Matt slung across his shoulder to a Boston Whaler tied at the dock and roll him in it. For one tense moment, Alex feared that he was going to drop Matt over the side between the power boat and the pilings.

After Miguel started the engine, Alex, with the automatic in hand, slipped out of the car and darted to the Whaler. In one long leap, she jumped from the dock to the stern and hunkered down.

When Miguel got off to untie the lines, the engine sputtered and stopped.

Alex huddled near Matt.

No, no, to come so far only to be caught at the last minute!

She covered Matt with the bathrobe and looked at Miguel and the men standing by the van. Miguel jumped back in the boat, pulled the choke, and managed to restart the engine. He looked at her with wide eyes and shook his head. The engine quit again.

"*Dios mio, ayudame,*" she heard him say.

The men began easing toward the boat. Alex lay as flat as she could, but in a boat without a cabin, she would be visible if they came much closer. One of them called to Miguel but Miguel waved his hand and continued his frantic efforts to restart the engine. Alex smelled gasoline.

The men, now less than twenty yards away, were close enough for her to see their features in the gray light. One man looked Caucasian with long blond hair that hung loosely about his shoulders. His eyes were narrow, their color indistinguishable, but they were focused on Miguel. The man's lips were moving.

"They're coming, Señora. They want to help me start the engine."

"Keep trying."

The other man, dark skinned, looked Spanish. His prominent belly preceded him up the dock. He, too, was looking intently at Miguel.

With a deafening roar, the engine came to life and continued to throb when Miguel throttled back. He waved them off and hopped on the dock to remove the lines. Once he was back on board, he thrust the Whaler away from the pilings and threw the boat in gear. When they exited the harbor, the sky appeared bright and new in the east.

As the small boat plowed through the heavy seas, Alex yelled over the din of the engine, "There's a boat out there, to the west. Someone is waiting for us. He'll help us get away."

Miguel nodded and took up a westerly heading. Alex knelt beside Matt, stroked his hair and murmured to him.

We're going to make it, she thought.

We're really going to make it. Please let the boat Matt told me about be there.

The storm had moved on, leaving a massive swell. When they rounded the western tip of the Island, there it was, a sizable power boat. As Miguel nosed the Whaler's bow closer to the motor yacht, Alex waved her arms and called out, "Is anybody there? We need help."

A tanned, slender man stepped outside the cabin and stared at them.

"No," he said. "I don't believe it."

"I'm Alex Spencer. My husband is hurt. Please, can we come aboard?"

The man remained fixed, his mouth gaping. Then someone else appeared, a stocky fellow with a carrot top and twinkling eyes.

"He did it!" she heard the burly, red-haired man say. "By God, he did it!" The big man grinned, raised a hairy fist and shouted, "Yes!"

CHAPTER SIXTY-THREE

Morgan Cay

Raoul, stunned for a moment, stared at the pillows and bunched-up towels.

She's on the run again, but not for long. Alfredo will bring her back, and this time I won't be so understanding. I've been too soft. She deserves the back of my hand. She'll have to learn the hard way.

He hurried downstairs and called one of his men on the telephone.

"Carlos, the woman has run away and Alfredo must be following her. Find them, bring both of them to me, and send someone to the guest house to tell Jorge that I want to see him."

Raoul hung up the receiver and pressed a button under his desk. In a few minutes, he heard thumps overhead as Consuelo climbed out of bed and put on her bathrobe. Soon he heard the soft pad of her slippers as she came down the stairs.

"Sí, Señor," she said, rubbing her eyes, "you require something?"

"Sorry to awaken you so early, Consuelo, but I need some coffee. It's been a long night."

"You want breakfast for you and the Señora?"

Raoul smiled.

"No, just coffee for me. I have something else in mind for Señora Spencer."

He stood up, opened the drapes, and stretched before sitting down again. He heard water running in the kitchen and not long after smelled coffee percolating.

What a night. I hope Jorge has found out where my cocaine is and has disposed of the gringo. I don't want her to know that he has been on the Island.

Consuelo appeared fifteen minutes later with a mug of coffee.

"Here, Señor, your coffee."

"Gracias, Consuelo."

"I'm going to get dressed now, Señor Chavez, but I will be right down in case you want something to eat."

"That's fine," he said absently as she poured the coffee. He blew on the contents before taking a sip. Consuelo turned and retreated, gently closing the door behind her.

I need some sleep.

He shuffled through some papers on his desk.

My age is showing. What is it they say, after thirty, it is all downhill.

He sipped his coffee and checked his watch. Sufficient time had elapsed for Carlos to find Alfredo Gonzalez and Alex.

There was a light tap on the office door and Raoul said, "*Entren.*"

Carlos and Alfredo entered; the latter sheepishly hung back.

"Ah, Alfredo, where is the woman?"

"The woman," Alfredo said and blinked, "I, uh, did not see her leave."

Raoul's face darkened.

"What did you say?"

"The woman, I did not see her leave the house. I don't know how she got by me."

"I know," Raoul said. "She's smarter than you, that's how. Either that, or you were not where you were supposed to be."

"I only went to my room for a little while, El Jefe. I promise you."

Raoul opened his top desk drawer and groped inside.

Jesus, someone's taken my gun."

"Both of you come here," he said and motioned to them. Raoul stood up and walked around his desk. With two abrupt movements he withdrew Carlos's gun from its holster and shot Alfredo between the eyes.

"*Idiota!*" Raoul said.

Carlos didn't move, uncertain about what would happen next.

"El Jefe…" he said.

"Where's Jorge?" Raoul said.

"I sent Diego to get him."

Raoul stepped over Alfredo's body and returned to his desk. Before he sat down, Consuelo called from the other side of the office door, "Señor Chavez, Señor Chavez, are you all right?"

"Sí, Sí, go back to your work."

"As you wish," she said and returned to the kitchen.

A few minutes later, Diego, flushed and breathless, flung open the office door.

"El Jefe, Jorge *esta muerto,* and the gringo, he is gone!"

"Jesus!" Raoul said as he slammed a fist on the desk, "Can't I count on anyone? Must I always handle things myself?"

"What happened?" Diego said when he saw Alfredo lying on the floor.

"It does not concern you," Raoul said with a wave of his hand. "Quick," he said, turning to Carlos, "get the men together, everyone, and look for the Americans. I want the entire Island searched!"

"Sí, El Jefe, at once."

"And take him with you," Raoul said glancing down at Alfredo.

Diego and Carlos dragged Alfredo from the room by his heels and closed the door behind them. His wound left a bright red stain on the Persian rug.

How can this happen? My best man, dead, and the woman, gone, just like that. The gringo, gone.

He stroked his chin.

They can't get very far.

He stood up and sat down again. How did the gringo get the upper hand? Jorge is, was, a resourceful man, an experienced assassin. Although he has been slipping lately, that's true. The crack was consuming him. I should have intervened. He should have taken care of the American at Robert's Cay and brought the cocaine back days ago. Before, it would have been an easy task. How did the gringo manage it? No matter. He will soon be found. I am going to make her watch while I personally eliminate him. I made a mistake with her. I allowed my feelings to cloud my judgment. I have been a fool, but I'll remedy that.

CHAPTER SIXTY-FOUR

Morgan Cay

Dwight and Jeremy groaned as they hoisted Matt from the power boat into the cockpit. Matt had been unconscious for over an hour, and Alex feared he was leaving her with each passing moment.

"God, he looks bad," Dwight said.

"He's lost a lot of blood," Alex said, "and he's bleeding from his ears and nose. We have to get him stateside."

"I think you're wrong," Jeremy said. "Spencer needs a doctor now. I'm sure we can find one that's not on the take. There's a GP in Mission Harbor who hasn't been bought by anyone. You remember, Dwight, that Albury guy."

"I think that would be a mistake, and a dangerous one," Dwight said.

Jeremy started to speak, hesitated, and bit down on his lower lip instead.

"We've gotta hurry," Alex said. "I'm sure they're looking for us right now."

Miguel sat by the stern quietly smoking a cigarette.

"What about him?" Jeremy said, motioning aft with his head.

"He has to stay with us," Alex said. "He helped me. We couldn't have gotten this far without him. Besides, he told me they'll kill him for allowing us to escape, and I promised him he could come with me."

"We can't take that guy to West Palm," Jeremy said.

"Now wait a minute," Dwight said. "The guy's probably a gold mine. He can tell us a lot about Chavez's operation. If need be, we can get him into the witness protection program."

"That spic doesn't know squat," Jeremy said. "Can't you see he's just a peon?"

"I don't know anything about him," Dwight said. "Christ, we haven't even talked to him yet."

"We're about to get massacred and now we have some low life scumbag to worry about. He'll slit our throats the minute we turn our backs."

"I doubt it," Dwight said. "Anyway, we have more important things to think about. We'd better get busy and haul ass before Raoul and his boys get here."

"I'm tellin' you, Dwight, you're makin' a big mistake," Jeremy said.

"And I'm telling you we don't have time to argue about this. He's comin' with us, okay?" Dwight said.

"Okay, okay, but you'll be sorry. Wait and see. Since I've been outvoted, I guess I'll start the engine. You take care of the anchor."

"I'll cut the Whaler loose first," Dwight said before he went forward.

Alex lay beside Matt in the V-berth and felt his feverish skin. She dabbed at his cracked, bleeding lips and mopped the blood that continued to seep from his nose and ears. She desperately wanted to embrace him, will some of her own life into his broken body.

"You're gonna be okay," she whispered in his ear. "I'm here, Matt, and we're on the boat with the man you told me about. We're leaving now and we're going to get you to a doctor."

She felt a catch in her throat and paused a few seconds before continuing.

"I love you, Matt. Please, please hang on."

The Mercury engine started on the first try. Alex exhaled and heard the thud of Dwight's heavy feet as he strained to raise the anchor. The chain rattled and clanked as it hit the deck.

"She's up!" she heard him call to Jeremy, and then the boat surged forward.

"Goddammit," she heard Dwight shout from the bow, "you almost knocked me overboard!"

CHAPTER SIXTY-FIVE

Morgan Cay

By eight a.m., the men had combed the Island in its entirety; every house, every shore, every road, every square inch of rugged ground.

"We have searched everywhere, El Jefe. I assure you, they are not on the Cay," Carlos said.

"They have to be here unless, unless they have left in a plane or a boat." Raoul said.

He tapped his right foot for a few seconds.

"The docks and airfields are where we have our strongest security," he said. "Surely they didn't get by Dominick and his men. Go to the terminal and account for every plane. We have had no incoming or outgoing flights in the last twenty-four hours because of the storm. Count the planes. Search them. Go to the dock. Check every boat, inside and out. Count them. *Comprende?*"

"Sí, El Jefe."

Raoul wondered how many more surprises the day held.

Could they have gotten off the Island together? How did they find each other?

He licked his lips and noticed his tongue tasted sour and furry.

God, I need to clean up, but I dare not leave the office right now.

He felt like a general who had been drawn into an unexpected battle.

The Americans have to be found, brought back to the Island. They must! It is bad enough to lose the cocaine and Jorge, to be outwitted by the gringo. But her, I have to get her back, finish what I started. I...

He raked his fingers through his hair, checked his watch. He had to admit that most of all, he was afraid of losing Alex.

"Damn that woman!" he said.

When the men reported back to him he would know how to proceed. In the meantime, he was forced to wait.

CHAPTER SIXTY-SIX

Bahama Bank

Jeremy aimed the *Fishy Business* west on a heading of 320 degrees. They were bound for Wayfarers Cay, where they could take on fuel before continuing across the Bahama Bank and out into the Gulf Stream.

"Goin' a little slow, aren't you?" said Dwight, who stood behind Jeremy.

"I don't know this part of the Bank all that well," Jeremy said over his shoulder. "According to the chart, this area has a lot of shoals. We really gotta be careful. Wouldn't want to damage the prop."

"We don't have time to be fuckin' careful," Dwight yelled over the engine noise. "We got a man who's dying and the hounds of hell are after us. Speed it up, man!"

Jeremy shook his head and inched the throttle forward a notch.

Miguel sat below decks at the dining table and sipped a cup of cold coffee he had poured from a pot he found in the sink. He looked around the cabin and listened to the murmur of the woman's voice as she spoke to the injured man in the V-berth.

Dwight stepped inside the cabin to talk to Miguel. "You speak English?" he asked him.

"Yes, Señor, a little."

"Will they come after us?"

"Of course. El Jefe will be angry. He not used to losing. His friend and high employee is dead, killed by the woman."

Dwight raised his eyebrows.

"She killed someone?"

"Sí, a most dangerous man."

"Incredible," Dwight said, "a regular Dirty Harriet."

Miguel looked puzzled.

"I was just wondering," Dwight said, "why did you decide to help them?"

"I had no choices. El Jefe would the killed me, made me take the anger for the death of the, his friend. And to speak with truth, Señor, I have try to get away from the Island and return to Colombia for much time but they no permit. This my only, uh, how you say, oppor…, no, chances, to save this life."

"Speaking of chances, do you think we'll outrun them?"

"I no think. They have, what you call them, the cigarette, no, another, uh, the like… Those fast boats. You cannot leave them. And they have many peoples who have help them everywhere, in the Islands and the U. S. of America."

"Well, you sure don't have to worry about us. We're the good guys."

"I pray, Señor."

Dwight's expression sobered when he heard the sound of the engine winding down. He hurried outside.

"What's up?" he asked Jeremy.

"I'm not sure, but we keep losing power. I'd better take it easy, nurse it along," Jeremy said, "and maybe it won't quit altogether. I told you we've been pushin' it too hard."

Dwight squinted and looked behind the stern. There were no other boats on the horizon, at least not yet.

"Here, let me see," he said and nudged Jeremy aside. Dwight gently pushed the throttle forward and felt the engine vibrate. He could almost hear the pistons going up and down, the valves opening and closing, the crank shaft turning. For a few minutes, he stood at the helm and steered the boat.

"Seems to be running okay now," he said.

"It was doin' it a minute ago, Dwight. I think we'd better take it easy. We'll be dead in the water if we don't watch out. And I mean that literally and figuratively speaking."

"Just keep the throttle down," Dwight said. "We'll be at Wayfarers Cay soon."

Jeremy looked stricken.

"Try to be an optimist for once," Dwight said as he patted Jeremy's shoulder. "We just might pull this off."

CHAPTER SIXTY-SEVEN

Morgan Cay

"We are certain, El Jefe, they are not on the Island," Carlos said. "A boat is missing, a Whaler, and Miguel cannot be found. They must have forced him to go with them."

Raoul did not blink. Instead, he squared his shoulders and stood erect.

"They cannot have gotten far in a small boat," he said. "It doesn't go very fast and in heavy seas they won't be able to cover much ground. Some of you," he said motioning with his hand, "head west and search for them. Dominick will be in charge. The rest of you, look east. They might try to get the cocaine at Robert's Cay or they may be heading directly for the U. S. Catch them and bring them to me. And be quick about it!"

"Not to worry, El Jefe, we'll find them," Dominick said.

Raoul realized nothing could make him feel better about Jorge or the fact that the Americans had escaped except to make them suffer long and hard by his own hand. He rested his elbows on the desk and laced his fingers together.

Maybe I have been in this business too long. How could I allow myself to become so soft? It was the woman, of course. Eventually she would have done what I asked, and willingly, but the gringo interfered.

Raoul clenched his teeth, closed his eyes.

But I will have my revenge. I won't kill the husband right away. His death will be slow and agonizing. And she will watch.

He decided to lie down for a while. He wanted to be rested when the Americans returned to the Island. He left his office and went upstairs to his room, where he showered and lay down on the bed. Raoul had instructed Consuelo to awaken him as soon as the couple was brought to the house.

He was glad that he had sent Carlos and Dominick in pursuit. They were dependable, sensible men. They had been with him a long time, almost as long as Jorge. Yes, Jorge. He would miss his old friend and would visit Jorge's sister in Medellin to convey the bad news of his untimely death.

Jorge has disgraced himself, appeared a fool. I should have recognized the signs. The cocaine had become his master. Jorge has been incompetent for some time. Another mistake in my judgment. In this business, friends are often lost. Only one's enemies remain.

His eyelids were heavy. He closed them. It felt good to let go for a moment.

CHAPTER SIXTY-EIGHT

Wayfarer's Cay

After the *Fishy Business* idled up to the fuel dock at Wayfarers Cay, Dwight found an attendant and asked him to fill the tank while Jeremy called headquarters on a pay phone. They had agreed that using the ship's radio at this point was simply too risky.

Spencer is still alive but just barely. I'm no doctor but I can see that the man is gravely injured. Maybe mortally injured. The woman, she's calm, together. If Spencer buys it on the trip home, she isn't the type to go nuts.

Jeremy, now that's a puzzle. He appears to be scared shitless, which is totally out of character. Over the years, we've been in a lot of tight spots but we've always managed to walk away from them relatively intact. True, Jeremy was shot once when that bust went sour, but that was years ago. Maybe he's remembering the bullet or maybe he just sees things the way they really are, hopeless. Let's face it, we can run but how far?

Jeremy talked on the phone for several minutes. When he returned to the boat, he grinned and tossed a cold beer to Dwight.

"Good news, buddy, the cavalry is on the way. The Coast Guard is sending a cutter to meet us. Smooth sailing from here on out."

"Keep it under your hat for a minute," Dwight said as he handed a wad of bills to the Bahamian, who had just finished pumping the gas.

"What did you tell them?" Dwight said after the attendant had stepped out of earshot,

"Oh, just that we had an injured man on board, that we needed a doctor, pronto."

"Did you mention the Colombian?"

"No, I didn't get into all that. We can explain about him later when we're face to face. You and I still have to get our stories straight. After all, we have more than not gone by the book. We've fuckin' thrown it out. I don't know about you but I don't want to lose my pension over this little escapade."

"You're right. After we're on our heading to West Palm, we can talk about it."

***

Alex relieved herself in the bathroom when Dwight and Jeremy got off the boat at Wayfarers Cay. Matt still held his own. His condition had not improved but then again he seemed no worse. She remained hopeful that he would be all right.

Alex felt safe with Dwight but she wasn't certain about the other guy, Jeremy. Something about him disturbed her. From the first moment they met, he seemed reluctant to help them. She splashed water on her face and smeared toothpaste on her teeth with an index finger.

Miguel slept on the port bunk, oblivious to what was going on around him. His posture throughout the ordeal had been one of resignation.

Dwight entered the cabin and offered her a Budweiser.

"Good news, Mrs. Spencer. Jeremy has arranged for a boat with a doctor to meet us. They should already be on their way out of West Palm."

Alex felt weak with relief.

Dwight extended the can of beer to her again.

"No, thanks."

"How's your husband doing?"

"About the same."

"Can I get you anything before we get underway?"

"I just want us to hurry up and get started. Can't we go any faster?"

"We had to take on a load of fuel so we can make it across the Gulf Stream at high speed. Jeremy's untying the boat now."

Alex glanced outside when she heard the engine start.

"Gotta' go and give him a hand," Dwight said. "Heat up the coffee. Might make you feel better to have something warm in your belly."

Dwight finished casting off the lines and Jeremy eased the boat away from the dock and threaded it through the pleasure craft anchored in the harbor. Their yellow quarantine flags indicating they had not cleared Customs snapped in the heavy air.

Taking up a heading of 276 degrees, Jeremy engaged the auto pilot and asked Dwight to keep a sharp look out. Inside the cabin, he found Alex cradling a mug of coffee in her hands.

"You must be exhausted," he said.

"Yes I am, but I understand help is on the way."

"That's right. It shouldn't be long now. Looks like your friend is sacked out," Jeremy said glancing at Miguel.

"He's earned it. We couldn't have gotten away if he hadn't helped us."

"Is that right? How's that?"

"I needed him to help me move Matt. I asked and he agreed. I think he's been a prisoner on the Island, in a manner of speaking, for some time. He seems like a gentle man."

"I see," Jeremy said as he looked down at his feet.

"And your husband, how is he?"

"I honestly don't know. I wish I did. He's still breathing, but barely. The bleeding from his nose has stopped, but I'm afraid there may be serious internal damage. He has some broken bones. He...he...has to be all right," she sobbed and covered her mouth with the back of her hand.

Jeremy sat down beside her and patted her knee.

"There, there," he said. "Things will work out. You'll see."

Alex dabbed at her eyes with a tissue and took a sip of coffee.

"What do you think of Raoul?"

"Raoul?"

"You know, the cartel boss, El Jefe, they call him."

"He didn't hurt me if that's what you mean."

"No, I wasn't thinking about that. Rather impressive, wouldn't you say?"

"He was okay, I guess."

"Just okay?"

"Why do you ask?"

"Oh, just curious. I've heard so many stories about him. They say he is quite intelligent."

Alex took another sip of coffee, stood up, and emptied the remainder into the sink.

"How long before the Coast Guard meets us?" she said.

"That depends on how fast they got underway."

Alex looked down as she washed her cup. She didn't want Jeremy to see her eyes.

Why is he so interested in Raoul? Idle curiosity? Why does this man trouble me so much?

The answers were buried somewhere but she knew that if she would quit trying so hard to unearth them, they would surface on their own. She dried the mug with a paper towel and returned it to the cupboard.

Chapter Sixty-nine

Morgan Cay

Raoul, awakened by a light tap on his bedroom door, sat up and squinted at his watch. He had slept for less than an hour.

"What is it?"

"Señor Chavez," Consuelo said in a low voice from the other side of the door, "Jose is downstairs. He says that he has an urgent message for you."

"I'll be right down."

"I will tell him."

Raoul eased off the bed and smoothed his tousled hair. His eyes burned, but he felt somewhat refreshed by his brief nap. After quickly dressing, he went downstairs where he found Jose by the front door pacing and clutching his baseball cap.

"*Que hay de nuevo?*" Raoul said.

"Very good news, El Jefe. Our man called. He reported that the Señora and her husband are aboard a boat called the *Fishy Business*, you know the one, and they are getting fuel at Wayfarers Cay. We were told they are en route to West Palm Beach. In fact, they should be underway as we speak."

"Have you informed Dominick and Carlos?"

"Not yet, El Jefe. I wanted to hear your instructions. What do you want me to tell them?"

"Radio them immediately and advise them that the Americans have been located at Wayfarers Cay on the boat called *Fishy Business*. Tell them they are west bound for Palm Beach. Instruct them to proceed with all due haste and intercept them before they reach the U. S. I want the Americans brought back to the Island. I am not concerned about anyone else."

"Sí, El Jefe, I will contact them immediately."

Raoul watched Jose hop into his Toyota truck and roar away. When he returned to his office, he sank into his chair. Frustrated by the events of the past twenty-four hours, his thoughts were a confusion of guarded optimism and fear. He had hope that the Americans, that she, would be brought back to the Island. Because of the previous blunders by him and his men, he was afraid that something might go wrong at the last minute and the woman and her husband would elude them. Ever since he heard that the cocaine was in the gringo's possession, there had been one ridiculous mistake after the other. And losses, serious losses. Not just the drugs. Jorge and two of the men were dead and one was missing.

I cannot allow the Americans to walk away from the wreckage they left behind. If they escape, my position will be in jeopardy. I will look like a fool and be vulnerable. I might as well send out hand-engraved invitations to my own funeral. Any further sign of weakness on my part will result in an attack by those in the ranks who have ambition and hunger for power.

It shouldn't be long now before I have my revenge. The Chinese say that he who sets out on a mission of revenge should first dig two graves. Not in this business.

CHAPTER SEVENTY

Gulf Stream

Ten feet and rising, the seas in the Gulf Stream hindered their passage. Dwight doubted they would be able to cover much ground before Raoul and his men showed up.

"How are we doing?" Alex asked Dwight as she clung to the side of the boat.

"Lousy, but we're making some headway. We ought to be in West Palm in a few hours. That shouldn't matter to you, though, because there's a cutter on the way. We'll rendezvous with them soon. They're on a reciprocal heading, which will bring them right to us. We ought to be able to see them when they're five miles or so from us."

"Matt has to see a doctor soon. Where's the Coast Guard?"

"Sorry, Mrs. Spencer, I have no way of knowing when the cutter will show up."

Alex looked back and scanned the horizon. They were ten miles out and the Islands were no longer visible off their stern. When she turned around, Jeremy emerged from the cabin with a gun in his hand and pointed it at Dwight.

"Hey, Jer, what gives?" Dwight said.

"Come back to idle and turn off the auto pilot."

Dwight throttled back and disengaged the auto pilot.

"What's this about? Have you lost your mind?"

"This is where you get off, old buddy," Jeremy said.

"What the fuck is the matter with you?" Dwight said.

"Nothing is the matter with me."

"I don't understand," Dwight said.

"And I thought you were such a smart boy."

Alex wondered if she could make enough noise to awaken Miguel. Suddenly she remembered what had been eluding her about Jeremy.

Of course, that voice. I heard it at Raoul's.

"I know what's going on," Alex said. "He's involved with them, with Raoul. He visited his house last night. I heard him talking to Jorge and Raoul in the office."

"Christ!" Dwight said as he took a step toward Jeremy.

"I don't want to have to shoot you," Jeremy said, "so I suggest you back up."

He gestured with the gun barrel.

"Come on, Jer, we're friends, partners for God's sake. We've been to hell and back together. Don't do this."

"Look, man, I'm sorry, okay? It's nothing personal, but you have to get off the boat."

Dwight looked behind him at the vast sea with its towering waves.

"It's fuckin' personal to me."

"Well, you can't stay here. You're a pain in the ass and sooner or later I would end up having to shoot you. I've got to turn around and meet Raoul's boys. They want the Spencer's and they'll pay me a bundle for handing them over. They're not gonna be wild about seeing you, old buddy. They'll kill you if I don't. So, as the conductor says, this is the end of the line."

"Is this about money?"

"Money and a future."

Dwight wiped his mouth with the back of a hand.

"How will you explain my absence to the boss?"

"That's easy. Lost overboard during a storm. An unfortunate acci-dent. Could happen to anybody."

"And Driggers?"

"They were on to him. Ate his fuckin' gun."

Dwight looked from Jeremy to Alex. Jeremy motioned with the gun barrel for Dwight to go over the side.

"Get off, Dwight, or I promise I'll shoot you and throw your fat ass over. I'm not gonna tell you again."

Alex tried to settle on a course of action. Desperate, she fell to the deck and grabbed one of Jeremy's legs. Jeremy lost his balance, reached for the wheel. In that brief instant, Dwight lunged. With one hand, he grasped Jeremy's throat, and with the other, he held onto the gun. Alex rolled out of the way. The struggle lasted only a few moments. Dwight, the heavier and stronger of the two, quickly extricated the automatic from Jeremy. The situation reversed, Jeremy now stood on the receiving end of the barrel.

"So," Dwight said, "where were we? Oh, yeah, you wanted me to go over the side. Well, my friend, it's your turn," Dwight said and glanced at the stern.

"Nice try, buddy, but you can't do it. You're one of the good guys, remember? It isn't in your personal code of ethics. As you have always pointed out, everyone deserves his day in court, even a low-life. Let the justice system take care of me, Dwight."

"Ah, Jeremy, you're full of shit and we're wasting time. You know we probably won't be able to outrun Raoul's boys, and they won't hurt you. You're one of the gang. But me, I'd be the first to go."

"You can't do it, partner. It isn't in you."

Dwight's face hardened as he stepped toward Jeremy.

"Quoting you from a moment ago, I'm only going to say this one more time before I shoot you, Cataglio. Get off."

"Dwight, I, uh…"

"Just think of it this way. I'm offering you more of a chance than you gave me. You just might get lucky and Raoul's men will pick you up. Aren't they right behind us?"

Now clear that he had no choice in the matter, Jeremy glanced at the depth finder. It flashed a series of meaningless numbers. After two hundred feet, the indicator was no longer accurate. He remembered the chart, that below the hull at least three or four hundred fathoms of water swirled between the boat and the sea bottom. But Dwight did have a point. Jeremy did have a good chance of being rescued by Raoul's men. In any event, he realized that Dwight wasn't bluffing.

"Okay, but give me a life vest. At least do that."

Dwight thought about it for a moment before agreeing.

"Mrs. Spencer, get Mr. Cataglio a life vest, there, inside the lazaret."

Alex raised the lid of the compartment and pulled out an orange kapok vest. She handed it to Dwight, who tossed it to Jeremy. Jeremy's hands trembled as he fumbled with the straps.

"Dwight, please…"

"Shut up and get off."

Jeremy climbed over the stern and slid into the choppy sea. His frightened eyes pleaded with them to reconsider as he drifted away from the boat. Dwight returned to the helm, and with an angry thrust, shoved the throttle forward. Alex gripped a stern cleat and watched as Jeremy's ashen face grew smaller. Soon she could only see a dot of orange, and then, it, too, was no longer visible.

"I'm sorry about your partner," she told Dwight.

"Me, too," he said and continued squinting straight ahead.

When Alex entered the cabin, she gasped. Miguel lay on the floor with his blood pooling around him. His throat had been cut. She ran to Matt in the V-berth. His breathing, though shallow, seemed no worse.

On deck, she reported Miguel's murder to Dwight, who brought the boat back to idle and went inside the cabin. Together, Alex and he carried the dead man to the stern and pitched him over. With wide eyes, Alex watched Miguel sink beneath the clear blue water. She wanted to look away but could not. His hands, buoyed by the sea, appeared to be reaching for the light, and his long, dark hair undulated in the current. Alex wondered how long it would take him to settle on the ocean floor a quarter of a mile below. Dwight touched her shoulder and asked her to take the helm.

"I'm not going to use the auto pilot again," he told her. "The sea is too sloppy and it's working too hard. The Gulf Stream is pushing us north. Hold a heading of 250 degrees. I have to contact the Coast Guard. We both know Jeremy's telephone call was to Raoul, not to any doctor. There is no help on the way."

Alex nodded and took the wheel. Somehow this didn't surprise her. She didn't think anything would ever surprise her again.

At the helm, she could barely hear Dwight's urgent message to the Coast Guard much less make out their garbled response. She silently prayed that they could understand him over the static and engine noise. Her hands gripped the wheel as she struggled to maintain course.

CHAPTER SEVENTY-ONE

Gulf Stream

Three forty-seven foot Aronow boats thundered out of Wayfarers Cay and took up a heading of 276 degrees for West Palm Beach. Powered by two one thousand horsepower turbo diesels, they roared across the water at a speed of seventy plus miles per hour.

Dominick commanded the lead boat. If he had been planning a trip to West Palm, he, too, would have plotted the same course. According to his calculations, they would overtake the *Fishy Business* in a matter of minutes.

The sleek boats streaked across the waves like lightening. Twenty-five miles out in the Gulf Stream, Dominick throttled back and waited for the others to catch up with him.

"There they are," he said when they arrived. He pointed to a speck in the distance. "We have a man on board but don't worry about him. El Jefe wants the American couple alive. The others are not important. Carlos, you approach from the north. Juan, from the south. I'll come up behind them from the east."

With the precision of a drill team, they separated and established their positions. In a few minutes it would all be over.

CHAPTER SEVENTY-TWO

Gulf Stream

Alex spotted a bright green and white boat on the horizon behind them.

"Dwight, come quick!"

He surfaced from the cabin with binoculars in hand and peered into them.

"Yep, there are two, no three boats. And here they come, the bastards, like the hounds from hell."

"Oh, God, what are we going to do?"

"First," Dwight said, "we engage the auto pilot; and second, you and I go below, close the hatches and secure them. I'm hoping they want you alive. Otherwise, we're screwed."

Alex looked at him for a moment, then swallowed a sob. She wanted to tell him how terrified she was, but what would be the point? She clamped the hatches while Dwight put two guns on the quarter berth and checked to make sure each one was loaded. Alex shut the door to the main cabin and bolted it.

"Now we wait," he said.

"Will they be here soon?"

"Sooner than the Coast Guard," he said. "I can promise you that."

They both listened. Over their Mercury engine, they heard the ominous thunder of the approaching speed boats.

At first, Raoul's men just circled them. Then a shot was fired. They shouted something in Spanish before someone yelled in broken English for them to stop or they would shoot the boat full of holes and sink it.

Alex glanced at Matt and wondered how she would get him out.

The V-berth hatch, maybe. I can open it if we sink.

"Once we're underwater, you'll never get it open," Dwight said as if he had read her mind. "With the water pressure, you'll never be able to raise it."

"I won't leave him."

"I know. I'll take care of him."

There were several reports before the engine on the *Fishy Business* finally sputtered and seized.

"Good shooting," Dwight said. "Now we're dead in the water."

"The Coast Guard, Dwight, are they coming?"

"I wish I knew. We'll have to sit tight and hold on for as long as we can."

"Maybe I can offer to go back to the Island. They might let you and Matt go."

"Don't bet on it. I suspect Raoul wants you and your husband so he can personally make examples of you."

When the Colombians turned off their engines, the calm unnerved Alex and Dwight more than the din of their motors. Several more shots fired in rapid succession shattered the silence. Minutes later, they heard the unmistakable sound of water trickling into the bilge.

"We're sinking!" she said and grabbed Dwight's arm.

"Sounds like little holes. We still have some time."

Alex studied the top of Matt's head. He hadn't moved in hours. Dwight and she stood facing each other as a slow stream of water invaded the hold. They heard the automatic bilge pump kick on.

"There," Dwight said as he patted her hand. "That ought to help, provided they don't shoot any more holes in her hull. Hopefully, they're just trying to scare us and don't really intend to sink the boat."

They heard more shouting in Spanish followed by another volley of shots.

"At least they haven't rammed us," Dwight said. "I don't guess they need to. Besides, no point in damaging those expensive rigs."

Alex nodded.

Overwhelmed, the pump could not keep up with the flood in the bilge and water began to spill over the floorboards. Alex watched as the sea began to claim the boat.

"Life vests?" Alex said.

"I'm afraid we don't need them. They'll either pick us up or kill us."

"What about Matt?"

"Sure. There's a spare under the V-berth. I'll try to get it on him without hurting him too much.

Alex looked on as Dwight rummaged in a compartment in the V-berth and came up with a mildewed kapok vest. He put it on Matt, who remained unconscious.

The water rose faster once it invaded the salon. It now reached Alex's knees. She tried to imagine them all surviving.

I am holding my breath. Dwight is carrying Matt and we are escaping from the upper hatch and swimming up, up, towards the sun.

Then they heard the hum of another engine. She looked at Dwight and her eyes asked the question, "the Coast Guard?"

Before Dwight could reply, a voice boomed over a loud speaker.

"This is the United States Coast Guard. Throw your weapons overboard and put your hands behind your head."

The sound of speed boat motors starting and several quick reports followed. They listened as the thunder of Raoul's boats gradually became a growl.

The water had risen to Alex's shoulders when Dwight hoisted Matt through the hatch and followed him out. As the sea enveloped the cabin, she thrust herself through the opening and into the light.

"Let me help you, ma'am," someone said, and hands reached for her and lifted her into a raft. Alex turned her head just in time to see the *Fishy Business* take one last gulp before it slid beneath the waves.

Once they were safely aboard the cutter, they whisked Matt to the ship's infirmary. While they waited for a medical report, Dwight and Alex told the captain about all that had transpired. When a corpsman appeared, he gave Alex cause for optimism. Matt had lost a lot of blood, had several broken bones along with a concussion, contusions and lacerations, but his blood pressure and oxygen levels were improving. The doctor gave Matt's recovery a prognosis of fair to good.

Wrapped in a flannel blanket, Alex felt herself growing heavy and distant, removed from the people around her. She lay down on a quarter berth, closed her eyes, and allowed the hum of the cutter's engines to lull her to sleep.

Printed in the United States
3686